PENGUIN BOOKS

THE CONSCIENCE OF THE RICH

C. P. Snow was born in Leicester in 1905 and educated at a secondary school. He started his career as a professional scientist, though writing was always his ultimate aim. He won a research scholarship to Cambridge, worked on molecular physics, and became a Fellow of his college in 1930. He continued his academic life in Cambridge until the beginning of the war, by which time he had already begun the 'Lewis Eliot' sequence of novels, the general title of which is *Strangers and Brothers*. The eleven books in the sequence are, in their correct order, which is not that of publication: *George Passant* (1940) – once known by the series title – *Time of Hope* (1949), *The Conscience of the Rich* (1958), *The Light and the Dark* (1947), *The Masters* (1951), *The New Men* (1954), *Homecomings* (1958), *The Affair* (1960), *Corridors of Power* (1964), *The Sleep of Reason* (1968) and *Last Things* (1970). His other novels include *The Search* (1934; revised 1938), *The Malcontents* (1972) and *In Their Wisdom* (1974). He has also written a collection of biographical portraits, *Variety of Men* (1967), a critical biography, *Trollope* (1975), and *The Realists* (1978).

In the war C. P. Snow became a civil servant, and because of his human and scientific knowledge was engaged in selecting scientific personnel. He has had further experience of these problems since the war, both in industry and as a Civil Service commissioner, for which he received a knighthood in 1957. His Rede Lecture on *The Two Cultures and the Scientific Revolution* (1959), his Godkin Lectures on *Science and Government* (1960), his address to the A.A.A.S., *The Moral Un-Neutrality of Science*, and his Fulton Lecture, *The State of Siege* (1968), have been widely discussed and are published in one volume, *Public Affairs* (1971). He received a baro[...] Parliamentary Secretary t[...] nology. In 1950 he married[...]

C. P. SNOW

THE CONSCIENCE
OF THE RICH

PENGUIN BOOKS

Penguin Books Ltd, Harmondsworth, Middlesex, England
Penguin Books, 625 Madison Avenue, New York, New York, 10022, U.S.A.
Penguin Books Australia Ltd, Ringwood, Victoria, Australia
Penguin Books Canada Ltd, 2801 John Street, Markham, Ontario, Canada L3R 1B4
Penguin Books (N.Z.) Ltd, 182–190 Wairau Road, Auckland 10, New Zealand

—

First published by Macmillan 1958
Published in Penguin Books 1961
Reprinted 1962, 1964, 1966, 1970, 1972, 1979

—

Copyright © C. P. Snow, 1958
All rights reserved

—

Made and printed in Great Britain
by Hazell Watson & Viney Ltd
Aylesbury, Bucks
Set in Linotype Baskerville

TO
PAMELA HANSFORD JOHNSON

CONTENTS

Part 1 : INSIDE A FAMILY

Part 2 : FATHER AND SON

CONTENTS
Part 3 : THE MARRIAGES

Part 4 : THE DANGERS

CONTENTS
Part 5 : ALONE

Part 1

INSIDE A FAMILY

Chapter 1

CONFIDENCES ON A SUMMER
EVENING

IT was a summer afternoon, the last day of the Bar final examinations. The doors had just swung open; I walked to my place as fast as I could without breaking into a run. For an instant I was touched again by the odour of the old Hall, blended from wooden panels, floor polish, and the after-smell of food; it was as musty as a boarding house, and yet the smell, during those days, became as powerful in making one's heart lift up and sink as that of the sea itself.

As I stared at the question-paper, I went through an initial moment in which the words, even the rubric 'Candidates are required to answer ...' appeared glaring but utterly unfamiliar. At the beginning of each examination I was possessed in this way: as though by a magnified version of one of those amnesias in which a single word – for example TAKE – looks as though we have never seen it before, and in which we have to reassure ourselves, staring at the word, that it occurs in the language and that we have used it, spelt exactly in that fashion, every day of our lives.

Then, all of a sudden, the strangeness vanished. I was reading, deciding, watching myself begin to write. The afternoon became a fervent, flushed, pulsing, and exuberant time. This I could do; I was immersed in a craftsman's pleasure. In the middle of the excitement I was at home.

Towards the end of the afternoon, the sunlight fell in a swathe across the room, picking out the motes like the beam from a cinema projector. I was cramped, tired, and the sweat was running down my temples; my hand shook as I stopped writing.

In that moment, I noticed Charles March sitting a little farther up the hall, across the gangway. His fair hair, just touching the beam of sunlight, set it into a blaze. His head was half turned, and I could see the clear profile of his clever, thin, fine-drawn face. As he wrote, hunched over his desk, his mouth was working.

I turned back to my paper, for the last spurt.

I had been a little disappointed at not meeting Charles during the course of the examination. We had only talked to one another a few times, when we happened to be eating dinners at the Inn on the same night; but I thought that at first sight we had found something like kinship in each other's company.

I knew little of the actual circumstances of his life, and the little I knew made the feeling of kinship seem distinctly out-of-place. He came from Cambridge to eat his dinner at the Inn, I from a bed-sitting room in a drab street in a provincial town. His family was very rich, I had gathered: I was spending the last pounds of a tiny legacy on this gamble at the Bar.

We had never met anywhere else but at the Inn dining-table. When I last saw him, we had half arranged to go out together one night during the examination. All I had heard from him, however, was a 'good luck' on the first morning, as we stood watching for the doors to open.

At last the invigilator called for our papers, and I stayed in the gangway, wringing the cramp out of my fingers and waiting for Charles to come along.

'How did you get on?' he said.

'It might have been worse, I suppose.' I asked about himself as we reached the door. He answered:

'Well, I'm afraid the man next to me is the real victim.'

'What's the matter?'

'He was trying to get a look at my paper most of the afternoon,' said Charles. 'If the poor devil managed it, I should think he'd probably fail.'

I laughed at him for touching wood. He began protesting, and then broke off:

'Look here, would it be a bore for you if we had tea somewhere? I mean, could you possibly bear it?'

I was already used to his anxious, repetitious, emphatic politeness; when I first heard it, it sounded sarcastic, not polite.

We went to a tea-shop close by. We were both very hot, and I was giddy with fatigue and the release from strain. We drank tea, spread the examination paper on the table and compared what we had done. Charles returned to my remark about touching wood:

'It's rather monstrous accusing me of that. If I'd shown the slightest sign of ordinary human competence –' Then he looked at me. 'But I don't know why we should talk about my performances. They're fairly dingy and they're not over-important. While yours must matter to you, mustn't they? I mean, matter seriously?'

'Yes, very much,' I said.

'Just how much? Can you tell me?'

In the light of his interest, which had become both kind and astringent, I was able to tell the truth: that I had spent the hundred-or-two pounds I had been left in order to read for the Bar; that I had been compelled to borrow some more, and was already in debt. There was no one, literally no one, I had to make it clear, to whom I could turn for either money or influence. So it rested upon this examination. If I did exceptionally well, and won a scholarship that would help me over the first years at the Bar, I might pull through; if not, I did not know what was to become of me.

'I see,' said Charles. 'Yes, it's too much to invest in one chance. Of course it is.' He paused. 'You've done pretty well, of course, you know that, don't you? I'm sure you have.' He pointed to the examination paper, still lying on the table-cloth. 'You're pretty confident up to a point, aren't you? Whether you've done well enough – I don't see that anyone can say.'

He gave me no more assurance than I could stand. It was exactly what I wanted to hear said. The tea-shop had grown darker as the sun dipped behind the buildings across the street. We both felt very much at ease. Charles suggested that we should have a meal and go to a theatre; he hesitated for a moment. Then he said:

'I should like you to be my guest tonight.' I demurred: because of the flicker, just for an instant, of some social shame. I remembered the things I usually forgot, that he was rich, elegantly dressed, with an accent, a manner in ordering tea, different from mine. Hurriedly Charles said:

'All right. I'll pay for the meal and you can buy the tickets. Do you agree? Will that be fair?' For a few minutes we were uncomfortable. Then Charles went to telephone his father's house, and came back with a friendly smile. Our ease returned. We walked through the streets towards the west, tired, relaxed, talkative. We talked about books. Charles had just finished the last volume of Proust. We talked about politics; we made harsh forecasts full of anger and hope. It was 1927, and we were both twenty-two.

He took me to a restaurant in Soho. Carefully, he studied the menu card; he looked up from it with a frown; he asked if his choice would suit me and ordered a modest dinner for us both. I knew that he had not forgotten my reluctance to be treated. But now, as we sat by the window (below, the first lights were springing up in the warm evening), his meticulous care seemed familiar, a private joke.

An hour later, we were walking down Shaftesbury Avenue to the theatre. When we arrived at the box office, Charles said:

'Just a minute.' He spoke to the girl inside: 'We asked you to keep seats for Mr Lewis Eliot. Have you got them ready?'

He turned to me, and said in an apologetic tone: 'I thought of it when I was ringing up my father. I decided we might as well be safe. You don't mind too much, do you?'

He stood aside from the grille in order that I could pay for the tickets. The girl gave them to me in an envelope. They were for the pit.

I could not help smiling as I joined him; his manoeuvres seemed now even more of a joke. They had made it impossible for me to be extravagant, that was all. As he caught my eye he also began to smile. As we stood in the foyer people passed us, one couple breaking into grins at the sight of ours.

We took our places as the house was filling up. The orchestra was playing something sweet, melancholy, and facile. I did not make an attempt to listen, but suddenly the music took me in charge. As I sat down, I had begun to think again of the examination – but on the instant all anxieties were washed away. Not listening as a musician would, but simply basking in the sound, I let myself sink into the sensation that all I wanted had come to pass. The day's apprehension disappeared within this trance; luxury and fame were drifting through my hands.

Then, just before the curtain went up, I glanced at Charles. Soon the play started, and his face was alive with attention; but for a second I thought that he, whom I had so much envied a few hours before, looked careworn and sad.

Chapter 2

INVITATION TO BRYANSTON SQUARE

THE results of the examination were published about a
month later. I had done just well enough to be given a
scholarship; Charles was lower in the list but still in the first
class, which, in view of the amount of work he had done,
was a more distinguished achievement than mine.

In September we began our year as pupils and at once saw
a good deal of each other. Charles met me the first day I
came to London, and our friendship seemed to have been
established a long time. He continued to ask about my affairs
from where we left off on the night of the examination.

'You're settled for this year, anyway? You've got £150?
You can just live on that, can't you?'

He got me to tell him stories of my family; he soon formed
a picture of my mother and chuckled over her. 'She must
have been an admirable character,' said Charles. But he
volunteered nothing about his own family or childhood.
When I asked one night, his manner became stiff. 'There's
nothing that you'd find particularly interesting,' he said.

He kept entertaining me at restaurants and clubs. One
evening he had to give me his telephone number; only then
did he admit that he had been living since the summer in
his father's house in Bryanston Square. It was strange to
feel so intimate with a friend of one's own age, and yet be
shut out.

We entered different chambers: I went to Herbert Getliffe
and he to someone called Hart, whom I knew by reputation
as one of the ablest men at the Common Law Bar. The first
weeks in chambers, for me at least, were lonely and pointless; there was nothing to do, and I was grateful when Getliffe appeared and with great gusto recommended some
irrelevant book, saying, 'You never know when it will come

in handy.' I was under-worked and over-anxious. I had taken two small rooms at the top of a lodging-house in Conway Street, near the Tottenham Court Road. Charles, guessing my state, drove round and fetched me out several nights a week. I wanted to discover why he, too, was harassed.

We each knew that the other was troubled when alone: we each knew that his secretiveness hurt me: yet those first nights in London and in Charles's company were in some ways the most exhilarating I had spent. For a young provincial, the life in London took on, of course, a glamour of its own. Restaurants and theatres and clubs were invested with a warm, romantic haze. And we saw them in a style different from anything I had experienced. The prickliness of the examination evening did not last; it was not much like me, anyway. If we were to go out at all, Charles had to pay.

I noticed that, after he had stopped protecting my feelings, he was not extravagant nor anything approaching it. At bottom, I thought, his tastes were simpler than mine. We ate and went out at night in a decent but not excessive comfort: Soho restaurants, the Carlton Grill, a couple of clubs, the circle and the back row of the stalls. It was decent and not luxurious; it was a scale of living that I had not yet seen.

All that helped. I liked pleasure and good things: and it meant more to me than just the good things themselves; it meant one side, a subsidiary but not negligible side, of the life I wanted to win. Like most young men on the rise, I was a bit of a snob at heart.

In fact, however, I should have gained almost as much exhilaration if I had been walking with Charles through the streets of my own town. There, in the past years as a student, I had made other intimate friends. But the closest of them was a very different person from myself; he saw the world, the people round him, his own passions, in a way which seemed strange to my temperament and which I had to learn step by step. While with Charles, right from our first meeting, I felt that he saw himself and other people much as I did; and he never exhausted his fund of interest.

That was the real excitement, during the first months of our friendship. The picture of those early nights which remained in my memory bore no reference to the dinners and shows, much as I gloated in them; instead, I remembered walking together down Regent Street late one night.

We had just left a coffee stall. Charles carried a mackintosh over his arms, he was stooping a little. He had begun to talk about the characters of Alyosha and Father Zossima. Didn't I think that no other writer but Dostoyevsky could have conveyed goodness in people as one feels it in them? That this was almost the only writer who had an immediate perception of goodness? Why could we accept it from him and doubt it from anybody else?

I could feel the fascination goodness held for him. I recognized what he meant; but at that age I should not have thought of it for myself. We began to argue, with a mixture of exasperation and understanding that often flared up between us. On the one side: isn't it just sentimentality carried out with such touch and such psychological imagination that we swallow it whole? On the other: aren't people like that, even if we choose to see their motives differently, even if we are sceptical about what goodness really means? Then Charles turned to me: his eyes were brighter than ever. They were dark grey, very sharp and intelligent.

'We're each feeling the other's right,' he said. 'The next time I talk about this, I shall appropriate most of what you're saying now – if you're safely out of the way. And you'll do the same, don't you admit it?'

As each day passed in chambers, I looked forward to the evening; but slowly I was managing to occupy myself, and I discovered several odd jobs to do for Getliffe, who soon began to keep me busy. It became clear that Charles was still idle. He seemed to be reading scarcely any law, and I knew quite early that he was unhappy about his career. He spoke of Hart with a kind of lukewarm respect, but was far more eager to hear my stories of Getliffe.

During those months, I still did not know when to expect Charles's concealments. His family, childhood – yes, as we spoke the blank came between us. About women and love and sex, he was franker than I was and knew more. He was not in love, I was: but we talked without any guards at all. When I spoke about my future, my hopes, he listened; if I asked him his, the secretiveness came back as though I had switched off a light. As an evasion he threw himself with intense vicarious interest into my relations with Herbert Getliffe.

As it happened, Getliffe was a tempting person to gossip about. It was hard not to be captivated by him occasionally: it was even harder not to speculate about his intentions, particularly if they had any effect on one's livelihood. I knew that, the first time he interviewed me in chambers, after I had already arranged to become his pupil. He was late for the appointment, and I waited in his room; it was a rainy summer afternoon, and looking down from the window I saw the empty gardens and the river. Getliffe hurried in, dragging his feet, his lip pushed out in an apologetic grin. Suddenly his expression changed into a fixed gaze from brown and lively eyes.

'Don't tell me your name,' he said. His voice was a little strident, he was short of breath. 'You're Ellis –' I corrected him. As though he had not heard my correction at all, he was saying 'You're Eliot.' Soon he was telling me:

'I make it a principle to take people like you. Who've started with nothing but their brains.'

He chuckled, suddenly, as though we were jointly doing someone down: 'It keeps the others up to it.'

'And' – his moods were quick, he was serious and full of responsibility again – 'we've got a duty towards you. One's got to look at it like that.'

Inside a quarter of an hour he had exhorted, advised, warned, and encouraged me. He finished up: 'As for the root of all evil – I shall have to charge you the ordinary pupil's fees. Hundred pounds for this year. This year only. You can pay in quarters. The advantage of the instalment system is that we can reconsider it for the fourth. If you've earned a bit of bread and butter before then.' He smiled, protruding his lip and saying: 'Yes! The labourer is worthy of his hire.'

I told Charles of this conversation in my first week in London. He said: 'His brother was a friend of mine at Cambridge. By the way, he's singularly unlike him. I was taken to dinner with your Herbert once, last year. Of course, he was the life and soul of the party. The point is, when he was talking to you I'm sure he believed every word he said. That's his strength. Don't you feel that's his strength?'

He added a few minutes later: 'I wish I'd known you were going to him, though.'

Then he knew he had made me more anxious: for the unreliability of Getliffe's temperament was one of those disagreeable truths which I could admit equably enough to myself, but was hurt to hear from anyone else. He said quickly: 'I really meant you might have done better at the Chancery Bar. But it'll make no difference. He'll be better in some ways than a solid cautious man could possibly be. It'll even itself out. It won't affect you too much, you agree, don't you?'

If I had mentioned it to Charles in the summer, he would have sent me to some other chambers, and I should have been spared a good deal. For this year, however, there were certain advantages in being with Getliffe. Quite early in the autumn, he began fetching me into his room two or three times each week. 'How's it going?' he would say, and when I mentioned a case, he would expound with a cheerful, invigorating enthusiasm, more often than not getting the details a trifle wrong (that first slip with my name was typical of his compendious but fuzzy memory). Then he would produce some papers for me: 'I'd like a note on that by the end of the week. Just to keep you from rusting.'

Often there were several days' work in one of those notes, and it was only by not meeting Charles and sitting up late that I could deliver it in time. Getliffe would glance through the pages, take them in with his quick, sparkling eyes, and say affably: 'You're getting on! You're getting on!'

The first time it happened, I was surprised to find the

substance of one of those drafts of mine appearing in the course of an opinion of his own. In most places he had not even altered the words.

The weeks went by, the new year arrived: and still Charles had told me little about himself. He had said no more about his family; he had never suggested that I should visit them. He offered no explanation, not even an excuse to save my face. It seemed strange, after he had taken such subtle pains over the most trivial things. It could not be reconciled with all the kind, warm-hearted, patient friendliness I had received at his hands.

At last he asked me. We were having tea in my room on a January afternoon. He spoke in a tone different from any I had heard him use: not diffident or anxious, but cold, as though angry that I was there to receive the invitation.

'I wonder if you would care to dine at my father's house next week?'

I looked at him. Neither of us spoke for a moment. Then he said: 'It might interest you to see the inside of a Jewish family.'

Chapter 3

MR MARCH WITH HIS CHILDREN

At the time, Charles was so distressed that I hurried to
accept and then turn the conversation away. It was later
before I could think over my surprise. For I had been surprised: although as soon as I heard him speak, I thought
myself a fool for not having guessed months before.

I remembered hearing Getliffe chat about 'the real Jewish
upper deck. They're too aristocratic for the likes of us, Eliot'
– and now I realized that he was referring to Charles. As it
happened, however, I had known scarcely a single Jew up to
the time I came to London. In the midland town where I was
born, there had been a few shops with Jewish names over
them; but I could not remember my parents and their friends
even so much as mention a Jewish person. There were none
living in the suburban backstreets; nor, when I got my first
invitations from professional families, were there any there.

I could think of just one exception. It was a boy in my
form at the grammar school. He stayed at the school only
a year or two: he was not clever, and left early: but for the
first term, before we were arranged in order of examination
results, we shared the same desk because our names came
next to each other in the list.

He was a knowing, cheerful little boy who brought large
packets of curious boiled sweets to school every Monday
morning and gave me a share in the midday break. In
Scripture lessons he retired to the back of the class, and
studied a primer on Hebrew. He assumed sometimes an air
of mystery about the secrets written in the Hebrew tongue;
it was only as a great treat, and under solemn promises never
to divulge it, that I gained permission to borrow the primer
in order to learn the alphabet.

I remembered him with affection. He was small, dark,

hook-nosed, his face already set in more adult lines than most of ours in the form. It was an ugly, amiable, precocious face; and on that one acquaintance, so it seemed, I had built up in my mind a standard of Jewish looks.

When I met Charles, it never occurred to me to compare him. He was tall and fair; his face was thin, with strong cheekbones; many people thought him handsome. After one knew that he was a Jew, it became not too difficult to pick out features that might conceivably be 'typical'. For a face so fine-drawn his nostrils spread a little more than one would expect, and his under-lip stood out more fully. But that was like water-divining, I thought, the difficulties of which were substantially reduced if one knew where the water was. After mixing with the Marches and their friends and know-ing them for years, I still sometimes wondered whether I should recognize Charles as a Jew if I now saw him for the first time.

I paid my first visit to Bryanston Square on a clear cold February night. I walked the mile and a half from my lodgings: along Wigmore Street the shops were locked, their windows shining: in the side-streets, the great houses stood dark, unlived-in now. Then streets and squares, cars by the kerb, lighted windows: at last I was walking round the square, staring up at numbers, working out how many houses before the Marches'.

I arrived at the corner house; over the portico there was engraved the inscription, in large plain letters, 17 BRYAN-STON SQUARE.

A footman opened the door, and the butler took my over-coat. With a twinge of self-consciousness, I thought it was probably the cheapest he had received for years. He led the way to the drawing-room, and Charles was at once intro-ducing me to his sister Katherine, who was about four years younger than himself. As she looked at me, her eyes were as bright as his; in both of them, they were the feature one noticed first. Her expression was eager, her skin fresh. At a first sight, it looked as though Charles's good looks had been transferred to a fuller, more placid face.

'I've been trying to bully Charles into taking me out to meet you,' she said after a few moments. 'You were becoming rather a legend, you know.'

'You're underestimating your own powers,' Charles said to her.

'What do you mean?'

'You've cross-questioned me about Lewis. You've done everything but track me. I never realized you had so much character.'

'It was the same with his Cambridge friends,' said Katherine. 'He was just as secretive. It's absolutely monstrous having him for a brother – if one happens to be an inquisitive person.'

She had picked up some of his tricks of speech. One could not miss the play of sympathy and affection between them. Charles was laughing, although he stood about restlessly waiting for their father to come in.

Katherine answered questions before I had asked them, as she saw my eyes looking curiously round the room. It was large and dazzlingly bright, very full of furniture, the side-tables and the far wall cluttered with photographs; opposite the window stood a full-length painting of Charles as a small boy. He was dressed for riding, and was standing against a background of the Row. The colouring was the reverse of timid – the hair bright gold, cheeks pink and white, eyes grey.

'He was rather a beautiful little boy, wasn't he?' she said. 'No one ever thought of painting me at that age. Or at any other, as far as that goes. I was a useful sensible shape from the start.'

Charles said:

'The reason they didn't paint you was that Mr L.' – (their father's first name was Leonard and I had already heard them call him by his nickname) – 'decided that there wasn't much chance of your surviving childhood anyway. And if he tempted fortune by having you painted, he was certain that you'd be absolutely condemned to death.'

I inspected the photographs on the far wall. They were

mostly nineteenth-century, some going back to daguerreo-type days.

'I can't help about those,' said Katherine. 'I don't know anything about them. I'm no good at ancestor worship.' She said it sharply, decisively.

Then she returned, with the repetitiveness that I was used to in Charles, to the reasons why she had not been painted — anxious to leave nothing to doubt, anxious not to be mis-understood.

It was now about a minute to eight, and Mr March came in. He came in very quickly, his arms swinging and his head lowered. As we shook hands, he smiled at me shyly and with warmth. He was bald, but the hair over his ears was much darker than his children's; his features were not so clearcut as theirs. His nose was larger, spread-out, snub, with a thick black moustache under it. When he spoke, he produced gestures that were lively, active, and peculiarly clumsy. They helped make his whole manner simple and direct — to my surprise, for I had expected him to seem formidable at once. But I had only to watch his eyes, even though the skin round them was reddened and wrinkled, to see they had once looked like Charles's and Katherine's and were still as sharp.

He was wearing a dinner jacket, though none of the rest of us had dressed. Charles had several times told me not to. Mr March noticed my glance.

'You mustn't mind my appearance,' he said. 'I'm too old to change my ways. You're all too bohemian for me. But when my children refuse to bring any of their friends to see their aged parent if they have to make themselves uncom-fortable, I'm compelled to stretch a point. I'd rather have you not looking like a penguin than not at all.'

The butler opened the door; we followed Katherine in to dinner. After blinking under the mass of candelabras in the drawing-room, I blinked again, for the opposite reason: for we might have been going into the shadows of a billiard-hall. The entire room, bigger even than the one we had just left, was lit only at the table and by a few wall-lights. On the walls I dimly saw paintings of generations of the family; later I discovered that the earliest, a picture of a dark full-bearded man, was finished in the 1730s, just after the family settled in England.

I sat on Mr March's left opposite Katherine, with Charles at my side; we took up only a segment of the table. A menu card lay by Mr March's place; he read it out to us with gusto and satisfaction : '*clear* soup, fillets of sole, lamb cutlets, caramel mousse, mushrooms on toast.'

The food was very good. Mr March began talking to me about Herbert Getliffe and the Bar; he already knew something of my career.

'My nephew Robert used to be extremely miserable when he was in your position,' said Mr March. 'My brother-in-law warned him he'd got to wait for his briefs, but Robert always was impatient, and I used to see him being disgorged from theatres every time I took my wife out for a spree. One night I met him on the steps of the St James's –'

'What's going to theatres got to do with his being impatient, Mr L.?' Katherine was beginning to laugh.

Mr March, getting into his stride, charged into a kind of anecdote that I was not ready for. I had read descriptions of total recall : Mr March got nearer to it than anyone I had heard. Each incident that he remembered seemed as important as any other incident (this meeting with his nephew Robert was completely casual and happened over twenty years before) : and he remembered them all with extravagant vividness. Time did not matter; something which happened fifty years ago suggested something which happened yesterday.

I was not ready for that kind of anecdote, but his children were. They set him after false hares, they interrupted, sometimes all three were talking at once. I found myself infected with Mr March's excitement, even anxious in case he should not get back to his starting-point.

Listening to the three of them for the first time, I felt dazed. Mr March's anecdotes were packed with references to his relatives and members of their large inter-married families. Occasionally these were explained, but usually taken for granted. He and his children had naturally loud voices, and in each other's presence they became louder still. Between Mr March and Charles I could feel a current of strain; perhaps between Mr March and Katherine also, I did not know; but the relations of all three were very close.

I kept looking from one to another of the clever, energetic, mobile faces. I knew that Charles had regretted inviting me; that, as we waited for his father to come in, he wished the evening were already over; yet now he was more alive than I had ever seen him.

'Yes, what was going to theatres to do with Robert being impatient?' asked Charles.

'If he hadn't been impatient, he wouldn't have gone to theatres,' said Mr March. 'You know he doesn't go now. And if his uncle Philip hadn't been so impatient, he wouldn't have made such a frightful ass of himself last Tuesday. That's my eldest brother, Philip' – he suddenly turned to me – 'I've never known him make such a frightful ass of himself since that night in 1899. The key was lost –'

'When, Mr L.? In 1899?' asked Katherine.

'What key?'

'Last Tuesday, of course. The key of my confounded case. I didn't possess a case in 1899. I used the bag that Hannah gave me. She never liked me passing it on to my then butler. So I told Philip the key was lost when I saw him in my club. They'd just made us trustees of this so-called charity, though why they want to add to my labours and give me enormous worry and shorten my life, I've never been able to understand.' (At that time Mr March was nearly sixty-three. He had retired thirty years before, when the family bank was sold.) 'Philip ought to expect it. They used to call him the longest-headed man on the Stock Exchange. Though since he levelled up on those Brazilian Railways, I have always doubted it.'

'Didn't you level up yourself, Mr L.?' said Katherine. 'Wasn't that the excuse you gave for not buying a car when they first came out?'

'While really he's always been terrified of them. You've never bought a car yet, have you?' said Charles.

'It depends what you mean by buying,' Mr March said hurriedly.

'That's trying to hedge,' said Charles. 'He can't escape, though. He's always hired them from year to year –' he explained to me. 'It must have cost ten times as much, but he felt that if he never really committed himself, he might find some excuse to stop. Incidentally, Mr L., it's exactly your idea of economy.'

'No! No!' Mr March was roaring with laughter, shouting, pointing his finger. 'I refuse to accept responsibility for moving vehicles, that's all. I also told Philip that I refused to accept responsibility if he took action before we considered the documents –'

'The documents in the case?'

'He stood me some tea – extremely bad teas they've taken to giving you in the club: they didn't even provide my special buns that afternoon – and I said we ought to consider the documents and then call at the banks. "When are you going to meet me at these various banks?" I said. He said I was worrying unnecessarily. My married daughter said exactly the same thing before her children went down with chicken-pox. So I told Philip that if he took action without sleeping on it, I refused to be a party to any foolishness that might ensue. I splashed off negotiations.'

'What did you do?' said Katherine.

'I *splashed* off negotiations,' said Mr March, as though it was the obvious, indeed the only word.

'Did Uncle Philip mind?'

'He was enormously relieved. Wasn't he enormously relieved?' Charles asked.

Mr March went on:

'Apart from his initial madheadedness, he took it very well. So I departed from the club. Owing to all these controversies, I was five minutes later than usual passing the clock at the corner; or it may have been fast, you can't trust the authorities to keep them properly. Then I got engaged in another controversy with the newsboy under the clock. I took a paper and he insisted I'd paid, but I told him I hadn't. I thought he was a stupid fellow. He must have mixed me up with a parson who was buying a paper at the same time. I tossed him double or quits, and I unfortunately lost. Then I arrived outside the house, and, just as I was thinking of a letter to Philip dissociating myself from his impulsive methods – I saw a light on in my dressing-room. So I ascended the stairs and found no one present in the room. John – that is my butler,' he remarked to me – 'came with me and I asked for an explanation. No one could offer anything satisfactory. We went into my bedroom and I asked the footman. Not that I've ever known him explain anything. He was under the window on all fours –'

'Oh God, Mr L.,' Katherine broke out. 'I've lost my grip. *Why* was the footman on all fours?'

'*Looking for the key*, of course,' Mr March shouted victoriously. 'It was still lost. John discovered it late that night –'

Mr March sailed into port by describing how the documents were read and showed Philip to have assumed one erroneous datum. But, as Mr March admitted, the datum was quite irrelevant to their transaction, and it was only in method that he had scored a decisive point of judgement.

We went back to the drawing-room for coffee. Mr March sat by the fire, radiant, bursting out into another piece of total recall. Nothing prevented him – I was thinking – from saying what he felt impelled to say; the only decorum he obeyed seemed to rest in purely formal things; he was an uncontrollably natural man, and yet when the coffee was two minutes late he felt a pang, as though something improper had happened.

We had not been sitting long in the drawing-room before Mr March was arranging a time-table for the next day. He visited his chauffeur first thing each morning, with written instructions of the times he and Katherine wanted the car; he felt the next day slipping out of his control unless he could compile the list the previous night.

'I suppose you're really going to the dance at last?' he said to Katherine.

'I'm not absolutely certain,' she said.

'I wish you'd make up your mind one way or the other. How can I keep Taylor in a suitable frame of mind tomorrow if he doesn't know whether he's on duty at eight o'clock or not?'

'Look. I can easily take her if she wants to go,' said Charles.

'I refuse to accept responsibility for my son's car,' said Mr March.

'But I'm pretty certain she'd definitely rather not,' said Charles. 'That's true, Katherine, isn't it?'

'I shan't get any pleasure from it myself. If I go it's only to oblige you, Mr L.,' said Katherine.

I glanced at her. For an instant I thought she was frightened of being a failure at the dance. It did not make much sense – she had pleasant looks, she was so fresh and warm. But she was only eighteen, there were the traces of a schoolgirl left in her: I imagined she could be shy of men, or dread they would have no use for her.

Suddenly, I knew that was not the reason. This dance must have a special meaning.

In fact, as I soon gathered, it was one of the regular dances arranged for the young men and girls of Jewish society in London; a means, as Mr March accepted with his usual realism, of helping to marry them off within their proper circle.

'I'll only go to oblige you,' said Katherine.

'I don't want you to oblige me, but I want you to go.'

'I'll promise to get myself there once before the end of the winter,' said Katherine.

'It's no use attending as though you were paying a visit to a mausoleum,' Mr March shouted.

'I'm certain I can't possibly like it,' she said.

'How do you know you won't like it? Florence thought she wouldn't like it till she tried.'

Florence was not, as I thought at the time, the other daughter – but merely a second cousin of Mr March's.

'I'll try to be unprejudiced when I do go,' she said. 'If you don't press me until I just want to get it over.'

'I'm not pressing you. Except that there are certain actions I require of my daughter –'

Charles broke in:

'That's putting her in a false position.' At once Katherine was left out of the quarrel. Mr March's temper flared against his son. He said:

'It's a position you ought to have adopted on your own account. You've only been there once or twice yourself. Though you knew what I required –'

'Don't you see it is for exactly the same reason that I only went once myself? You're asking her to spend her time with totally uncongenial people –'

'What do you mean, uncongenial?'

Charles said:

'She'll only be miserable if you insist.'

Mr March shouted:

'I don't know why you're specially competent to judge.'

'I'm afraid I know,' said Charles.

'I refuse to recognize it for a minute.'

Katherine was flushed and worried, as she looked from one to the other. Now that the anger was concentrated between them, with her left out, it had taken on a different tone.

Charles began to speak quietly to Mr March. I said to Katherine to take her attention away:

'Don't you think any mass of people sounds rather forbidding? But one can usually find a few who make it tolerable, when one actually arrives.'

She gave an uncomfortable smile. The quarrel, however, seemed to have died down. Soon Mr March said, with no sign that he had been shouting angrily a few minutes before:

'The chief feature of these dances occurred one night when I escorted your mother. I was feeling festive, because we'd recently become engaged. It was 1898, though my sister Caroline always said we were as good as engaged after seder night in '96. She wasn't at this dance, but your mother's sister Nellie was, unfortunately as it turned out. We'd been dancing very vigorously, proper old-fashioned dancing that you're all too degenerate to approve of. So I went outside to mop my brow. When I came back into the room your mother and her sister were sitting down on the other side. Someone stopped me and said: "Mr March, I must felicitate you on your engagement." I didn't like him, but I said "Thank you very much"; I thought I might as well be civil. Then he said: "Isn't your fiancée sitting over there?" And I agreed. He went on – he was a talkative fellow – and said: "I suppose she's the pretty one on the left." ' Mr March simmered with laughter. 'Of course, he'd fallen into the trap. That was her sister. No one ever thought my wife was the prettier one. But I liked her more.'

At exactly 10.40 Mr March started to his feet and said good-night. 'You'll visit us again, I hope,' he said, in a manner so simple and natural that it seemed more than a form. Then, with equal attention to the task in hand, he set off on a tour of inspection round the room; he pulled aside each curtain to make sure that the window behind it was latched for the night. His final words were to Charles:

'Don't forget to lock this door. When you decide to retire.'

When he had left, Charles explained:

'The idea is, you imagine a burglar getting through the windows. In spite of the fact that Mr L. has seen they're locked and bolted. Then, having got through the window, the burglar discovers with amazement that the door is locked on the other side.'

Katherine smiled.

'But he was more tolerable than I expected tonight, I must say,' she said. 'I thought there might be a scene. I was afraid it might be embarrassing for you,' she said to me.

'Yes,' said Charles. Then he asked her: 'You are satisfied, aren't you? You do feel that things are coming out better?'

'Thanks to the way you coped,' she said.

In a few minutes she went to bed, and soon Charles and I

walked out into the square. I told him how much I liked them both.

'I'm enormously glad,' he said. His face was lit up with a blaze of pleasure; for a second, he looked boyish and happy.

We talked about Mr March. Charles pointed back to the house: several windows were still lighted. 'He's waiting to hear me come in,' he said. 'Then he'll trot downstairs to see that the door is properly fastened.' Charles was speaking with fondness; but I noticed that he found it easier to talk of Mr March's eccentric side. He was using this joke, this legend of Mr March, to distract first my eyes, and then his own.

When I mentioned Katherine again, he broke out without any reserve.

'I'm devoted to her, of course. As it happened, we were bound to have a lot in common. It was exciting when I suddenly discovered that she was growing up.' Then he said: 'I couldn't let her be sent to this dance – without trying to stop it. You could see it wasn't just ordinary diffidence, couldn't you?'

I said: 'As soon as she spoke.'

'If a man she liked wanted to take her to a dance, she might be nervous, and then I'd definitely bully her into going,' said Charles. 'It would do her good to be flirted with. But this is different. It means something important to her. If she goes, she's accepting –' He hesitated. He had suddenly begun to speak with obsessive force. He said: 'If she goes, she'll find it harder to keep on terms with everything she wants to be.'

Chapter 4

A SIGN OF WEALTH

CHARLES seemed to be afraid that, during our conversation about Katherine, he had given himself away. He did not refer to it again until, in curious circumstances, he made a confession. That happened some months later than my introduction to his family, on the night after his first case.

Meanwhile, Mr March and Katherine welcomed me at Bryanston Square, and I went there often.

On the surface, of course, we were novelties to each other – I as much to them as they to me. They had never known a poor young man. Mr March once or twice took an opportunity to put me at my ease; on one occasion, I had written to him apologizing for having caused some trouble (my rooms became uninhabitable owing to a burst gas-pipe, and I stayed a couple of nights at Bryanston Square). He replied in a letter which covered two sheets of writing paper; his handwriting was firm, his style rather like his speech, but sometimes both eloquent and stately; he said '... as you know, no one deplores more than I the indifference to manners and common decency displayed by the younger generation. But I am glad to make an exception of yourself, who are always the height of punctiliousness and good form. ...' It was untrue, by any conceivable standard. It delighted me to read it; it gave me the special pleasure of being flattered on a vulnerable spot.

On my side, I was often fascinated by the sheer machinery of their lives. They were the first rich family I had known; in those first months, it was their wealth that took my attention more, not their Jewishness. It was the signs of wealth that I kept absorbing – yes, with a kind of romantic inflation, as though I had been one of Balzac's young men.

I should have done the same if they had not been Jews at

36

all; yet I had already seen the meaning which being Jews had for both Charles and Katherine. They had not spoken of it. I dared not hurt them by saying a word. I could not forget Charles's invitation to 'see the inside of a Jewish family' nor Katherine's face as they quarrelled about the dance. This silence, which got in the way of our intimacy, had the minor result of misleading me. I did not appreciate for a long time how eminent the family was. I picked up some facts, that Mr March's brother Philip was the second baronet, that both Philip and his father had sat as Conservative members: but no one mentioned, or let me infer, that the Marches were one of the greatest of Anglo-Jewish houses.

About their luxuries, however, they were as amused as I was. They were both quick at seeing their everyday actions through fresh eyes.

Katherine said one night as she came down to dinner: 'I thought of you in my bath, Lewis. I just remembered that I've never run one single bath for myself in the whole of my life.'

One afternoon at Bryanston Square, I made another discovery. Charles and I were alone in the drawing-room. There came a tap on the door, and a small elderly man entered the room, wearing a cloth cap. I thought he could scarcely be a servant: Charles took no notice, and went on talking. The man walked up to the clock over the fireplace, opened it, wound it up, and went away.

'Whoever is that?' I asked.

'Oh,' said Charles, 'that's the clock man.'

Charles looked surprised, then began to smile as I asked more questions. The clock man had no other connexion with the house; he was appointed to come in on one afternoon a week, and wind up and supervise all the clocks. He was engaged on the same terms by other houses in the square; like many of the Marches' servants, he would be recommended from one relative to another—their butlers and chief parlourmaids usually began as junior servants in another March household. Charles claimed to have heard one of his aunts ask: 'I wonder if you can tell me of a good reliable clock man?'

It seemed bizarre, more so than any of the open signs of wealth. As Charles said: 'I suppose it is the sort of thing anyone would expect Mr L. to do himself. Putting on his deerstalker hat for the purpose.'

But there was one sign of wealth that neither Charles nor I could face so easily.

Our year as pupils ended in September; at the end of it, Charles remained in Hart's chambers, scarcely mentioning the fact; Getliffe let me stay on in his 'paying a nominal rent. Just as a matter of principle'. He had not referred again to any remission of pupil's fees; he promised to find me some work, and several times I heard the phrase 'the labourer is worthy of his hire'.

In fact, I was doing the same work that winter as when I was still a pupil. I told myself that nothing worth having could possibly come yet. Just as I had done the year before, I attended many cases, as though it were better to be in court as a spectator than not at all. Charles, just as he had done the year before, came with me to hear Getliffe in the King's Bench Courts. One day, it was all according to the usual pattern. Getliffe for once was not late, but he was no less flurried-looking. His wig was grimy, and he pushed it askew. As usual, when he spoke he gave the impression of being both nervous and at home. He used short and breathless sentences and occasionally broke into his impudent shame-faced smile. The case was merely a matter of disentangling some intricate precedent and he was doing it clumsily and at length. Yet the judge was kind to him, most people were on his side.

When they went in to lunch, Charles and I walked in the Temple gardens, just as we had often done the year before.

'One thing about him,' said Charles, 'he does enjoy what he's doing. Don't you agree? He thoroughly enjoys coming into court and wearing his wig. Even though he's a bit nervous. Of course he enjoys being a bit nervous. He's completely happy playing at being a lawyer.'

Then he smiled, and his eyes shone.

'But still, I refuse to let him take me in altogether. It will be monstrous if he wins this case. It will be absolutely monstrous.'

Charles began to argue, at his most incisive, what Getliffe's case should have been. He could not forget what he called the 'muddiness' of Getliffe's mind: even though he felt humorously tender to him as he heard him speak, even though he could not escape the envy that a carefree spontaneous nature evokes in one more constrained.

'Ah well,' I said, 'I wouldn't mind putting up a bit of muddiness myself – if I could get a foot in first.'

Charles was intent on the pure argument; for him, usually so quick, it took moments to realize that I had spoken bitterly. We were further apart than usual; here, more than anywhere, each felt estranged from the other; as our careers came nearer, we began to know for the first time that we were being driven different ways. Then he said:

'I suppose you feel that you're wasting months of your life.'

'Don't you? Don't you?'

'I might waste more than months.' He paused, and went on: 'Don't you think that even Getliffe sometimes wonders whether he's been such a success after all?'

'I'd prefer it to none at all.'

'That's over-simple,' said Charles. 'Or else I'm making excuses in advance. Do you mean that?'

'How much are you looking forward to your first case?' I said.

'Not very much,' said Charles. 'Not in your fashion. I don't know. I may be glad when it comes.'

Within a month of that conversation, his first case came. Something different, that is, from the guinea visits to the police courts, which we had both made: instead, a breach of contract, legally interesting although the amounts involved were small, arrived in Hart's chambers. The plaintiff knew one of Charles's uncles, and Hart himself; Hart, who had married Charles's cousin, suggested that young March was the most brilliant of the family and only needed some encouragement. So the case came to Charles. There was nothing sensational about it; it was a chance for which, that winter, I would have given an ear.

Charles could see the depth, the rancour, of my envy. One of the nights we studied the papers together, he looked at me with eyes dark and hard.

'I'm just realizing how true it is,' he said, 'that it's not so easy to forgive someone, when you're taking a monstrously unfair advantage over him.' Trying to compensate for my envy, I spent evenings with him over the case. He was so restless, so anxious, that it was uncomfortable to be near: to begin with, I envied him even that. To have a real event to be anxious about! Then I suspected that this was not just ordinary anxiety.

He worked hard, but he was tense all the time, getting out of bed at night to make sure he had written a point down. If and when my first case came, I thought, I should do the same. But I should still be in high spirits – while one had only to listen to Charles's voice to hear something inexplicably harsh, not only anxious but abnormally strained.

As the hearing drew nearer (it was fixed for the middle of January) he seemed to find a little relief in violent, trivial worries about the case: 'I shall put up the dimmest opening,' he said, 'that's ever been heard in a court of law. Can't you imagine the heights of dimness that I shall manage to reach?'

Several times, as I heard him reiterate these anxieties, I thought how they would have deceived me only a short time before. Charles was the most restrained of his family; but, like Mr March and Katherine, he did not try to be stoical in little things. Many acquaintances felt that their worries (over, for instance, this opening speech, or catching a train, or whether someone had overheard an indiscreet remark) could only be indulged in by weak and unavailing people. It was tempting to regard them as part of the sapping process of luxury. It was tempting: it seemed sociologically just:

but in fact, when affliction came, not petty worry, each of the three Marches was stoical in the end.

Katherine knew this, although on those nights at Bryanston Square, while Charles was waiting for his case to come on, she watched him with pain. I wondered if she understood better than I why he was so tense. Whether she understood or not, her own nerves were strung up. But she could still tease him about the symptoms of fuss; as she did so one evening, she repeated in my presence the latest story of Mr March's fussing, which was only a few months old.

As I knew, Mr March always expressed gloomy concern if one of his children had a sore throat: he would enquire after it repeatedly, with the most lugubrious expression: 'Wouldn't it be better if I sent for a practitioner? Not that I pretend to have much faith in any of them. Wouldn't it be better if I sent for one tonight?' In the same way, he profoundly doubted anyone's ability to get to the correct station in time to catch an appropriate train: travelling could only be achieved by a kind of battle against the railways, in which he sat like a general surrounded by maps and time-tables, drawing up days before any journey an elaborate chart of possible contingencies.

In the past summer, he had spent himself prodigiously over a journey of Katherine's. She had never been away alone up to this time; even now, it was scarcely alone in any but Mr March's sense of the word, as she was going on a cruise down the Adriatic, in a party organized by her young women's club. Mr March opposed on principle; and, when she got her way, occupied a good part of a night in making certain what would happen if she missed the party at Victoria on the first morning.

Three days after the party started, Mr March received a telegram. It reached him half an hour after breakfast and read: *Regret Katherine ill in — hospital Venice food poisoning suspected urgent you should join her.* It was signed by the secretary of the club. Mr March said in a business-like tone to Charles: 'Your sister's ill. I may be away some time', and caught the eleven o'clock boat train.

He arrived at the hospital the following midday; he interviewed the doctors, decided it was nothing grave, and then began to grumble at the heat. He was wearing his black coat and striped trousers, and he had arrived in a Venetian July.

He saw Katherine, said: 'I refuse to believe there's anything wrong', and walked off to find an English doctor. He had all his life expressed distrust of 'those foreign practitioners'. When he talked to an English one, however, he decided that he was probably incompetent and that the Italians 'seemed level-headed fellows'. So Mr March accepted the position; he could do nothing more; he retired to his hotel and sat in his shirt sleeves looking at the Grand Canal.

In a couple of days Mr March and the Italian doctors agreed that Katherine could be safely moved to the hotel. Mr March arranged everything with competence; as soon as Katherine began to walk about, he said, with an air of conviction and scorn:

'I knew there was never anything wrong.'

They stayed in Venice for a fortnight. From the moment of his arrival, he had behaved with equanimity. When she recovered, however, the air of sensible friendliness suddenly broke: and it broke in a characteristic way. Katherine slept in the room next to Mr March's: like his, its windows gave on to the Canal: to Mr March's horror, she wanted to leave them open all night. Mr March angrily protested. Katherine pointed out that no gondolier could get in without climbing from the balcony beneath: and that, in any case, her jewellery had been deposited in the manager's safe and there was nothing valuable to steal.

Mr March stamped up and down the room. 'My dear girl,' he shouted, 'it's not your valuables I'm thinking of, it's your virtue.' Katherine stuck to her point. An hour later, when they were both in bed, she heard his voice come loudly through the wall:

'How sharper than a serpent's tooth. . . .' The last words sounded, at first hearing, as though they were an invention of her own. But like most of the March stories, this was discussed in Mr March's presence: he protested, chuckled, added to it, and it must have been substantially true. In fact, if Mr March felt like King Lear, he acted upon it, even if the occasion seemed to others inadequate.

The story must have been true, except for what they each left out. They left out what none of us would find it necessary to tell in a family story: the fact that there was deep feeling in the quarrel, though the occasion was so absurd: that Katherine, arguing with her father, felt more overawed and frightened than she could admit: that Mr March felt a moment of anxiety, such as we all know as we see someone beginning to slip from the power of our possessive love.

Chapter 5

CONFESSION

CHARLES'S case lasted for a day and a half. From the beginning, lawyers thought it impossible that anyone could win it: at times, particularly on the second morning, I found my judgement wavering – was he going to prove us wrong after all? His manner was restless, sometimes diffident, sometimes sharp and ruthless: I knew – it was not an unqualified pleasure for me to know – that I did not often hear a case argued with such drive and clarity.

Mr March sat through every word. As he watched his son, his face lost its expression of lively, fluid interest, and became tightened into one that was nervous, preoccupied, and rigid. He took me out to lunch on the first day; his mood was quieter than usual, and he was glad to have someone to talk to.

'My daughter Katherine has mysteriously refused to put in an appearance,' he said. 'She did not account for her actions, but the reason is, of course, that she couldn't bear to watch my son making a frightful ass of himself in public. I must say that I can sympathize with her attitude. When he contrived to get himself into the team at school, I used to feel that propriety demanded that I should be represented in person: but invariably I wished that I could take a long walk behind the pavilion when he came out to bat.'

Mr March went on:

'I also considered today that propriety demanded that I should be present in person. Even though it might entail seeing my son make a frightful ass of himself upon an important occasion. So far as I can gather with my ignorance of your profession, however, he appears to have avoided disaster so far. Hannah might not think so, but I fail to see why she is specially competent to judge.'

44

I told him how well Charles had done; Mr March gave a delighted and curiously humble smile.

'I'm extremely glad to have your opinion,' he said. 'This is the first time that I've been able to consider the prospect of any of my family emerging into the public eye.' He added, in a matter-of-fact tone: 'I could never have cut anything of a dash myself. My son may conceivably find it easier.'

We walked back to the court, Mr March still nervous and proud. For the first time I had seen how much he was living again in his son.

*

In the last hours of the case, Charles's cross-examination of an expert witness secured most attention. Several people later commented on how formidable a cross-examiner he would become. Actually, his own strain gave him an added edge; but still, he enjoyed those minutes. He loved argument: he was sometimes ashamed of the harshness that leapt to his tongue, but when he let himself go, argument made him fierce, cheerful, quite spontaneous and self-forgetful. The court had just admired him in one of those moods.

In the end, Charles lost the case, but the judge paid a compliment to 'the able manner, if I may say so, in which the case has been handled by the plaintiff's counsel.'

As we left the court, men collected round Charles, congratulating him. I joined them and did the same, before I went back to chambers.

'I want to see you rather specially. I'll come round tomorrow night,' said Charles. 'Can you manage to stay in?'

On my way to the Inn, I wondered what he was coming for. He had looked flushed and smiling: perhaps his success – my envy kept gnawing, as sharp, as dominating as neuralgia – had settled him at last. I walked along the back streets down from the Strand; it was a grey afternoon, and a mizzle of rain was greasing the pavement. I thought about Charles's future compared with mine. In natural gifts there was not much in it. He was at least as clever, and had a better legal mind; perhaps I was the more speculative. In strength of character we were about the same. In everything but natural gifts, he had so much start that I was left at the post.

I had one advantage, though. Neither of us was the kind of man whom his career would completely satisfy. Charles had read for the Bar because he could not find a vocation; I had always known that, in the very long run, I wanted other things. The difference was, I had to behave as though the doubt did not exist. To earn a living, I had to work as though I was single-minded. Until I made some money and some sort of name, I could not even let myself look round. Charles often envied that simplification, that compulsory simplification, which being poor imposed upon my life.

Nevertheless, anyone in his senses would put his money on Charles, I told myself that afternoon. As Herbert Getliffe remarked when I arrived and told him of the result: 'Mark my words, Eliot, that young friend of ours will go a long way.' He went on: 'He was lucky to get the job, of course. The boys on the Jewish upper deck are doing a bit of pulling together. Don't you wish you were in that racket, Eliot?'

He looked harassed, responsible, sincere.

'I must see if I can find you a snippet for yourself one of these days. The trouble is, one owes a duty to one's clients. One can't forget that, much as one would like to –'

The next night, I waited in my room for Charles. It was a room which bore only a remote resemblance to Mr March's drawing-room. The satin was wearing through on the two arm-chairs; the room was unheated all day, and even by the fire at night it struck empty and chill, with the vestige of a smell of hair-lotion drifting up from the barber's shop down below. Charles was late: at last I heard his car draw up below, and his footsteps on the stairs. As soon as he entered, I was struck by the expression on his face. The strain had left him. He apologized for keeping me; I knew that he was tired, relaxed, and content.

He sat in the other chair, at the opposite side of the fire-place. Nothing had been said except for his apologies. He stretched himself in the chair, and smiled. He said:

'Lewis, I shan't go on with the Bar.'

I exclaimed. After a moment, I said: 'You've not settled anything, have you?'

'What do you think?' He was still smiling.

'You know you'd do well at it,' I began. 'Better than any of us –'

'I'm sure that's nonsense,' he said. 'But in any case, it isn't the point. You know it isn't the point, don't you?'

He had not come for advice. His mind was made up. There was no anxiety or hesitation left in his manner. He was speaking more calmly, with more strength and authority, than I had ever heard him speak.

'I was very glad that I didn't disgrace myself yesterday,' he said. 'Because one of the reasons for giving up the law wasn't exactly pleasing to one's self-respect. I knew it all along: I wanted to escape because I was frightened. I was frightened that I shouldn't succeed.'

'I don't believe much in that,' I said.

'You mustn't minimize it.' He smiled at me. 'Remember, I'm a much more diffident person than you are. As well as being much more spiritually arrogant. I hate competing unless I'm certain that I'm going to win. The pastime I really enjoy most is dominoes, right hand against left. So I wanted to slip out: but I should have felt cheap doing it.'

I nodded.

'What would have happened if you hadn't done so well yesterday?'

'Do you think I've enough character to go on until I'd satisfied myself?' He chuckled. 'I wonder if I or anyone else could really have stuck on doggedly at the Bar until they felt sufficiently justified. It would have been rather heroic: but it would also have been slightly mad. Don't you agree it would have been mad? No, I'm sure I should have given it up whatever had happened. But if I'd been a complete failure yesterday, I should have felt pretty inferior because I was escaping. Now I don't, at any rate to the same extent.' He went on: 'Of course, you know what I think about the law.'

He meant the law as an occupation: for a time we went

over our past arguments: I knew as well as he did how he found the law sterile, how he could not feel value in such a life. Then Charles said:

'Well, those were two reasons I've thought about for months. You can't dismiss them altogether. I shall always have a slight suspicion that I ran away. But, like all the other reasons one thinks about for months, they had just about as much effect on my actions as Mr L.'s patent medicines have on his superb health. It was something quite different – that I didn't need or want to think about – that made it certain I should have to break away.'

He looked straight at me.

'I think you've realized it for long enough,' he said. 'You remember the first time I talked to you about Katherine?'

'Yes.'

'I was afraid afterwards that you must have noticed something,' he said, with a grim smile. 'It was the first time you came to our house, of course. I was very much upset because she was being sent to that dance against her will. I was pretending to be concerned only about her welfare. I was talking about her, and trying to believe that I was being detached and dispassionate. You've done the same thing yourself, haven't you? It was the sort of occasion when one sits with a furrowed brow trying to work out someone else's salvation – and knows all the time that one's talking about oneself.'

'Yes,' I said.

'Probably you understand,' said Charles, 'without my saying any more. But I want to explain myself. It's curiously difficult to speak, still. Even tonight, when I'm extremely happy, I'm still not quite free.'

He said, slowly:

'The Bar represented part of an environment that I can't accept for myself. You see, I can't say it simply. If I stayed at the Bar, I should be admitting that I belonged to the world' – he hesitated – 'of rich and influential Jews. That is the world in which most people want to keep me. Most people, both inside it and outside. If I stayed at the Bar, I should get cases from Jewish solicitors, I should become one of the gang. And people outside would dismiss me, not that they need so much excuse, as another bright young Jew. Do you think it's tolerable to be set aside like that?'

There was a silence. He went on:

'I haven't enjoyed being a Jew. Since I was a child, I haven't been allowed to forget – that other people see me through different eyes. They label me with a difference that I can't accept. I know that I sometimes make myself feel a stranger, I know that very well. But still, other people have made me feel a stranger far more often than I have myself. It isn't their fault. It's simply a fact. But it's a fact that interferes with your spirits and nags at you. Sometimes it torments you – particularly when you're young. I went to Cambridge desperately anxious to make friends who would be so intimate that I could forget it. I was aching for that kind of personal success – to be liked for the person I believed myself to be. I thought, if I couldn't be liked in that way, there was nothing for it: I might as well go straight back to the ghetto.'

He stopped suddenly, and smiled. He looked very tired, but full of relief.

As I listened, I was swept on by his feeling, and at the same time surprised. I had noticed something, but nothing like all he had credited me with. I had seen him wince before, but took it to be the kind of wound I had known in myself through being born poor; I too had sometimes been looking out for snubs. In me, that was not much of a wound, though: it had never triggered off a passion. Now I was swept along by his, moved and yet with a tinge of astonishment or doubt.

'What shall you do?' I said, after a silence. 'Do you know what your career's to be?'

'Most people will assume that I intend to drift round and become completely idle.'

Then I asked if anyone else knew of his abandoning the Bar. He shook his head.

'Mr L. will be disappointed, of course,' he said.

'He was talking to me yesterday,' I said. 'He was delighted

about the case. He's set his heart on your being a success in the world.'

For a moment, Charles was angry.

'You're exaggerating that,' he said. 'You forget that he'd get equally excited if any of his relations made a public appearance of any kind.' Then he added, in a different tone:

'I hope you're not right.'

I was startled by the concern which had suddenly entered his voice: he seemed affected more strongly than either of us could explain that night.

Chapter 6

FULL DINNER PARTY

WITHIN a few days of Charles's visit, he told me that he had broken the news to Mr March. He also told me how Mr March had responded: he wanted to convince me that his father had accepted the position without distress. In fact, Mr March's behaviour seemed to have been odd in the extreme.

His first reply was: 'I don't believe a word of it.' This was said in a flat, dejected tone, so Charles admitted: but at once Mr March began to grumble, almost as though he were parodying himself: 'You ought to have chosen a more suitable time to tell me. You might have known that hearing this would put me out of step for the day.' Then he added again: 'In any case, I don't believe a word of it.'

For several days he refused to discuss the matter. He seemed to be pretending that he had forgotten it. At the same time, he kept asking with concern ·about his son's health and spirits; one day at lunch, without any preamble, he offered Charles a handsome increase of his allowance to pay for a holiday.

Mr March still went about the house as though he had not so much as heard Charles's intention. It was not until the next full family dinner party that he had to face it.

Each Friday night, when they were in London, Mr March and his brothers took it in turn to give a dinner party to the entire family: the entire family in its widest sense, their wives, their sisters and their sisters' husbands, the children of them all, remoter relations. When I first knew the Marches, it was rare for a 'Friday night' to be attended by less than thirty, and fifty had been reached at least once since 1918.

The tradition of these parties went back continuously to

the eighteenth century; for the past hundred years they had been held according to the same pattern, every week from September to the end of the London season.

As luck would have it, I was invited for that night. As a rule, friends of the family were asked only if they were staying in the house; it was by a slight extension of the principle that Mr March invited me.

Getliffe's brother Francis, whose friendship with Charles began in their undergraduate days, had been living at Bryanston Square for the week. When I arrived there for tea on the Thursday, the drawing-room was empty. It was Francis who was the first to join me. He came in with long, plunging, masterful strides, strides too long for a shortish man. His face was clearly drawn, fastidious, quixotic, with no kind of family resemblance to Herbert's, who was his father's son by a first marriage. He had not a trace of Herbert's clowning tricky matiness. Indeed, that afternoon he was nervous in the Marches' house, though he often stayed there.

He disliked being diffident; he had trained himself into a commanding impatient manner; and yet most people at that time felt him to be delicate underneath. He was two years older than Charles; he was a scientist, and the year before had been elected a fellow of their college.

'Will you dine with me tomorrow, Lewis?' he asked. 'They've got their usual party on here, and it'd be less trouble if I got out of the way.'

'Of course,' I said.

'Good work,' said Francis. Then he asked, a little awkwardly, how I was getting on with his brother.

'He's very stimulating,' I said.

'I can believe that,' said Francis. 'But has he put you in the way of any briefs?'

'No,' I said.

Francis cursed, and flushed under his dark sunburnt skin. He was both a scrupulous and a kind-hearted man.

Just then Charles and Katherine came in. As we began tea, Francis said, with an exaggerated casualness: 'By the

way, I've arranged to dine out with Lewis tomorrow night.
You'll forgive me, won't you? It'll give you more room for
the party.'

Katherine's face was open in disappointment.

'I hoped you would come,' she said.

'I should be in the way,' said Francis. 'It will definitely be
much better if I disappear.'

Katherine recovered herself, and said:

'You are more or less expected to come, you know. Mr L.
will say "If I am obliged to have the fellow residing in my
house, I can't send him away while we make beasts of ourselves." He'll certainly expect you to come.'

'I don't think I should do you credit,' he said.

'You'll find points of interest, I promise you,' she said.

'I shouldn't know many of them, you see —'

'Look here,' said Katherine, 'do you want another Gentile
to keep you company? I'm certain Lewis will oblige, won't
you?'

She turned to me: as I heard that gibe of hers, I felt how
fond she was of him.

Since Charles had spoken to me about Jewishness, so had
she. It was no longer a forbidden subject. 'It was a bit hard,'
Katherine had said, 'to be stopped riding one's scooter in
the Park on Saturday because it was the Sabbath, and then
on Sunday too. It seemed to me monstrously unjust.' She
had gone on: 'But the point was, you were being treated
differently from everyone else. You wouldn't have minded
anything but that. As it was, you kept thinking about every
single case.' Less proud than Charles, she had talked about
her moments of shame: but she was still vulnerable. It was
not till she teased Francis about being a Gentile that I heard
her speak equably, as though it did not matter any more.

'It's a bit hard on him,' said Francis. He broke into a smile
that, all of a sudden, narrowed his eyes, creased his cheeks,
and made his whole expression warm: 'I'd better tell you,
I'm feeling very shy.'

Charles broke in:

'It'll be slightly bizarre, but you must come. Even if it's

only to oblige Lewis. I'm sure he can't resist the temptation. Incidentally, even if it weren't so tempting, he wouldn't be able to refuse it.' Charles went on: 'Lewis is temperamentally incapable of refusing any invitation, whether he wants to go or not. Isn't that true?'

Katherine asked Mr March as soon as he entered the house. He came into the room and invited us both. I knew he felt it irregular; he did not want either of us at a family party; but his natural warmth prevailed. 'Eight o'clock sharp,' he said. 'And you must both dress suitably for once. For this occasion, I can't possibly let you off.'

I had never seen the house anything but empty before that Friday night. Cars were drawn up bonnet to stern in the square; from the hall one heard the clash of March voices; the drawing-room was full. There was already an orchestra-like effect of voices and laughs: this was the week's exchange of family news. Every day, the Marches told each other the latest pieces of family gossip; Mr March would meet his brother Philip at the club, Philip would tell his wife, she would ring up her children; but it was on Friday night that the stories were crystallized, argued over, and finally passed into the common stock.

Several of the characters in Mr March's sagas were that night present in the flesh. Sir Philip, a spare man, the furrows of whose face seemed engraved not by anxiety but by a stiff, caustic humour – he took for granted his position as head of the family and here, in his brother's house, he walked round the entire company, giving everyone a handshake and a switched-on truculent smile. Mr March's favourite sister Caroline, and her husband Lionel Hart, a brother of Charles's former master. Their son Robert, who, despite Mr March's pessimistic forecasts, had been for years successfully practising in company law. Florence Simon, the cousin who 'thought she wouldn't like it till she tried'. A large family of Herbert Marches, the children of the youngest brother. Mr March's eldest daughter Evelyn, plump and pleasant-looking in a different fashion from Katherine, much darker and brown-eyed. She had married the editor of a

Jewish paper, who was not present. Charles and Katherine said she was happy, but Mr March sometimes referred to her marriage with gloom.

There were many unusual faces. Three or four looked, in the stereotyped sense, Jewish. Some of the older women were enormous. Both in face and figure, the party seemed the most unstandardized one could imagine. Beauty, grotesque oddity, gigantic fatness – the family went to all extremes. There was scarcely anyone there whom, for one reason or another, one would not look at twice.

Unfortunately for me, Mr March's eldest sister, Hannah, was not there. I wanted to see her, as she entered his narrative as a symbol of disapproval and the self-appointed leader of all oppositions. There was a legend of Mr March, on his way to his honeymoon at Mentone, putting his head out of the window at Saint Raphael and sniffing the air: then he turned to his bride and said: 'The air is quite different here. Hannah would say it isn't, but it is.'

*

The dining-room was no more clearly lit than usual when we went in; the table had been lengthened to contain the party. Mr March placed Philip on his left hand, and Philip's wife on his right: then the brothers and sisters in order of seniority: Charles at the far end of the table, and the younger people near him. I sat a place or two from Charles between Florence Simon and one of the Herbert March girls.

Voices rose and blared as, looking down the table, I saw faces coming out of the shadows: I felt a glow because these Friday nights had gone on for so long. It was the warm romantic glow, the feeling of past time: the glow which made one of those dead and gone Friday nights become more enchanted in our minds than it ever was to sit through. I felt exactly as I sometimes did at dinner at the Inn, or when I was Francis's guest at his High Table. The chain of lives – odd glimmers ran through my head, the fragments of information which had come down about the first English Marches sitting round their dinner-table in the City, just over their bank. The two original March families dined together on the Friday in the week they arrived in London from Deventer.

How they had first got established in Holland, where they had come from before that, there was no record nor any tradition – not even of how they derived their name. In Spain March could have been a Jewish name, but there was no evidence that these Marches ever lived there. The first mention of them in the archives was mid-seventeenth-century: they were already in Holland, already one of the leading families of the Ashkenazim (the Northern group of Jews, as opposed to the Sephardim who lived in Spain and round the Mediterranean coasts).

They were well-off when they left Deventer. During the last half of the eighteenth century, Friday night by Friday night, these parties went on, families walking to each other's houses across the narrow City streets; their friends and relatives, the family of Levi Barend Cohen, the Rothschilds, the Montefiores, lived close by.

The nineteenth century came in; all those families, like those of the Gentile bankers, moved westward; and the Marches' dinners took place now round Holborn. It was already the fourth generation since Deventer; the children were no longer given Jewish first names. A honeymoon couple travelled in postchaises along the French roads as soon as the war was over, and Charlotte March wrote in 1816: 'it must be admitted that in the arts of the toilette and the cuisine France excels our country: but we can hearten ourselves as English people that in *everything* essential we are infinitely superior to a country which shows so many profligacies that it is charitable to attribute them to their infamous revolution.' This though they stayed with their Rothschild uncle in Paris; that pair thought of themselves as English, differing as little from their acquaintances as the Roman Catholic families who, when Charlotte wrote, were still hoping to be emancipated.

Victoria's reign began. Round the dinner-table, the Marches were sometimes indignant at Jewish disabilities;

David Salomons was not allowed to take his seat in Parliament. There was also talk, even in the forties, of liberalizing themselves; one March became a Christian. Apart from him, no March had married 'out of the faith': nor indeed out of their own circle of Anglo-Jewish families. That was still true down to the people round this table; except for one defection, by a woman cousin of Mr March's, thirty years before.

The March bank flourished; many of the families moved to the neighbourhood of Bryanston Square; by the seventies, one of Mr March's uncles was holding Friday dinners at No. 17. The universities and Parliament became open, and Mr March's father went into the House. England was the least anti-Semitic of countries; when the news of the pogroms arrived from Russia in 1880, the Lord Mayor opened a fund for Jewish relief. Half the University of Oxford signed a protest. The outrages seemed an anachronistic horror to decent prosperous Englishmen. The Marches sent thousands of pounds to the Lord Mayor's fund. Yet that news was only a quiver, a remote quiver, in the distant world.

By then the Marches had reached their full prosperity; on Friday nights cabs made their way under the gaslight to the great town houses. The Marches were secure, they were part of the country, they lived almost exactly the lives of other wealthy men.

The century passed out: its last twenty years, and the next fourteen, were the best time for wealthy men to be alive. The Marches developed as prodigally as the other rich.

Those were the heroic days of Friday nights. A whole set of stories collected round them, most of which originated when Mr March was a young man. Of Uncle Henry March, who owned race-horses and was a friend of the Prince of Wales; how he regretted all his life his slowness in repartee, and after each Friday night used to wake his wife in bed so that she should jot down answers which had just occurred to him. Of his brother Justin, who, to celebrate a Harrow victory, rode to his house on one of the horses that drew the heavy roller at Lord's; and who, when only nine people attended one of his Friday nights, took hold of the tablecloth

57

and pulled the whole dinner service to the ground. Of their cousin, Alfred March Hart, the balletomane who helped sponsor Diaghilev's first season in London: who as an old man, hearing someone at a Friday night during the war hope for a Lansdowne peace, rose to his feet and began: 'I am a very old man: and I hope the war will continue for many years after my death.'

They were the sort of stories that one finds in any family that has been prosperous for two hundred years. For me they evoked the imaginary land which exists just before one's childhood. Often as I heard them I felt something like homesick – homesick for a time before I was born, for a society which would have thought my father's home about as primitive as a Trobriand Islander's.

*

The dinner began. At the head of the table, Philip and Mr March were talking about expectations for the Budget. Mr March suggested that supertax would be applied at a lower limit.

'I don't believe it,' said Philip. 'That's on a par with your idea for the new trust, Leonard.'

Mr March chuckled.

'I should like to remind you that your last idea didn't bring in sufficient for your requirements. Also that you made an exhibition of yourself over that same trust. That was the time your husband wrote a letter so precipitately –' He turned to his sister-in-law and began to tell the story which I heard on my first visit to Bryanston Square.

'It's fantastic to imagine Winston doing anything of the kind,' Philip interrupted him. 'After what he said to the unfortunate George. I wouldn't believe it if George weren't much too incompetent to invent the story.'

The table quietened down. Philip gave the actual words. It was the first time I had heard behind-the-scenes gossip at that level: Philip endowed it with a special authority.

The elder Marches listened with satisfaction as Philip settled the question of supertax. Most of them were not only academically interested; there was a great deal of wealth in the room. Exactly how much, I should have liked very much to know, but about their fortunes they were more reticent than about anything else. None of the younger generation, at our end of the table, could do more than guess. Apparently no individual March had ever been enormously rich. There had probably never been a million pounds at any one man's disposal. So far as one could judge from wills, settlements, and their style of life, most of the fortunes at this dinner-table would be between £100,000 and £500,000.

Philip was talking about the next election:

'We've left it too late. We're a set of bunglers. Our fellows had better stick it out until they're bound to go.'

'What's going to happen?' said Caroline.

'We shall get the sack,' said Philip.

'Does that mean a Socialist Government?' asked Florence Simon of Charles.

'What else do you think it can mean?' Mr March exclaimed down the table. 'Now that your Aunt Winifred's wretched party has come to the end that they've always richly deserved.'

He was chuckling at Winifred, Herbert March's wife, who was the only Liberal of the older generation. The Marches had been Conservatives for a hundred years; when they stood for Parliament, it was as supporters of Salisbury, Balfour, Bonar Law; their political attitudes were those of other rich men.

At our end of the table, opinion moved a good way to the left. Herbert March's daughter Margaret, who had not long since graduated at Oxford, was working as secretary to a Labour member. She was the most practical of them, the only professional: Charles took her side in argument, was more radical than she was, and Katherine followed suit. Most of the others had undertaken to vote against Sir Philip's party. Of course, many other Marches had passed through a liberal phase in their youth – but to them that night, to me watching them, this seemed something harder, more likely to last.

We had finished the pheasant. Philip and Mr March put politics aside, and began talking about one of their nieces by marriage, who was reported to be living apart from her husband. She had always possessed a reputation for good looks: 'the best-looking girl in the family, Herbert said, though I never knew why he was specially competent to judge,' said Mr March. She had stayed unmarried until she was over thirty.

She was said to have had a good many offers, 'but no one ever established where they came from,' said Mr March. 'The only reason I believed in them was that Hannah didn't.' And then, to everyone's surprise, she had married someone quite poor, unattractive and undistinguished. 'She married him,' Philip announced, 'because he was the only man who didn't look when she was getting over a stile.' His grin was caustic; but his dignity had broken for a moment, and there was a randy glitter in his eyes.

They were arguing about what had gone wrong with the marriage, when their sister Caroline, who was deaf, suddenly caught a word and said:

'Were you talking about Charles?' Mr March shook his head, but she went on:

'I hope he realizes he's making an ass of himself. Albert Hart won't hear of his giving up the Bar.'

'It's all unsettled, there's nothing whatever to report,' said Mr March quickly.

Mr March had been compelled to speak loudly, even for a March, to make her understand. His voice silenced everyone else, and the entire table heard Caroline's next question.

'Why is it unsettled? Why has he taken to bees in his bonnet just when he might be becoming some use in the world?'

'The whole matter's been exaggerated,' said Mr March. 'Albert always was given to premature discussion –'

'What's this? What's this?' said Philip.

'I mentioned it to you. She's not made a discovery. I mentioned that my son Charles was going through a period of not being entirely satisfied with his progress at the Bar. Nothing has been concealed.'

Katherine was looking at Charles with a frown of distress.

'I expect he's got over it now. You're all serene, aren't you, Charles?' Philip asked down the table: his tone was dry but friendly.

'I'm quite happy, Uncle Philip.'

'You're getting down to it properly now, aren't you?'

'The whole matter's been grossly exaggerated,' Mr March broke in, rapidly, as though signalling to Charles.

'I expect I can take it that your father's right,' said Philip. There was a pause.

'I'm sorry. I should like to agree. But you'd find out sooner or later. It's no use my pretending that I shall work at the Bar.'

'What's behind all this? They tell me you've made a good start. What's the matter with you?'

Charles hesitated again.

'You've got one nephew at the Bar, Uncle Philip.' Charles looked at Robert. 'Do you want all your nephews there too? Cutting each other's throats –'

He seemed to be passing it off casually, his tone was light; but Caroline, who was watching his face without hearing the words, broke out:

'I didn't mean to turn you into a board meeting. This comes of being so abominably deaf. Leonard, do you remember the day when Hannah thought I was deafer than I am?'

We went back to our pudding. Katherine had flushed: Charles smiled at her, but did not speak. He stopped the footman from filling his glass again. Most of us, after the questions ceased, had been glad of another drink, including Francis, who had been putting down his wine unobtrusively but steadily since dinner began.

The table became noisier than at any time that evening; the interruption seemed over; Charles's neighbours were laughing as he talked.

Florence Simon plucked at my sleeve. She was a woman

of thirty, with abstracted brown eyes and a long sharp nose; all through dinner I had got nowhere with her; whatever I said, she had been vague and shy. Now her eyes were bright, she had thought of something to say.

'I wish you'd been at the dinner last Friday. It was much more interesting then.'

'Was it?' I said.

'Oh, we had some really good general conversation,' said Florence Simon. She relapsed into silence, giving me a kind, judicious, and contented smile.

Chapter 7

TWO KINDS OF ANGER

By half past eleven Katherine could speak to Charles at last. She had just said some goodbyes, and only Francis and I were left with them in the drawing-room.

'It was atrociously bad luck,' she burst out.

'I was glad it didn't go on any longer,' said Charles.

'It must have been intolerable,' she cried.

'Well,' said Charles, 'I was just coming to the state when I could hear my own voice getting rougher.'

'The family have never heard anyone put Uncle Philip off before.'

'I thought he was perfectly good-tempered,' Charles replied. He was being matter-of-fact in the face of the excitement. 'He's merely used to being told what he wants to know.'

'He's still talking to Mr L. in his study. There are several of them still there, you know,' she went on.

'Didn't you expect that?' Charles smiled at her.

'It's absolutely maddening,' she broke out again, 'this fluke happening just when Mr L. was ready to accept it.'

Charles was silent for a moment. Then he said:

'I'm not certain that he was.'

'You told me so,' said Katherine. 'But still – you're going to have a foul time. I wish to God I could help.'

She went on:

'He thinks the world of Uncle Philip, of course. Did you notice that he pretended to have told him? He'd obviously just muttered "my son Charles is mumpish" and was hoping that nobody would notice that you never appeared in court –'

'Is there anything I can do?' said Francis. His voice was a little thick. In his embarrassment at dinner, he had been drinking more than the rest of us; now, when he wanted to

63

be useful and protective, he looked as though the light was dazzling him.

Charles shook his head and said no.

'You're sure?' said Francis, trying to speak with his usual crispness. Again Charles said no.

'In that case,' said Francis, 'it might be wiser if the rest of us left you to it.'

'I'd rather you didn't,' said Charles. 'I'd rather Mr L. found you all here.'

For a second it sounded as if he were trying to avoid a scene. Listening to his tone, I suddenly felt that that was the opposite of the truth.

He went on speaking to Francis. Katherine smiled at them anxiously, then turned to me.

'By the way, according to your theory, the mass of people at dinner must have sounded very forbidding,' she said. 'Did you find a few who made it tolerable? When you actually arrived?'

The question was incomprehensible, and yet she was clearly expecting me to understand. 'Your theory': I could not imagine what she meant.

'Don't you remember,' she said, 'saying that to me the first time we met? When I was being shunted off to the Jewish dance. I won't swear to the actual words, but I'm pretty certain they're nearly right. I thought over them a good many times afterwards, you see. I wondered whether you meant to take me down a peg or two for being too superior.'

It was the sort of attentive memory, the sort of extravagant thin-skinnedness, that I should have become accustomed to; but a new example still surprised me just as much.

'As a matter of fact,' said Katherine, 'I decided that you probably didn't mean that.'

Then Mr March entered. He went straight to Charles, paying no attention to the rest of us: he stood in front of Charles's chair.

'Now you see what you're responsible for,' he said. Charles got up.

'You know how sorry I am that you're involved, Mr L.,' Charles said.

'I haven't got time to speculate whether you're sorry or not. I've just been listening to my brothers telling me that you're making a fool of yourself. As though I wasn't perfectly aware of it already. I expressed exactly the same point of view myself but unfortunately I haven't succeeded in making much impression on you.'

'No one could have done more than you did.'

'A great many people could have done enormously more. Do you think my father listened to Herbert when he got up to his monkey tricks and wanted to study music? An astonishingly bad musician he would have made if you can judge by his singing in the drawing-room when we were children. Hannah said that he was only asked to sing because he was the youngest child. Anyone else would have done enormously more. In any case, I never gave my permission as you appear to have assumed. You may have thought the matter was closed, but that doesn't affect the issue.'

'It's no good reopening it, Mr L. I'm sorry.'

'Certainly it's some good reopening it. After tonight, I haven't any option.'

Charles suddenly broke out:

'You admit that tonight is making the difference?'

'I never allowed you to think that the matter was closed. But in addition to that, I don't propose to ignore –'

'The position is this: when we were left to ourselves, you disapproved of what I wanted and you brought up every fair argument there was. If it had been possible, you know that I should have given way. Now other people are taking a hand. I know what they mean to you, but I don't recognize their claim to interfere. Do you think I can possibly do for them what I wouldn't do for you alone?'

'You talk about them as if they were strangers. They're treated better by an outsider who's just married into us, like that abominable woman who married your cousin Alfred. They're your family –'

'They've no right to affect my life.'

'I won't have the family dismissed as strangers.'

'I should feel more justified in going against your wishes – now you've been influenced by them,' said Charles, 'than when you were speaking for yourself.' They were standing close together. There came a cough, and to my astonishment Francis began to speak.

'Will you forgive me for saying something, Mr March?'

His face was pallid under the sunburn; there was a film of sweat on his forehead. But he managed to make himself speak soberly: the words came out strained, uncomfortable, but positive.

Mr March, who had been totally indifferent to his presence or mine, did not notice anything unusual. With a mixture of irritableness and courtesy, Mr March said:

'My dear fellow, I'm always glad to hear your observations.'

'I assure you,' said Francis, uttering with care, 'that Charles would have gone further to meet your wishes than for any other reason. I completely agree with you that he's wrong to give up the Bar. I think it's sheer nonsense. I've told him so. I've argued with him since I first heard about it. But I haven't got him to change his mind. The only argument which would make him think twice was about the effect on yourself.'

Mr March regarded him with an expression that dubiously lightened; the frown of anger had become puzzled, and Mr March said, his voice more subdued than since he entered the room:

'That was civil of him, anyway.'

He went on:

'I don't know what's happening to the family. My generation weren't a patch on my father's. And as for yours, there's not one of you who'll get a couple of inches in the obituary column. My uncle Henry said that just before he died in '27, and all I could reply was "After all, you can say this for them. They don't drink, and they don't womanize."'

Mr March spoke straight to Charles:

'You might be the only chance of rescuing them from

mediocrity. There's always been a consensus of opinion that you wouldn't disgrace yourself at the Bar. Ever since your preparatory schoolmaster said you had a legal head: though he was wrong in his prognostications about all your cousins. I don't know what I've done to deserve the most unsatisfactory children in the whole family. First your sister made her regrettable marriage. Of her there's nothing good to report. Then you choose to behave in this fashion. And neither you nor your sister Katherine have ever made any attempt to fit into the life of the people round you. You've always been utterly unsociable. You've never taken the part everyone wanted you to take. You've not had the slightest consideration for what the family thinks of me. You wouldn't cross the road to keep me in good repute. I've been more criticized about my children than anyone in the family since 1902, the time Justin's daughter married out of the faith. Justin had a worse time than anyone. He couldn't bear to inspect the wedding presents. It was always rumoured that he sent some secretly himself to cover up a few of the gaps. Since Justin, no one has been disapproved of as I have.'

Mr March sat down, in an armchair close to one of the side tables. For a second, I thought the quarrel was over. Then Charles said:

'I wish it weren't so, for your sake.'

Charles had spoken simply and with feeling: in reply, Mr March flushed to a depth of anger he had not reached that night. He clutched at the arm of his chair as he leant forward; in doing so, he swept off an ashtray from the little table. The rug was shot with cigarette-stubs and match-ends. Charles bent to clear them.

'Don't pick them up,' Mr March shouted. Charles replaced the ashtray, and put one or two stubs in it.

'Don't pick them up, I tell you,' Mr March cried with such an increase of rage that Charles hesitated.

'I refuse to have you perform duties for my sake. I refuse to listen to you expressing polite regrets for my sake. You appear to consider yourself completely separate from me in all respects. I am not prepared to tolerate that attitude.'

'What do you mean?' Charles's voice had become angry and hard.

'I am not prepared to tolerate your attitude that you can dissociate yourself from me in all your concerns. Even if I survive criticism from the family on your account, that isn't to admit that you've separated yourself from me.'

'I come to you for advice,' said Charles.

'Advice! You can go to the family lawyer for advice. Though I never knew why we've stood a fellow so long-winded as Morris for so long,' cried Mr March. 'I'm not prepared to be treated as a minor variety of family lawyer by my son. I shall have to consider taking actions that will make that clear.'

Charles broke out:

'Do you imagine for a moment that you can coerce me back to the law?'

Mr March said:

'I do not propose to let you abandon yourself to your own devices.'

Everyone was surprised by the calm, ambiguous answer and by Mr March's expression. As Charles's face darkened, Mr March looked almost placid. He seemed something like triumphant, from the instant he evoked an outburst as angry as his own. He went on quietly:

'I want something for you. I wish I could know that you'll get something that I've always wanted for you.' He checked himself. Abruptly he broke off; he looked round at us as though there had been no disagreement whatever, and began an anecdote about a Friday night years before.

Part 2

FATHER AND SON

Chapter 8

THE COST OF HELP

FOR some time after the quarrel I did not get a clear account of Mr March's behaviour. According to Katherine, he was so depressed that he stopped grumbling; he listened to criticisms from his brothers and sisters, but even these he did not pass on. Weeks went by before he began to greet Charles at meals with: 'If you're determined to persist in your misguided notions, what alternative proposal have you to offer?' One afternoon, when I was in the drawing-room, Mr March burst in after his daily visit to the club and cried:

'I'm being persecuted on account of my son's fandango.'

That was all I heard directly. When I dined with them, there were times when he seemed melancholy, but his level of spirits was so high that I could not be sure. One day Charles mentioned to me that he thought Mr March had begun to worry about Katherine. I fancied that I could recall the signs.

As for Charles himself, none of his family had any idea what he was intending, or whether he was intending anything at all. He put on a front of cheerfulness and good temper in his father's presence. His days had become as lazy as Katherine's. He stayed in bed till midday, talked to her most afternoons, went dancing at night. Many of his acquaintances thought, just as he had predicted, that he was settling down to the life of a rich and idle young man.

They should have watched his manner as he set me going on my career.

By the early summer I still had had nothing like a serious case, and I was getting worn down with anxiety. Then Charles took charge of my affairs. He handled them with astuteness and nerve. He risked snubs, which he could not have done on his own behalf, and got me invited to the famous June party at the Holfords'. At the same time he approached Albert Hart and through him met the solicitors who sent Hart the majority of his work. One of them was glad to oblige Philip March's nephew, and said he would like to meet me; another, one of the best-known Jewish solicitors in London, promised to be present at the Holfords' party. There were other skeins, concealed from me, in Charles's plans. They took up his entire attention. As he devoted himself to them, Charles was continuously angry with me.

A few minutes before the Holfords' party, where he planned for me to make a good impression, there was an edge to his voice. I was sitting in his bedroom at Bryanston Square while he knotted his white tie in front of the mirror. I mentioned a story of Charles's grandfather that Mr March had just told me – 'he must have been a very able man,' I said.

'Obviously he must have been,' said Charles. He was still looking into the mirror, smoothing down his thick, fair, wiry hair. 'But he didn't do so much after all. He was a rather successful banker. And acquired the position that a rather successful banker could in that period, if he happened to be a competent man. Don't you agree?'

I was referring to Mr March's account, but Charles interrupted: 'Oh, I know he'd got some human qualities. The point is, he didn't do so much. Look, don't you admit those jobs he spent his life on are really pretty frivolous? I mean, the traditional jobs of my sort of people. The Stock Exchange and banking and amateur politics when you've made enough money. Can you imagine taking them up if you had a free choice?'

'No,' I said.

Charles turned round.

'And if you had a free choice, can you imagine taking up – the profession you're anxious to be successful at?'

I did not answer.

'You can't imagine it. Don't you admit that you can't?' Charles said, with an angry, contemptuous, sadic smile.

'Not if I'd been given a completely free choice, perhaps.'

'Of course you can't. You don't want just money. You'll realize that if you make some. You don't want the sort of meaningless status that appeals to Herbert Getliffe. You'll realize that if you get it. Granted that you want to satisfy yourself instead, it's not a job a reasonable man would choose. Don't you agree?'

In my suspense that night, those 'ifs' were cruel: we each knew it. I was both hurt and angry. I could have told him that he was speaking out of bitter discontent. Did I admit to myself what kind of discontent it was? He was angry that I had direct ambitions and might satisfy them. I ought also to have known that he wanted to lead a useful life. He could not confide it or get rid of it, but he had a longing for the good. We faced each other, on the edge of quarrelling. He sounded arrogant, impatient, cruel; he was angry with me because we were different.

As he drove me to Belgrave Square through the June dusk, Charles suddenly turned as anxious as I was myself. He wanted me to be at ease; he wanted me to forget the doubts that he had raised by his own words five minutes before; he kept reiterating facts about the Holfords and their guests, and conversational gambits I could use with Albert Hart.

When we arrived in the crowded drawing-room, Charles took me to Hart's side as soon as my introduction to Lady Holford was over. He reminded Hart about me. He set us talking. Hart was an uneasy nervous man who broke into flashes of speech: he liked Charles, it was clear, and even more he liked having someone he knew at this party, so unfluctuating in its noise-level, so ornate. In a few minutes, we moved out through the great French windows, down the steps, into the sunken garden. A waiter brought us three balloon glasses and put into each a couple of inches of brandy.

'His lordship's compliments,' the waiter said to Charles, 'and he wishes to say that this is *not* Napoleon brandy. But it is reasonably old.'

As soon as the waiter turned to ascend the steps, Charles

looked at Albert Hart and winked. Charles's face became gay, the more as he saw Hart and me beginning to make contact. Soon Charles left us to 'do his duty' in the house, and Hart and I enjoyed comparing the display round us to the subdued opulence of a March Friday night. He was supple, gossipy, devoted to his work and still, at the age of fifty or more, overawed when he went into society. I felt his heart warm to me when I told him that this was the first time I had set foot in a London garden. He was shrewd, he was trying to find out whether there was anything in me: he also had a taste for sly jokes at the Holfords' expense, he was glad to have someone there to listen.

The garden was filling up. Hart was joined by his friend the solicitor, who at once asked me some leading questions about Herbert Getliffe. I had to try to be both forthcoming and discreet; but Hart was already friendly, and I thought the other man was ready to approve of me. The conversation returned to the Holfords: I began to feel happy as I watched the people round us, the lights at the bottom of the garden, the profound blue of the London evening sky.

Two women, mother and daughter, acquaintances of Hart and the Marches, joined us for a time. The girl was to be presented at Court the next month and the mention of royalty stimulated Albert Hart. He remembered a story of Holford, who was said, in the first hey-day of his success, to have let drop at one of his parties: 'I suppose my daughter may as well be presented this year. It must be a bore for the monarchs, though, to see faces they know so well.'

That must have happened a few years before the Holfords' title finally submerged their name. They first appeared in England in 1860, and they were then called Samuel; they hyphenated themselves to Samuel-Wigmore within ten years, and had dropped the Samuel by the end of the century. They had made a fortune out of cigarettes, and the man in whose garden we were standing could have bought up the entire March family. Their entertainments had been flamboyant thirty years before, and had grown steadily grander; although they boasted of their acquaintance with royalty, they genuinely had royal acquaintances to boast of. This 'little evening party in the garden' (in the largest garden within a mile of Hyde Park Corner) took place each year in June, just as a sign, so Albert Hart said, that they might do some less simple entertaining later in the year.

Though they had disguised their name and though nine out of ten of their guests were Gentiles, they had remained faithful Jews. And, though their success had been on a different scale, they still looked up to the Marches as one of the senior Jewish families in England, while they were newcomers. Invitations to their parties went to the Marches as a matter of right, but the Marches rarely attended. Charles would not have thought of coming that night, but for me: and yet, when he accepted the invitation and asked if he might bring a friend, the Holfords chose to forget his family's stiffness. They seemed to feel that Jewish society was still hierarchical, that rank still meant something. It was not by accident that Holford's message about the brandy had been sent to Charles.

It was curious to see two different social codes collide, I thought, taking my last sip of old, but not Napoleon, brandy. I felt satisfied with the evening. I felt so satisfied that when I caught sight of Charles again I did not care how much deference the Holfords gave him. He was standing at the top of the steps above the garden. A dark-haired girl was looking up at him. The light from an open window picked out the glass in his hand, the gardenia in his buttonhole, and threw his features into relief.

Then he came down the steps, and found our group. His eyes met mine, searching for how things had gone. It was not hard for him to see that I was pleased.

A moment afterwards, the lights round the garden suddenly went out. In the warm darkness we were left mystified; people asked each other what was happening. What was happening was soon known, as three gigantic Catherine wheels spurted out of the distance. Lord Holford was producing a firework display, extravagant, varied and, as we came to realize, inordinately long.

A case came to me not long after that party: not from the man I talked to there, but from another solicitor who sent a considerable amount of work to Hart and whom Charles had arranged for me to meet.

It was not such an important case as Charles's, but far better than anything I could reasonably expect. I had to prosecute in a libel action. It was not difficult, the case was fairly self-evident; but I had not much time, as someone else had thrown up the brief through illness, and with a case so good it would be disastrous not to win.

In fact, I did win, though I stumbled in the last stages. Charles had helped me prepare, and was present all through the hearing. I saw his face, clouded and frowning, as, with the case nearly won, I went off on a side-line that seemed tempting. A witness was obstinate, I knew that I might have done the case harm; but I was able to recover and make some pretence of passing it off.

When I got the verdict, I joined Charles. He congratulated me, and then, his eyes bright, said:

'I'm glad. But what possessed you to draw that absurd red herring?'

I defended myself. I said it had not been as bad as that.

'Oh, you did very well. Henriques [the solicitor] is satisfied with you; you're a good investment.'

His glance kept its glint. 'But still, you did lose sight of the point for five minutes, didn't you? It was a classical example of using two arguments where one would do, don't you agree?'

I felt let down. All in all I had done well: I wanted praise, not his kind of candour. He was fond of telling the truth, I thought with no detachment at all, especially when it was unpleasant.

Herbert Getliffe did just the opposite. He was fond of rejoicing with him who rejoices. He behaved as though he had won the case, instead of me, and immediately set about improvising a celebratory supper ('each man to pay for himself and partner. I always believe in Dutch treat,' he told me, with energy and sincerity). Over the telephone, at four hours' notice, he invited guests, most of whom were only acquaintances of mine. Charles could not come, and Getliffe whistled and clucked his tongue in disapprobation. 'He ought to have put everything else off, on a night like this! But you'll find, Eliot, that some people take one view of the responsibilities of friendship, and some take another.' He added, in his most reflective, earnest, and affectionate tone: 'Of course some chaps in the position of young March would have done something for you in the way of introductions – instead of letting you sink or swim. I don't believe in flattering myself, Eliot, but I must say it was a providential thing that you came to my chambers, so that you had one well-wisher at any rate to look after you a bit –'

With genuine feeling he developed the theme. He was so sincere, so full of emotion, that he found it impossible to remember that he had done nothing for me whatsoever; listening, I found it nearly as impossible myself.

At the meal, I began by being jubilant and boastful, trying to impress my neighbour, a cool and handsome girl. Getting nowhere, I went on boasting, still exalted: yet I felt this party was becoming a joke against me, and as we stood about when we had finished eating I was smiling to myself.

It was then that I caught sight of a young woman watching me: she too was smiling, but with what looked like sympathy. All I knew about her was that her name was Ann Simon, and I had met her for the first time that night. I went across to her.

'You ought to be pleased, oughtn't you?' she said. Her tone was kind, a little shy, almost deferential. As I looked at her, I was struck by a contrast. Her face was open and intelligent, with bright-blue eyes folded at the inner corners; under her left eye was a mole. Against her thick dark hair, her temples seemed delicate and white. One could call her pretty, certainly good-looking, but at the first glance one was thinking of the character in her face. That was where the contrast came, for her figure was elegant, soft and supple, more carefully and expensively dressed, so I thought, than any woman in the room. Her manner was at the same time direct and shy, warm but not at all flirtatious. I found myself talking to her as an ally.

Yes, I ought to be pleased, I said, it had been an important day for me. But this celebration wasn't exactly what I might have imagined. The young woman I was fond of was not there, nor were any of my friends. On the other hand, Getliffe and some of his chums were having a remarkably good time.

'I suppose,' she said, 'you couldn't have arranged anything in advance, could you? I mean, you couldn't have got your friends to stand by?'

'I was touching wood too hard,' I replied.

She nodded her head in comprehension. It would have been easy to tell her about my love-affair. She asked about my friends: I mentioned Charles March, and asked if she knew the family. Yes, she did, and she had met him once. It was agreeable standing there talking to her, and I thought she felt so too. We were the same age; she was kind and clever and we were not making any demands on each other. Meeting her seemed a good end to that day.

I told Charles about her. He was not sure who she was, but he was interested in her effect on me. Just then we had sharper eyes for each other than for ourselves. He saw that I had fallen deeply in love too early, and that Sheila had already left a mark on my life: he saw also that, too much committed to Sheila as I was, I often felt disproportionate gratitude to women who gave me what she could not. Such as ordinary simple friendliness, which was what I had received from Ann Simon.

With him, I saw just as clearly that he wanted to find someone to love: or rather he wanted to lose himself in someone. It was the opposite of my experience. Why he had missed it, I could not imagine: but now that he was consciously looking for it, I thought his chances were getting less.

That summer he went on living his idle life. He spent days at Lord's and Wimbledon; took a season-ticket for the ballet; flirted with a young woman he met at a coming-out dance;

arrived a good many times at Bryanston Square when the door was already unlocked for the morning.

The mantelpiece in his sitting-room was shining with invitations. Less than half came from Jewish houses. He was a highly eligible match, and hostesses were anxious to secure him. That year, he was eager to accept. His car drove with the others to Grosvenor Square, Knightsbridge, the houses round the Park. It was a hot brilliant summer, and sometimes I used to walk past those houses, whose lights shone out while the sky was still bright. Dance-tunes sounded through the open windows, and girls' voices as they walked under the awning from the street.

Charles found someone to flirt with; but he did not find what he was looking for. Just before he went down to Mr March's country house for the summer, he was sharper-tempered than I had known him.

Chapter 9

WEEKEND IN THE COUNTRY

ONE afternoon in July, as I sat in the drawing-room at Bryanston Square, Mr March entered even more quickly than usual, said: 'I'm always glad to have your company. But I've a great many worries to occupy me now,' and went out again.

It sounded ominous: but I discovered that he was talking about the yearly move to Haslingfield, his country house in Hampshire. I also discovered that each year this move produced the same state of subdued commotion. Mr March sat in his study for hours every day for a fortnight 'seeing if it's possible to get anything safely down to that confounded house', but what he did no one knew. The elder servants became infected with the atmosphere of imminent catastrophe – all except the butler who, finding me alone on one of these occasions, suddenly said: 'I shouldn't take much notice of Mr March, sir. He'd die if he didn't worry. Believe me he would.'

I was asked down to Haslingfield for the last week-end in August. That year, for the first time, Katherine was acting as hostess, 'not entirely a job to look for,' she wrote. 'Mr L. may have intended it as a compliment, or as a sign that I'm getting on in years – but he still regards it as unlikely that any guests will receive or answer my invitations, or, if by any miracle they do come, that they'll ever go away. However, I've invited Ann Simon for the same week-end as you. Mr L. resisted having her, apparently on the grounds that she was a bit of a social come-down: actually her father's a highly successful doctor. Still, it's better to have Mr L. angry about her than about other topics. Anyway, she's coming. I thought you talked as though you were interested in her, when you met her after your first case. ...'

80

Incidentally, that first case was now not my only one. Another small job had come my way in July, and at the end of the month the solicitor whom I met at the Holfords' sent me a case which any young man at my stage would have thought himself lucky to get. It was to be heard in the autumn, and through August I had been working at it obsessively hard.

Katherine had asked me to come down early, and so I took the train on the Friday afternoon, tired but encouraged. This case would get me known a bit; I had a foot in; the next year looked brighter. The Surrey fields passed by in the sunshine, the carriage cushions smelt stuffy in the heat, and I felt happy, sleepy, and without any premonition at all.

Charles met me with his car at Farnham. He was sun-burned, and his hair slightly bleached. For a second, I thought his face had aged in the last two years. Before I could ask him anything, he was talking – with the special insistence, I thought, of someone who wants to keep questions away.

'I've been doing absolutely nothing,' he said, 'except play tennis and read.'

As he drove through the lanes towards Hampshire, he let off a string of questions about the books he had just been reading. What did I think of the Sacco-Vanzetti case? What did the jury actually tell themselves when they were alone? How cynical can any of them have allowed themselves to be?

He had been reading the evidence: he drove with one hand, and used the other to draw diagrams in the air – the place where Sacco and Vanzetti were proved to stand and the street down which 'eye-witnesses' were later shown to have been travelling. 'Going at this pace,' said Charles, driving faster, 'identifying a man out of sight, roughly behind that clump of pines. Those seem to be the facts. How did the jury and those witnesses – most of them ordinary decent people, you must assume that – face what they were doing? Face it in their own minds, I mean?'

It was the kind of detective story in real life, full of concrete facts and edged with injustice, that he could not resist. Far more than me, he had a passionate personal interest in justice for its own sake.

That afternoon, though, he was using it to distract us both. 'Nothing's happening,' he said, when I asked him about himself. 'Nothing in the world.' Quickly, as though in self-defence, he pounced on me with another question about a book.

When I asked after Katherine, he glanced at me without expression. 'She's very well,' he said. 'She's very well indeed.'

'What do you mean?'

He shook his head. 'You'd better see for yourself.'

'Is she all right?'

'I think she's very happy.'

When I pressed him, he would not say any more. He returned to talk about literature, as he drove into a dark alley of trees; I noticed high banks, patches of sunshine, rabbit holes; I was listening, and at the same time trying to calculate the distance from the lodge. It turned out to be three miles to the house: 'the advantage being,' Charles said, 'that Mr L. can take his constitutional within his own territories.'

Mr March and Katherine were waiting in the courtyard.

'Glad to see you arrive safely in my son's car,' said Mr March. 'I wanted to send the chauffeur, but was overruled. I should have refused to answer for the consequences.'

He took me into the drawing-room, bigger and lighter than at Bryanston Square. A great bay of windows gave on to the terrace; below lay the tennis court, the shadow of a tree just beginning to touch one of the service lines. The view stretched, lush and wooded, to the blue Surrey hills; the English view, every square yard man-made, and yet with neither a house nor a path in sight.

Katherine poured out the tea. Mr March glanced at me.

'You're looking seedy,' he said. 'No! I'm prepared to believe that you can be allowed out of quarantine – if you admit that you've been living in a cellar.'

'I've been working hard, Mr L.,' I said.

'I'm very glad to hear it. It makes a great contrast to my deplorable family. I don't propose to make any observations upon my son. As for my daughter, I suppose she can hardly be expected to perform any serious function – but she can't even write foolproof letters to my guests. I detected her making a frightful ass of herself again on Tuesday; she admitted that she hadn't sent Charles's friend Francis Getliffe a list of the trains to Farnham.'

Mr March seemed in good spirits. Katherine said: 'For the fifth time, Mr L., I didn't send Francis the trains because he knows them as well as you do.' She smiled. 'And I object to being referred to as though I was feeble-minded. Why can't I be expected to perform any serious function?'

'Women can't,' said Mr March. 'Apart from any particular reflection on you as shown by these various incompetences.'

The evening flowed on. Dinner in the late summer half-twilight was just as at Bryanston Square, with Mr March dressed and no one else: the routine was not altered, we went in on the stroke of eight, Mr March declaimed the menu. He talked on, as though he had been compulsorily silent for some time. Sir Philip had just been made a Parliamentary Secretary. Mr March's astonishment and pride were each enormous. 'I never thought any son of my father would reach the heights of a Minister. Possibly they considered,' he added thoughtfully, 'that, as the Government is obviously about to go out in ignominy, it didn't matter much whom they put in. Still, my father would have been extremely gratified.' His reflections on Philip set him going on the main narrative-stream of his own journey round the world in the eighties, with subsidiary streams of, first, the attempt of Philip's wife, 'the biggest snob in the family', to invite the Queen to tea: second, the adventures of Hannah and the Belgian refugees, 'the only useful thing she ever tried to do, and of course she said it was a success: but no one else believed her': third, his morning walk with Katherine yesterday, and her ignorance of the difficulties of moving back to Bryanston Square (in time for the Jewish New Year in September).

Only the cricket scores were allowed to interrupt him when we moved back to the drawing-room. It was still very warm, and the butler brought in iced drinks after the coffee. We lay back, sipping them: but the heat did not quieten Mr March.

Then, at 10.40 exactly, he broke off and performed his evening ritual. The whole household was in for the night, and so he went round the house with the butler to examine all the doors, after giving Charles instructions about the drawing-room windows. At last we heard him go upstairs to bed.

Charles asked Katherine when the other two would arrive: he said (I did not catch the meaning for a moment): 'I still think you could have found a more ingenious excuse.' 'That's monstrous,' said Katherine. She smiled. Her hair was tousled over her forehead; she usually managed to become untidy, I thought, by this time of night. She appealed to me: 'I told you Mr L. is prepared to disapprove of Ann in advance, for reasons best known to himself. So I decided we wanted someone else to soothe him down – and Francis is the obvious choice, you can't deny it. It's a perfectly good excuse.' 'You only decided it was good,' Charles said, 'after concealing it from me for two days.'

'Privilege of hostess.' Katherine smiled again. 'Ah well – Lewis, don't you agree that Mr L. is getting more vigorous the older he becomes? I shall have to marry before he's exhausted me completely.'

She was laughing: but, as we listened to those words 'I shall have to marry . . .' and heard their caressing pleasure, we knew that she was in love.

Soon she went to bed herself.

'She liked being told that it was a bad excuse,' I said.

Charles said:

'She's only realized quite recently, I think.'

'When did you?'

'Shouldn't you say,' said Charles, 'that she's been getting fond of him for months?'

'He's very fond of her,' I said.

'Are you sure?'

I nodded. Charles broke out:

'I just can't tell whether he's in love, perhaps it's harder for me to tell than anyone.'

For a time we were silent. Then I asked, because the thought was in both our minds:

'How much has Mr L. noticed?'

'I've absolutely no idea.'

We were each thinking of her chances of being happy. Neither of us knew whether Francis wanted to marry her. If he did, I could not foresee what it would mean, her marrying a Gentile.

Nevertheless, as Charles spoke of her, there was a trace of envy in his voice. Partly because he might be losing her; but mainly, I thought that night, because she had been taken up by an overmastering emotion, because she had lost herself and been swept away.

We talked until late: of Katherine, Francis, Mr March, my work, and again of the books he had been reading. He had no news of his own.

Chapter 10

A WALK WITH MR MARCH

AT last we tiptoed up the broad slippery staircase, and went
to our rooms. But in my case not to sleep, immediately at
least; for the bedrooms at Haslingfield carried comfort to
such a point that it was difficult to sleep at all.

There was a rack of books, picked by Charles, several of
which were just out – a Huxley, the latest of the Scott-
Moncrieff translations, the books we had talked about that
afternoon. There was a plate of sandwiches, a plate of fruit,
a plate of biscuits. A Thermos flask of tea and one of iced
lemonade. A small bottle of brandy. After one had had a
snack, read a book or two, and finished off the drinks, one
could snatch a few hours' sleep – until, quite early in the
morning, a footman began padding about the room, taking
out clothes and drawing curtains. Which for me, who liked
sleeping in the dark, finished the night for good.

There was nothing for it but to get up. Although I arrived
in the breakfast-room early, one place at the table had
already been occupied; Mr March had been and gone. As
I chose my breakfast from the dishes on the sideboard, I was
puzzled for a moment. There were several plates of fried
tongue, none of bacon. For a visitor used to rich houses, that
was the only unfamiliar thing at Bryanston Square and
Haslingfield.

Katherine and Charles both came down late to breakfast.
Twice, while I was sitting alone, Mr March entered rapidly,
said 'Good morning' without stopping, and changed the
newspaper he was holding out in front of him; first *The
Times* for the *Daily Telegraph*, and then the *Daily Telegraph* for the *Manchester Guardian*.

It was another hot day. Katherine was complaining at the
prospect of her five-mile walk with Mr March before lunch;

why does he insist on a companion, she said, pretending that she was only complaining as a joke. I thought that, as she waited for Francis to arrive, she did not relish being alone with Mr March. So I volunteered; and at exactly half past eleven we set off down the drive at Mr March's walking pace, which was not less than four miles an hour. He wore his deerstalker, and before we had walked four hundred yards took it off, saying: 'I must mop my bald pate.' Several times he groaned, without slowing down: 'I'm cracking up! I'm cracking up!'

Nothing interrupted his walking, he neither slackened nor quickened his pace. The only interruptions to his talking were those he made himself. His feats of total recall were as disconcerting as ever. For the first time I heard, out of the blue, the end of that gnomic story about his nephew Robert on the steps of the St James's, which had tantalized me on my first visit to Bryanston Square. It appeared that Robert, tired of waiting for briefs, had taken to going to theatres, not just to pass the time or because of a disinterested passion for drama, but because he had conceived the idea of filling up his leisure by writing a play: all he was doing was study the technique. In Mr March's view, this procedure was ill-judged, since he regarded it as axiomatic that Robert did not possess a shred of talent.

We turned at the lodge gates and made off by a path among the trees. Mr March chuckled and pointed back to the lodge.

'My son Charles,' he said, 'got himself into an unfortunate predicament a fortnight ago last Saturday. I had Oliver Mendl staying with me for the weekend. Of course I knew that he obeyed the Lawgiver more strictly than I do myself. His father was just the same. When he visited us, I used to have to open his letters on Saturday morning. Though I noticed that he always read them quick enough if he thought they contained anything to his advantage. Oliver invited Charles to come for a stroll, and in the circumstances Charles couldn't very well refuse. It looked very threatening that morning. I said so as soon as I woke up: I was ten minutes later than usual, because my daughter Katherine had kept me awake by inconsiderately having a bath before she went to bed the previous night. She accuses me of shouting through the wall "You've done me in. I shall never get to sleep again, never again". I strongly advised them to take overcoats or at least umbrellas. However, they preferred their own opinion and they'd just reached the lodge when it started to rain with violence. The only drop of rain we've had since July 19: remember you're only allowed four inches in your bath. Charles showed more gumption than you might expect: he suggested ringing up from the lodge and asking Taylor to bring a car. It might have been a ridiculous suggestion, of course: you can't expect to get a car unless you make proper arrangements in advance. As it happened, Taylor was not occupied between 10.30 and 12 that morning. So Charles could have obtained his car, but unfortunately he didn't. Because Oliver begged him to order the car for himself, but depressed Charles by adding: "Of course I can't use it today, I shall have to walk." The Lawgiver forbade people of my religion to make journeys on the Sabbath: why, I've never been able to understand. Well, though I oughtn't to pay him compliments, my son Charles is a polite young man with people he doesn't know well. Hannah says he isn't, but she's only seen him when she's present herself. On this occasion he felt compelled to walk back with Oliver. We heard an infernal noise when they got back, and I went out and found him standing on a towel in the hall. He expressed himself angrily whenever I pointed out how he could have avoided disaster.'

Mr March was beaming with laughter. Then he added, quietly, and to my complete surprise:

'Of course, he's not bad-tempered as a rule. He wouldn't have minded so much if it hadn't been caused by the religion.'

He went on: 'Herbert was the same forty years ago. At the time when he was getting up to his monkey tricks about studying music. He didn't much like to be reminded that he belonged to our religion.'

Mr March added:

'Of course, Herbert found that troubles of that nature passed away as he got older. I am inclined to think that the thickening of one's skin is the only conceivable advantage of becoming old. If my son's trouble was entirely due to his thin skin, I should cease to have periods of worry about him. But it isn't so.'

Mr March talked no more on our walk home. We arrived at the house a few minutes before his standard time of 12.45, and found Katherine eating an early lunch before going out to meet Ann Simon.

Chapter 11

MR MARCH ENDS A REFLECTION

CHARLES and I were alone at lunch with Mr March, who was still half-saddened, half-anxious, as he had been on the way home. I was certain by now that he was innocent about Katherine. As he talked to Charles, he had no thought of trouble from her. His concern was all for his son; he did not imagine any other danger to his peace of mind.

He told some stories, but they were shot through with his affection for Charles. Because he was in that mood, he told us more than I had heard of his early life. At once one knew, more sharply than on the day he watched Charles's case, how much of himself he was re-creating in his son.

He described his own career. He talked, not as vivaciously as usual, but with his natural lack of pretence. 'I never made much progress,' he said.

His father and Philip's, the first Sir Philip, had been the most effective of all the Marches; he had controlled the March firm of foreign bankers and brokers when it was at its peak. 'And in my father's days,' said Mr March, 'they counted as more than a business house. Of course it would be different now. Everything's on too big a scale for a private firm. Look at the Rothschilds. They used to be the most influential family in Europe. And they've kept going after we finished, they've not done badly, and what are they now? Just merchant bankers in a fairly lucrative way of business.'

When his father died, Mr March, who would have preferred to go to the university, was brought in to fill a vacancy in the firm. 'It was a good opening,' he said to us, nearly fifty years after. 'I wasn't attracted specially to business, but I hadn't any particular inclinations. I hoped you would have,' he said to Charles.

It was not during this conversation, but previously, that I had the curiosity to ask him about the routine of foreign banking, when he first joined the firm. There had still been an air about it, so it seemed. Each morning, the letters came in from the Marches' correspondents: there had been two in Paris, and one in each of the other European capitals, including 'the very capable fellow at St Petersburg. We never believed he was a Russian'. Since the bank started, they had depended on their correspondents, a group of men very similar in gifts and outlook to the foreign-based journalists of the twentieth century. In 1880 the Marches were still better informed, over a whole area of facts where politics and economics fused, than any newspaper. The March correspondents acquired a curious mixture of cynicism and world-view. Just because their finding the truth could be measured in terms of money, they learned what the truth was. All through 1870 one of the Paris correspondents was predicting war, and war in which the French army would be outclassed: Mr March's father cleared some hundred thousand pounds. Right through the nineteenth century, up to the end of the bank in 1896, the foreign letters added sarcastic footnotes to history: they were unmoral, factual, hard-baked, much more hard-baked because they did not set out to be.

The secret correspondent declined in value as communications got faster. The Marches' telephone number was London 2; but they did not time their moves as certainly as when Mr March's father opened his despatches in the morning. Mr March gallantly telephoned in French to Paris and Brussels every day as the bourses opened; but as the nineties passed by, neither his uncles nor Philip, nor he above all, felt they were in touch, even as much in touch as ten years before.

Of course the scale of things was altering under their hands. Their loans of a million pounds or so to the Argentine or Brazil no longer went very far; they were coming near to a world of preposterous size – a world dangerous, mad, exciting beyond measure, and, as Mr March decided, no place for a financier of distinctly anxious temperament. It was about this time that the legend sprang up of his only being able to control his worry by balancing the firm's accounts each night.

They might have stayed in longer, but for a characteristic weakness against which Mr March struggled in vain. They would never take anyone outside the family into the firm. As Mr March argued and quarrelled with his uncles, he kept protesting that one man of a different sort from the Marches might vitalize them. But they were loyal to the family: the Marches had started the bank a hundred years before, they had controlled it ever since, they could not give power to a stranger. In fact, as they were good pickers of men, Mr March's policy would probably have made them richer; but, whatever happened, neither they nor any other 'merchant banker in a fairly lucrative way of business' would have stayed in usefully for long: the twentieth century needed, not single millions, but tens and hundreds of millions, and could only be financed by the joint stock banks.

So they ceased business in 1896. They had not made much money in the nineties, but each of the five partners retired with a comfortable fortune. Mr March was just thirty-two. As the three of us sat at lunch he was talking of that time.

'I was still a bachelor,' he said, 'I thought I possessed enough for my requirements. But it was a pity, a firm like ours terminating after a hundred years. I sometimes think we should have continued. But we hadn't improved our position noticeably since my father died. Of course if I had been like him, I should have carried on successfully. But I didn't do much. My temperament was quite unsuitable for business. I was too shy and anxious.'

He was accepting himself as always, but his eyes did not leave Charles and he was speaking with regret. Success, in the world of his father and uncles, meant multiplying one's fortune and adding to one's influence among solid men. Mr March, not valuing it as much as they did, knew nevertheless that he would have pursued it if his temperament had not let him down; he would have kept the firm going, or joined others, as his brother Philip had done. While in fact he had come to terms with himself and retired. He had been happier, he had followed his nature; but he made no excuses, and it meant admitting to himself that, compared with those others, he was not so good a man.

'I was too shy and anxious' – he had taken himself for granted and lived unrestrainedly according to his own comfort. Like many people who are obsessed by every detail in the world outside, he was driven to simplify his life. Business was unbearable with a real anxiety every day, and instead he let himself loose on anxieties such as locking the door at night. Like many people sensitized to others' feelings, he was driven to escape more and more from company – except of those he had known so long that they did not count. More than any other March, he came to live entirely inside the family. He retired from any competition (Charles had said the same of himself the night he announced he was abandoning the law), met few new faces, and enjoyed himself as he felt inclined.

His happiness grew as he lived at the centre of his family, and his own most extravagant stories began with his marriage. It was a good start, as he stood with his bride on Victoria Station, to arrange for a cab to meet their train on Monday afternoon exactly one month later. After they had been a week at Mentone, another thought occurred to him of a contingency left unprovided for. He walked alone to the post office and sent off a telegram, reserving for his wife a place next to himself in the Jewish Cemetery at Golders Green.

Thus he plunged among twenty-five years of marriage – not at all tranquil years, because he could not be tranquil anywhere, but full of the life he wanted and in which he breathed his native air. He was passionately fond of his wife, and he was occupied with plenty of excitements, major and minor; the major excitements about his children as they grew up, and the minor ones of his fortune, Bryanston Square, Haslingfield, the servants, the whole economico-personal system of which he was the core.

He had not been bored. He had enjoyed his life. He still enjoyed it. He would have taken it over again on the same terms, and gone through it with as much zest.

And yet, it was foreign to his nature not to be frank with himself, and he felt that he had paid a price. Underneath this life which suited him, which soaked up the violence underneath and let him become luxuriantly himself, he knew that he had lost some self-respect. He had been happier than most men, but it meant that he chose to run away from the contest.

Even Mr March, the most realistic of men, could not always forgive himself for his own nature. He could not quite forget the illusion, which we all have, most strongly when we are young, that every kind of action is possible to us if only we use our will. He felt as we all do, when we have slowly come to terms with our temperament and no longer try to be different from ourselves; we may be happier now, but we cannot help looking back to the days when we struggled against the sight of our limitations, when, miserable and conflict-ridden perhaps, we still in flashes of hope held the whole world in our hands. For the loss, as we come to know ourselves, is that now we know what we can never do.

Mr March felt envious of himself as a young man, not yet reconciled, not yet abdicating from his hopes of success. There were times when he called himself a failure. It was then that he invested all those rejected hopes in Charles; for everything that one aspired to, and had to dismiss as one discovered one's weakness, could be built up again in a son. Could be built up more extravagantly, as a matter of fact; because, even in youth, the frailties of one's own temperament were always liable to bring one back to realism, while the frailties of a son's could be laughed off.

For a long time Mr March secretly expected a great deal from Charles's gifts, more than he expressed during any of their arguments when Charles gave up the law. I remembered the end of that evening, after their quarrel, when suddenly he said 'I have always wanted something for you' and broke off the conversation, as though he were ashamed.

This afternoon at Haslingfield he was speaking in the same tone, concerned, simple, and with no trace of reproach. Months had passed. So far as he knew, Charles was still idle and ready to follow his own escape; Mr March could see his son also driven to waste himself. As he told us of his career at the bank, Mr March was speaking of his fears for Charles. When he let us see his own regret, he was desperately anxious that he and his son should not be too much alike. He looked at Charles as he told his stories, in a voice more subdued than I had heard it. 'After all,' he said, '*I* didn't do much. *I* wasn't the man to make much of my opportunities.'

Chapter 12

FIRST AND SECOND SIGHT

AFTER lunch Mr March left us, and Charles and I went out to the deck-chairs in the garden. It was glaring and hot out of doors, by contrast with the shaded dining-room. Charles, affected by his father's self-description, sat by me without speaking.

I heard a car run up the drive. A quarter of an hour later, Ann and Katherine came down from the house towards us. I noticed that Ann's walk had the kind of stiff-legged grace one sometimes saw in actresses, as though it had been studied and controlled. By Katherine's side, it made her look a fashionable woman: she was wearing a yellow summer frock, and carrying a parasol: she was still too far off for us to see her face.

When they came up to us, and she was introduced to Charles, it was a surprise, just as it had been on the night of Getliffe's party, to see her smile, natural, direct, and shy. In the same manner, both direct and shy, she said to him:

'We've met before, haven't we?'

Charles, standing up, her hand in his, said:

'I believe we have.'

He added:

'Yes, I remember the evening.'

She had spoken to him with friendliness. Although he was polite, I did not hear the same tone in his voice. He looked at Katherine. There was a glint in his eye I did not understand.

Ann lay back in her deck-chair, and for an instant closed her eyes, basking in the heat. With her face on one side, the line between dark hair and temple was sharp, the skin paper-white under the bright sun. She looked prettier than I had seen her. Charles was glancing at her: I could not tell whether he was attracted: the moment we began to talk, he was provoked.

Sitting up, she asked me a question about Herbert Getliffe, going back to our conversation at the party.

'I've heard a bit more about him since then,' she said.

'What have you heard?'

She hesitated; she seemed both interested and uneasy.

'I couldn't help wondering —'

'What about?'

'Well, why you ever chose to work with him.'

Charles interrupted:

'You'd better tell us why you think he shouldn't.'

'I warn you that you're going to meet his brother soon,' said Katherine.

'Look, I'm sorry,' Ann said to her, 'if Herbert Getliffe is a friend of yours.'

'No. I've never met the man,' said Katherine, who was nevertheless blushing.

'You've gone too far to back out, you know,' Charles broke in again. 'What have you really got against Herbert Getliffe?'

Ann looked straight at him.

'I don't want to overdo it,' she said uncomfortably and steadily. 'I can only go on what I've been told — but isn't he the worst lawyer who's ever earned £4,000 a year?'

'Where did you hear that?' asked Charles.

'I was told by a man I know.'

Charles's eyes were bright, he was ready (I found the irony agreeable) to defend Getliffe with spirit. 'I suppose,' he said, 'your friend isn't by any chance a less successful rival at the Bar?'

'His name is Ronald Porson. He happens to have been practising out in Singapore,' said Ann.

'He's really a very unsuccessful rival, isn't he?'

'He's a far more intelligent person than Getliffe,' she said. With Charles getting at her, her diffidence had not become greater, but much less. Just as his voice had an edge to it, so had hers.

'Even if that's so,' Charles teased her, 'for success, you know, intelligence is a very minor gift.'

'I should like to know what you do claim for Getliffe.'

'He's got intuition,' said Charles.

'What do you really mean by that?'

'Why,' said Charles, with his sharpest smile, 'you must know what intuition is. At any rate, you must have read about it in books.'

Ann gazed at him without expression, her eyes clear blue. For a second it seemed that she was going to make it a quarrel. She shrugged her shoulders, laughed, and lay back again in the sun.

Soon Katherine asked her to play a game of tennis. Ann tried to get out of it, saying how bad she was. I imagined that it was her normal shyness, until we saw her play. Katherine, who had a useful forehand drive, banged the ball past her. By the end of the fourth game, we realized that Ann was not only outclassed but already tired.

'Are you sure that you ought to be doing this?' called Charles.

'It's all right.' She was panting.

'Are you sure that you're quite fit?'

'Not perfectly. But I want to go on.'

'We'd better stop,' said Katherine.

'If you do, I shall claim the game.' She was still short of breath, but her face was set in an obstinate, headstrong smile.

She served. They played another game. Charles was watching her with a frown. At the end of the set he went on to the court. She was giddy, and clutched his arm; he took her to her chair. Soon she was moving her head from side to side, as though making sure that the giddiness had passed. She smiled at Charles. He said in relief:

'Why didn't you behave reasonably?'

'This is ridiculous,' said Ann.

He scolded her:

'Why did you insist on playing on after you'd tired yourself out?'

'I was ill in the spring, you see.' She was explaining her collapse.

'Would it upset you,' said Charles, 'if I sent for a doctor?'

'I'd ask you to if I needed one, I promise you I would.'

'Just to relieve my own mind?'

'I'd ask you to, if there was the slightest need.'

'There really isn't any?'

'You'll only irritate one if you fetch him.'

'I don't mind that —'

'You haven't had a doctor as a father, have you?'

'You really don't think there's any need? You know enough about yourself to be sure?' Charles reiterated.

Their sparring had vanished. They were speaking with confidence in each other.

'You see,' said Ann, 'I used to have these bouts before. They're passing off now.'

Just then Mr March walked down after his afternoon sleep. Before he reached us, he was watching Ann and his son. Then he looked only at Ann, and his manner to her, from the moment Katherine introduced them, impressed us all.

'I am delighted to have you adorning my house,' said Mr March. 'It isn't often that my house has been so charmingly adorned.'

It was a speech of deliberate gallantry. It was so emphatic that Ann became flustered; she smiled back, but she could not make much of a reply.

Mr March went on:

'I hope my son has not been excessively negligent in entertaining you until I arrived.'

'Not at all,' said Ann, still at a loss.

'I am relieved to hear it,' said Mr March.

'But I didn't give Katherine much of a game at tennis,' she said over-brightly, casting round for words.

'You shouldn't let them inveigle you into action too soon after your arrival. I might remark that you're paler than you ought to be, no doubt as a result of their lack of consideration.'

'I've been looked after very nicely, Mr March –'

'It's extremely polite of you to say so,' he said.

'Really I have.' She was getting over the first impact, and she answered without constraint, smiling both at him and Charles.

Soon afterwards Francis arrived, and I watched Katherine's eyes as his plunging stride brought him through the drawing-room, over the terrace, down to the lawn. Tea was brought out to us, and we ate raspberries and cream in the sunshine.

After tea we played tennis; then, when Mr March went in to dress, Katherine took Francis for a walk round the rose-garden, and I left the other two together. I strolled down the drive before going to my room; the stocks were beginning to smell, now the heat of the day was passing, and the scent came to me as though to heighten, and at the same time to touch with languor, the emotions I had been living among that afternoon.

When I left Ann and Charles, their faces had been softened and glowing. No one would say that either was in love; but each was in the state when they knew at least that love was possible. They were still safe; they need not meet again; he could still choose not to ask her, she could still refuse; and yet, while they did not know each other, while they were still free, there was a promise of joy.

It seemed a long time since I had known that state, I thought, as the smell of the stocks set me indulging my own mood. It had gone too soon, and I had discovered other meanings in love. I wondered how long it would last for them.

Evening was falling, and as I turned back towards the house its upper windows shone like blazing shields in the last of the sunlight. Looking up, I felt a trace of worry about Francis and Katherine; I felt a trace of self-pity because Charles and Ann might be lucky; but really, walking back to the house through the warm air, I was enjoying being a spectator, I was excited about it all.

Chapter 13

GAMBLE

At dinner Mr March was not subdued and acceptant, as he had been at that table a few hours before. Instead, he intervened in each conversation and produced some of his more unpredictable retorts. So far as I could notice, his glance did not stay too long on Katherine, whose face was fresh with happiness as she talked to Francis. He interrupted her, but only as he interrupted the rest of us, in order to stay the centre of attention. It was hard to be sure whether his high spirits were genuine or not.

Once or twice Mr March waited for a response from Ann, who sat, dressed all in black except for an aquamarine brooch on her breast, at his right hand. She was quiet, she was deferential, she laughed at his stories, but it was not until after dinner that Mr March forced her into an argument.

We had moved into the drawing-room, and Mr March sent for the footman to open more windows. There we sat, the lights on, the curtains undrawn and the windows open, while Mr March proceeded by way of the day's temperature to talk to Francis, who was going to Corsica for a month's holiday before the October term.

'I hope you will insist on ignoring any salad they may be misguided enough to offer you. My daughter last year failed to show competent discretion in that respect. Caroline made a similar frightful ass of herself just before the earthquake at Messina. The disaster might have been avoided if she had possessed the gumption to keep sufficiently suspicious of all foreigners –'

'If you mean me, Mr. L.,' Katherine said, 'I've proved to you that being ill in Venice can't have had anything to do with what I ate abroad.'

'I refuse to accept your assurances,' said Mr March. 'I hope you too will refuse to accept my daughter's assurances,' he said to Francis. In each remark he made to Francis, Katherine was listening for an undertone: but she heard none, and protested loudly because she was relieved. Mr March shouted her down, and went on talking to Francis: 'I should be sorry if my daughter's example lured you into risks that would probably be fatal to your health.'

'As I've spent an hour before dinner trying to persuade him not to climb mountains without a guide,' said Katherine, 'I call that rather hard.'

'She definitely disapproves of the trip,' said Francis. 'She can't be blamed for not discouraging me enough.'

'I should advise you to ignore any of her suggestions for your welfare,' said Mr March.

It sounded no more than genial back-chat. Katherine kept showing her concern for Francis. She could not resist showing it: to do so was a delight. Yet Mr March gave no sign that he saw him as a menace.

Mr March left off talking to Francis, and addressed us all:

'My experience is that foreigners can always tempt one to abandon any sensible habit. I have never been able to understand why it is considered necessary to intrude oneself among them on the pretext of obtaining pleasure. Hannah always said that she came to life abroad, but I don't believe that she was competent to judge. Since I married my wife I have preferred to live in my own houses where foreigners are unlikely to penetrate. The more I am compelled to hear of foreign countries, the less I like them. I am sure that my charming guest will agree with me,' he said confidentially to Ann.

Ann was embarrassed. 'I don't think I should go quite as far as that, Mr March,' she said.

'You'll come to it in time, you'll come to it in time,' cried Mr March. 'Why, you must be too young to remember the catastrophe foreigners involved us in fifteen years ago.'

'I was nine,' she said.

'I am surprised to hear that you weren't even more of an infant. I should be prepared to guarantee that you will keep your present youth and beauty until you are superannuated. But still you can't conceivably remember the origins of that unfortunate catastrophe. You can't remember how we were bamboozled by foreigners and entangled in continental concerns that were no affair of ours –'

Mr March went on to develop a commentary, jingoistic and reactionary, on the circumstances of the 1914–18 war. He had the habit of pretending to be at the extreme limit of reaction, just because he knew that Charles's friends were nearly all of them on the left. But we did not argue with him; when politics came up among the senior Marches, we usually avoided trouble and kept our mouths shut.

As she listened, Ann was frowning. She glanced at Charles, then at me, as though expecting us to contradict. When Mr March paused for a breathing space, she hesitated; she started to talk and checked herself. But the next time he stopped, she did not hesitate. In a tone timid, gentle but determined, she said:

'I'm sorry, Mr March, but I'm afraid I can't believe it.'

'I should be glad to be enlightened on what you do believe,' said Mr March, preserving his gallant manner.

Still quietly and uneasily, Ann told him, without any covering up, that she did not accept any of his views about the war, or nations, or the causes of politics.

'I suppose you're going to tell me next that we can't understand anything unless we take account of what those people call the class struggle.'

Mr March's voice had become loud; his face was heavy with anger.

Ann's tone was more subdued, but she continued without hesitation:

'I'm afraid I should have to say just that.'

'Economic poppycock,' Mr March burst out.

'It's a tenable theory, Mr L.,' Charles interrupted. 'You can't dispose of it by clamour.'

'My guest can't dispose of it by claptrap,' said Mr March.

Then he suppressed his temper, and spoke to Ann in his most friendly and simple way:

'Obviously we take different views of the world. I presume that you think it will improve?'

'Yes,' said Ann.

'You are optimistic, as you should be at your age. I am inclined to consider that it will continue to get worse. I console myself that it will last my time.'

'Yes,' Mr March added, as he glanced round the bright room, 'it will last my time.'

He had spoken in a tone matter-of-fact and yet elegiac. He did not want to argue with Ann any more. But then I saw that Ann was not ready to let it go. Her eyes were bright. For all her shyness, she was not prepared to be discreet, as I was. Perhaps she was contemptuous of that kind of discretion. I had an impression that she was gambling.

'I'm sure it won't last mine,' she said.

Mr March was taken aback, and she added:

'I'm also sure that it oughtn't to.'

'You anticipate that there will be a violent change within your lifetime?' said Mr March.

'Of course,' said Ann, with absolute conviction.

She had spoken with such force that we were all silent for an instant. Then Mr March said:

'You've no right to anticipate it.'

'Of course she has,' Charles broke in. 'She wants a good world. This is the only way in which she can see it happening.' He smiled at her. 'The only doubt is whether the world afterwards would be worth it.'

'I'm sure of that,' she said.

'You've no right to be sure,' said Mr March.

'Why don't you think I have?' she asked quietly.

'Because women would be better advised not to concern themselves with these matters.'

Mr March had spoken with acute irritability, but Ann broke suddenly into laughter. It was laughter so spontaneous, so unresentfully accepting the joke against herself, that Mr March was first taken at a loss and then reassured. He watched her eyes screw up, her self-control dissolve, as she abandoned herself to laughter. She looked very young.

Charles took the chance to smooth the party down. He acted as impresario for Mr March and led him on to his best stories. At first Mr March was still disturbed: but he was melted by his son's care, and by the warmth and well-being we could all feel that night in Charles.

Katherine joined in. Between them they poured all their attention on to Mr March, as though making up for the exhilaration of the last few hours.

They succeeded in getting Mr March on to the subject of Ann's family. He told her: 'Of course, you're not one of the real Simons,' and she proved that she was a distant cousin of the Florence Simon whom I had met at the family dinner at Bryanston Square and who even Mr March had to admit was 'real'. From then till 10.40 Mr March explored in what remote degree he and Ann were related; stories of fourth and fifth cousins 'making frightful asses of themselves' forty years ago became immersed in the timeless continuum in which Mr March, more extravagantly than on a normal night, let himself go.

When Mr March had rattled each door in the hall and gone upstairs, Katherine said to Ann:

'Well, I hope you're not too bothered after all that.' Ann shook her head.

'Did you want me to keep out?' she said to Charles. Charles was smiling. Francis asked:

'What would your own father have said if a strange young woman had started talking about the revolution?'

'Didn't you agree with me?' she said, quite sharply. She knew that Francis was on her side: he was as radical as his fellow scientists. Deferential as she often sounded, she was not to be browbeaten. Then she smiled too.

'I won't do it again,' she said. 'But tonight was a special occasion.'

Again I had the impression that she had been gambling. Whatever the gamble had been, it was over now, and she was relaxed.

Making it up with Francis, she said to him: 'As for my father, he wouldn't have had the spirit to argue. Even when I was growing up, he'd managed to tire himself out.'

Although she seemed to be speaking to Francis, she was really speaking to Charles. One could guess from her tone that she loved him. One could guess too that she was not often relaxed enough to talk like this. She smiled again, almost as though her upper lip were twitching, and said:

'Can you remember the agony you went through when your father was first proved wrong?'

It was Katherine who answered her:

'I don't know,' she said. 'We were used to the whole family proving each other wrong, weren't we?'

'But I think I know what you mean,' Charles was saying to Ann.

'I've never forgotten,' said Ann. 'It was the day after my birthday – I was nine. Someone came in to dinner, a friend of mother's. He said to my father: "You call yourself a doctor. You remember how you swore last week that the sea was blue because of the salts that it dissolved? Well, I asked one of the men at school. He laughed and said it was a ridiculous idea." Then he gave the proper explanation. I never have been able to remember it to this day.' Ann went on: 'I've re-learned it several times, but it's no good. I told myself in bed that night that of course father was right. But I knew he wasn't. I knew people were laughing because he didn't know why the sea was blue. Every time I remembered that night for years, I wanted to shut my eyes.'

Charles said to Katherine:

'We know what that's like, don't we?' He turned back to Ann. 'But when I've felt like that, it wasn't over quite the same things.'

'Not over your father?'

Charles hesitated and said:

'Not in the same way.'

'What was it about then?'

'Mostly about being a Jew,' said Charles.

'Curiously enough,' said Ann, 'I never felt that.'

'Which is no doubt why I met you,' said Charles, 'on my one and only appearance at the Jewish dance.'

He looked at me; this was the trick of fortune I had not recognized that afternoon. He was smiling at his own expense, and his expression, sarcastic and gay, brought back the first night I dined at Bryanston Square, when he talked 'with a furrowed brow' of Katherine being sent to the dance. Tonight he seemed free of that past.

'You were lucky to escape,' said Charles. 'There've been times when I've disliked other Jews – simply because I suffered through being one.'

'Yes,' said Katherine.

'I couldn't help it, but it was degrading to feel oneself doing it,' he said.

'Yes,' said Katherine again.

'I think you would have behaved better,' Charles said to Ann.

'No,' she said. 'I've hated my father sometimes because of the misery I've been through on his account.'

We all confided about our childhoods, but it was Charles and Ann, and sometimes Katherine, who spoke most about the moments of shame – not grief or sorrow, but shame. The kind of shame we all know, but which had been more vivid to them than to most of us : the kind of shame which, when one remembers it, makes one stop dead in one's tracks, and jam one's eyelids tight to shut it out.

They went on with those confidences until Ann went to bed. It was late, and Francis followed not long after. Katherine made an excuse and ran out, and from the drawing-room Charles and I heard her speak to Francis at the bottom of the stairs. For several minutes we heard their voices. Then Katherine rejoined us, and gave Charles a radiant smile. We opened the long windows, and walked on to the terrace. It was an August night of extreme beauty, the moon just about to rise over the hills. A meteor flashed among the many stars to the south.

No one spoke. Katherine threw her arm round Charles's shoulders, smiled at him, and sighed.

Chapter 14

BORROWING A ROOM

Early in October, when the March household had returned to London, Katherine started gossip percolating through the family, just by having Francis Getliffe three or four times to dinner at Bryanston Square. We speculated often upon when the gossip would reach Mr March: we became more and more puzzled as to whether he was truly oblivious.

On an autumn night, warm and misty, with leaves sometimes spinning down in the windless air, Charles and I were walking through the square. He had not been talking much. Out of the blue he said:

'I've got a favour to ask you.'

'What is it?'

He was speaking with diffidence, with unusual stiffness.

'I don't want you to say yes out of good-nature. It may be too much of an intrusion –'

'If you tell me what it is –'

'I don't want you to say yes on the spot.'

'What in God's name is it?'

At last he said:

'Well, we wondered whether you could bear it, if Ann and I met in your rooms –'

He produced time-tables, which he had been thinking out, so I suspected, for days beforehand, of how they could fit in with my movements, of how they need not inconvenience me.

Up to that night we had said nothing about Ann. Hearing him forced to break his secretiveness open, I was both touched and amused. I was amused also to find him facing a problem that vexed me and my impoverished friends when I was younger – of 'somewhere to go' with a young woman. In our innocence we thought the problem would have solved itself if we had money. While in fact Charles, with all the March houses at his disposal, could get no privacy at all – less than we used to get in the dingy streets of the provincial town.

Walking with Charles that night, and other nights that autumn, I felt as one does with a friend in love – protective, superior, a little irritated, envious. His tongue was softened by happiness. He was full of hopes. Those hopes! He would not have dared to confess them. He would have blushed because they were so impossibly golden, romantic – and above all vague. They had no edge or limit, they were just a vista of grand, continuing, and perfect rapture.

Charles was by nature both guarded and subtle. His imagination was a realistic one. If I had confessed any such hopes as uplifted him that autumn, he would have riddled them with sarcasm. They would have sounded jejune by contrast to his own style. Yet now he fed on them for hours, they were part of the greatest happiness he had ever known.

As the autumn passed, I saw a good deal of Charles and Ann together. Inquisitive as I was, I did not know for certain what was happening to them. Then one evening when I returned to my flat they were still there. They were sitting by the fire; they greeted me; they did not tell me anything. Yet looking at them I felt jealous because they were so happy.

Ann said, gazing round the room as though she was noticing it for the first time:

'Why does Lewis make this place look like a station waiting-room?' Charles smiled at her, and she went on:

'We ought to take care of him for once, oughtn't we? Let's take care of him.'

She spoke with the absorbed kindness of the supremely happy: kindness which was not really directed towards me, but which was an overflow of her own joy.

I thought then that it had taken Ann longer than anyone else to recognize that she was in love: though from that afternoon at Haslingfield the barriers dropped away, and she gave him her trust. She had not known before that she could let the barriers fall like that; except with her father, she had not entrusted herself to another human being. To all of us round her, there seemed no doubt about it; each moment she was living through had become enhanced. Yet it was some time before she said to herself: 'I am in love.'

Of course, that conscious recognition to oneself – particularly in a character like Ann's – is a more important stage than we sometimes allow. Until it has happened, this present desire may still swim with others, there are plenty more we have never brought to light. But when once it is made conscious, there is no way of drawing back; the love must be lived out.

That moment, when Ann first thought 'I am in love' (to Charles it happened at once, during the week-end at Haslingfield), was more decisive for them than the dates which on the surface seemed to mark so much: of the first kiss, of when they first made love. Seeing them that night, when it was all settled, I guessed that it came later than the rest of us suspected: and that, as soon as it came, there was no retreat. They knew – they told each other with the painful and extreme pleasure of surrender – that fate had caught them.

Chapter 15

BELIEVING ONE'S EARS

A DAY or two after I had watched Charles and Ann in my own sitting-room, she took me out to dinner alone. She took me out to a sumptuous dinner; shy as she could be, she was used to making her money work for her, and she led me to a corner table in Claridge's; more unashamed of riches than Charles, more lavish and generous, she persuaded me to eat an expensive meal and drink a bottle of wine to myself. Meanwhile she was getting me to talk about Charles.

For a time I was reticent. He was too secretive to tolerate being discussed, even with her, perhaps most of all with her.

Very gently she said:

'All I should like to know is what *you* think he really wants.' She did not mean about herself: that was taken for granted and not mentioned all night. There she was as delicate and proud as he was; she did not even suggest that they would get married. But about the rest of his life she was tender and not so delicate. She wanted anything she could learn about him which would help him. As she pressed me, her face open, her manner affectionate and submissive, I could realize the core of will within her.

What had he been like when I first knew him? What had he thought of doing with himself? What had he really felt when he gave up the Bar?

'He would always have hated the Bar,' I said. 'He was dead right to get out of it.'

'Of course he was,' said Ann.

'And yet,' I said, 'he's not so unambitious as he seems.'

'Aren't you reading yourself into him?' she said, suddenly sharp.

'Do you think he likes being idle?' I retorted.

'Don't you think' – she was gazing straight at me – 'there are other ways of not being idle?'

She took up the attack.

'Would you really say,' she went on, 'that he wants success on the terms that you want it, or most other men do?'

I hesitated.

'No,' I said. 'Perhaps not quite.'

'Not quite?' She was smiling. As she asked the question, I knew how tenacious and passionate she was.

'Not at all. Not in the ordinary sense,' I had to admit.

She smiled again, sitting relaxed in her corner. Once more she asked me in detail what he had done about giving up the Bar. She needed anything I could tell her about him; nothing was trivial; she was bringing her whole self to bear. When she had finished with me, she became silent. It was some time afterwards before she said:

'Have you got an idea of what he really wants?'

'Has he?'

She would not answer; but I was sure she thought he had. Alone with her, I knew for certain how single-minded her love was. She had no room for anyone but him. She liked me, she was friendly and comradely, she had good manners, she wanted to know how I was getting on: but really this was a business dinner. She was securing me as an ally, just because I was his intimate friend: she was picking my brains: that was all.

I was thinking, I had never seen her flirt. Only once had I seen her so much as give any meaning to another man's name: that was the first afternoon at Haslingfield, when Charles was baiting her and she replied by praising Ronald Porson. She had done it to defend herself, to provoke Charles. Apart from that, although she was admired by several other men, she had not let Charles worry about them.

Actually Porson was pressing her to marry him. She had talked of him to me once: he had meant little to her, but he had been infatuated with her for years: she felt a last shred of responsibility for him on that account. She found it hard to say the final no. From her description, he seemed to be an eccentric, violent character, and I thought that perhaps his oddity had found some niche in her imagination.

That night at Claridge's, I was on the point of asking her about him, when by chance I said something about politics. At once she was on to it; she was eager to discover whether I was an ally there also. In a few minutes I discovered that she was not playing. This was not just a rich young woman's fancy.

I had not been able to understand her outburst at Haslingfield; I was still puzzled by it, after this talk with her alone; but at least I respected her in a way that I had not reckoned on. Most of the radicalism of the younger Marches I could not take seriously, after being brought up in a different climate, the climate of those born poor. But Ann was different again.

As we argued that night, I could not help but see that there was nothing dilettante about her. This was real politics. She knew more than I did. She was more committed.

I respected her: on many things we agreed: it was a curious pleasure to agree on politics, to see her pretty face across the table, to feel that her warmth and force were on one's side. But, even then, it seemed a bit of a mystery. Much more so when I thought about it in cold blood. Why did politics mean so much to her? Why was she like this? What was she after?

I could not find any sort of answer. To another of that night's mysteries I did however get an answer – when, just before Christmas, I came back to my room late in the evening. As I got to the landing, I saw a crack of light under the door. When I went in, I had an impression they had waited for me. Ann was sitting in a chair by the fire, Charles on the rug at her feet. She was running her fingers through his hair. They went on talking as I laid down a brief. For an instant, I fancied I caught the words from Ann 'when you've finished at hospital'. I thought I must have misheard. But, as I came to sit down in the other armchair, she used the same phrase, unmistakably, again.

It seemed to me fantastic. It seemed so fantastic that I was just going to ask. But Ann then said:

'We're thinking that Charles might become a doctor.'

'That's going a bit far,' said Charles, who was in high spirits. But chiefly I noticed Ann's pleasure — soft, intense, youthful.

'Don't you think it would be a good idea?' she said.

Charles teased her for her enthusiasm, but she did not let it go. 'You wanted him to know, didn't you?' she said.

'It's only the barest possibility, you understand?' said Charles to me.

'But he wants to hear what you think.' Ann also was speaking to me.

Charles insisted that we keep secret even the most remote mention of the idea. As she promised, a smile flickered on Ann's happy face, and the sight of it made Charles, after an instant's lag and as though reluctantly, smile too.

Chapter 16

CHOICE OF A PROFESSION

ONE afternoon in January, I went to tea at Bryanston Square and discovered that Charles had just confided in Katherine. I discovered it through their habit of repeating themselves. When I arrived, they were talking of a rumour that Aunt Caroline had been making enquiries about Francis Getliffe: how often did he go to Bryanston Square? How often did he go when Charles was otherwise engaged? Katherine was agitated and excited. There was another rumour that Caroline was considering whether she ought to speak to Mr March. Was it true? Then Katherine said, harking back to what they had been saying:

'I suppose he won't mind this idea of yours. Don't you agree that he won't mind it?'

'Can you give me a good reason why he should?'

'It will be a shock to him, you realize that?' she said. She looked at me, and went on: 'Does Lewis know anything about this, by the way?'

'He's had a bit of warning.' Charles then said to me: 'I've told Katherine this afternoon that I'm going to try to become a doctor.'

Since that hint in my room he had not asked my advice nor anyone else's. Only Ann had been inside his secret. He was presenting us, just as he had done when he gave up the law, with a resolution already made. By the time he told us, it was made once for all, and the rest of us could take it or leave it.

Katherine was frowning. 'I can't understand why you should do this.'

'It isn't as difficult as all that, is it?'

'You could do so many things.'

'I've evaded them so far with singular sucess,' said Charles.

115

'Is it the best scheme?' Katherine said. 'Don't you think he'll be wasted, Lewis?'

'It's exactly to prevent myself being wasted that I've thought of this.' Charles looked at her with a sarcastic, affectionate grin. 'I agree, I wouldn't like to feel that I had wasted my time altogether. The chief advantage of becoming a doctor is precisely that it might prevent me doing that. I shall still be some use in a dim way even if I turn out to be completely obscure. It's the only occupation I can find where you can be absolutely undistinguished and still flatter yourself a bit.'

'That's all very well for one of nature's saints,' said Katherine. 'But are you sure it's your line?'

Charles did not answer. He hesitated. He was embarrassed. Sharply, he went on to a new line:

'I've told you, there's a perfectly good practical reason. You both know, I'm hoping that Ann will marry me. We've got to look a reasonable way ahead. I suppose Mr L. will make me independent when I'm twenty-five, that is in April. He's always promised to do that, or when I marry, "whichever shall be the earlier", as he insists on saying. And I suppose I shall come into his money in time. But don't you see? I daren't count on any of this lasting many years. If I come into Mr L.'s money, I daren't count on that lasting many years. Too much may happen in the world. It's not exactly likely we shall be able to live on investments all our lives. Well, I think there's more security as a doctor than as anything else I could take up. Whatever happens to the world, it's rather unlikely that a doctor will starve.'

Those words sounded strange, in the drawing-room at Bryanston Square, from the heir to one of the March fortunes. But we had already begun to speak in those terms. On this winter evening when Charles was talking, such an anxiety seemed, of course, remote, not quite real, not comparable for an instant with that which Katherine felt when she saw a letter from Aunt Caroline waiting for Mr March.

*

When Charles told Mr March a few days later, he gave the same justification – the desire to be some use, the need to be secure, though he did not mention Ann's name.

For some time, Charles's insight failed him; he did not understand how his father had responded. Mr March began by opposing: but that was nothing unusual, and Charles was not disturbed. Mr March's first remarks were on the plane of reason. He put forward entirely sensible arguments why Charles could not hope to become a doctor. He was nearly twenty-five. At best he would be well into the thirties before he was qualified. He had had no serious scientific education, and was, like all the Marches, clumsy with his hands. It would be an intolerable self-discipline to go through years of uncongenial study. 'You might begin it,' said Mr March, 'but you'd give it up after a few months. You've never shown the slightest disposition to persevere with anything when you're not interested. You've never shown the slightest disposition to persevere with anything at all. I refuse to believe that you're remotely capable of it.'

That was the end of the first discussion. Mr March's tone had become not quite so reasonable. As never before in all their quarrels over his career, Charles heard a gibe behind it. Mr March used to speak about his son's idleness with sympathy and regret. For the first time a gibe sprang out, harsh, almost triumphant.

Even so, Charles was slow to see what Mr March was feeling. The arguments went on, and became angrier. Mr March ceased to speak with caution; he was behaving not like a man troubled, or even sad and wounded, but one in a storm of savage distress. It seemed fantastic, but at last Charles had to admit that he had not seen his father in a state as dark as this before.

When Charles told me about it, he was enough upset to stay late in my room, retracing the arguments, trying to find a motive for Mr March's behaviour. Charles was having to guard his own temper. He was resentful because he had provoked a response like this – a response deeper, angrier, and more ravaged than anyone in his senses could have expected.

It was no use my telling Charles that this was a torment of passion; he knew that as well and better than I did. He knew too that, as with so many of the torments of passion, Mr March's distress was bitter out of all proportion to what appeared to have provoked it. It seemed just like love, I thought to myself, when a trivial neglect, such as not receiving a letter for a day or two, may suddenly make one seethe with anguish and hatred: the event, of course, being a trigger and not a cause. So Mr March heard Charles say that he was going to abandon a life of idleness and become a doctor, and was immediately shaken by passion such as no other action of his son had ever roused.

For day after day he got less controlled, not more. One night Charles was so worn down that I walked back with him, some time after one in the morning, to Bryanston Square. As we stood outside, he asked if I would mind coming in, he would like to go on talking. Before we had sat five minutes in the drawing-room, there was a heavy shuffle outside and Mr March pushed open the door.

Just by itself his appearance would have been bizarre. He was wearing red square-toed slippers and a bright-blue dressing-gown on which glittered rising-sun decorations, as though he was covered with the insignia of an unknown order. But the extraordinary thing about him was his face. For some reason difficult to understand, he had covered his eyelids, the skin under the eyes, in fact all the skin within the orbital area, with white ointment. He looked something like the end-man in an old-fashioned minstrel show.

He was scowling: his courtesy had been swept away, and he entered the room without any sign that I existed. He said to Charles: 'I've been considering the observations you insist on making –'

'Can't we leave it for tonight, Mr L.?' Charles's tone was tired, but even-tempered and respectful.

'We can only leave it if you abandon your ridiculous intentions. I should like to be assured that that is what you are now proposing.'

'I'm sorry.'

'In that case I want to inform you again that your intentions are nothing but a ridiculous fit of crankiness. I've listened to your maunderings about wanting your life to be useful. Herbert never maundered as crankily as that, to do him justice, which shows what you've come down to. I should like to know why you consider it's specially incumbent on you to decide in what particular fashion your life ought to be useful.'

'I've told you, I shouldn't be on terms with myself –'

'Stuff and nonsense. Why are you specially competent to decide that one man's life is useful and another's isn't? Was my father's life useful? Is my brother Philip's? Is John's [the butler's]? I suppose that I'm expected to believe that my brother Philip's life isn't as useful as any twopenny ha'penny practitioner's.'

Charles stayed silent. Mr March flapped the arms of his dressing-gown and his eyes were furious in their white surround.

'Is that what I am expected to believe?' he cried.

'I don't expect you to believe it for yourself, Mr L.,' said Charles with restraint. 'I don't expect you to believe it for Uncle Philip. All I want you to accept is that it does happen to be true for me.'

'All I want you to accept,' shouted Mr March, 'is that it is a piece of pernicious cranky nonsense.'

The furore in the room made it hard to stay still. Yet it was true that Mr March could not credit that a balanced man should want to go to extravagant lengths to feel that his life was useful. He could not begin to understand the sense of social guilt, the sick conscience, which were real in Charles. To Mr March, who by temperament accepted life as it was, who was solid in the rich man's life of a former day, such a reason seemed just perverse. He could not believe that his son's temperament was at this point radically different from his own.

Without warning he began a new attack – from Charles's expression new to him, not only new but beyond comparison more offensive.

'I've been considering the origin of this pernicious non-sense,' said Mr March. His tone had suddenly dropped, not to a conversational level, but to something lower, like a hard whisper. It was a tone completely unexpected, coming from him, and the effect was jarring, almost sinister.

'I don't know what you mean,' said Charles.

'I refuse to be persuaded that you came to these ridiculous conclusions by yourself.'

'What do you mean to suggest?'

For the first time, Charles had raised his voice. Mr March kept his low.

'I have been considering how many of these conclusions can be attributed to another person.'

'Who would that be?' Charles burst out.

'My guest of last summer. Ann Simon.'

Mr March had not seen her since Haslingfield. Charles had told him nothing of their meetings: her name had been mentioned very seldom. Yet all of a sudden Mr March showed that he had been thinking of her with suspicion, with an elaborate, harsh, and jealous suspicion.

'Is she or is she not,' Mr March said, in a grating, obsessed tone, 'the daughter of a practitioner herself?'

'Of course she is.'

'Is she or is she not the kind of young woman who would encourage a man to go in for highfalutin nonsense?'

'Don't you think this had better stop straight away?' Charles said.

'Has she or has she not attempted to seduce you into adopting her own pestilential opinions?'

White with anger, Charles stood up, and went towards the door. For the first time that night, Mr March addressed a remark to me:

'Isn't this young woman set on making my son what she'd have the insolence to call a useful member of society?'

I did not reply, and in an instant Mr March was asking another obsessed question at Charles's back.

'How many times have you seen her since she visited my house?'

Charles turned round. Trying to command himself, he said, with dignity, with something like affection:

'It will be worse if we don't leave it, don't you see?'

'How many times,' cried Mr March, 'have you seen her this last week?'

Charles looked at him, and to my astonishment Mr March said nothing more, did not wait for an answer, but rushed out of the room, his slippers scuffling.

The next day, however, Mr March repeated the questions again. Charles became enraged. At last his control broke down. He said curtly that there was no point in talking further. Without an explanation or excuse, he went out of the house.

When Charles had left, Mr March was subdued for a few hours. He did not know where his son had gone. His fury returned and he vented it on Katherine. 'Why hasn't Ann Simon been invited to my house?' he burst into the drawing-room shouting. 'I hold you responsible for not inviting her. If she had visited my house, I could have stopped this foolery before it showed signs of danger. I tell you, I insist on Ann Simon being invited here at once. I insist on seeing her before the weekend.'

Katherine invited her, but had to report to Mr March that Ann replied she was busy every day that week and could not come. Mr March did not say another angry word to Katherine. His silence was sombre and brooding.

Chapter 17

A REASON FOR ESCAPE

For forty-eight hours after he left Bryanston Square, no one knew where Charles was. Katherine was distracted with anxiety; on the second afternoon, Ann rang me up and asked if I could tell her anything. There had not been a silence between them before.

He came to my rooms that night. I had taken a brief home from chambers and was still working on it at ten o'clock. I had not heard him on the stairs, and the first I knew was that he stood inside the room, the shoulders of his coat glistening from the rain.

'May I sleep on your sofa tonight?' he asked. He was tired, he wanted the question to be accepted as casually as he tried to ask it. In order to prevent any talk of himself, he asked what I was doing, picked up the brief and read it with his intense and penetrating attention. He had begun to read before he threw off his overcoat; he stood on the carpet where, only a month before, I had seen him sit at Ann's feet by the fire.

'What line are you taking?' he asked. 'Have you got anything written down?'

I gave him my sketch of the case. He read it, still with abnormal concentration. He looked at me, his eyes bright with a smile both contemptuous and resentful.

'Yes,' he said. 'You ought to win it that way. Unless you show more than usual incompetence when you get on your feet. But you oughtn't to be satisfied with the case you've made, don't you realize that? I should say you're doing it slightly better than the average young counsel at your stage. Do you think that's fair? I know you're cleverer than this attempt suggests. But I sometimes wonder whether you'll ever convey to the people in authority how clever you really are. You're missing the chance to make this case slightly more impressive than your previous ones, don't you admit it? If you just look here, you'll see –'

He set to work upon my draft. Impatiently, but with extreme thoroughness and accuracy, he reshaped it; he altered the form, pared down the argument in the middle, brought in the details so that the line of the case stood out from beginning to end. It was criticism that was more than criticism, it was a re-creation of the case. He did it so brutally that it was not easy to endure.

I tried to shut out pique and vanity. I thought how strange it was that, at this crisis of his conflict with his father, in which they were quarrelling over his new profession, he could immerse himself in the problems of the one he had deliberately thrown away. He would never go back; he was determined to find his own salvation; yet was there perhaps the residue of a wish that he could return to the time before the break was made?

'Well,' said Charles, 'that's slightly less meaningless. It's not specially elegant – but it will do you a bit less harm than your first draft would have done, don't you admit that?'

It was nearly midnight, and neither of us had eaten for a long time. I took him to a dingy café close by. Charles looked at the window, steamy in the cold, wet night, smelt the frying onions, heard the rattle of dominoes in the inside room. 'Do you often come here?' he asked, but he saw, from the way the proprietor spoke to me, and the nods I exchanged, what the answer was. This was a side of my life he scarcely knew – the back streets, the cheap cafés, the ramshackle poverty, which I still took for granted.

We sat in an alcove, eating our plates of sausage and mash. Charles said:

'You haven't many ties, have you?'

'I've got those I make myself,' I said.

'They're not so intolerable,' said Charles. 'You're lucky. You've been so much more alone than I ever have. You've had such incomparably greater privacy. Most of the things you've done have affected no one but yourself. I tell you, Lewis, you're lucky.'

His eyes were gleaming.

'They think I'm irresponsible to have gone off like this. They're right. And they think I'm naturally not an irresponsible person. It might be better if I were. Can't they imagine how anyone comes to a point where he wants to throw off every scrap of responsibility – and just go where no one knows him? Can't they imagine how one's aching to hide somewhere where no one notices anything one does?'

'That's why,' he said, 'you're lucky to have no ties.'

He could not break, he was telling me, from his: for a night or two he had escaped, behaved completely out of character, shown no consideration or feeling or even manners: but he was drawn back to the conflict of his home. For a night or two he had escaped from the attempts to confine him, not only his father's but also Ann's. He was drawn back. But, sitting in the alcove of the smoky café, his face pale against the tarnished purple plush, his eyes brilliant with lack of sleep, Charles talked little of his father or Ann. He was unassuageably angry with himself. Why had he behaved in this fashion? – without dignity, without courage, without warmth. He could not explain it. He felt, not only self-despising, but mystified.

He talked of himself, but he said nothing I had not heard before. He went over the arguments for the way he had chosen. He was exhausted, unhappy, nothing he said could satisfy him. We walked the streets in the cold rain, it was late before we went to bed, but he had not reached any kind of release.

In the morning, grey and dark, we sat over our breakfast. He had been dreaming, he said, and he looked absent, as though still preoccupied and weighed down by his dream. Suddenly he rose, went to my desk and took hold of the brief on which we had worked the night before. He turned to me, his lips pulled sideways in a smile, and said: 'I was unpleasant about this yesterday.' It was not an apology. 'You know what it is not to be able to stop being cruel. One hates it but goes on.'

At that moment we both knew, without another word, why he had escaped. He had not really escaped from the conflict: he had escaped from what he might do within it.

He knew – it was a link between us, for I also knew – what it was like to be cruel. To be impelled to be cruel, and to enjoy it. Other young men could let it ride, could take themselves for granted, but not he. He could not accept it as part of himself. It had to be watched and guarded against. With the force, freshness, and hope of which he was capable, he longed to put it aside, to be kind and selfless as he believed he could be kind and selfless. When he spoke of wanting to lead a 'useful' life, he really meant something stronger; but he was still young enough, and so were the rest of us, to be inhibited and prudish about the words we used. He said 'useful'; but what he really meant was 'good'. When Ann fought shy of my questions about what he hoped for, we both had an idea: he wanted to lead a good life, that was all.

I sometimes thought it was those who were tempted to be cruel who most wanted to be good.

Charles wanted to dull his sadic edge. He knew the glitter which radiated from him in a fit of malice. He was willing to become dull, humdrum, pedestrian, in order not to feel that special exhilaration of the nerves. For long periods he succeeded. By the time of that quarrel, he was gentler than when I first knew him. But he could not trust himself. To others the edge, the cruel glitter, might seem dead, but he had to live with his own nature.

So he was frightened of his conflict with his father. He must be free, he must find his own way, he must fulfil his love for Ann; but he needed desperately that he should prevail without trouble, without the harsh excitement that he could feel latent in his own heart. Neither Ann nor his father must suffer through him.

In the grey bleak light of that winter morning, he stood, still heavy from his dream, and knew why he had run away. Yet he believed that he could keep them safe. Those fits of temptation seemed like a visitor to his true self. They faded before the steady warmth and strength which ran more richly in him than in most men. With all the reassurance of that warmth and strength, he believed that he could keep them safe.

'I shall go to stay with Francis for a few days,' he said. 'Then I'll come back to Mr L.'s. I'll let them know today, of course. It's monstrous to have given them this absurd piece of worry.'

Chapter 18

MR MARCH ASKS A QUESTION

As soon as Mr March heard from his son, he insisted once more that Katherine should invite Ann to the house. Again Ann refused. Katherine was frightened to bring the reply to Mr March, but he received it without expression.

Hearing what had happened, I met Ann and told her it was a mistake to have declined the invitation. We were sitting in a Soho pub. Her eyes were sparkling, as though she were laughing it off.

'Why shouldn't I?'

She spoke so lightly that I went on without concealing anything: I said that Mr March suspected her influence, and that for all their sakes she ought to calm him down.

Then I realized that I had completely misread her. It was anger that made her eyes bright; she was not only indignant, but outraged.

'I'm very glad that I didn't go,' she said.

'It will make things worse.'

'No,' she said with fierceness. 'He's got to see that Charles has decided for himself.'

'He'll never believe it,' I told her.

'I can't help that.'

'Can't you try?'

'No.' Her tone was dismissive and hard. 'I should have thought you knew that Charles had made his choice. I should have thought you knew that it was right for him.'

'I'm not asking you to make me realize it –' I began.

'Any sane father would realize it too. If Mr March insists on making a nuisance of himself, I can't help it.'

She added that she had rung up Charles to ask whether she might refuse the invitation – and he had said yes. The pleasure, the submissive pleasure, with which she spoke of asking Charles's permission glowed against the hardness she had just shown about Mr March.

She had been angry with me also, for telling her what she already knew. But she was tired by the conflict over Charles; she found it a relief to make it up with me and talk about him. She told me something, more than either of them had done before, about their plans for marriage. It was still not settled. Recently, there had been a reason for delay, with Charles deciding on his career; but Ann told me that, months before, he had been pressing her to marry him. I did not doubt her for a second, but it puzzled me. The delay had been on her side. Yet she returned his passion. That night, in the middle of trouble, she spoke like an adoring woman who might be abandoned by her lover.

'I wish it were all over,' she said to me. 'I wish he and I were together by ourselves.'

Her face was strained. It occurred to me that hers was the kind of strength which would snap rather than give way. To divert her, I arranged to take her to a concert the following night.

When I spoke to Katherine, in order to find out whether Mr March had taken any more steps, I mentioned that Ann was only putting a face on things by act of will.

Katherine said impatiently: 'I often wish Charles had found someone a bit more ordinary.'

As Ann and I walked to our seats at the Queen's Hall next evening, I noticed how many men's eyes were drawn to her. When the first piece had started and I was composing myself, because the music meant nothing to me, for two hours of day-dreaming, I looked at her: she was wearing a new red evening frock, the skin of her throat was white, she had closed her eyes as she had done in the sun at Haslingfield.

In the interval, we moved down the aisle on our way out. Suddenly, with a start of astonishment and alarm, I saw Mr March coming towards us. Ann saw him at the same instant. Neither of us had any doubt that he had followed her there to force this meeting. All we could do was walk on. As I waited for the moment of meeting, I was thinking 'how did he learn we were here?' The question nagged at me, meaninglessly important, fretting with anxiety, 'how did he learn we were here?'

Mr March stood in our way. He looked at Ann, and said good evening to us both. Then, addressing himself entirely to Ann, he said without any explanation: 'I'm glad to see you here tonight. I haven't had the pleasure of your company since you graced my establishment in the country. My children, for some reason best known to themselves, have deprived me of the opportunity of renewing our acquaintance.'

'I'm sorry that I couldn't come this week, Mr March. Katherine asked me,' said Ann.

'It was at my special request that my daughter asked you. I see no reason why my house should not claim an occasional evening of your time,' said Mr March. From the first word his manner reminded me of his reception of her at Haslingfield: except that now he made more demands on her. 'I recall that shortly after our first acquaintance we had an unfortunate difference of opinion upon the future of the world. I should consider the views you expressed even more pernicious if they prevented you from coming to my house again.'

Ann made a polite mutter.

'I am expecting you to come tonight,' said Mr March. 'I expect you both to give me the pleasure of your company when these performers have finished. I don't think you can refuse to call in at my house for an hour or so.'

Ann's expression stayed open and steady: but her eyes looked childishly young, just as I had seen others' at a sudden shock.

'I shall have the pleasure of escorting you,' said Mr March. For the first time, he turned to me: 'Lewis, I rely on you to see that when the performers have exhausted themselves you both find your way towards my car.'

Ann sat by my side through the rest of the concert without any restless tic at all, as though keeping herself deliberately still.

The drive to Bryanston Square was quiet. I sat in front and only once or twice heard any words pass between the two behind. Even when he did speak, Mr March's voice was unusually low. It was still not his full voice that he used in giving orders to the butler, as soon as we entered the house.

'Tell my daughter to join us in my study. See that something to eat and drink is provided for my guests. Tell Taylor he is to wait with the car to take Miss Simon home.' He took Ann's arm, eagerly, perhaps roughly, and led her across the hall.

His study was the darkest room in the house, the wallpaper a deep brown, the bookshelves full of leather-bound collections that came down from his ancestors, together with the *Encyclopaedia Britannica*, the *Jewish Encyclopaedia*, and rows of works of reference. A bright fire was blazing, though the room still seemed cavernous. A tray of sandwiches and glasses was brought in after us, and Katherine followed. At the sight of her face, I knew the answer to the nagging question 'how did he know where to find us?' She must have let fall, after my conversation with her, that I was taking Ann to the concert. I felt an instant of irrelevant satisfaction, as one does when a name one has forgotten suddenly clicks back to mind.

'I am not aware what refreshment you consider appropriate for this time of night,' said Mr March to Ann, as he sat down in his armchair on the opposite side of the fireplace. 'I hope you will ask for anything that may not be provided.'

Ann absently let him give her a brandy-and-soda, and sipped at it.

'I want to ask you,' said Mr March, 'why my son is contemplating a completely unsuitable career.'

Chapter 19

FATHER AND SON

'I want to ask you,' said Mr March, 'why my son is contemplating a completely unsuitable career.'

The firelight glowed on Ann's face. She did not show any change of expression. Politely she answered:

'I really don't know why you're asking me that.'

'I'm asking you,' said Mr March, 'because there is no one else qualified to give an opinion.'

'There is only one person who can give an opinion, you know,' said Ann.

'Who may that be?'

'Why, Charles himself.' She answered once more in a deferential tone, but Mr March's voice was growing harsh as he said:

'I do not consider that my son is responsible for his actions in this respect.'

'I wish you'd believe that he's entirely responsible.'

'I acknowledge your remark,' Mr March shot out furiously. 'I repeat that he is not responsible for this preposterous nonsense. You regard me as being considerably blinder than I am. From the moment I heard of it, I knew that he was committing it at your instigation. You have forced him into it for reasons of your own.'

'I assure you that isn't true,' said Ann. Mr March burst out again, but she went on, her manner still respectful, but with firmness and anger underneath:

'Charles has discussed his future with me, I won't pretend he hasn't. I won't pretend that I haven't told him what I think. As a matter of fact I do believe that becoming a doctor is absolutely right for him. But the idea was entirely his own. Neither I nor anyone else has any influence over him when it comes to deciding his actions. As far as I'm concerned, I shouldn't choose to have it otherwise.'

She was sitting back in her chair, and the flickering of the bright fire threw shadows on her cheeks and heightened the moulding of the bones. As she replied, Mr March's frown had darkened. He was maddened at not being able to upset her. Then he said: 'You are much too modest. You are aware that you are an exceedingly attractive woman. I have no doubt that you have tested your power of twisting men round your little finger. I have no doubt that you are testing it on my son now. I can imagine that he is enough in your power to be willing to throw away all I had hoped for him.'

'I can't think you know him,' said Ann.

'I know,' said Mr March, looking at her with an intense and bitter stare, 'that many men would do the same. They would do any nonsense you might want them to.'

'I shouldn't have any use for a man who did what I told him,' she said.

'Then you have no use for my son?' shouted Mr March, in a tone that was suddenly triumphant and full of hope.

'He would never do what I told him.'

'What is your attitude towards him?'

'I love him,' she said.

Mr March groaned.

Ann had spoken straight out, almost roughly, as though it was something that had to be settled once for all. Perhaps she was provoked, because she could feel him torn by a double jealousy.

She was taking away his son, destroying all his hopes: this was the loss which kept biting into his thoughts. But there was another. He was jealous of his son for winning Ann. He too had been attracted by her. That had been evident under the gallantry he showed her at Haslingfield. There was nothing strange about it. Mr March was still a vigorous man. He could imagine by instinct exactly what his son felt for her, down to the deep level where passion and emotion are one. He could imagine it because, with the slightest turn of opportunity, he could have felt it so himself.

So Mr March groaned, as though it were a physical shock.

'If that is true,' he said, bringing himself back to the other loss, 'I find it even more astonishing that you express approval of his absurd intention. Even though you refuse to accept responsibility for it, from what you have just said, I am more certain than ever that the responsibility is yours, and yours alone.'

'I was glad when he decided to become a doctor, of course I was. He knew I should be glad. That is all,' she said.

'Glad? Glad? What justification have you for feeling glad except that you are responsible for it yourself? Are you incapable of realizing that he is ruining any reasonable prospects he might have had? Even if he goes through with this absurd intention —'

'He will go through with it.' For the first time she interrupted him.

'What then? You think my son ought to be satisfied to be a mediocre practitioner?'

'He'll be happier about himself,' said Ann.

There was a silence. A lull came over them. Katherine and I said a few words: Ann even talked of the music she had heard. Then Mr March began to start on his accusations again. A few minutes later, we heard a noise in the hall. As we listened, the clock on the mantelpiece struck midnight. The door opened, and Charles came into the room.

'I was given no warning to expect you back,' said Mr March.

'I only decided to come a couple of hours ago,' said Charles.

He looked at Katherine, and I guessed that she had let him know, as soon as she realized what her gaffe had meant.

Charles drew up a chair by the side of Ann's.

Mr March's expression was harsh, sombre, and guilty. He said:

'I met your friend Ann Simon being escorted by Lewis Eliot to the Queen's Hall. A remarkably undistinguished evening the performers entertained us with, by the way.

So I invited them here for refreshments, before they went to their respective homes.'

'I see,' said Charles.

Mr March paused, then said:

'I have taken the opportunity to give Ann Simon my views on your present intentions. I have also asked her for an explanation as to why you have conceived such a ridiculous project.'

'I should have preferred you to do that in front of me,' said Charles.

'I refuse to listen to criticisms from my son upon my behaviour in my own house,' said Mr March.

'I shall make them,' said Charles, 'if you insist on intruding on my privacy. Don't you see that this is an intolerable intrusion, don't you see that?'

'Your privacy? Do you expect me to accept that your ruining your life is simply a private concern of your own?'

'Yes,' said Charles.

'I refuse to tolerate it in any circumstances,' Mr March said. 'Particularly when you're not acting as a free agent, and are simply letting this young woman gratify some of her misguided tastes.'

'You must leave her out of it.'

'I've told Mr March,' said Ann, 'that I'm very glad about your decision. But I've told him that I had nothing to do with your making it, and couldn't have had.'

'I shall leave her out of this matter when I have any reason to believe that she's not the source and origin of it all. If she enjoys wearing the trousers, she's got to be prepared to answer for the results.'

Up to that instant, Charles's manner had been stern without relief, and his voice hard and constrained. Suddenly he broke for a second into a singular smile. It was a smile partly sarcastic, partly amused: it was edged by the nearness of Ann, by his sense of the absurd, as though, after Mr March's last remark, nothing could be so absurd again. Then the argument went on.

With their usual repetitiveness they went over the practical reasons time and time again: underneath one heard the assertion of Mr March's power, the claims of his affection, the anguish of his jealousies, the passion of his hopes, and in Charles, his claustrophobic desire to be free, his longing for release in love with Ann, his search for the good, his untameable impulse to find his own way, whatever its cost to others and himself. At least twice Charles was on the point of an outburst, such as he had struggled against. He did not let it come to light; he had mastered himself enough for that.

At half past one, Mr March sent Katherine to bed, and a little later made a last appeal.

'I have not alluded to the opinion of the family,' he said.

'You know they could not even begin to count,' said Charles.

'I must remind you that they will occupy a place in my regard as long as I live,' said Mr March. 'But I was aware you allowed yourself to entertain no feeling for them. You did not leave me any illusions on the point when you made known your intention not to continue for the time being at the Bar.'

He was talking more quietly and affectionately than at any time that night.

'You even had the civility to say,' Mr March went on, 'that you would pay considerably more attention to my wishes than to theirs. You expressed yourself as having some concern about me.'

'I meant it,' said Charles.

'You did not pretend that your actions had no effect on my happiness.'

'No.'

'I should like to inform you that if you carry out your present intention, it will have a considerable effect on my happiness.'

Charles looked at Ann, and then at his father.

'I wish it were not so,' said Charles. 'But I can't alter my mind.'

'You realize what it means for me?'

'I'm afraid I do,' said Charles.

Until that moment they might have been repeating their quarrel on the first Friday night I attended, the quarrel to which Mr March had just referred. All of a sudden it took a different turn. Immediately he heard Charles's answer, Mr March got up from his chair. He said:

'Then I must use my own means.'

He said goodbye to Ann with his old courtesy, and even now there was a spark of the gallant in it. He asked me to see her into the car, and retired to his study with Charles. The door closed behind them.

As Ann got ready to go, I saw that she was radiant, full of joy. I told her that I would stay in case Charles wanted someone to talk to. She pressed my hand and said:

'And thank you for taking me to the concert. You can see what being kind lets you in for, can't you?'

She was happy beyond caring. The car was ready, and she walked down the steps, straight-backed, not hurrying. I switched on the lights in the drawing-room. It was brilliant after the dark study. The fire had gone out hours ago, and there was nothing but ashes in the grate. The cold, the bright light, made me shiver. I tried to read. Once, perhaps twice, I heard through the walls a voice raised in anger.

An hour passed before Charles entered. He asked me for a cigarette, and had almost smoked it before he spoke again. Then he said, in a level, neutral tone: 'He's revoked his promise to make me independent.'

He went on:

'I've told you before, he was going to make over some money to me when I was twenty-five. He's just admitted that it has always been his intention.'

I asked what Mr March had said. He had repeated, Charles replied, that up to that night he had been arranging to transfer a substantial sum to Charles on his twenty-fifth birthday – something like £40,000. He had now altered his mind. He was prepared to continue paying Charles his allowance. But he was determined to make no irrevocable gift.

'I said that I might want to get married soon,' said Charles. 'He replied that he could not let that influence his judgement. He was not going to make me independent while I insisted on going in for misguided fooleries.'

The lines in Charles's face were cut deep.

'I can understand,' he said, 'that he wants me to lead the life he's imagined for me. I know I must be a desperate disappointment. You know, don't you, that for a long time I've tried to soften it as much as I possibly could? You do know that? But I tell you, I shan't find this easy to accept.'

I felt a sense of danger which I could not have explained. I could not even have said which of them I was frightened for.

Charles asked me:

'Do you think he wants to stop me marrying?'

I hesitated.

'Do you think he wants to stop me marrying Ann?'

'He wouldn't have chosen her for you,' I said, after a pause. His insight was too keen for him not to have seen both of Mr March's jealousies: but they were best left unspoken.

'What shall you do?' I said.

Suddenly his heaviness and anger dropped away, and he gave a smile.

'What do you think I shall do? Do you think I could stop now?'

Part 3

THE MARRIAGES

Chapter 20

THE COMING-OUT DANCE

Mr March did not have another talk in private with Charles that winter. In company they took on their old manner to each other, and no one outside guessed what had happened. Charles had begun to work for his first M.B., but the news was not allowed to leak out, any more than that of his assignations with Ann.

Meanwhile, tongues all over the March family had kept busy about Katherine and Francis Getliffe. Charles received a hint from Caroline's son, Robert; Katherine from someone at her club; Herbert Getliffe became inquisitive about his brother. For a long time, despite false alarms, the gossip seemed not to have been taken seriously by Mr March's brothers and sisters; certainly none of them had given him an official family warning.

When the invitations were issued for the coming-out dance of one of the Herbert March girls, we wondered again how far the gossip had spread. For that family scarcely knew Francis Getliffe; and yet he had been invited. Katherine threshed out with Charles what this could mean. Was it an innuendo? It looked like it. But invitations had gone out all over the place; the Holfords had been sent one, even Herbert Getliffe through the Hart connexion, I myself. Francis's might have been sent in perfect innocence and good nature.

Katherine still remained suspicious. For days before the dance she and Charles re-examined each clue with their native subtlety, repetitiveness, realism, and psychological gusto. One thing alone was certain, said Charles, grinning at his own expense: that for once his passion for secrecy had been successful, with the result that Ronald Porson had been invited, obviously as the appropriate partner for Ann.

This piece of consideration did not seem funny to Ann

herself. Her pride rose at being labelled with the wrong man. It was her own fault. Porson was still pressing her, begging her to marry him; she had not yet brought herself to send him away. Nevertheless, when the Herbert Marches picked him out as her partner, she was angry with them for making her face her own bad behaviour.

On the night itself, Herbert March's larger drawing-room had been converted into a ballroom. We stood round the floor waiting for the band to begin. The shoulders of young women gleamed, the jewels of old ones sparkled, under the bright lights: loud March voices were carried over the floor: the Holfords, the Harts, the Getliffes, formed a group round their host, while his sister Caroline, standing elephantine in their midst, pulled up her lorgnon and through it surveyed the room.

It was a room on the same scale as those at Bryanston Square, but brighter and more fashionable. The whole house was a little less massive, the decoration a little more modern, than Mr March's, and the company less exclusively family than anywhere else in the March circle. One remembered Mr March's stories about Herbert as the rebel of an older generation.

Standing in front of a pot of geraniums, Mr March himself was telling Sir Philip an anecdote with obscure glee. It was the obscure glee that usually possessed him when someone committed a *faux pas* against the Jewish faith. 'The new parson from the church round the corner paid me a visit the other day,' said Mr March. 'I thought it was uncommonly civil of him, but I was slightly surprised to have to entertain anyone of his persuasion. The last parson I was obliged to talk to descended from the ship at Honolulu when I was going round the world in '88. He was an extremely boring fellow. Well, as soon as I decently could, I asked this one why he had given me the pleasure of his company. And he had an unfortunate stammer, but gradually it emerged that he wanted a contribution for his Easter offering. So I said, I should like to be informed if you still pray on certain occasions for Jews, Turks, and other infidels. He had to admit that he did. I replied that being a Jew I might be excused for finding the phrase a little invidious, and I couldn't make a donation for his present purposes. But I didn't want to embarrass him because he'd chosen an unfortunate occasion. So I said: "Come again at Christmas. We've got some common ground, you know. I'll give you something then." '

Just then Caroline's son Robert brought Ann to be introduced to Sir Philip. As usual, she was one of the smartest women in the room; as usual, she stayed quiet, let Sir Philip and Robert talk, got over her shyness just enough to put in a question. Mr March broke in:

'This is the first time I have seen you since you were good enough to come to my house after a concert, which you possibly remember.'

'Yes, Mr March,' said Ann.

'She is rather competed for, Uncle Leonard,' said Robert. He was a middle-aged man, bald, with a face more predatory than any other of the Marches – predatory but not clever. As soon as he spoke, Mr March resented his flirtatious air; and Mr March's own manner became more formidable and at the same time more intimate.

'I am well aware that it would be astonishing if she had time to spare for elderly acquaintances,' he said brusquely and, ignoring Robert, turned to Ann. 'I take it that my son Charles has been lucky enough to secure a certain fraction of your leisure.'

'I've seen him quite often,' she said.

'I assumed that must be so.'

Then the music started up. Robert took her on to the floor. I went to find a partner. As the first hour passed and I danced with various March cousins and visitors, I noticed that Charles and Ann had danced together only once. Whoever they had as partners, they were each followed by a good many sharp, attentive eyes. She was striking-looking in any company. And to some there, particularly among the women, he was the most interesting of the younger Marches.

Katherine and Francis, on the other hand, had decided

that it was no use pretending to avoid each other. It seemed the sensible thing to take the polite average of dances together. As they did so, one could not fail to realize that some of the March aunts were watching them. Several times I saw Caroline's lorgnon flash, and even to me she shoved in an enquiry, when we happened to visit the refreshment table at the same time.

'How well do you know this young fellow Francis Getliffe?' she said.

I tried to pass it off, for she was too deaf to talk to quietly, and there were several people round us.

'I want to know,' said Caroline, 'whether he's engaged yet?'

'I don't think so,' I said.

'Why isn't he? He must be getting on for thirty. What has he been doing with himself?'

I smiled: it was easier than producing a non-committal shout.

She went on with the interrogation. She had hoped that Francis might be entangled elsewhere. That hope extinguished, she was framing her plan of campaign.

When I returned to the drawing-room, Ann was dancing with Albert Hart, and Charles with the cousin for whom the dance was being held, a good-looking, strapping girl. For the first time that night, I found Katherine free. She whispered at once, as we went on to the floor:

'It's slightly embarrassing being under inspection, isn't it? You would have expected Francis to mind tremendously, wouldn't you have expected him to? But he seems to be enjoying himself.'

She was so happy, despite her anxiety, despite the prying eyes, that it was obvious how well — when she and Francis were together — the night was going. She went on:

'You know, I wish Charles and Ann would decide what they want to happen. They've got to settle down some time, and it won't get any easier. It's preposterous that she should have this man Porson trailing after her tonight.'

She looked up at me. 'I think she enjoys it — am I being

unfair? I expect I envy her, of course. Mind you, I know she's made a colossal difference to Charles.

Then she glanced across the room, where Francis was talking to Mr March.

'But it is a superb party, don't you think?' she burst out. 'Francis dances abominably, but I forgive him even that. It means that I'm nothing like so jealous when I see him dancing with other women. I can always console myself with how disappointed they must be when they get a fairly nice-looking young man for a partner – at least I think he's fairly nice-looking – and he promptly insists on putting his foot on their toes.'

She was bubbling with happiness.

'It is a superb party, Lewis,' she said. She was silent for a moment, and I saw that she was smiling.

'What are you thinking?' I said.

She chuckled outright.

'I've remembered what I used to feel about the young men Charles brought to the house. I never believed that they could possibly want to see me. I thought they only came because they wanted to see Charles or needed a house to stay in when they were in London.

I was sorry when the dance ended; at that time, as I watched others happy in love, I was sometimes envious – but not of Katherine. It was difficult to begrudge her any luck that came her way.

The next dance I watched by the side of Mr March and Sir Philip. Mr March was studying his dance programme before the band began.

'Though why they find it necessary to issue programmes to the superannuated members of the party, I have never been able to understand,' he said to me. 'Possibly so that the superannuated can imbibe the names of these productions that your generation are accustomed to regard as tunes.'

The band struck up, couples went on to the floor; Charles was dancing with Ann, Katherine with Francis. Mr March stopped talking; he let his programme swing by the pencil;

he watched them. Katherine was smiling into Francis's face; Charles and Ann were dancing without speaking.

Philip also was watching.

'How many times,' he asked Mr March, 'has Katherine been to the regular dance this year?'

'She has missed occasionally.'

'How many times has she been?'

'I can't be expected to recollect particulars of her attendance,' said Mr March.

Philip went on asking; Mr March fidgeted with his programme and gave irascible replies. If he had been suppressing his knowledge about Katherine and Francis, he could do so no longer.

Philip's glance followed Katherine round the room. But even as he answered the questions, Mr March did not look in her direction. His expression was fixed and anxious: he had eyes for no one but his son.

'I should like you to meet Ronald Porson,' Ann said, as shortly afterwards I delivered a girl to her partner in the corner of the room. Ann, sitting with Porson close by, smiled at both him and me, making herself act as though this was a casual night out.

'I've heard about you,' said Porson. 'Don't you go about picking up the pieces after Getliffe? I suppose I oughtn't to speak to you about your boss —'

'Yes, I've been with him since I came to London,' I said.

'You have my blessing,' said Porson. 'And by God you'll need it.'

His voice was loud, his manner hearty and assertive, though tonight he was preoccupied. He kept looking at Ann, but his eyes flickered nervously away, if he caught hers. His appearance surprised me after what I had heard; he was a short, plethoric man with a ruddy face. His left cheek often broke into a twitch which, instead of putting one off, happened to make his expression companionable and humorous.

The room had cleared for an interval, and Charles was almost alone on the floor. Several times Ann's attention strayed to him, and then she said to Porson:

'Have you ever met Charles March, by any chance? He's the nephew of your host tonight. You've heard me talk about him. Perhaps you ought to be introduced.'

'I might as well,' said Porson.

He did not glance at Charles; I was sure that he had already identified him. Ann beckoned to Charles: Porson went on talking to me as he came up. It was not until they shook hands that Porson raised his eyes and looked into Charles's face.

'Are you enjoying this do tonight?' he said. 'Are you enjoying yourself?'

For a moment Charles did not answer. Before he spoke, Ann had turned to him. 'Ronald is thinking of starting a practice in London,' she said. 'I've been trying to persuade him that before he makes up his mind he really must get some up-to-date advice. He happens to know Getliffe, I mean Herbert Getliffe, quite well. He doesn't think much of him, but I don't see that ought to matter: he might be useful.'

'Getliffe's not gone far enough,' said Ronald. 'I dislike crawling unless it's worth while.'

'It can't do any harm.' Ann looked at Charles.

'It can't do any harm,' said Charles. 'Isn't that the point? I know it's an intolerable nuisance, going to people for this kind of purpose –'

'I dislike crawling in any case,' said Ronald. 'Particularly to men I don't care for and whose ability I despise.'

'He's climbing pretty fast, isn't he?' Ann was asking me.

'There are private reasons, which you know enough to guess,' Ronald said to her, 'which make it certain that, before I asked Getliffe for a favour, I'd sooner sweep the streets.'

I said:

'There are plenty of other people you could talk to, aren't there?'

'Albert Hart would give you a pretty sensible judgement,' said Charles. 'If ever you'd like me to introduce you –'

'I'm not prepared to go on my knees except for a very good reason.'

'I should feel exactly the same,' said Charles. 'But still, that never prevents one, does it, from pointing out that some-one else is doing too much for honour.'

Ronald laughed. After his first remark, he seemed surprised that he was actually liking Charles's company.

'Ah well, my boy,' said Ronald, 'I might stretch a point some day. But I insist on tapping my own sources first –' Then he turned to Ann:

'I'm going to take you home soon, aren't I?'

'Yes,' said Ann.

'Are you ready to come now?'

'I think I'd like to wait half an hour,' said Ann.

'You'll be ready then? You'll remember, won't you?'

'Yes,' said Ann.

His masterfulness had dropped right away; suddenly he asserted himself by saying to me in a loud voice:

'Well, my lad, I'm going to take you away and give you some advice.'

We went to the study, where whisky bottles and glasses were laid out. Ronald said:

'Now you must develop a master plan too. Of course, you can't expect it to be on such a scale as mine, but I'm damned if we can't work out something for you. We must use some of my connexions.'

He was at home, now he was giving help instead of taking it. His smile became domineering and good-natured; he could even put aside his obsession with Ann while he was giving me advice. Yet, though his connexions were genuine enough, the advice was vague; his voice was throaty with worldly wisdom, but he was really an unworldly man. He was far more lost than Ann believed, I thought.

In time he left off advising me, took another drink, put an arm round my shoulders as we stood by the mantelpiece, told me a dirty story, and confided his ambitions. 'It's incredible that they shouldn't recognize me soon,' he said in his master-ful tone. Those ambitions, like the advice, turned out to be quite vague; he was forty, but he did not know what he wanted to do. When I enquired about details his manner was still overbearing, but he seemed to be longing for something as humble as a respectable status and a bare living at the Bar.

Soon he said, with a return of anxiety:

'We'd better be making our way back, old boy. Ann wants me to take her home tonight.'

When we returned to the dance-room, Ann and Charles were standing together. Ronald said to her:

'Do you feel you can tear yourself away yet?'

'I'd just like the next dance with Lewis,' said Ann.

Ronald gave an impersonation of nonchalance, heavy and painful.

'In that case I can use another drink,' he said.

He went away before the band began to play.

Neither Charles nor Ann spoke. When she looked at him, he gave her a smile which was intimate but not happy. Then Charles's gaze was diverted to the other end of the room, where his aunt Caroline had just buttonholed Mr March. He watched them walk up and down, Caroline protruding her great bosom like a shelf as she inclined her less deaf ear to catch Mr March's replies. Charles had no doubt that she was catechizing him about Katherine.

'I was afraid that they wouldn't leave him in peace,' he said.

As Ann and I were dancing, I asked her what Mr March would be forced to do. But she was scarcely attending: her mind was elsewhere: all she said was: 'Charles has too much trouble with his family, hasn't he?'

We danced round, the conversation ground to a stop. Then, to my surprise, she settled more softly in my arms, and said:

'I shan't be sorry when tonight is over.'

'What's the matter?'

She looked straight up at me, but slipped away from the question.

'I always used to dread meeting people till I got in the middle of them, didn't you?'

'Not much,' I said.

'Don't you really mind?'

'I'm nervous of lots of things you're not,' I said. 'But not of that.'

'Do you know,' said Ann, 'I used to make excuses to stay by myself. Not so long ago, either. As a matter of fact, last summer, I very nearly didn't go to Haslingfield.'

As we danced on, she said in a low voice:

'Yes. I very nearly didn't go. That would have altered things.'

I asked again:

'What's the matter?'

After a pause, she replied:

'You've seen Ronald now, haven't you?'

Then I guessed that all night she had been screwing herself up to make the final break. This was the night when she had to tell him that he had no hope.

I said that she should never have come with him at all.

'Perhaps,' said Ann. 'I'd better get it over.'

Then she softened again, and as she spoke of Charles she pressed my hand. 'I shall have to go off with Ronald now. I shan't be able to talk to Charles. Will you tell him that everything is well? You'll remember, won't you? I don't want him to go home alone without being told that.'

Ronald came to Ann as soon as we left the floor. She went to say goodbye to Herbert March's wife: Ronald and I walked into the hall, where we met Getliffe on the point of leaving. Before he saw us, he was trying to smooth down the fur of his old top hat. He said to me: 'As soon as my wife comes, I depart from the shores of Canaan. But I must say they've done us pretty well.' Then he noticed Ronald. 'Why, I didn't realize it was you. It must be years since we met. Though I've always wanted to keep in touch with you. Everything satisfactory with the job?'

'It's been a complete success,' said Ronald. 'I've never regretted going out east for a minute.'

'I'm very glad to hear that,' said Getliffe earnestly. 'Look here, if you're not ashamed of your old friends, we ought to get together some time. Why, I've scarcely had a glass of water with you since we used to tune up the old Feathers — I don't believe you've forgotten the place.'

They fixed nothing, but Getliffe shook hands with both of us, though he was bound to see me the next morning, and said:

'The best of everything. Pleasant dreams.'

The Getliffes had gone when Ronald and Ann had finished their goodbyes. Charles and I waited with them in the hall while someone moved a car. At last they went out into the road, and Ann said to Charles: 'I shall see you soon.' Charles watched her climb into Ronald's car and draw her coat round her shoulders; she was talking to him as they drove away.

We went back to the dance for half an hour, and it was strange, after breathing the heavy air that descends sometimes on to any passion, to be making conversation to young girls — young girls pleased to find a partner, or else proud that they had not missed a dance all night.

One or two, as they noticed their cousin Charles dancing with Ann, must have wondered if they were in love: but they would have been surprised if they had known the pain and decision that had been going on under their noses in this house.

The dance was almost over when Charles and I began to walk the few hundred yards to Bryanston Square. It had been a wet day; the pavements were glistening, though now the rain had stopped. After the ballroom the air was cool on our cheeks.

Charles said that he was worried about Mr March and Katherine. He questioned me on what Caroline had said. But I saw that he was distracted, and he soon fell quiet.

When I gave him Ann's message, his face lit up.

'Life's very unfair.' He smiled. In a single instant he had become brilliantly cheerful. 'If I'd been capable of more civilized behaviour, she'd never have needed to think of me.'

'You made Porson feel flattered,' I said. 'I thought that was rather gallant.'

'No,' said Charles. 'I was behaving with the sort of excellence when I could almost see myself shine. And it's easy to take in everybody except oneself and the person to whom it matters most.'

Suddenly he said:

'It's ridiculous, you know, but I'm jealous of him. Though she's never loved him in the slightest. Still, I was jealous when I met him. Ann knew that from every word I said. That's why she sent me that message. She wanted to save me from a dismal night.'

He took my arm, and broke out with a warm, unexpected affection.

'I wish you'd been saved more, Lewis. You know so much more about that kind of suffering than I hope I ever shall.'

We had reached Bryanston Square. Mr March was long since home, and the house stood in darkness. Charles and I stayed under the lamp, just opposite the railings.

'It's curious,' said Charles, 'how the unexpected things catch one off one's guard. I went there tonight, knowing that I had to get him to talk and make him as comfortable as I could and so on. But there was one thing I hadn't reckoned with; it was the sight of them together in his car, just ready to drive away. For a second I felt that I had utterly lost her.'

Chapter 21

WHISPERS IN THE EARLY MORNING

THE day after the coming-out dance, Katherine had to face
a scene with her father.

'Your Aunt Caroline wants you to spend a month in her
house,' Mr March said the moment she arrived at breakfast.
'There is a consensus of opinion that you don't meet enough
people.'

'Shall I go?' said Katherine, so equably that Mr March
became more angry.

'I naturally didn't consider your refusing.'

'Of course I'll go,' said Katherine.

Until she went to stay with Caroline, Mr March behaved
as though Katherine's presence was irritating. Several of
his relations had followed the lead of Caroline and Philip
and advised him to 'keep an eye on Charles's friend Francis
Getliffe'. The sight of Francis and Katherine together had
impressed most of Mr March's brothers and sisters. With
their own particular brand of worldliness, they decided that
Leonard could not be too careful, the young fellow might
think he had a chance of her money.

Katherine duly spent her month at Caroline's, and there,
each night at dinner, was produced a selection of the eligible
young men in the March world. It was all magnificent in
its opulence and heavy-footedness. At the end of her stay
Katherine returned with a collection of anecdotes to Bryanston Square. The anecdotes she had to keep for Charles. It
struck everyone that Mr March did not enquire what had
happened, and irascibly brushed aside any mention that
Katherine made.

In July, on the customary date, Mr March moved his
household to Haslingfield. I was invited there in August,

and found, on the evening I arrived, that Katherine was still trying to imagine Charles's life as a doctor.

'I know you'll go through with it now,' she said. 'But I just can't see what it will be like, you know. It's too far-fetched for me.'

'You just want to purr away in comfort,' said Charles.

'You ought to be able to be happy, and get your dash of comfort into the bargain,' she said.

'I call that animal content,' said Charles.

'I only wish you could have it,' she said.

Beneath the backchat their voices showed their fondness and concern. Between them there flowed a current of intimacy – it was not only his future they were talking of. Katherine was at once apprehensive and happy, so happy that she had become maternally concerned for Charles. Two years earlier, she would have hero-worshipped him.

They told me nothing that evening. Mr March appeared to be in something like his old spirits; his manner to his son was not constrained, and he talked about a holiday abroad which Charles had spoken of, and then shelved, as 'my son's misguided expedition to gather energy for purposes which he was never able to justify. Like the time my Uncle Natty gave them all a fright by trying to go on the stage. But it was always rumoured that he had his eye on an actress. So he went to London University and they made him a knight.'

'It sounds rather easy, Mr L.,' said Charles.

'No! No!' said Mr March. 'He went to London University and became a professor and a member of their financial board. I always thought he was a superficial fellow. He went slightly off his head, of course, and they gave him his knighthood just before he died.'

Lying half awake the next morning, after the footman had drawn the curtains, I heard the whisper of conversation in Charles's room next door. I could distinguish Charles's voice and Katherine's, hers raised and animated, and I caught one whole reply from Charles: 'I can easily ring him up at Cambridge.' When Katherine came down to breakfast I said:

'What conspiracy are you busy with now?'

She blushed. 'What do you mean?'

'Consultations before breakfast –'

'Lewis, you didn't hear? You can't possibly have heard, can you?'

Then Charles entered, and she said:

'Lewis pretends he overheard us this morning. He's probably bluffing, but I'm not quite sure.' She turned to me, smiling and excited: 'If you really do know, it's absolutely essential you shouldn't breathe a word.'

Charles said to Katherine:

'You're rather hoping he does know, aren't you? I mean, you wouldn't be entirely displeased to give yourself away.'

'You suggested telling him.' They were smiling at each other. Katherine burst out: 'Look here, I insist on being put out of my misery. Did you hear or didn't you?'

'No,' I said. 'I can see you're very cheerful, and it's about Francis. I couldn't very well help seeing that, could I? But I don't know exactly what's happening.'

'Is this a double bluff?' she said.

'You'd better tell him,' said Charles.

'Well,' said Katherine, 'it's important for me. You'll be discreet, won't you?'

I said yes.

'As a matter of fact,' she said, 'about a fortnight ago Francis asked me to marry him.'

I said how glad I was. Her delight seemed to become even greater as she shared the news. She had been forced to restrain herself for a good many days, except to Charles. 'When it came to the point,' said Katherine, smiling lazily, 'Francis was different from what any of you would expect.'

'Now did you know?' she harped back.

'No.'

'But you see why I'm anxious that Charles shouldn't do anything more to upset Mr L. – till my marriage is settled. If Charles begins to talk about his career or his independence again, it will only make things more difficult. Of course, I shall be the chief affliction. If I'm to have the slightest hope of getting away with it, Mr L. mustn't feel there's anything else wrong with his family.'

Charles caught my eye.

'Don't you see, Lewis,' she said, 'I still have the worst time in front of me? Somehow I must break the news to Mr L.'

'How much does he know?'

She shook her head.

'It will be the biggest disaster he's ever had,' she said.

I said:

'Are you sure of that?'

Katherine said to Charles:

'Don't you agree? Don't you agree that I'm right?'

Charles did not answer.

Katherine said:

'I'm positive that I'm right. Lewis, you simply can't understand what this will mean to him.'

She spoke to Charles: 'You know, I feel gross asking you to think of the slightest point that might affect my chances. But, as things have turned out, I can't do anything else. I must have a clear field, mustn't I?'

'I've been telling you so for days,' Charles teased her.

'You see, Lewis,' said Katherine, 'I shall marry Francis whatever happens. I knew I should never have a minute's doubt – if ever he asked me. I'm not a self-sacrificing person, and however much it upsets Mr L. it's more important for me than for him. I'm worried about him, but I shan't feel that I've done wrong.'

'Yes,' I said.

'If the worst comes to the worst,' she said, 'we can live on what Francis earns. It won't exactly support me in the condition I've been accustomed to. But still –'

'Francis is pretty proud,' said Charles. 'He's not as sensible as he tries to appear. He'd like to have you without a penny.'

'He's always taken the gloomiest view and expected to keep me,' said Katherine. 'At any rate, that's settled. We shall be married by December. But it's obvious that I want to placate Mr L. as much as I humanly can. I'm prepared to be thrown out if there's no other way, but it would be an enormous horror for us both. I expect I should feel it even more than I think now.'

'Yes, you would,' said Charles.

'You know it, don't you?' She looked at him.

Then Katherine said:

'Whatever happens, Mr L. must be told soon.'

Chapter 22

INVITATION

As soon as I got back to London after that week-end, Ann asked me to dine with her. Once more she took me out in luxury, this time to the Ritz. I took it for granted, going out with her, that the waiters would know her by name: I was not surprised when other diners bowed to her. As usual, she set herself out to buy me expensive food and wine.

Looking at her across the table, I had no idea what she wanted to talk to me about that night. Not Katherine's marriage, I was sure. Not Charles, at least directly, it soon seemed. No, the first person she began to mention was Ronald Porson. She wanted to tell me that he had given up trying to see her: that even he accepted that it was over and done with. As she told me, Ann was referring back to the coming-out dance three months before, when I blamed her for letting Ronald's attendance drag on: she wanted me to admit that she had been firm. Laughing at her, I saw the shyness wiped away from her face as though it had been make-up; and yet my piece of criticism rankled, she might have just been listening to it.

At the same time she was giving me something like a warning about Porson. She said that now he bore a grudge against the Marches, and he was a man who could not stop his grudges breaking out; she talked about him with a kind of remorseful understanding, because she could not love him back.

She knew him well, she was fond of him, she was afraid of what he might do. Although he had got nowhere himself, she told me, he had some influence; his father had been an ambassador, he had his successful acquaintances.

'What can he do?' I said with scepticism.

'Would you like him as an enemy?' she replied.

But it was not really Porson she had got me there to talk about. Politics: the depression was deepening all over Europe: had I been following the German election? She was in earnest. All she said was business-like. She had a clear sight of what was coming. She was better informed than I was. It was not quite like the politics I used to talk with my friends in the provincial town; we had been born poor, we spoke with the edge of those who rubbed their noses against the shop windows and watched others comfortable within; she had known none of that. She was more generous than we were, but she hoped as much.

As we talked – we were not so much arguing as agreeing – I felt a curious excitement in the air. Her voice at the same time quickened and sank to something like a whisper; her blue eyes had gone wide open, were staring at me, or past me, with the kind of stare that one sees in someone who is obsessed by the thought of making love. In fact, it might have been the beginning of a love-affair.

Yet she was totally in love with Charles: I was just as single-minded in my love for Sheila: that was why Ann and I could keep up a friendship without trouble to either of us.

The excitement tightened, and I was completely at a loss. She whispered:

'Look, Lewis. Isn't it time you came in with us?'

'What do you mean?'

'Isn't it time you came into the party?'

When at last I heard the question, I thought I had been a fool. Nevertheless, up to that evening she had been discreet, even with me; she had talked like someone on the left, but so did many of our friends, none of whom were communists in theory, let alone members of what she called 'the party'.

I looked at her. The strain had ended. She was brave, headstrong, and full of faith.

I owed her an honest answer. Trying to give it to her, I felt at a disadvantage just because she was brave and full of faith. I felt at a disadvantage, too, because I happened not to be well that night. Giving her reasons why I could not come in I did not make either a good or an honest job of it.

Yet I did manage to make the one point that mattered most to me. She wasn't as interested as I was, I told her, in the nature of power and those who held the power. The more I thought of it, the less I liked it. Any régime of her kind just had to give its bosses great power without any check. Granted that they were aiming at good things, it was still too dangerous. People with power began to get detached from anything but power itself. No one could be trusted with power for long.

For a time she argued back with the standard replies, which we both knew by heart, then she gave up.

'You're too cynical,' she said.

'I'm not in the least cynical.'

'You're too pessimistic.'

'I don't think so, in the long run.' But I wished that my hopes were as certain as hers.

She was disappointed with me, and put out, but she wasted no more time. This was what she had come for, and she had failed. She had a business-like gift of cutting her losses. She decided that in my own fashion, I was as obstinate as she was.

She asked me to order more brandy: even after a disappointment, she liked giving me a good time. In a voice still lowered, but not excited by now, only brisk, she said:

'You'll keep this absolutely quiet, of course, won't you?'

She meant about herself and the party. She spoke with trust. In the same tone I said:

'Of course.'

I went on:

'It's the sort of secret I'm not bad at keeping.'

She looked at me, her face open and gentle, and said: 'Nor am I.'

We both laughed. After the argument, we were glad to feel comradely again. She asked me (I thought it was a relief to her to be straightforward) whether I had suspected she was a member.

'No,' I said, and then suddenly a thought crossed my mind.

'You're pretty good at keeping your mouth shut, aren't you?' I said. 'But that first night at Haslingfield – why did you give everyone such a hint?'

Her reply did not come at once. At last she said:

'I think I knew already that Charles was going to be important to me.'

'And so –'

'And so I couldn't let them take me in on entirely false pretences, could I?'

I was pleased to think that, at the time, I had been somewhere near the truth. There was a streak of the gambler in her. She did not like being careful; even though she had to be, it seemed to her, more than to most of us, cowardly, impure, dishonourable. It was really part of her to tell the truth. That night at Haslingfield, a cardinal night for her, she had believed she could tell the truth and get away with it.

But there was no one outside the party, apart from Charles and me, who knew that she was in it – so she told me as we finished our last drinks at the Ritz. She had made clear to Charles exactly what she did, before their affair began. That I should have expected from her: what interested me was that she had made no attempt to invite him in. She had not tried to persuade him, even to the extent she had tried with me. It seemed that she did not want to influence him. She had taken care that he knew the exact truth about her. That done, she longed just to make him happy.

Chapter 23

KATHERINE TELLS MR MARCH

KATHERINE put off breaking the news to her father. It was the second week in October before she told him. The family were together at Bryanston Square, and Mr March, having written his usual hundred letters for the Jewish New Year, had been grumbling because others' greetings were so late. Katherine waited until the festival had passed by.

I had tea at Bryanston Square the day she finally brought herself to the pitch. We were alone. Francis had not long left for Cambridge, after staying the week-end in the house. She told me that she meant to face Mr March that night.

'I'm extremely embarrassed,' she said. 'No, I'm more than embarrassed, I'm definitely frightened. It's absurd to feel oneself being as frightened as this.'

She added: 'I can't shake off an absurd fear that when I do try to tell him, I shall find myself go absolutely dumb. I've been rehearsing some kind of an opening all day. To tell you the honest truth, I've been rehearsing it ever since Francis proposed. I never thought I should put it off as long.'

The next evening she and Charles came round to my rooms. She said at once: 'I've got it over. I think it's all right. But –'

'It's all right so far,' said Charles.

Mr March had been at moments extravagantly himself, and Katherine could laugh at some of his remarks: yet she was still shaken.

Immediately after dinner she had said to Mr March, falling back on the sentence she had rehearsed:

'I'm sorry, Mr L., but I've something to tell you that I'm afraid will make you rather unhappy.'

Mr March replied:

'I hope it isn't what I suppose it must be.'

They went into his study, and Katherine heard her own information sound blunt and cut-and-dried. It took only a minute or two, and then she said:

'Naturally, I'm tremendously happy about it myself. I'm not going to try and hide that from you, Mr L. I'm only sorry that it's going to make you slightly miserable.'

Mr March said:

'Of course, I wish you'd never been born.'

Katherine felt that he was saying simply and sincerely what he meant. She felt it again, when he said:

'My children have brought me nothing but disgrace.'

'I know I've given you a lot of trouble,' said Katherine.

'Nothing you've done matters by the side of what you are informing me of now.'

'I was afraid of that.'

'Afraid? Afraid? You knew that you were proposing something that I should never get over. You never gave a moment's thought to the fact that you'd make me a reproach for the rest of my life.'

'I've thought of nothing else for weeks, Mr L.,' she said.

'And you are determined to persevere?' he shouted.

'I can't do anything else.'

Mr March spoke in a calmer tone:

'I suppose I can't stop it. He can presumably maintain you in some sort of squalor. Not that I have any objection to his profession. It's all very well for men who are prepared to sacrifice all their material requirements. Though I can't understand how they venture to support their wives. How much does this fellow earn?'

'About eight hundred a year.'

'Twopence a week,' said Mr March. 'It's enough for you to contemplate existing on, unfortunately. I suppose I can't stop it. It was exactly the same when your Aunt Hetty insisted on marrying the painter. He took to drink before they'd been married three years.'

He broke off:

'I'm obliged to say, though I couldn't disapprove more strongly, that I've no particular objection to this fellow on personal grounds. He seems quiet, and he's surprisingly level-headed, apart from whatever proficiency he may have at his academic pursuits. I realize that he exercises himself on mountains, but he doesn't look particularly strong.'

'He's as tough as I am,' said Katherine.

'The doctors said you were delicate when you were young,' said Mr March. 'They said the same about me in '79. If they had been right in either case, I might have been spared this intolerable state of affairs you're bringing on me. I say, I haven't any strong personal objection to the fellow. I could put up with his poverty, since he's pursuing a career which isn't discreditable. I should be willing to give you my approval apart from the fact that makes it impossible, as you must have known all along. It would be different if he were a member of our religion.'

'I realize that,' she said.

'What's the use of realizing it?' said Mr March. 'When you come and tell me that you are determined to marry him. What's the use of realizing it? When you're determined to do the thing that I shall never get over.'

Then he said:

'I know it's not so easy for a woman to refuse. If he'd satisfied the essential condition, I shouldn't have blamed you for accepting him on the spot. After all, you mightn't get a second chance.'

It was strange, Katherine felt as though she were noticing it for the first time, to see his distress suddenly streaked with domestic realism. Rather excessively so in this case, she grumbled to Charles and me, since she was not quite twenty-one, 'and not so completely repulsive as Mr L. seems to assume'. In the same realistic way, he appeared to be convinced that there was nothing for him to do. He cut the interview short, and neither Charles nor Katherine saw him again that night; Katherine took Charles off to the billiard-room, and they played for hours.

In the morning they arranged to come down to breakfast at the same time. As soon as they had sat down, Mr March came in, banging the door behind him.

'You never show the slightest consideration,' he said. 'You announce your intentions at night just before I'm going to bed. You might have known that it would keep me awake.'

Charles was reassured when he heard that first outburst. He tried to speak casually:

'What is the proper time to upset you, Mr L.? We should like an accurate answer for future reference.'

Mr March gave a reluctant chuckle.

'After dinner is the worst time of all,' said Mr March. 'If I must have an ungrateful family, the best thing they can do is not to interfere with my health. It was exactly the same when Evelyn contracted her lamentable marriage. She was thoughtless enough to tell me at half past ten at night. So that I actually got to bed late in addition to finding it impossible to sleep.'

'I'm extremely sorry,' said Katherine.

'That's the least you should be,' said Mr March. He turned on her: 'You go on expressing your sorrow uselessly while you persist in making it intolerable for me to show myself in the streets.'

Charles had to intervene.

'This comes,' he said, 'of letting your children bring their disreputable friends to the house.'

'I've tried to consider where I'm to blame,' said Mr March. 'But no precautions that I might have been expected to take would have been certain to spare me from the present position.'

That afternoon Charles said that Mr March would tolerate the marriage 'so long as no one else interferes'.

They argued about Mr March's state of mind. How deeply had he been wounded? None of us could be certain. They were surprised that he was not more crushed. True, he had a lively affection for Francis, and respect for his accomplishments. Possessive though he was, he was instinctively too healthy a man not to want to see his daughters married. But neither Charles nor Katherine could feel sure to what extent he had been afflicted, afflicted in himself apart from minding about other people's opinion, because Francis was not a Jew.

I did not have much doubt. I had so little doubt that to Katherine certainly, to Charles almost as much, I seemed right out of sympathy. Katherine told me flat that I could not understand. For I believed that Mr March was hurt a good deal less than by the first quarrel with Charles, at the time when he abandoned the law: and incomparably less than by the struggle over Ann and Charles's future. The suffering he felt now was on a different level, was on the level of self-respect and his external face to the world. It was not the deep organic suffering that he knew over his son, when he felt that a part of his own being was torn away.

Both on the first day and in the week after, he seemed far more preoccupied with the family's criticism than with any distress of his own. He became irascible and hunted, and kept exploding about the esteem he would lose as soon as the news got out. In fact, Mr March tried to delay the news getting outside the house. He did not object to seeing Francis and arranging the settlement; he greeted him with the cry: 'I've nothing against you personally. But I entirely disapprove.' Afterwards he said to Charles: 'The astonishing thing is, he knows something about business. He doesn't like imprudent methods any more than I do myself.'

But he invented excuses for delaying the announcement from day to day. He could not write to his relations for a few days, he said, since he had just written all round for the New Year. It might be better to wait for one of Herbert's daughters, whose engagement was just coming out, 'if the man doesn't fight shy, as I strongly suspect,' said Mr March. 'Hannah thought she'd hooked a man once. I never believed it was possible.' He would not put an announcement in *The Times* until he had let the family know: and he dreaded the thought of publication even more than anything Philip and Hannah and Caroline might say. For he knew himself how after the first glance at the news, he read in order the deaths, the births, and the forthcoming marriages. He could imagine too clearly how people throughout the Marches' world would do the same one morning and suddenly ask: 'Who's this Francis Getliffe that's going to marry Leonard March's daughter? Does it mean that she can be marrying "out"?'

A fortnight passed after Katherine broke the news, and then one day Mr March ordered the car in the afternoon. It was a break in his daily time-table such as neither Charles nor Katherine could remember. His temper muttered volcanically at lunch, and he refused to say where he was going. At night they realized that he had at last confessed to his sister Caroline.

'She had furnished herself with an absurd ear-trumpet,' said Mr March. 'It was bad enough being obliged to divulge my family's disgrace without having to bawl it into this contraption of hers. Your mother made the same mistake when she bought a fur in Paris on the ridiculous assumption that it was cheaper than in London –'

'Sorry, Mr L.,' said Charles. 'What mistake?'

'Of not being able to resist articles in foreign shops, of course. My sister Caroline succumbed to the temptation when she was in Vienna recently. She caught sight of this apparatus in one of the latest shops. Women are unstable in these matters.'

'You are being a bit hard,' said Katherine. 'She probably gets on better –'

'Nonsense,' said Mr March. 'She found it exactly as difficut to comprehend what I was trying to say. Then she was polite enough to remark that I ought not to hold myself entirely to blame, and that these disappointments were bound to occur in the family, and that they'd all come round to it in time.'

Actually Caroline, just by being as tactless as usual, cheered him up; in his heart, he had expected a far more violent outcry. He was so much relieved that he indulged in louder complaints.

'I can't dissociate myself from the responsibility according to her advice. I remember that she regarded it as my responsibility when she suggested that fishing trip for you at her house. Not that I ever had the slightest faith in her averting the disaster. I suppose I must have brought it on myself. Though I can't decide where I went wrong with my family. If I'd made you' – he said to Katherine – 'take your proper place at dances and other entertainments, I doubt whether it would have served any useful purpose.'

'I'm sure it wouldn't,' she said. 'Mr L., you mustn't blame yourself because your family is unsatisfactory. It's just original sin.'

'Everyone else's children have managed to avoid being a reproach. Except Justin's daughter who did what you're doing in even more disastrous circumstances. The less said of her the better. I suppose I'm bound to accept responsibility for what you call original sin. Even though my wishes have never had the slightest effect on your lamentable progress.'

The next day, he told the news to Philip, who received it both robustly and sadly; that night, with great commotion and expressions of anger, Mr March drew up the announcement for *The Times*. He sat in his study with the door open, shouting, 'Go away, don't you see I'm busy!' when Charles approached. 'I'm busy with an extremely distasteful operation.' Then, a moment afterwards, Mr March rushed into the drawing-room. 'Well, how does the fellow want to appear? I suppose he possesses some first names. ...' Several times Mr March dashed into the drawing-room again: at last, standing by the open door, he read out his composition – ' "A marriage has been arranged ..." '

'That's done,' said Mr March, and, instead of leaving the letter for the butler to collect, he took it to the post himself.

Katherine was thinking of getting up the next morning, when Mr March flung open the door.

'It's not my fault this has happened,' he said. 'It's your mother's fault. I never wanted another child. She made me.'

Chapter 24

A PIECE OF NEWS

FROM the morning of the announcement, Mr March was immersed in letters, notes, conversations, and telephone calls. Since he had feared more than the worst, he became cheerful as he answered 'what they are civil enough to term "congratulations"'. Most of the March family wrote in a friendly way, though there were rumours that one cousin had threatened not to attend the wedding. Hannah was reported to have said: 'I never thought she'd find anyone at all. Even someone ineligible. Mind you, she's not married him yet.'

For several days Mr March did not receive any setback; Katherine thought she had been lucky.

Then Herbert Getliffe spoke to me one evening, in chambers, just before I went off to dine at Bryanston Square. He entered the room I worked in looking worried and abashed, and said:

'There's something I want to say to you, L.S.'

Recently he had taken to calling me by my initials, though no one else did; as a rule, I was amused, but not that night, following him into his own room, for his alarm had already reached me. He sat at his desk: the smoke from his pipe whirled above the reading lamp; his face was ominous, and the smell of the tobacco became ominous too.

'I want a bit of help, L.S.,' he said. 'They're getting at me. You've got to come along and clear up the mess. I may as well tell you at once that it can turn out badly for your friends.'

His misery was as immediate as a child's. It was hard to resist him when he asked for comfort.

'Your friend Mr Porson is trying to raise the dust,' said Getliffe. 'You know something about him, don't you? He was called at the same time as I was. But he didn't find this wicked city needed his services enough to keep him in liquor, so he went off to lay down the law in the colonies. Well, he's suddenly taken it into his head that I've been making more money than is good for me. He's decided that I've used some confidential knowledge to make a packet on the side. You remember the Whitehall people asked me for an opinion last year? You gave me a hand yourself. Remind me to settle up with you about that. The labourer is worthy of his hire. Well, Master Porson is trying to bully them into an enquiry about some of my investments. Involving me and other people who are too busy to want to go down to Whitehall to answer pointless questions. But I don't like it, L.S. I can't prevent these things worrying me. I ought to tell you that Porson is a man who can't forgive one for being successful. You'll find them yourself as you go up the ladder. But you'll also find that more people than not will lend half an ear to Porson and company when they start throwing darts. That's the world, and it's no use pretending it isn't. That's why I want you to help me out.'

He wanted support from someone. He quite forgot, he made me forget, that he was the older man.

He gave me his own version of what Porson had discovered. It was not altogether easy to follow. Getliffe gave as much trouble as any of the evasive clients about whom he had ever grumbled. All I learned for sure that night was that he had been asked an opinion by a government department eighteen months before; while giving it, he had guessed (Porson said he had been told as an official secret) a Cabinet decision about a new government contract; two of his brothers-in-law had bought large holdings in the firm of Howard & Hazlehurst; they had done well out of it.

After telling me this story, Getliffe said:

'Well, Mr Porson has just broken out in a new place. I've been told that he's trying to persuade some pundit to ask a question in the House. Porson's had the face to tell me so in as many words.

'I warn you,' Getliffe went on, 'it's possible he may bring it off, L.S. I can talk to you frankly now you're going up the hill a bit. Of course, I don't worry much for myself. It may be a little difficult even for me, but it's a mistake to worry too much about the doings of people who would like to step into one's goloshes. I want you to believe that I'm thinking entirely of the effect on some of your friends. And particularly on my young brother. It's for their sakes that I want everyone to use their influence to calm Porson down.'

He knew that I had met Porson occasionally since the coming-out dance.

'If I can get the chance,' I said, 'I'll talk to him. Though it won't be easy. I don't know him well.'

'You mustn't get the impression that I'm exaggerating. Porson could make things awkward for your friends. You see, my name couldn't help but be brought in, whatever he did. That wouldn't be good for my brother. The Chosen People don't like public appearances. There are one or two members of the March family who would specially dislike this one. I give you fair warning. It's uncomfortable for all of us.'

He was speaking with a severe expression, almost as though I was responsible for the danger. When he wanted your help, he sometimes appealed, sometimes threatened you with his own anxiety: anything to get the weight from his shoulders to yours. Then he said:

'I can't make out why Porson has got into this state. I always thought he was unbalanced. I don't like to believe that he's trying to bring the place down on our heads simply because he hates me. After all, I've managed to get on with most of my fellow men. I don't like being hated, L.S. Even by that madman. It's a nasty sensation, and when people say they don't mind being hated they're just whistling to keep their spirits up. So I prefer to think something else may be moving Mr Porson. I shouldn't be altogether surprised. Didn't the young woman Ann Simon turn him down pretty flat not long ago? You may find that's got something to do with it.'

He warned me again not to think that he was exaggerating the trouble. In fact, I was uneasy. He was shrewd, despite (or partly because of) his excessively labile nature. He was not a man over-inclined to anxiety. I had often seen him badgered, I had often seen him inducing others to extricate him from troubles – but the troubles were real, the consequences of living his mercurial, tricky life.

When I left him, it was nearly eight o'clock, and I had to go to Bryanston Square by taxi. As I waited while the Regent Street lights jostled by, rain throbbing against the windows, I was listening for the strike of eight. There was no chance of a word with Charles before dinner: I was greeted with genial shouts by Mr March: 'You've made a frightful ass of yourself. You're three minutes late. Anyone knows that you must allow five minutes extra on nights of this appalling nature.'

We went straight in to dinner. I was enough of a favourite of his not to be allowed to forget that I was late. Meanwhile I saw Charles several times, and Katherine once, looking in my direction: Charles at least knew that something was on my mind.

As luck would have it, Mr March was in more expansive form than for weeks past. Margaret March, whom I had met at my first Friday night, was there as well as Francis. After disposing temporarily of the topic of my incompetence, Mr March spent most of the night talking to Francis about buying a house.

The two of them were happy discussing plans and prices. Mr March occasionally burst out into accounts of his own struggles with Haslingfield and Bryanston Square. 'One trouble you won't have,' he said, 'since you are camping out in your Bohemian fashion, is that you won't surround yourself with a mass of ponderable material that you'll never extricate yourself from.' The internal furniture of Bryanston Square had been valued years before at £15,000; but Mr March was lamenting that he could not sell it for as many shillings.

Houses of this size were relics of another age, now that

people 'camped out in a Bohemian fashion', as Mr March insisted on referring to the style in which Katherine and Francis proposed to live. So the solid furniture of the March houses had become almost worthless, and Mr March and his brothers spent considerable ingenuity in persuading one another to accept the bulky articles that they unwillingly received as legacies, as their older relations died off. Several of Mr March's stories on this night, told mainly for Francis to appreciate, finished up with the formula: 'I pointed out it was far more use to him than it was to me. And so I was willing to sacrifice it, provided he paid the cost of transport.'

When Mr March went to bed, Margaret settled down in her armchair. She was older than the rest of us, but still not married; she had a similar handsomeness to Charles's, and a similar hard, ruthless mind. Yet underneath, at the thought of any of our marriages, she was full of feeling. That night, she noticed the constraint in the air. Naturally she put it down to Mr March. So she said to Katherine:

'I'm sure he has come round now. I'm positive you haven't got anything to fear.'

'I suppose not,' said Katherine.

Margaret had spoken warmly and protectively. She was surprised, a little put out, to feel us all still in suspense. She turned for confirmation to Charles:

'Don't you agree that she's safe enough?'

'She ought to be,' said Charles.

'I wouldn't have believed that Mr L. could come round so quickly.' Like her cousins, Margaret was not above plucking away at the same nerve. 'He's now drawn up your settlement good and proper, hasn't he?'

'Yes, he's gone as far as that,' Katherine replied.

Charles kept watching me, knowing I was not going to speak while Margaret was there. But Katherine was not so much on edge. At the mention of the settlement, she began to smile. 'I've actually got it here,' she said to Margaret.

She went to the writing-desk and brought out a sealed

envelope. She broke the seal and looked over the document inside. It was printed, and ran into several pages.

'I still think this is extremely funny,' she said.

'You don't know what I shall become as I get older,' Francis said, and they laughed at each other.

'The point is,' Katherine went on, 'that really Mr L. has the greatest possible confidence in Francis. Apart from his not being a Jew. Actually, Francis would have been a far more suitable child for Mr L. than Charles. He wouldn't have rebelled anything like as much.'

'I should have managed,' said Francis. His cheeks were creased by a smile, but he meant it. He would have found his way to his science somehow; he would have been radical, but he would have kept quiet. That night his quixotic, fine-drawn expression was less evident than it used to be; he looked composed and well.

'Well,' said Katherine, 'it's obvious that Mr L. approves of the man. But as soon as he drew up my settlement' – she pointed to the sheet in front of her – 'he at once acted on the assumption that I was an imbecile and Francis was a crook. He's taken every possible precaution to see that Francis never touches a penny. The settlement never gives him a chance. When I die, the money goes straight to our children. If Francis outlives me, he receives a small tip for watching his sons inherit their slice of their grandfather's estate.'

All the marriage settlements in the family followed the same pattern; no one but a March should handle March money. Katherine and Charles had been amused, but nevertheless they took for granted the whole apparatus as an ordinary part of a marriage: while in the property-less world into which I had been born, no one would have known what a marriage settlement was.

I mentioned that I had never seen one. Katherine was just going to show me theirs, but Francis said: 'I think Mr L. would be shocked – even though it's Lewis.'

'You mean you'd be shocked yourself,' said Katherine, but slipped the papers into the envelope again.

It was nearly midnight, and Margaret rose to go.

As she said goodbye, she noticed that I was staying. Her bright eyes looked keenly, uncomfortably round, worried because there was something wrong, self-conscious because she had been in the way.

We heard the butler taking her across the hall.

'What's the matter?' said Charles, the moment the door clanged. 'What's the matter?'

'Is anything wrong with Sheila?' said Katherine.

'It's nothing like that,' I said. I told the story.

Katherine cried:

'Will he bring it out in the next three weeks? Before we're married?'

'No one knows,' I said. 'In any case, we may all be taking it too seriously –'

'I'm not sure,' said Charles. 'Herbert Getliffe is right, it's the sort of affair the family wouldn't like. You mustn't worry,' he said to Katherine. 'It ought to be possible to stop Porson yet.'

'That must be tried,' said Francis. 'There's plenty to do. We'll break the jobs down in a minute.'

Suddenly he had taken charge. He had the decision, the capacity for action, of a highly strung man who had been able to master his nerves. It was easy at that instant to understand the influence he had had on Charles when they were undergraduates, with Francis two years older.

He spoke straight to Katherine as though they were alone.

'The first thing is, we must prepare for the worst. We've got to assume that he'll act on it. It's better to assume that right away. If he does, we shan't let the family make any difference.'

'That's easier said than done,' said Katherine. 'But – no, we shan't.'

'Good work,' said Francis, and took her hand. 'Now let's get down to it. Lewis, tell us the practical steps Porson can take. If he wants to make as much fuss as possible. We want all the details you can give us.'

Sharply he asked me: could Porson start anything more damaging than a parliamentary question? How long did it take to get a parliamentary question asked? Could it be delayed? Could we find out the moment it began to pass through the department?

Francis arranged that on the next day I should try to see Porson. Charles would see Albert Hart, who might have an acquaintance in the department. Francis himself would speak to his brother.

That settled, Francis looked at Katherine, and said with a smile, tart and yet distressed:

'I'm sorry that my brother should be responsible for this. It isn't altogether his fault. Ever since I can remember, I've been listening to his latest manoeuvre. He's got too much energy for one man. That's what has made him a success.'

He had just surprised me by being more effective than any of us. Now he surprised me again – by showing something he had never shown before, his true relation to his half-brother.

Occasionally he had not been able to disguise his shame and anger at one of Herbert's tricks: but he had usually spoken of him very much as Charles used to speak, with amusement at his exploits, with indifference, with humorous disapproval. His apology to Katherine had torn that cover aside. Now we saw the affection, the indulgent, irritated, and above all admiring affection, which a man like Herbert Getliffe so often inspires in his nearest circle; so that Herbert's children, for example, would come to worship him and make his extravaganzas into a romance. That was true even of Francis, so responsible and upright.

Francis soon controlled his smile, so that the distress was no longer visible. His expression became commanding and active.

'It's clear what must be done,' he said. 'I think it's all set. You'll do what you can with Porson, Lewis? I don't like to involve you in this business, but if it can be stopped it would be convenient.'

'It probably can be stopped,' said Charles. He was trying to reassure Katherine on a different plane from Francis's. 'I'll see Ann first thing tomorrow. She may know more about Porson. And there is something I might be able to say to the family myself.'

Chapter 25

THE SMELL OF WET LEAVES
IN THE SQUARE

FROM the night of Getliffe's warning, there were nineteen days before the wedding. On the first of them I could not find Ronald Porson, but within forty-eight hours of the news from Getliffe I had managed to have a long talk with him. I was able to assure Katherine that there did not seem much to fear.

Since we met at the coming-out dance, I had got on well with Porson. He was boastful, violent, uncontrolled; but he had the wild generosity one often finds in misfit lives, and I was the only one of his new circle who was still struggling. With me he could advise, help, and patronize to his heart's content. And with me he could stick a flower in his button-hole, swing his stick, and lead the way to a shopgirl who had taken his fancy: he was a man at ease only with women beneath him in the social scale.

Ann had punctured his sexual vanity, as was so easy to do. He had talked to me about her with violent resentment and with love. He was more easily given to warm hate than anyone I knew.

So I did not dare ask him to call off his attack on Getliffe in order not to risk disturbing Katherine's marriage. He was capable of such inordinate good nature that he might have agreed on the spot, even for a girl he scarcely knew; but on the other hand, because she was connected with Charles and Ann, he might have burst out against them all. Instead I felt it was safe to talk only of Herbert Getliffe and of what Porson was now planning.

To my surprise he was very little interested: he seemed to have given up the idea of a parliamentary question, if he had ever entertained it. He mentioned Ann affectionately, and

I suspected she had gone to see him the day before. He was full of his scheme for going on to the midland circuit.

For some reason or other his anger had burned itself out. So I told Katherine, and Charles agreed that there seemed no danger from him. He had heard something more about Ronald, also reassuring, from Ann, though exactly what I did not learn.

For a day or two there seemed nothing to worry over. Katherine had to show Francis off to some of her relations, and recaptured the fun of being engaged, which, since Mr March first came round, she had been revelling in.

Then, though Ronald Porson made no move, rumours spread through the Marches. One reached Charles; Katherine heard others hinted at. It was known that the Getliffe brothers had been discussed on the past Friday night, when Mr March happened to be away. No one was sure how the rumours started; but it became clear that Sir Philip knew more about Herbert Getliffe than anyone in the family did, and had described him with caustic contempt.

Both Charles and Katherine accepted that without question. Philip had his code of integrity. It was a worldly code, but a strict one. He did not forgive an offence against it. He was indignant that Herbert Getliffe should have laid himself open to suspicion, whether the suspicion was justified or not.

All the family were impressed by his indignation. Charles and Katherine were told by several of their cousins to expect him to visit Mr March. Katherine waited in anxiety. Night after night she could not get to sleep, and Charles played billiards with her at Bryanston Square. For three mornings running, Mr March grumbled at them; then he suddenly stopped, the day after Philip's visit.

Philip called at Bryanston Square on a Tuesday afternoon: the wedding was fixed for ten days ahead. He went into Mr March's study, and they were there alone for a couple of hours. On his way out, Philip looked into the drawing-room, said good afternoon to Charles and Katherine, but would not stay for tea and did not refer once to seeing her at her wedding.

When Philip left, they waited for Mr March; they expected him to break out immediately about what he proposed to do. But he did not come near them all the evening: the butler said that he was still in the study: at dinner he spoke little to them, though he made one remark about 'a visit from my brother about your regrettable connexions'.

When Katherine tried to use the opening, he said bad-temperedly:

'I have been persecuted enough for one day. It is typical of my family that when they wish to make representations to me, they select the only relative whom I have ever respected.'

By the time I arrived for tea the next day, Charles had already heard, from various members of the family, versions of the scene between Mr March and Philip; the versions differed a good deal, but contained a similar core. They all agreed that Mr March had put up a resistance so strong that it surprised the family. He had made no attempt to challenge the facts about Herbert Getliffe, but protested, with extreme irritability, that 'though I refuse to defend my daughter's unfortunate choice, I have no intention of penalizing the man because of the sharp practice of his half-brother'. According to one account, he had expressed his own liking and trust for Francis; and certainly, with his accustomed practicality, he had said that it was far too late to intervene now. 'If you had wanted me to refuse to recognize the marriage, you should have communicated your opinion in decent time.'

It sounded final. Charles, piecing together the stories, was relieved, but he was not quite reassured: even less so was Katherine. Mr March had brazened matters out, as though he were ready to defy the family. But his mood since had been sombre, not defiant; and they knew he was hurt, more than by the family's disapproval which Philip represented, by his feeling for Philip himself.

They knew the depth of his feeling. Warm-hearted as he was, yet with no intimate friends outside the family, this was the strongest of his human bonds, after his love for his children. When he had spoken the night before of 'the only relative whom I have ever respected', he was trying to mask, and at the same time relieve, his sadness. He made it sound like an outburst of ill-temper, an exaggerated phrase; but it was really a cry of pain.

So Charles and Katherine kept coming back to Philip's effect on Mr March. It was not till after tea that Charles said:

'It's possible that I may be able to help with Uncle Philip.' He asked me to take Katherine out for the evening: he would see Mr March, and persuade him to invite Philip for dinner.

Katherine looked puzzled as he made these plans. Charles said:

'It may help you. You see, Ann has promised to marry me. I think I ought to tell them at once.'

'Did you expect to be able to tell them this?' Katherine burst out. 'You said something – you remember – the night Lewis brought the news?'

Charles did not reply, but said:

'It may smooth things over with Uncle Philip.'

'Of course it will,' said Katherine, suddenly full of hope. 'It will put Mr L. right with the family. Your making a perfectly respectable marriage. And he ought to be glad about it himself.'

Charles looked across at me.

'Of course, he ought to be glad about it,' Katherine went on. 'I know he thinks she's got too much influence over you. But she's everything he could possibly wish, isn't she? He likes her, doesn't he?'

'Yes,' said Charles. 'Yes. In any case, he ought to be told at once.'

Then he got up from his chair, and added in a tone now vigorous and eager:

'I want to tell him tonight.'

Charles had become impatient. He scarcely had time to listen to our congratulations. He asked me again to take

Katherine away for the evening, and before we were out of the house he had entered Mr March's study.

It was pouring with rain, and we went by taxi to our restaurant, and even then got wet as we crossed the pavement. But Katherine, without taking off her coat, went straight to the telephone to ring up Francis at Cambridge. In a few minutes she returned, her eyes shining, her hair still damp.

She was anxious, but her capacity for enjoyment was so great that it carried both of us along. In her bizarrely sheltered life, she had never dined out with a man alone, except Francis. She was interested in everything, the decoration of the restaurant, the relations between the pairs of people dining, my choice of food. It was her own sort of first-hand interest, as though no one had ever been out to dinner before.

With the same zest, she kept returning to the news Charles was at that moment telling Mr March. 'Lewis, when did he propose? It must have been what he hinted at that night, don't you agree? That was a week ago – don't you admit he's had it up his sleeve ever since?'

She chuckled fondly. Then she asked me:

'Lewis, do you think she'll make him happy?'

I told her what I thought: they would be happier together than either with anyone else. She was not satisfied. Did that mean I had my doubts? I said that Charles had been luckier than he ever expected. Katherine asked if Ann was not too complicated. I said that I guessed that in love she was quite simple.

Katherine broke out:

'If she makes him happy then everything is perfect. Lewis, you've just said that he never expected to be so lucky. What I am positive about is that he never expected a wife who would please the family. Don't you agree that's the astonishing part of it? That's why I'm fantastically hopeful tonight. I don't pretend that Mr L. and Uncle Philip will think she's a tremendous catch. She doesn't come from our group of families, and she's only moderately rich. But they'll have to admit that she passes. After all, most of Mr L.'s nephews have done worse for themselves. And I don't think it will be counted against her that she's very pretty. She's been admired in the family already.'

I took her to a theatre, so that we should get back to Bryanston Square late enough for Charles to be waiting for us. On the way back her anxiety recurred, but Charles met us in the hall and his smile dispelled it.

'I'm pretty certain that all is well,' he said in a low voice.

She kissed him. He stopped her talking there, and we went into the drawing-room.

'I'm pretty certain all is well,' he repeated. 'You mustn't think it's due to me. It would have come all right anyhow – don't you really believe that yourself?'

When she questioned him, he admitted that Philip had been pleased with the news. There had been considerable talk about the Getliffes and Porson. Mr March and Philip had parted on good terms.

We both noticed that Katherine suddenly looked very tired. Charles told her so; she was too much excited to deny it, and went obediently, first to the telephone and then to bed.

Charles's smile, as we heard the final tinkle of the call, and then her step upstairs, was tender towards her. His whole expression was open and happy: yet, despite the tender smile, it was not gentle. It was open and fiercely happy. He jumped up and went to the window. His movements were full of energy.

'Look,' he said, 'I think it has cleared up now. I'd very much like a stroll. Do you think you could bear it?'

*

It was just such a night as that on which we walked home after the coming-out dance. The rain had stopped: there was a smell of wet leaves from the garden in the square. The smell recalled to Charles the excitement, the misgivings, the promise of that night, as well as the essence of other nights, forgotten now. In an instant he was overcome by past emotion, and did not want to speak.

It was some time before I broke the silence.

'So you think Katherine is safe?' I said.

'Yes,' said Charles. 'It's quite true what I told her. I think the wedding would have come off without any more trouble – any more trouble in the open, anyway. But I'm glad I talked to them. Uncle Philip did seem to be placated. He was completely surprised about Ann. He said that I'd never been seen with her in public. He couldn't remember hearing anyone in the family couple our names together.'

Charles smiled. He broke off:

'By the way, he is very angry about this Getliffe business. I suppose he's sufficiently patriarchal to feel that all attachments to the family ought to come up to his standard of propriety. That must be the reason, don't you agree? It pleased him more than you'd think, when I said that Porson had probably got tired of his own indignation.'

Charles went on:

'And Uncle Philip was genuinely delighted about Ann. He decided that she would be a credit to us. He also said' – Charles laughed – 'that he did hear she was a bit of a crank, but he didn't take that seriously.'

'And Mr L.?'

Charles hesitated.

'He was not so pleased. Did you expect him to be?'

'What did he say?'

'Something rather strange. Something like – "I always knew it was inevitable. I have no objections to raise".'

In a moment, he said:

'Of course he was extremely glad that Uncle Philip is coming round. That is going to be the most important thing for him.'

Then Charles broke into his good-natured, malicious grin:

'It struck me as pleasing that I should be soothing the family. It struck me as even more pleasing that I should be doing it by announcing that I intended to marry in as orthodox a manner as my father did.' The malicious smile still flickered. 'There is also a certain beauty,' he reflected, 'in the fact that, after all the fuss I've made from time to time, I should be eager to tell my father so.'

'Ah well,' he said, 'it's settled. It is superb to have it settled.'

Just as when he saw Ann at Haslingfield he smiled because he had first met her at the Jewish dance — so tonight he was amused that he of all men, who had once winced at the word 'Jew', should now be parading his engagement to a Jewess, should be insisting to his father that he was conforming as a Jewish son. It was a sarcastic touch of fate completely in his style; but it was more than that.

All of a sudden I realized why he had been so fiercely happy that day, why he had gained a release of energy, why as he walked with me he felt that his life was in his own hands. To him the day had been a special one — though all the rest of us had had our attention fixed on Katherine and her father, and had forgotten Charles except as a tactful influence in the background.

In Charles's own mind, the day marked the end of the obsession which had preyed on him since he was a child. It marked the death of a shame. He felt absolutely free. Everything seemed open to him. He felt his whole nature to be fresh, simple, and at one.

We walked across Bayswater Road and into the Park. His stride was long and full of spring. He was talking eagerly, of his future with Ann, of what he hoped to do. He was more spontaneous, frank, and trustful than I had ever known him. He had forgotten, or put aside for the night, any thought of his conflict with his father over Ann.

In the darkness I listened to his voice, lively, resonant, happy. I thought of this shame which had occupied so much of his conscious life. It had gone, so it seemed to him, because he had fallen in love with Ann, and thus that evening could tell his father, with unqualified happiness, that he was going to marry her — and, more than that, could use the fact that he was marrying a Jewess in order to ease the way for Katherine.

So Charles was talking with boyish spontaneity, completely off his guard, his secrecies thrown away. I felt a great affection for him. Perhaps the affection was greater because I did not see his state that night quite as he did himself. For me there was something unprotected about his openness and confidence.

I remembered his confession when he gave up the law. I had felt two things then, and I felt them more acutely now: that this shame had tormented him, and that at the same time he had used it as an excuse. Charles would always, I thought, have been prouder and more self-distrustful, harsher and more vulnerable to shame, than most of us. In his youth, he would in any case have gone through his torments. But even he, for all his insight, wanted to mollify and excuse them. Even he found it difficult to recognize his sadic harshness, his self-distrust, above all his vulnerability, as part of his essential 'I'.

Some years before, I had had a friend, George Passant, who put the blame for the diffidence and violence of his character on to his humble origin. His vision of himself was more self-indulgent than Charles's. Yet Charles's insight did not prevent him from seizing at a similar excuse. He had felt passionately, as we have all felt, that everything would have been possible for him, life would have been utterly harmonious, he would have been successful and good 'if only it had not been for this accident'. Charles had felt often enough 'I should have been free, I should have had my fate in my hands – if only I had not been born a Jew.'

It was not true. It was an excuse. Even to himself it was an excuse which could not endure. For his vulnerability (unlike George Passant's) was of the kind that is mended by time; for years the winces of shame had become less sharp. It seemed to him that by telling his father and Philip he was marrying a Jewess he had conquered his obsession. I should have said that it was conquered by the passing of time itself and the flow of life. In any case, he could no longer believe in the excuse. That night for him signalized the moment of release, which really had been creeping on imperceptibly for years.

He was light with his sense of release. He felt that night that now he was truly free.

That was why I was stirred by a rush of affection for him. For he would be more unprotected in the future than he had been when the excuse still dominated him. In cold blood, when the light and warmth of release had died down, he would be left face to face with his own nature. Tonight he could feel fresh, simple, and at one; tomorrow he would begin to see again the contradictions within.

Chapter 26

MR MARCH CROSSES THE ROOM

Up till the day of the wedding, rumours still ran through the family, but I heard from Charles that Philip had sent an expensive present. I also heard on the wedding morning that Mr March was in low spirits but 'curiously relieved' to be getting ready to go to the register office.

When I arrived at Bryanston Square after the wedding, to which not even his brothers were invited, I thought Mr March was beginning to enjoy himself. Nearly all the family had come to the reception and, soon after being 'disgorged from obscurity' (his way of referring to the marriage in a register office) he seemed able to forget that this was different from any ordinary wedding.

In the drawing-room Mr March stood surrounded by his relatives. There were at least a hundred people there: the furniture had been removed and trestle-tables installed round two of the walls and under the windows, in order to carry the presents. The presents were packed tightly and arranged according to an order of precedence that had cost Katherine, in the middle of her suspense, considerable anxiety; for, having breathed in that atmosphere all her life, she could not help but know the heart-burnings that Aunt Caroline would feel if her Venetian glasses ('she hasn't done you very handsomely,' said Mr March, who made no pretence about what he considered an unsatisfactory present) were not placed near the magnificent Flemish tapestry from the Herbert Marches, or Philip's gift of a Ming vase.

The tables glittered with silver and glass; it was an assembly of goods as elaborate, costly, ingenious, and beautiful as London could show. At any rate, Mr March considered that the presents 'came up to expectations'. Hannah, so someone reported, had decided that they 'weren't up to much'; but, as that had been her verdict in all the March weddings that Mr March could remember, it merely reassured him that his daughter's was not continuously regarded as unique.

There were few of those absences of presents which had embarrassed the cousin whose daughter married a Gentile twenty years before. 'That appears to be ancient history,' said Mr March to Katherine, when presents had arrived from all his close relations and some of his fears proved groundless. The two or three lacunae among his cousins he received robustly: 'George is using his religious scruples to save his pocket. Not that he's saving much — judging from the knick-knack that he sent to Philip's daughter.' At the reception itself, he repeated the retort to Philip himself, and they both chuckled.

Philip had already gone out of his way to be affable. He had greeted Ann with special friendliness, and had even given a stiff smile towards Herbert Getliffe. He seemed set, in the midst of the family, on suppressing the rumours of the last fortnight.

Mr March responded at once to the signs of friendship. He began to refer with cheerfulness and affection to 'my son-in-law at Cambridge', meaning Francis, who was standing with Katherine a few feet away. A large knot of Mr March's brothers and sisters and their children had gathered round him, and he was drawn into higher spirits as the audience grew.

'I refuse to disclose my contribution,' he said, after Philip had been chaffing him about the absence of any present of his own. Everyone knew that Mr March had given them a house, but he had decided not to admit it. Philip was taking advantage of the old family legend that Leonard was particularly close with money.

'You might have produced half a dozen fish forks,' said Philip.

'I refuse to accept responsibility for their diet,' said Mr March. 'I gave Hetty some decanters for her wedding and she always blamed me for the regrettable events afterwards.'

'You could have bought them something for their house,' said Herbert.

'You could have passed on a piece of your surplus furniture,' said Philip. 'So long as Katherine's forgotten that you ever owned it.'

'There must have been something you could have bought for the house,' said Herbert's wife.

Mr March chuckled, and went off at a tangent. 'They insist on living in some residence in the provinces, owing to the nature of my son-in-law's occupation –'

Katherine interrupted 'I wish you wouldn't make it sound like coal-mining, Mr L.' But he was sailing on:

'A month ago I went to inspect some of their possible places of abode. My son Charles told me the eleven-fifty went from King's Cross, and it goes from Liverpool Street, of course. However, I never had the slightest faith in his competence; naturally I had consulted the time-table before I asked him, and so arrived at the station in comfortable time. Incidentally, in twenty-five minutes my daughter and son-in-law will be compelled to leave to catch the boat train. On my honeymoon I had already left for the train at the corresponding time, allowing for the additional slowness of the cab as a means of conveyance. People always say Mentone is a particularly quiet resort, but I've never found it so. The first time I visited it was on my honeymoon with its general air of unrest. The second time my wife had some jewellery stolen and I was compelled to undergo some interviews with a detective. I never had any confidence in him, but the jewellery was returned several months later. The third time passed without incident. Having arrived despite Charles's attempt to make my journey impossible –'

'Where? When?' shouted several of his audience.

'At my daughter's future domicile in the provinces. On the occasion under discussion,' replied Mr March without losing way, 'I proceeded to inspect the three residences which were considered possibilties by the couple principally concerned –' Philip and the others threw in remarks, they gave

Mr March the centre of the stage, and he was letting himself go.

Then, just after he had triumphantly ended that story and begun another, he looked across the room. Outside the large noisy crowd over which his own voice was prevailing, there were two or three knots of people, not so full of gusto – and Ann by the window, talking to Margaret March.

Mr March broke off his story, hesitated, and watched them. As Mr March stared at Ann, the room happened to become quiet. Mr March said loudly

'I've scarcely spoken to my future daughter-in-law. I must go and have a word with her.'

Slightly flushed, he crossed the room, swinging his arms in his quick, awkward gait.

'Why haven't you talked to me, young woman? Why am I being deserted on this public occasion?'

He took her to the centre of the carpet, and there they stood.

Mr March showed no sign at all of the gallant, elaborately courteous manner which he had first used to her in company. He was speaking to her, here in public view, intimately, simply, brusquely.

'I shall have to see about your own wedding before long,' he said.

'Yes,' said Ann.

'The sooner the better,' said Mr March. 'Since we are to be related in this manner.'

Ann looked at him. His expression had become sad and resigned. His head was bent down in a posture unlike his normal one, a posture dejected, subdued.

'Now, whatever happens,' he said, 'we must bear with each other.'

Ann was still looking at him, and he took her hand. They went on talking, and some of us moved towards them. Katherine began teasing him about arranging another wedding in the middle of this. For a second he was silent, then he straightened himself and recovered his gaiety. Katherine was continuing to talk of weddings, funerals, and Mr March's *Times* reading habits.

'You can't help paying attention to them,' he told her, 'when you reach my venerable years. I've attended a considerable number of both in my time. And I've also been informed of a great many births. Most of the results of which survived,' Mr March reflected. 'Even my cousin Oscar's child – even that lived long enough for me to give it the usual mug.'

Chapter 27

'MY FAVOURITE CHILD'

AFTER Katherine's wedding it seemed as though Mr March was groping round to heal the breach with his son. We had watched him cross the room to Ann at the wedding breakfast; he was acting not happily, not with an easy mind, but impelled to remove some of the weight that had for months, even through the excitement over Katherine, been pressing him down.

I intruded so far as to tell Charles that he ought to forget the night of the concert, and meet his father more than halfway. Charles himself was happy in the prospect of his marriage, which was fixed for three months ahead. He was also gratified that he could discipline himself enough to work patiently at his medicine; he had done it for a year, and he had no misgivings left. So that he was ready to listen to everything I said. His natural kindness, his deep feeling for his father now shone out. He wanted Mr March to be happy for the rest of his life. He would respond to any overture his father made. I tried to persuade him to go to his father, on his own initiative, and ask to be made independent. I did not need to give him reasons. Speaking to him, I had no sort of foresight. If I had been asked, I should just have said that if a man like Charles had to put up with domination, no good could come of it.

'Do it,' I pressed him, 'as though nothing had been said. As though the question hadn't ever been mentioned before. I believe that he will agree. He's in danger of losing more than you are, you know.'

Charles knew all that I meant. But he hesitated. As we talked his face became lined. If Mr March refused, the situation was worse than before. If Mr March refused, it would be even harder for Ann. They would know that all that was left was to put a civil face on things.

Nevertheless, I pressed him to go. He promised everything else but would not definitely promise that.

Then Mr March himself showed us the colour of his thoughts when he talked to Charles one Friday night in January.

It was Mr March's turn that night to give the family dinner party, and he invited me without any prompting, saying: 'You might oblige me by filling one of the gaps at my table.' He had never done so before; I felt the invitation on his own account marked a break with things Mr March had known.

The dinner party itself had changed since the first I went to. It was neither so lively nor so large. There were only eighteen pople this time sitting round the great table at Bryanston Square. Some of the absences were caused by illness, as Mr March's generation was getting old; Herbert had just had a thrombosis. Florence Simon was married now, and living out of London. While Katherine's marriage not only kept her away, but at least two of Mr March's cousins.

Philip's glance went round the room, noticing those relatives who had attended his own house the week before but who had not come that night. He said nothing of it to Mr March, and instead chaffed him, as he had done at the wedding, with the dry, elder-brotherly friendliness that had been constant all their lives. But even Philip's sharp tongue did not make the party go; family gossip never began to flow at its usual rate; by a quarter to eleven the last car had driven away.

Mr March came into the drawing-room, where Charles and I were sitting. We were sitting as we had been on the night of Charles's quarrel with his father, after that different dinner party three years before. Mr March sat down and stretched out his hands to the fire.

'I never expected to see a Friday night in my own house finished in time for me to have only ten minutes less than my usual allowance,' he said.

'Mr. L.,' said Charles, 'don't you remember saying they were nothing like they used to be, even in Uncle Philip's house? You said that months ago.'

'I appreciate your intention,' said Mr March, 'but I am unable to accept it entirely. I never expected to find myself in danger of being in Justin's position. After his daughter's marriage he did not venture to hold a Friday night until we were able to reassure him that there would be an adequate attendance. Which we were unable to do until a considerable number of years afterwards. I confess that I am surprised at not having a similar experience.'

'They respect you too much to treat you in the same way,' said Charles.

'It's not respect,' said Mr March. 'It's the family that has changed. It's curious to see the family changing in my own life-time. I've already seen most things pass that we used to regard as completely permanent features of the world.'

He spoke, with regret, in a matter-of-fact, acceptant, almost cheerful tone. He added:

'As for respect, the nearest I approach it is that at synagogue people are always ready to commiserate on the misfortunes which have happened to me through my children. Last Saturday one fellow insisted on keeping me talking in the rain. He said: "Mr March, I should like you to know I am as upset as you must be to see the Marches fall from their old position." I acknowledged his remark. The fellow was making it impossible for me to cover myself with my umbrella. He said: "We all feel the decline of our great houses." I said that it was very civil of him. He said: "Think of your family. Your father was a great man. And his brothers were known outside our community. But your generation, Mr March – I know you will excuse me for speaking frankly – you have just been living on the esteem of your father. What have any of you done compared with the old Marches?" I brought up the name of my brother Philip, but this man replied: "He was lucky enough to be the eldest son of your father. That's all. And you and your brothers weren't even that, again speaking frankly, Mr March." '

'Who was this man?' Charles asked.

'I refuse to disclose his name,' said Mr March, still reporting the conversation in such a matter-of-fact way that Charles had to follow suit.

'Is he the man,' said Charles, 'who called you a radical reformer because you wanted to let women into the synagogue?'

'Of course not,' said Mr March. 'In any case, that was Hannah's fault. He proceeded to say: "You and your brothers did nothing to add to the family reputation. While among all your children and nephews and nieces, is there one who won't subtract something from the family name? Think of your own children. Your son's just an idler about town. One daughter married a man who lives by his pen. The other daughter has inflicted this great sorrow upon us. Whatever can happen to the next generation of Marches? What about your grandchildren?" '

'I must say,' said Charles, 'that he sounds a vaguely disagreeable companion.'

'He was just being frank,' said Mr March.

'If that's frankness,' said Charles, 'give me a bit of dissimulation.'

'It was possibly true,' said Mr March, 'though I thought it was rather pungently expressed. And I wished he had delivered himself before synagogue when it wasn't raining.'

'I am inclined to think,' he added, 'that he represents what a number of my acquaintances are saying.'

'They're not worth considering.'

'No,' said Mr March. 'I can't help considering anything that is said about the family's position. These lamentations show how general opinion is preparing to dispose of the family. As I remarked previously, it's curious to see such changes occur in my own life-time.'

Charles looked at him, astonished by the fortitude with which Mr March could see part of his world destroyed. He was realistic as ever: nostalgic also (for that was the other side of his realistic temperament), hankering after the world that was gone or going, but not pretending for a moment that it could be saved. His fortitude was stoical: but Charles knew there was nothing light about it. It came out in matter-of-fact terms, but it was only separated from melancholy because the pulse of his vitality was still throbbing deep and strong.

'You might blame me more than you do,' said Charles.

'I don't propose to,' said Mr March. 'I don't know how much either you or I can be held to blame. In any case, I should not consider the investigation profitable. We have arrived at the position we are now in. And I lay no claim to a philosophical turn of mind, but I have noticed one result of things changing outside. One has to fall back on those attachments that can't change so rapidly. After his daughter's marriage and its regrettable consequences, Justin always devoted himself entirely to his wife.'

Mr March gazed at his son, and added:

'Since I am deprived of other consolations, I find that I attach more value to your continued existence.'

*

For days afterwards, I kept trying to persuade Charles that now was the time to go to his father. Now if ever was the time. Sometimes he was nearly persuaded. Sometimes he advanced the old arguments. He was not obstinate, he was not resenting my intrusion. He was gripped by an indecision so deep that it seemed physical, not controllable by will. He said: 'I admit that he spoke with complete sincerity. He always does. He desperately wants everything to be right between us. But you notice that he didn't mention my marrying Ann? You noticed that, didn't you?'

Katherine joined in my efforts, warmly, anxiously, emphatically, when she came to Bryanston Square for a weekend in February. It was two months since her honeymoon, and there was a physical change in her face, as though some of the muscles had been relaxed. She was tranquil, happy, more positive than we had known her. When Charles had told Mr March of his engagement, she had shown less than her usual insight; she had even expected Mr March to be pleased. But now she saw the situation with clear eyes. It was worth the risk, she argued; it was the one step which could set them free with each other.

Once she grew angry with Charles, and told him that he would surely do it if only Ann were not holding him back. Her concern was so naked and intimate that he did not take offence. She continued to persuade him. For half an hour one night, I thought she had succeeded. Then, suddenly, his mood changed. In fatigue and resignation, he said, smiling at her with extreme affection:

'I'm sorry, my dear. I'd do anything else. But I can't do it.'

She knew that the decision was final. She called to see me the next evening in my rooms.

'Lewis,' she said, 'I've asked Charles if he minds my speaking to Mr L.'

'What did he say?'

'He welcomed it. Oh, it's wretched, don't you think it's wretched? He was within an inch of going himself, and yet he simply can't. I'm appallingly diffident about talking to Mr L. myself. But if I don't, I should feel cowardly for ever. Don't you agree?'

Katherine promised to return after she had talked to Mr March. I waited in a fret of apprehension, thinking time after time that it was her footsteps on the stairs. When she came at last, I knew that all had gone wrong.

She sat down heavily.

'He was absolutely unreasonable,' she said. 'He wouldn't even begin to listen to reason. His mind seemed absolutely shut.'

She had told him that he could not treat Charles like a child; he was a grown man; this attempt to keep him dependent was bound to make a gulf between them. Mr March replied that he did not propose to let such considerations influence his actions. She had told him that his actions were stupid as well as wrong. They could not even have the practical effect he wanted. Charles was committed to becoming a doctor now; and he would marry Ann in April, come what might. Mr March replied that he was aware of these facts; he did not propose to discontinue Charles's allowance, which might hinder his son's activities, but he refused, by making him independent, to give any sign of approval to either of his major follies. Katherine begged him to think of his own future relations with Ann. She was going to be his daughter-in-law. For the rest of his life he would meet her. Mr March said that he did not propose to consider the opinions of that young woman on the matter.

He was not angry, but utterly set in his purpose. He even told her that he needed his son's affection more than he had ever done; he said, quite naturally, that he had told Charles so. But, on the issue before them, he would not make the slightest concession.

'I do not believe,' Katherine burst out, 'that it would have made any difference if Charles had gone himself. I shall always console myself with that. I tell you, I'm sure it's true.'

She had finished by asking him to explain the contrast between his gentleness over her own marriage, and this fantastic harshness to Charles. Mr March had not answered for a long time. Then he said, in a sombre tone:

'He was always my favourite child.'

Katherine stayed with me for a long time, in order to put off breaking the news to Charles.

Part 4

THE DANGERS

Chapter 28

SEVENTIETH BIRTHDAY

MR MARCH's seventieth birthday was due in the May of 1936, and for weeks beforehand he had been calling on his younger relatives and friends, insisting that they keep the night of the twenty-second free. It was the only birthday he had celebrated since he was a child; usually he would not have the day so much as mentioned. But some caprice made him want everyone to realize that he was seventy. Many of the very young had not seen him as extravagant as this.

They had heard the family legends of Uncle Leonard, but they had not often been inside his house, except for the formal Friday nights. Since the marriages of Katherine and Charles five years before, he had given up entertaining the young.

For his seventieth birthday party, we were each invited, not only by a call from Mr March in person, but also by a long letter in his own hand. Presents were prohibited with violence. None of us knew how large the dinner was to be until we arrived at Bryanston Square; the house was brighter than I ever remembered it, lights streaming on to the square, cocktails, which Mr March had not allowed there before, being drunk in the drawing-room. Mr March was moving from one young relative to another, his coat-tails flapping behind him. Wherever he went one heard noise and laughter.

As we waited for dinner, there were about fifty people standing in the room. None of Mr March's contemporaries was there; by another caprice of Mr March's, none of them had been invited. Perhaps, I thought, he did not want to be reminded that his generation of Marches was dying.

Since Charles married, Herbert and his wife had both died, and Caroline's husband. Hannah was still alive, but bed-ridden. Of Mr March's contemporaries, only Philip and Caroline were left at Friday nights.

At the birthday party, Margaret March and I seemed to be the oldest of the guests, and we were just over thirty. The majority of them were Mr March's youngest nephews and nieces and second cousins. To make up the number which he had set himself, Mr March had asked several to bring their young men and women.

Mr March walked among them, cordial to everyone, lingering once or twice appreciatively by the prettier girls. His spirits were not damped by Katherine's absence; she had had to cry off at a few hours' notice, since one of her children had measles. 'I should see no reason to anticipate serious consequences at this stage,' said Mr March, 'if it were not for the practitioners whom they insist on employing. They are reported to be competent, but I refuse to accept responsibility for their performances. I thought it wise to send my daughter an account of their careers, so far as I could discover them from the professional records, and draw special attention to those features I did not consider up to snuff.'

He added:

'I have to admit that I have not yet discovered a practitioner whose record appeared to me to be up to snuff in all respects.'

He returned to a knot of nephews and nieces in order to answer their chaff about presents. Why had he refused to allow us to give him any? Because the material objects offered on these occasions were always of singular uselessness. Books? All the books approved of by young persons of cultivated taste produce nothing but the deepest depression. Had he really received no presents from anyone? 'Well,' said Mr March, 'my second-cousin-once-removed Harry Stein didn't obey my instructions. He ignored the hint and sent me a box of cigars. If the fellow wants to be civil, I suppose I can't deprive him of the pleasure.'

Instead of receiving presents on his birthday, Mr March had decided to give some. Someone asked him whether this was true, and he said: 'I refuse either to deny or confirm.'

Under pressure, he admitted that 'the juvenile members of the family had received a contribution towards their confectionery' that morning. But he became his most secretive when people wanted him to say exactly what he had given, and to how many. It came out later that each person under twenty-one in the March family, that is the March family in its widest sense, had found waiting for them at breakfast that morning a cheque for *Seventy Pounds Exactly*.

Mr March stood in his drawing-room, retorted to the questions of his nieces, sent the footmen hurrying about the bright room with trays of cocktails, sipped a glass of sherry. As I watched him, I thought how well preserved he still looked. His moustache had whitened in the last few years, the wings of hair above his ears were scantier and greyer, the veins on his temples stood out; but his step, his brusque, quick, clumsy movements, the resonance of his laughter, were still a robust man's.

He seemed gayer than I had seen him for a long time. Even the entrance of Ann did not seem to produce any strain. It was a long time since she had been inside his home. There had been no break, but since Mr March made his last unconceding answer to Charles before their marriage, she had without a word spoken slipped away. That night, as she went up to shake hands with Mr March, he greeted her in a curt, matter-of-fact fashion. His manner seemed to suggest, not that they only met on the most formal occasions within the March family life, but simply that there was no need of explanations between them. He asked Margaret March to introduce her to a group in the corner of the room, and despatched a footman after her.

He kept Charles by him a little longer, and teased him affectionately and without rancour. 'May I enquire about the vital statistics of Pimlico and similar unsalubrious neighhourhoods?'

'They're not much affected yet,' said Charles, also with good humour.

'I refuse to take responsibility for any deterioration,' said Mr March.

'Well, that will be bad for everyone's morale, won't it, Mr L.?' Charles replied.

Mr March chuckled. Just listening to them, no one would have guessed their story. Then Mr March moved off to meet Caroline's grandchildren.

For a second Charles was left alone, until two cousins joined him. He stood there, in the centre of his father's drawing-room, looking a little older than his age: his forehead had lined, but his expression was keen, healthy, and settled: his face had taken on the shape it would wear until he was old.

His father's reference to 'Pimlico and similar unsalubrious neighbourhoods' meant that, not long after he graduated as a doctor, Charles had bought a partnership in a practice down by the river. Whether he bought it with Ann's money, none of us knew. It was certain that Mr March had made no contribution.

Charles himself was lighting a cigarette for a girl and as he straightened himself he looked at Ann. I followed his eyes. She had altered less than most of us; she had kept her open, youthful good looks. She was listening to a young man with the attention, gentle, friendly, and positive, that I remembered so well. As he watched, there was a spark in Charles's eye. Their love had stayed not only strong but brilliant. For them both, except that they had still had no child, it had turned out the best of marriages.

There were two tables laid in the dining-room, and the butler went to Charles and told him that he and Ann were expected to preside at the smaller. Mr March was left free to have two bright, pert, pretty nieces sitting one on each hand. Between the two tables stood four standard lamps, brought in for the occasion; Mr March caused a commotion by demanding that two of them be removed, as soon as we had sat down. 'This room has been appallingly dark during my occupancy of thirty-eight years,' he said loudly. 'It was even darker in my uncle Francis's time. Now the first time it's ever been properly lit, the confounded lights are arranged so as to obscure my view of half my guests.'

The lights were removed. Mr March surveyed the whole party with a satisfied, possessive, and triumphant smile. There were fifty-seven people in the room. Mr March announced, and again over the fish, that he had reserved one and a half rows of the stalls at 'some theatre whose name you will be informed of in due course'.

Margaret teased him about this sudden burst of secrecy: she produced the theory that he refused to go to the sort of play admired by his children's 'intellectual friends', and so was luring us somewhere of his own choice.

'No! No!' said Mr March. Other members of the family joined in, shouting and laughing. Mr March's voice rose above them.

'No! No! My motives are being misinterpreted. But I will say this, if any of you want to be depressed tonight, you'd better stay in the house and read one of the books approved of by your literary friends. Not that I don't admire 'em –' he said to me, 'but now I'm getting old I find I don't want to be reminded of the unpleasant circumstances which afflicted me when I was young.'

'So that you find that you worry less than you used to, do you?' said one of the bright, pretty nieces.

Several people in the know were chuckling, for the night's celebration had been arranged with an expenditure of anxiety unusual even for Mr March.

'I worry dreadfully,' said Mr March complacently. 'I've never known anyone worry more dreadfully than I do.'

'Not so badly as you used to, though,' said Margaret.

'Worse. Much worse,' said Mr March. 'I've learnt to control myself, that's all.'

He chuckled, as loudly as anyone. 'I've also learned to avoid occasions that I dislike. The only advantage of getting old,' said Mr March, 'is that you're not faced by so many occasions that you're bound to dislike, if you're too shy and diffident a person.

'There are a corresponding number of disadvantages, of course,' Mr March went on. 'I shall shortly have to abandon my club because the people I know are dropping off one by one, and it's an unnecessary strain on the memory to burden yourself with new faces — a very ugly face, by the way, that fellow possesses that my brother Philip has just got into the club. It's a an unnecessary strain to burden yourself with new faces for a period of time that can't be worth the effort. It's curious also how soon people are forgotten in the club when they're dead. When I die they'll discontinue my special brand of tea-buns next day.'

For a few moments the reflection sobered him. Before the end of the meal, he was enjoying himself again. On the way to the play, which turned out to be a revival of one of Lonsdale's, he enjoyed marshalling the cars, re-collecting the party on the steps of the theatre, taking the middle seat of the second row of the stalls. In the first interval he came out with Margaret March, and said with the utmost gratification: 'I call it a very mediocre play.'

Margaret protested, but Mr March overbore her in his most sincere and genial manner:

'It is extremely mediocre.' He turned to me thoughtfully. 'I believe you could write a play not much worse than that.'

While he was talking, Margaret noticed her Aunt Caroline coming down from the circle by herself. We saw the gleam of her lorgnon as she sighted her brother. She had become enormously fat, and her flesh shook as she made her way down.

'I heard from a good many quarters,' she said to Mr March, 'that you were giving yourself a spree tonight. So I decided to come and inspect you.'

She could not resist the time-honoured joke about his meanness: was that why he had not invited the older Marches? Mr March grinned, but his manner was defensive.

She protruded a large silver ear-trumpet at him as he replied.

'Birthday parties have always been understood to come into a special category,' he said. 'I've never had any of you to my house on my birthday since I was married — except Hannah, and, needless to say, she invited herself.'

Just before we returned to our seats, Caroline said casually in her loud voice:

'By the way, I had dinner with Philip. The poor fellow would have been here with me, but he's afraid he's got his gout coming on. He gave me a message for you. He said that, in case I missed you, you'd find the same message waiting at your house.'

As she rummaged in her handbag for an envelope, she did not seem specially interested, nor Mr March specially concerned. But, as he read the note, his face darkened with anxiety, and he said to his sister:

'I shall need your company in the next interval.'

Mr March was on his feet in the stalls as the curtain came down at the end of the second act. He met his sister, and I watched them walk back and forth on the far side of the foyer. She walked slowly, with her ponderous tread, and her silver trumpet flew to and from her ear.

To my surprise, Mr March beckoned me to them. Their conversation had looked comic from a distance: at close quarters there was nothing comic in Mr March's expression.

'I wanted to ask you, Lewis, whether you have any recent knowledge of the activites of my daughter's brother-in-law? I mean the fellow Herbert Getliffe.'

The question was unexpected: Mr March asked it in a flat and heavy tone.

'No, I've not seen much of him lately,' I said. 'I've dined with him once or twice, but that's all.'

'You can't give us any information upon how he can be affecting the position of my brother Philip?'

I was astonished. I said that I could not imagine it.

'So far as I can infer from the only information I possess,' said Mr March, 'this preposterous situation is connected with certain gossip which was circulating at the time of my daughter's marriage. You may remember that there was a certain amount of gossip at that time.'

I nodded. 'But that was five years ago.'

'I do not pretend to any greater enlightenment than you do. My brother has however sent a note asking for my advice, which is an entirely unprecedented occurrence. I have been trying to discover the reason for this occurrence from my sister, but she has not proved illuminating.'

Caroline caught this last sentence.

'I still think you're making a mountain out of a molehill,' she boomed.

'You said that twice about my son,' said Mr March. He was silent for a moment, then turned to me with a sad, friendly, and trusting smile. 'I rely on you for the discretion and kindness you have always shown towards my family.'

The second bell sounded, and Mr March began to walk into the theatre. He said to me:

'I should be obliged if you would find my son's wife. I should like a word with her.'

I brought Ann to him in the aisle of the stalls. Without any explanation, he asked her:

'Do you still see Ronald Porson?'

'Do you know him?' she asked.

'Do you still see him?'

'Very occasionally.'

He began to ask her another question, something about Ronald Porson and Getliffe, in a voice which had become low but intensely angry. As he did so, the lights of the theatre were dimming, and Ann left to find her seat.

After the play was over, when we stood outside the theatre, Mr March was no calmer. He did not attempt to ask more questions, he just let his temper go. It was raining, the fleet of cars in which his party had arrived could not get round to the front of the theatre. Mr March watched car after car drive up to the pavement, and his temper grew worse.

'In former days,' he complained, 'there wasn't this congestion of owner-drivers from the suburbs. Owner-drivers are making the town intolerable for genuine inhabitants. A genuine inhabitant used to be able to reckon on returning to his house within a quarter of an hour of being disgorged from any suitable place of entertainment.

The cars did not arrive: Mr March borrowed an umbrella from the commissionaire and went out into the middle of the road. The lights of taxis, golden bars on the wet asphalt, lit him up as he looked furiously round. Drivers honked at him as he stamped in front of them back to the theatre steps.

'It's intolerable,' he cried. 'They're taking my night's rest away from me now. They're changing everything under my feet, and I'm too old to change my ways. I suppose my existence has been prolonged unnecessarily already. Though Lionel Hart didn't think so, when he had a blood transfusion on his seventy-eighth birthday. They're changing everything under my feet.' He thudded the umbrella point against the pavement. 'I remarked at dinner-time, when I was under the illusion that I had completed seventy years without disaster, about not wanting to be reminded of the unpleasant circumstances which afflicted me when I was young. But when you're young you don't lose your sleep at night on account of your attachments. When you begin to do that, it makes you realize that you have lived too long.'

Chapter 29

REASSURANCE

THE morning after his birthday party, Mr March rang me up: would I be good enough to spare him an hour of my time, as soon as I could arrange it without prejudice to my duties? I went round to Bryanston Square immediately, and was taken into Mr March's study. I had not entered that room since the night he interrogated Ann.

'I appreciate your courtesy in visiting me without delay,' said Mr March. His eyes were bloodshot and the skin under them had darkened in the last few hours. 'I have to apologize, of course, for trespassing on your valuable time, but you are the only person whose opinion is of any appreciable value to me in the present regrettable circumstances. Owing to your acquaintance with the fellow Getliffe, and other factors which I need not specify.'

He had already been out to see Philip that morning; Philip was in bed and and in pain, and had not been able to present all the facts. One thing, however, was clear to Mr March. Philip had now become certain about the nature of Herbert Getliffe's transactions, some time before Katherine's wedding. There was no doubt in Philip's mind that Getliffe had, while giving legal advice to a ministry, acquired knowledge in advance of a government contract. Getliffe had known that the contract was going to the firm of Howard & Hazlehurst; his relations had duly bought large holdings. That had happened. On the main points Porson had been right, though he had muddled some of the details.

That story would not by itself have worried Mr March. It was a piece of sharp practice by a rising barrister, but it was seven years old. By this time the Marches had completely accepted Francis Getliffe. There were, however, other stories which worried Mr March much more.

The first was that 'obnoxious propagandists', as Mr March kept referring to them, were passing the word round that a similar leakage had just occurred, and that Getliffe and his friends were again involved. According to Sir Philip, this news was going round the lobbies and clubs; it was still secret but there was a threat that it would soon break.

The second story was that not only Getliffe and his friends were involved, but so were several junior ministers. Philip had been taken back into the government three years before, into the same parliamentary secretaryship he had held for a few months in 1929. On Friday nights he had loved gossiping like a man in office, mentioning his colleagues' names. The 'obnoxious propagandists' were now mentioning some of those names, including that of Hawtin, one of the ablest youngish men in the government. They were being brought into the scandal. 'It's like another Marconi case,' said Mr March, harking back to a time when he felt more at home.

Philip had told him that among the names being mentioned was Philip's own.

Mr March was puzzled and distressed, more lost than angry. He would have liked to explode into rage, and dismiss the scandal as 'mischievious nonsense invented by agitators for their own purposes'. He had begun so, that morning: but stopped suddenly when he found Sir Philip fretted and impatient.

I have never seen my brother Philip so much affected by any incident in his public life,' said Mr March. 'I was inclined at first to attribute his depressed state to his disease, but I was forced to realize that he is sick in mind apart from his physical discomfort. I had never realized that he was capable of being sick in mind. From the earliest time I can remember, I always envied him as not being vulnerable to the weaknesses that afflicted me.'

He was profoundly shaken at having to console Philip – Philip, whom throughout their lives he had thought self-sufficient. He went on:

'I do not profess to understand why he should take this criminal nonsense so much to heart. I did not need to be assured by my eldest brother that he had not taken advantage of his official position. But he was sufficientlly overwrought to insist on assuring me that he had completely given up any transactions of any kind whatsoever since he re-entered the government and that he had not made a single purchase of stock for the last twelve months.

Philip had said that he did not know whether the stories of Herbert Getliffe's recent coups were true or not. Mr March was mystified by these stories, and so was I. Was there anything in them?

It was in both our minds how Philip had taken action against Getliffe at the time of Katherine's marriage.

I promised Mr March that I would try to find out what Getliffe had been up to. It was not such an easy job for me as it would have been once. Since my marriage four years before, I had left Getliffe's chambers; I had given up legal practice and spent half my time teaching law at Francis Getliffe's college and the other half in London as a consultant to a big firm.

I promised also that I would try to find out who was spreading the gossip, and why.

I began to realize that, of all Mr March's anxieties, that was the deepest. From all he had picked up, the gossip had originated with people who were familiar with Getliffe and his circle. Perhaps they were familiar with Sir Philip and his colleagues too: that did not seem so clear. It sounded like Ronald Porson: yet the scandal had, according to Philip, been started by the extreme left. It was not just malicious gossip, it was no more nor less than a piece of politics, he said. From what Mr March had heard of Porson, that ruled him out.

Mr March concealed his thoughts from me: but after a time I had no doubt – he was dark with a suspiciousness that seemed quite unrealistic, with a fear that seemed on the edge of paranoia – that he was thinking of Ann.

It was this fear, I was sure next day, that drove him to see Charles.

I had promised to make enquiries about Getliffe within twenty-four hours and return to Bryanston Square for dinner on the night following; when I arrived, I found Mr March and Charles alone in the drawing-room. There was a silence as though neither had spoken for some minutes. Mr March roused himself, and said: 'I asked my son to join us for dinner. As you see, he has found it possible to do so.'

Charles said:

'It happens to be a good night for me, Mr L. My partner is always at home on Wednesdays.'

Mr March did not reply. Charles looked at me with a frown, enquiring and concerned. It was clear that Mr March had not yet spoken.

We went into the dining-room with little conversation. Charles made an effort to get Mr March talking, and himself told a story of Katherine: Mr March sat absently at the head of the table.

Suddenly, Mr. March said:

'Lewis, I should like to learn the results of your investigations.'

'I'm afraid they haven't got anywhere yet,' I said. 'Herbert Getliffe is out of London. He'll be back early next week, and I've arranged to see him then. I'm also trying to see Porson on the same day.'

Mr March inclined his head.

'I know that in the circumstances you will not permit any unnecessary delay.' He turned to Charles. 'You realize what I am referring to?'

'I haven't the slightest idea,' said Charles.

'It is desirable that I should enlighten you,' said Mr March. 'My brother Philip is being attacked by scurrilous gossip from various sources. This attack appears to be aimed at his personal honour and his public position. It is connected, in some way about which I am not in a position to give you precise details, with the speculations of my son-in-law

Francis Getliffe's brother. Anyone in my family will recollect a previous occasion on which that subject exercised a certain importance. My brother is being attacked for similar mispractices, though in his case they would be more reprehensible, since they would imply that he took advantage of his official position for these purposes.'

Mr March stopped, then asked in a loud harsh voice: 'I wish to ask you, what do you know of these attacks?'

'Nothing. Nothing whatever,' said Charles. His tone was unresentful, almost amused, and utterly candid. 'They sound very improbable.'

Mr March's relief was manifest and radiant. Then his face darkened again.

'I take it, your wife is still active politically?'

Charles looked surprised; it was years since they had argued over Ann's beliefs: in those days, Mr March had spoken as though her politics were academic. Nevertheless Charles replied at once:

'Yes, she is.'

'I am very sorry to hear it.'

Mr March was looking absent and sombre again.

Charles said, in a considerate, respectful, but unyielding tone:

'I ought to say that I think she's doing good most of the time.'

By that year, men like Charles and Francis Getliffe and me had not much doubt about what was in store. It seemed to us that there was no choice except war with Hitler – or rather that any other choice was going to be worse than the war. That conviction was separating us from our elders, even those we liked, such as Mr March and Sir Philip.

In the struggle, which was growing bitter, we felt that Ann and her party were on our side. While Sir Philip went confidently about Whitehall and talked to the family on Friday nights as though their world were invulnerable, placid, and permanent. Both he and Mr March were men of judgement: they were more detached and realistic than most of their class: they were Jews. But they could not believe what was coming. To us, they seemed often not to care.

Mr March did not reply to Charles, but asked abruptly:
'What does your wife know of these attacks?'

'I should think as little as I do.' Charles's tone was once more open and candid, so candid that Mr March was entirely reassured.

Charles asked for the full story, and Mr March told it him: as he spoke, Mr March's manner had become animated, but he finished:

'I must impress on you, that my brother Philip takes this with the utmost seriousness. My first inclination was not to give it serious attention. But my brother's demeanour made me adopt a different attitude.'

'I don't understand him,' said Charles. 'It wouldn't be hard to make up a good many kinds of attack on Uncle Philip: but, if I'd been thinking of something improbable, I couldn't have invented anything as improbable as this.' He was speaking light-heartedly. He asked more questions about Getliffe, some of them sarcastic, so that Mr March chuckled. He went on: 'About Uncle Philip – aren't all people in public life absurdly sensitive to the slightest breath of criticism? Isn't that the explanation? Don't you really think that Uncle Philip sticks his Press cuttings into an album every morning before he gets up? If you are as interested as that in your public personality, it must be uncomfortable when people are blackguarding you – even on singularly fantastic grounds. It's that kind of discomfort he's frightened of, don't you admit it?'

Mr March broke into laughter. He had become carefree in a way that made his black anxiety of a quarter of an hour before difficult to bring back to mind. He was, in fact, carefree as I had not seen him in his son's presence for years past. The last few minutes – after Charles showed his ignorance of the attacks – had seemed like the first days I saw them together. Mr March's cares were dispelled; he grinned at his son's teasing, he paid it back with teasing of his own. It was like old days. As we said good night, Mr March remarked cheerfully to Charles: 'You're making a frightful ass of yourself, living in your unsalubrious abode by the river, I refuse to accept any responsibility for the effects on your health. But I'm always glad to see you in my house.'

Chapter 30

A WALK FROM BRYANSTON SQUARE
TO PIMLICO

It was a fine, warm night, and Charles and I decided to walk home. I had a house in Chelsea by this time, and so we could go the same way. As we crossed over to the park, Charles said:

'You'd heard all this commotion about Uncle Philip before?'

I told him that it had begun at the birthday party. 'It's a curious story,' he said.

He was not actively interested. He was sorry that Philip should be disturbed, but he did not feel himself involved. I thought of asking him to mention it to Ann, and considered that it was wiser not to. Soon he changed the subject.

The night air was soft, the park was spotted with couples lying mouth-to-mouth. We walked slowly, tired and comfortably relaxed. With the pleasure of an old intimacy, we talked as we had not done for years. Of our marriages, so different in all that had happened to us and yet both childless. 'Yes,' said Charles, with comradeship, 'it will be sad if neither of us leaves a son to follow him.'

We talked of our careers, and for the first time Charles told me how he felt about being a doctor. We had just left the park, and were waiting to cross the road at the end of Piccadilly. Cars were hooting by, and Charles had to pause until he could make himself heard.

'Often I've disliked it strongly, of course,' he said. 'More often I've found it extremely dull. You'd expect so, wouldn't you? There's a fair amount of human interest, of course, but one's got to be patient to get even that. A G.P. isn't dealing continually with crises of life and death, you know. Nine-tenths of his time he's seeing people with colds and nerves and indigestion and rheumatism. That's the basis of the job, and if you're looking for human interest, people exhibit slightly less of it when they've a bad cold than when they haven't.'

As we walked down Grosvenor Place, Charles went on: 'A doctor has his moments, but most of his time it can't be interesting. It just can't. The percentage of ordinary workaday tedium is bound to be high. And I suspect that's true of any job, isn't it? One always hears them described with their high moments heightened a bit; it's nice to hear, but it's quite different when you begin living them. Don't you agree? Don't you admit that's true? Look, Lewis, you possess a great capacity for getting interest out of what you're doing: I've never met anyone with a greater: but tell the truth, isn't your own job – aren't the various jobs you've tackled – mostly tedious when you come to live them?'

We argued for a time. Charles said:

'Anyway, doctoring is tedious for nine hours out of every ten. Anyone who tells you it isn't either doesn't know what excitement is or suffers from an overdose of romantic imagination. And for me it's also tedious in rather a different way. I don't think you'll sympathize much with this. But I mean that it doesn't give me anything hard to bite on men-tally. I've got a taste for thinking: but I shouldn't be any worse a doctor if I were a much more stupid man.'

Since we began our walk, he had been talking without guard. He was not trying to protect or disguise himself, and at this point he did not attempt to conceal his intellectual arrogance, his certainty of his own intellectual power, his regret as he felt that power rusting.

'So you see,' Charles gave a smile. 'I'm resigned to being distinctly bored for the rest of my life.'

'But there are compensations,' I said.

'Yes,' said Charles, 'there are compensations.'

'There are compensations,' he repeated. 'Each month I count up my earnings very carefully. Last month I made over eighty pounds – if they all pay me. You've no idea how pleasant it is to earn your own living. It's a pleasure you can only really appreciate if you've been supported in luxury ever since you were born.' He smiled broadly, and added:

'There are other compensations too. People show such confidence in one. It's nice to be able to justify that sometimes. Once or twice in the last few weeks I've felt some use.'

We had crossed in front of Victoria Station and came out into Wilton Road. I asked:

'Charles, if you had your time again, would you make the same choice?'

'Without any doubt,' he said.

I looked at him under the light of a street lamp. He had become older than any of us. He was carrying a mackintosh; he was stooping more than he used to. At that moment – while he was saying, his eyes glinting maliciously at his own expense: 'If I had my time again, I might not even take quite so long to make up my mind' – I was moved back to the evening in Regent Street long ago, when we argued about goodness. I felt the shock that assails one as one suddenly sees an intimate in a transfiguring light, the shock of utter familiarity and utter surprise. Here was Charles, whom I knew so well, whom I took for granted with the ease of a long friendship – and at the same time, I was thinking with incredulity, as though I had never met him before, what a curious choice he had made.

In Antrobus Street the light was glowing over the night-bell. We said good-night in front of his house, and I began to walk west along the Embankment. The night was so caressingly warm that I wanted to linger, looking at the river. There was an oily swell on the dark water, and on the swell the bands of reflected light slowly swayed. I could see the red and green eyes of lamps on the bridges up the river. I stayed there, watching the bands of light sway on the water, and, as I watched, among the day-dreams drifting through my mind were memories and thoughts about Charles.

The river smell was carried on a breath of air. Down towards Chelsea the water glistened and a red light flashed. Leaning on the Embankment, I thought that, in a different time, when the conscience of the rich was not so sick, Charles might not have sacrificed himself, at least not so completely. Some of his abnegation one could attribute to his time, just as some of his surface quirks, his outbursts of arrogance and diffidence, one could attribute to his being born a Jew.

But none of that seemed to me to matter very much, compared with what I thought I had seen in him, walking in the Wilton Road half an hour before.

I thought I had seen a nature which, at the deepest, was never sure of love. Never sure of receiving it: perhaps never sure of giving it: vulnerable and at the same time resenting any approach.

It was the kind of nature which could have broken his life — for men with that flaw at the root often spend their lives in pursuing unrequited love, or indulging their cruelty on others, or tormenting themselves with jealousy, or retiring into loneliness and spiritual pride. But in Charles this deepest self was housed in a temperament in all other respects strong, active, healthy, full of vigour. It was that blazing contrast which I had seen, or imagined that I had seen.

Perhaps it was that contrast which made him want to search for the good.

He had always been fascinated by the idea of goodness. Was it because he was living constantly with a part of himself which he hated? To know what goodness means, perhaps one needs to have lain awake at night, hating one's own nature. The sweet, the harmonious, the untempted, have no reason to hate their natures; it is the others, the guilty or the sadic — it seemed to me most of all the sadic — who are driven to find what goodness is.

But men like Charles did not find it in themselves. It was not as easy as all that. He wanted to be good; so his active nature led him to want to do good. He was living a useful life now — but that was all. No one felt that as a result he had reached a state of goodness: he never felt it for a moment himself. He knew that, with his insight and sarcastic honesty. He would have liked to feel goodness in himself — he would have liked to believe that others felt it. But he knew that in fact others often felt a sense of strain, because he was acting against part of his nature. They did not feel he was apt for a life of abnegation. They distrusted his conscience, and looked back with regret to the days before it dominated him – to the days, indeed, in which they remembered him as gay, malicious, idle, brilliant.

I looked down at the water, not wanting to drag myself away. I had never felt more fond of him, and into my thoughts there flickered and passed scenes in which he had taken part, the night of our examination years before, quarrels in Bryanston Square, a glimpse of him walking with his arm round Ann. I thought I had seen in him that night some of the goodness he admired. But not in the way he had searched for it. Instead, there was a sparkle of good in the irony with which he viewed his own efforts; in the disillusioned certainty with which he knew that he at least was right to be useful, that he could have chosen no other way, even if it now seemed prosaic, lacking in the radiance which others attained by chance.

Most of all there was a sparkle of good in the state to which his struggle with his own nature had brought him. He could still hate himself. Through that hatred, and not through his conscience, through the nights when he had lain awake darkened by remorse, he had taken into his blood the sarcastic astringent experience of life which shone out of him as he comforted another's self-reproach and lack of self-forgiveness.

Chapter 31

A SUCCESS AND A FAILURE

I DID not see Mr March again before the day I had arranged
to meet Herbert Getliffe, but I received an anxious note,
saying that he hoped I would persevere with my enquiries
and relieve his mind as soon as I had information. The lull
of reassurance was over and his worry was nagging at him
again. There were few states more infectious than anxiety, I
thought, as I walked through the courts to Getliffe's chambers, with an edge to my own nerves.

Getliffe had taken silk a year before. There he was, sitting
at his great desk, where I had sat beside him often enough,
Four briefs were untied in front of him; on a side table stood
perhaps thirty more, these neatly stacked and the pink rib-
bons tied. I caught sight of a lavish fee on the top one – it
might not have been accidental that it was that fee a visitor
could see.

For two or three minutes after I was shown in, Getliffe
stared intently at the brief he was studying. His brow was
furrowed, his neck stiff with concentration; he was the model
of a man absorbed. This was a new mannerism altogether.
At last he looked up.

'Heavens, you're here, are you, L.S.?' he said. 'I'm afraid
I was so completely up to the eyes that I just didn't realize.
Well, it's good to see you, L.S.'

I asked him how his practice was going since he took
silk.

'I mustn't grumble,' said Getliffe, sweeping an arm towards the briefs on the side table. 'No, I mustn't grumble. It
was a grave decision to take; I should like you to remember
what a grave decision it was. I could have rubbed on for ever
as a junior, and it would have kept me in shoe-leather' – his
dignity cracked for a second – 'and the occasional nice new

hat.' Then he settled 'himself even more impressively. 'But two considerations influenced me, L.S. I thought of the increased chances it would give one to give promising young men their first jump on the ladder. One could be more useful to a lot more young men. Young men in the position you were, when you first came looking for a friendly eye. Believe me, I thought of you personally, L.S., when I was making the decision. You know how much I like helping brilliant young men. Perhaps that was the most important consideration. The other was that one owes a duty to one's profession and if one can keep oneself alive as a counsel of His Majesty, one ought not to refuse the responsibility.'

No one could have enjoyed it more, I thought. No one could have more enjoyed throwing himself into this new, serious, senatorial part. He added: 'Of course, if one keeps one's head above water, one gets certain consolations for the responsibility. I'm thankful to say that may happen.' He chuckled. 'I haven't had to cut off my evening glass of beer. And it's fun to take my wife round the town and order a dollop of champagne without doing sums in the head.' He was in triumphant form. He felt he was going to arrive. He kept giving me heavy homilies, such as were due from a man of weight. He believed them, just as he believed in everything he said while he was saying it.

After a time I said:

'By the way, I came to ask you something.'

'If there is any help I can give you, L.S.,' said Getliffe, 'you have only to ask. Ask away.'

'You remember the trouble that happened just before your brother's wedding?'

'What trouble?'

'Rumours were going round about some investments in Howard & Hazlehurst.'

Getliffe looked at me sternly.

'Who are Howard & Hazlehurst?' he said.

He seemed to believe that he had forgotten. I reminded him of our conversation that evening in chambers, when he was frightened that Porson would expose the deal.

'I remember it vaguely,' said Getliffe. He went on reprovingly: 'I always thought that you exaggerated the danger. You're a bit too highly strung for the rough and tumble, you know. I think you were very wise to remove yourself most of your time to a place with ivy round the walls. One has to be very strong for this kind of life.' He paused. 'Yes, I remember it vaguely. I'm sorry to say that poor old Porson has gone right down the hill since then.'

'I wanted to ask you,' I said, 'if you'd heard that some similar rumours were going round now.'

'I have been told of some nonsense or other,' said Getliffe in a firm and confident tone. 'They appear to be saying that I used inside knowledge last year. I've ignored it so far: but if they go on I shall have to protect myself. One owes a duty to one's position.'

'Have they the slightest excuse to go on?'

'I shouldn't let everyone ask me that question, L. S.,' said Getliffe reproachfully. 'But we know each other well enough to pass it. You've seen me do things that I hope and believe I couldn't do nowadays. So I'll answer you. They haven't the slightest excuse, either in law or out of it. I've never had a cleaner sheet than I've had the last two years. And if I can prove these people are throwing mud, they'll find it a more expensive game than snooker.' He looked at me steadily with his brown, opaque eyes. He said:

'I can't answer for anyone else. I can't answer for March, Hawtin, or the ministerial bigwigs, but I'm glad to say that my own sheet is absolutely clean. A good deal cleaner, I might tell you, than some of our common acquaintances' about the time that you were dragging up just now. I suppose you know that old Sir Philip did himself remarkably well out of the Howard & Hazlehurst affair? He was much too slim to have anything to do with Howard & Hazlehurst, of course. No, he just bought a whole great wad in a rocky little company whose shares were down to twopence and a kiss from everyone on the board. Well, Howard & Hazlehurst took over that company six months later. They wanted it for their new contract. Those shares are now 41s. 6d. and as safe as young Aunt Fanny. Our friends in Israel must have made a packet.'

His manner became weighty again, as he went on:

'I must tell you that I strongly disapprove. I strongly disapproved when it happened, though I was a younger man then and I hadn't done as well as I have now. I don't believe anyone in an official position ought to have any dealings, that is, speculative dealings, on the Stock Exchange. And I should like to advise you against it, L.S. There must be times in your little consultancy when you gain a bit of inside knowledge that a not-too-scrupulous man could turn into money. I dare say you'd bring it off every now and then. But you'll be happier if you don't do it. I don't know what you collect from your little consultancy and that job of yours with the ivy round the walls. But I advise you to be content with it, whatever it is. I'm content with mine, I don't mind telling you.'

We went out for lunch. As usual, I paid. When I left him, on my way to find Porson at an address in Notting Hill, two thoughts were chasing each other through my mind. Getliffe was speaking the truth about his 'clean sheet' in recent years. His protests were for once innocent, not brazen; it was a luxury for him to have such a clear conscience. The rumours about him seemed to be quite false. That surprised me; but it did not surprise me anything like so much as his revelation about Sir Philip. I did not know how much to believe; remembering Mr March's report of his visit to Philip's bedside, I was sure there was something in it.

Porson had given me an address in Notting Hill. When I reached it, I was met by his landlady, who said that he had been called away that morning: he had left a message that he would write again and fix another rendezvous. The house was decrepit, the landlady was suspicious of me, on guard for Porson; he was living in a flat up the third flight of shabby stairs.

I called on friends who might have heard the gossip – radical journalists, civil servants, barristers who knew Getliffe. Several of them had picked up the rumours, but no one told me anything new. Some were excited because there was scandal in the air. Even when one man said: 'I don't like the idea of a Dreyfus case started by the left,' his eyes were bright and glowing.

Then I told Mr March what I had found out. The rumours, I said, all referred to a leakage within the past year. I told him that Herbert Getliffe seemed not to be in any way responsible this time. If even one of these rumours was brought into the open, it looked entirely safe to sue straight away. But I also told Mr March that, though I could not see the bearing, he ought to hear Getliffe's story about Sir Philip.

Mr March listened in silence. At the end he said: 'I am deeply obliged to you for your friendly services.' His expression was not relieved, but he said: 'I may inform you that my brother Philip yesterday appeared to think that the affair was blowing over. I have always found that persons in public life become liable to a quite unwarranted optimism.' Mr March himself showed no optimism.

I waited three weeks before I heard from Porson. Then a note came in his tall fluent hand, which said: 'I expect you have guessed what chase has kept me away from London. I will tell you about her when I meet you. I insist on going to the University match, and shall return in time for the first day. Do you feel like joining me, even though your respectable friends may see us there and count it against you?'

I found him on the first morning, sitting on the top of the stand at the Nursery end. I had not seen him for two years, and I was shocked by the change. Under his eyes, screwed up in the sunlight, the pouches were embossed, heavy, purplish-brown. His colour was higher and more plethoric than ever, and the twitch convulsed his face every time he spoke. His suit was old, shiny at the cuffs, but he was wearing a carnation in his buttonhole and an Authentic tie. He welcomed me with a hearty aggressive show of pleasure. 'Ah well, my boy, I'm glad you haven't boycotted me. I need some company, the way these people are patting about.' His face twitched as he looked irascibly out to the pitch. 'It's going to be bloody dull. I hope it won't mean your being crossed off many visiting lists if some of your friends notice you're here with me. Anyway, it's bloody good to see you.'

We sat there in the sun most of that day. In his loud, resonant, angry voice Porson told me of his misfortunes. Three years before, he had lost a case in which Herbert Getliffe was leading for the other side. He had never worked up a steady practice. But he persuaded himself that, until that time, he was just on the point of success. Even now he could not admit that he had mismanaged the case. It was intolerable for him to remember that he had been out-manoeuvred by Getliffe, on the one occasion they had been on opposite sides in court. But he could not help admitting that for three years past the solicitors had fought shy of him. He went out of his way to admit it, pressing on the aching tooth, in a loud, rancorous tone that rang round the top of the stand at Lord's.

Often his discontent vented itself on the batsmen. A young man was playing a useful, elegant innings. It was pretty cricket, but Porson was not appeased. 'What does he think he's playing at?' he demanded. 'What does he think he's doing? I insist these boys ought to be taught to hit the bloody ball.'

At the close of play we walked down to Baker Street, and Porson became quieter in the hot, calm evening, in the light which softened the faces in the streets. He confided the reason he had been away from London. A girl half his age had fallen in love with him, and they had been staying together by the sea. 'The way it began was the most wonderful thing that has ever happened to me,' he said. 'She was old —'s secretary, and I used to borrow her sometimes. Not that I need a secretary nowadays. Ah well, she came in one morning, and I hadn't the least idea, my boy. She just threw her arms round my neck and said she loved me. I couldn't believe it, I told her that she wanted a nice young man who'd make her a decent husband. She said she wanted me. She thought that I was so clever and so masterful and so kind. And she was sure I ought to have been happy if some woman hadn't treated me badly. She thought she could make it up for me.' He looked at me with an expression humble, bewildered, incredulous. 'I tell you, my boy, I do believe she loved me a little. I've chased a few women, but I don't think that's ever happened to me before. I've been glad if they've liked me. I've been prepared to pay for my fun and when they got tired I've sent them away with a bit of jewellery and a smack on the behind.'

We walked on a few steps. He said:

'I hope I haven't done the girl any harm. She wasn't really my cup of tea. Ah well, she's not losing much. It can't matter much to anyone, losing me.'

He insisted on taking me to the Savoy and giving me a lavish dinner. I could not refuse, for fear of reminding him that now I was comfortably off and that he was living on his capital. He exulted in being generous; it gave him an overbearing pleasure to press food and drink on me. 'You can use another drink,' he kept on saying. 'And so can I. By God, we'll have another bottle of champagne.'

Soon he became drunk, vehemently drunk. He abandoned himself to hates and wishes. He boasted of the things he could still do; there was still time to gain triumphs at the Bar and, he said, 'show them how wrong they are. Show them just where their bloody intrigues and prejudices have led them. Just because I'm not a pansy or a Jew they've preferred to ignore me. I tell you, my lad, you've got to be a pansy or a Jew to get a chance in this bloody country.' Drunkenly he saw lurid, romantic conspiracies directed at himself; drunkenly he talked politics. It was the crudest kind of reactionary politics, inflamed by drink, hate, and failure. He talked of women: he boasted of his conquests now, instead of speaking as he had done on the way to Baker Street. Boastfully he talked of nights in the past. Yet his tongue was far less coarse than when he talked politics, less coarse than most men's when talking sex. He was a man whom people disliked for being aggressive, boastful, rancorous, and vulgar; he was all those things; but, when he thought of women, he became delicate, diffident, and naïf.

Throughout the day, I had not mentioned why I had written to him. Partly because I had an affection for him, and wanted him to feel I was with him for his own sake: partly because I thought it was not safe to talk while he was in a resentful mood. At last I risked asking when he had last seen Ann. He answered, gently enough, in the spring: he remembered the exact date. I went on to ask whether he knew what she was doing politically nowadays.

He stared at me with an over-intent, over-steady gaze, as though if I moved my head he might fall down. He said: 'If you want to talk about her, you'd better come to my blasted flat. It's only a temporary place, of course. I shall insist on somewhere better soon.'

As we got into the taxi, he repeated, with drunken fury:

'I shall insist on somewhere better soon. It's not the sort of place most of your friends are living in.' He went on: 'I can't talk about her until I've cooled down.'

After he had climbed the shabby stairs of the house in Notting Hill, I looked at his little sitting-room. It was crowded with furniture. There was a glass-fronted bookcase, another glass-fronted case full of china, two tables, a desk, a divan. Yet each piece was dusted and shining: I suddenly realized that he must be obsessively tidy. It might have been the room of a finicky old maid.

On the table by the divan stood a photograph of Ann. She did not photograph well. Her face looked flat, undistinguished, lifeless; there was no sign of the moulding of her cheekbones. Anyone who only knew her from her photograph would not have thought her so much as good-looking. As I turned away, I saw Porson's face. He was still looking at the picture with eyes clouded and bloodshot with drink, and his expression was rapt.

'You loved her very much, didn't you?' I said.

He did not reply immediately. Then he said:

'I still do.'

He added.

'I think I always shall.'

A little later, he said:

'I should like to tell you something. It may sound incredible to you, but I should like to tell you. I believe she'll come to me some day. She can't be happy with her husband. She's loyal, she's told me that she is happy, but I've never credited it. Anyway, she knows that I'm waiting for her if ever she wants to come. She knows that I'd do anything for her. By God, she knows that will always be true.'

He wanted us both to start drinking again, but I dissuaded him.

We sat on the divan and I led him back to my question about Ann's political actions. His face became sullen and pained.

'I never liked them, of course. But I attribute them entirely to her blasted husband. If she were really happy with him, she would have given them up. It stands to reason. If she had married me, I believe I should have made her happy, and these things wouldn't have interested her any more. I insist on attributing them to that blasted March.' He told me many facts about her, most of which I knew.

Then he told me something which I did not know – that she was one of the group that produced the *Note*. The *Note* was a private news-sheet, cyclostyled like an old-fashioned school magazine, distributed through the post, on the model of one or two others of that time. It was run by an acquaintance of mine called Humphrey Seymour; he was a communist, but he had been born into the ruling world and still moved within it. In fact, the charm of the *Note* (it was subscribed to by many who had no idea of its politics) was that its news seemed to come from right inside the ruling world. Some of the news, so Porson told me, was provided by Ann.

'Of course she can go anywhere,' he said. 'She was brought up in the right places, and she's got the entrée wherever she wants. And I don't put that down to the Jews, I might tell you. It's just because she makes herself liked wherever she goes.'

Ronald Porson was still doing the detective work of love; he followed her track from dinner-party to dinner-party;

often he could see where she had picked up a piece of information for use in the *Note*.

'That's why I had to refuse her something for the first time in my life,' he said.

'Why?' It did not seem likely to be interesting: the heavy drunken sentiment was wearing me down.

'She's an honourable person, isn't she?'

I nodded, but he came back at me fiercely.

'I don't want to be humoured,' he shouted. 'Despite her blasted politics, isn't she the soul of honour, yes or no?'

I thought, and gave a serious answer.

'Yes.'

'And I am too, aren't I? Damn you, am I an honourable man, yes or no?'

'Yes.' Again, in a curious sense, it was dead true.

'Well then. The last time I saw her, I told you it was in the spring, she wanted to see me at short notice. That's what she'll do when she comes back to me. And she reminded me that I once found out some pretty stories about that shyster Getliffe – found out how he'd played the markets and laughed at decent people who respect positions of trust and got away with the whole blasted shoot. Well, Ann wanted all the details. She told me – that's where her honour comes in, that's where she'd never think of going behind my back – is that true, yes or no?'

After I had answered, his voice quietened, and he said: 'She asked me for the details. She told me that she might want to use them.'

He was by this time speaking in a throbbing whisper, but it seemed loud.

'I couldn't give her them,' said Ronald Porson. He wiped trickles of sweat from his cheeks. 'I've not refused her anything before, but I couldn't do that. I didn't like refusing, but it stuck in my gullet to help that blasted group of reds. I insist they've got at her, of course. She's always had a good heart and they've taken advantage of it. I insist on putting the blame on to them and her blasted husband. And I refuse to help them impose on her. I've never said no to anything she's asked me before, but I couldn't stomach helping those reds in their blasted games. I've no use for Getliffe, he's a bloody charlatan and a bloody crook, and the sooner he's exposed the better. But I insist that the reds aren't the people to do it.' He paused. 'I was tempted when she asked me. I don't want to say no to her again. Ah well! I expect she understands.

Chapter 32

TWO KINDS OF SELF-CONTROL

THE next morning I rang up Ann and asked if I could see her at once. The same evening I arrived at Antrobus Street at half past six, in the middle of Charles's surgery hour. She was waiting for me in her drawing-room; outside the house was dingy, but the room struck bright. It was her own taste, I thought, as I glanced at the Dufys on the cream-papered walls. She herself looked both calm and pretty. Her first words were: 'We know what you've come for, don't we?' She gazed at me with steady blue eyes, without expression. I said.

'Do you? It will be easier if you do.'

'It can't be very easy, can it?'

'How in God's name,' I said, 'did you come to get into this mess?'

'No.' She sounded more equable and business-like than I did; she was not going to begin on those terms. 'It isn't as simple as that.'

I settled myself to wait for her.

'I suppose,' I said, 'you haven't decided what to do?'

'We're not certain yet.'

She was saying 'we' again. Business-like as she sounded, she was making it clear that Charles knew everything. She was glad to bring him in. It was the only sign of emotion she had shown so far.

'Of course,' she said, 'you've come about the Getliffe affair?'

I nodded.

'I knew it.'

'You've been mixed up in that, haven't you?' I asked.

'Oh yes.'

'Didn't you see what it was going to mean?'

235

She was unmoved. 'Not everything, no,' she said.

'I can't understand what you were trying to do.'

'I'm not sure,' she said, 'how much I can tell you.'

'I don't even understand what the line is,' I said.

Deliberately I was using a bit of her own jargon. She looked at me, knowing that I was not unsophisticated politically, knowing that I had an idea how 'the party' went about its work.

She began to explain, keeping back little, so far as I could judge, though some of the manoeuvres still puzzled me. The 'line', she said, I ought to know: it was to get rid of this government and rally all the anti-fascists to do so, whoever they were, Churchillites, middle-of-the-roaders, labour people, intellectuals. Unless we did just that, this government would sell the pass altogether, she said. Unless we got rid of it, Hitler and his fascists would have power on a scale no one had had before: that meant the end of us all, liberals and men of good will, Gentiles and Jews.

'Jews first,' said Ann in a neutral tone. 'Mr March and his friends might remember that.'

She looked at me and said:

'The point is, we've got to get people acting now. You can't disagree about that, can you?'

'No,' I said. I was speaking out of conviction. 'I can't disagree with that.'

'There isn't much time,' she said.

That was where the *Note* got its orders. Its job was to damage personal credit: it was to chase any scandal anywhere near the government, or even the chance of any scandal. It was not to run straight into libels, but it would take risks that an ordinary newspaper would not. Oddly enough, it was better placed than an ordinary newspaper to collect some kinds of scandal: Ann and another colleague and Seymour himself most of all had acquaintances deep in official society, at nearly all levels except at the very top.

Yet, I began to ask her, what were they hoping for? A few thousand cyclostyled sheets – what was the circulation of the paper?

'Nineteen thousand,' she said.

A bit of scandal going to a few thousand people – what was the use of that?

'It helps,' she said. Once more she spoke without expression, with the absence of outward emotion which had surprised, and indeed harassed me, since I arrived. Nevertheless I felt within her a kind of satisfaction which those who only look on at politics never reach. It was a satisfaction made up of a sense of action, of love of action, and of humility. It did not occur to her to argue that the *Note*'s significance was greater than it seemed, that its public was an influential one, that what it said in its messy sheets got round. No: this was the job she had been set, and she was devoted to it. It was as humble as that.

Early in the year, she told me, someone had collected a piece of gossip about Hawtin, the man Mr March had mentioned. Hawtin, like Sir Philip, was a parliamentary secretary: but, unlike Sir Philip, he was not an old man getting his last job, but a young one on the rise. He also happened to be a focus of detestation for the left. The gossip was that he had made money because he knew where an armaments contract was to be placed. But Seymour and his friends, Ann said, could not prove it. They could not get at him; they tried all their usual sources, but found nothing to go on. I gathered that one or two of their sources were shady, and some not so much shady as irregular in a most unexpected way: I was almost sure they had an informant in the civil service. When they were at a loss, someone discovered that Hawtin, who was a lawyer by profession, had once had business dealings with Herbert Getliffe. It was then that Ann recalled what she had heard against Getliffe years before. At once she brought out the stories in the *Note* office: this had been a real scandal, she could track it down and get it tied and labelled.

'Why didn't you remember?' I said.

'What was there to remember?'

'Didn't you think how Philip March's name kept coming in, when we were all worried before Katherine's wedding?'

237

'I didn't give it a thought,' she replied.

'Why not?'

'I had plenty of things against him, but I could never have imagined he'd have got mixed up in a wretched business like this, could you have done?'

I took her at her word. I asked her:

'But you must have imagined that if you dug up the Getliffe affair –'

'What do you mean?'

'If you did that, it was coming close to home.'

I meant that it would damage Katherine through her husband: Ann knew what I meant, and did not pretend.

'I thought of that, of course I did. But we wanted the exact dope on Getliffe just as a lead-in to the job. It was a good time ago, I didn't think we should want to use it.'

'Did you think there was a risk?'

She looked straight at me.

'Yes, I thought there was a risk. I didn't think it was very real.'

'Are they going to use it?' I asked.

'I don't know. It's possible.'

'How possible?'

'It's just about as likely as not.'

All the time I had been with her, I had had a feeling that I scarcely knew her at all. It was not her politics that struck so strange: I expected all that. I expected her sense of duty. It was not that she had been unfriendly or ambiguous. On the contrary, she had been precise, direct, completely in command of herself. It had been I who was showing the temper and wear-and-tear. What made her seem so strange was just that control. Her voice had not given a quiver of strain. Her head had stayed erect, unnaturally still, as though the muscles of her neck were stiff.

To my astonishment, she did not know the exact position about the original Getliffe scandal. Porson had refused to tell her the details, and she had not discovered them from anyone else: when she failed, the *Note* had set another person on the same search. It was characteristic of them that she had not been told whom he had been talking to, or whether he had got all the facts. I asked again if the *Note* were going to use the story. She gave the same answer as before.

'Can it be stopped?' I broke out.

'I could go to Humphrey Seymour —'

'You'd better not waste any time.'

'I don't want to go unless it's necessary.'

She meant: this was her work, these people were her allies, it was bitter to get in their way.

'It's irresponsible,' I said, 'not to go to him at once.'

'We've got different ideas of responsibility, haven't we?'

'Not so completely different,' I said. 'If your people really begin splashing Philip March's name about, you know what it will mean.'

'I haven't any special concern for Philip,' she said. 'He's a reactionary old man. If he has had his fingers in this business, then he deserves what comes to him.'

'I wasn't thinking so much of him.' I paused. 'But Mr March?'

She replied:

'You know what happened between us. Since then I haven't felt that he had any claim on me.'

I paused again. Then I said:

'Have you thought what it would mean for Charles?'

Her eyes stayed steady, looking into mine. For a second I totally misread her face. She had spoken of Mr March in a reasonable tone, but one hardened, I thought, with resentment, the memory of an injustice still fresh. Her eyes were sparkling; she seemed just about to smile. Instead her throat and cheeks reddened: her brow went smooth with anger. At last her control had broken, and she said:

'I won't tolerate any interference between Charles and me. Go and make your own wife love you as much as I love Charles. If she's capable of recognizing who you are. Then I might listen to anything you say about my marriage.'

I did not speak.

Ann said: 'I'm sorry. That was an unforgivable thing to say.'

Slowly – I was not thinking of her or Charles – I replied:
'You wouldn't have said it unless –' I stopped, my own
thoughts ran away with me. I made another effort: 'Unless
you were afraid of what you might do to Charles.'

We both sat silent. I was leaning forward, my chin in my
hands. I scarcely noticed that she had crossed the room
until I felt her arm round my shoulders.

'I'm desperately sorry,' she said.

I tried to talk to her again.

'I still think,' I said, 'that you ought to speak to Seymour
pretty soon.'

'It's not easy. Don't you see it's not easy?'

I told her that she would have to do it. She pressed my
hand and went back to her chair. We sat opposite each other,
not speaking again, until Charles came in.

She sprang up. He took her in his arms and kissed her. She
asked how the surgery had gone. He told her something
about a case, his arms still round her, and asked about herself. They were absorbed in each other. No one could have
seen them that night without being moved by the depth and
freshness of their love.

Over his shoulder Charles glanced at me, sitting in the
pool of light from the reading-lamp.

'Hallo,' he said. 'You're looking pale.'

'It's nothing.'

'Are you sure?'

'I tell you, it's nothing. No, I've been talking to Ann about
this Getliffe business.'

He glanced at Ann. 'I expected that was it,' he said.

They sat side by side on the sofa. Without waiting for any
kind of preliminaries, I said:

'I've been telling Ann she ought to go straight to Seymour.'

To my astonishment, Charles began to smile.

'Why is that funny?' I was on edge.

'Did you know he was at school with me? It's strange, I
shouldn't have guessed that he'd crop up again –'

He was still smiling at what seemed to be a memory.

'I'm quite sure,' I said, 'that Ann ought to go round to the *Note* tomorrow.'

'That's getting a bit frantic, isn't it?' Charles said, in a friendly tone.

I could not help overstating my case. 'Tomorrow,' I repeated, getting more emphatic because I could not find a reason.

'You don't want to go along unless it's the last resort, do you?' said Charles to Ann, and their eyes met in trust.

The curious thing was, Charles did not seem much worried. Ann was so torn that she had said something I should not be able to forget. That apart, I was acutely anxious. Yet Charles, who was himself given to anxiety, who had much more foresight than most men, seemed almost immune from what was affecting us. True, he was much further from politics than Ann was, a good deal further even than I was myself. Nevertheless, it was strange to see him so unruffled, giving us the drinks which, in the grip of the argument, Ann had not thought of. With a kind of temperate irritation, he said:

'I must say, the thing which I really dislike is that we misled Mr L. Quite unintentionally, of course, but it's the sort of thing any of us would dislike, wouldn't they?'

He meant, when Mr March told him of the rumours about Sir Philip and he had said that neither he nor Ann had any knowledge of them. It had been true then: at the time, Ann was trying to find out about Getliffe and no one but Getliffe. But it would not have been true a week or two later.

'I've explained the position to him now, of course,' he said.

'Did he accept it?' I asked.

'As much as he could accept anything,' said Charles.

'When did you talk to him?'

Charles gave me the date. I had seen Mr March since, but he had not mentioned a word about it.

'I also explained Ann's connexion with the *Note*,' said Charles. 'I thought it was right to do that.'

For a few seconds it was all quiet. Then Ann said to him:

'Look, if you think Lewis is right and I ought to tell the *Note* about it –'

'It means making a private plea, doesn't it? And you wouldn't want to unless it's really dangerous?'

'Of course I shouldn't want to.' She added, talking to him as though I was not there: 'I'll do it tomorrow if you think I ought to.'

Suddenly I felt that she wanted him to tell her to. He was hesitating. He could have settled it for her, but he seemed reluctant or disinclined.

He knew, of course, better than I did how much political action, the paper itself, meant to her. But it was not only consideration and empathy that held him back. Nearly all the Marches, seeing his hesitation, would have had no doubt about it: he was under her influence, she was the stronger, he did what she told him.

The truth was just the opposite. Often he behaved to her, as now, with what seemed to many people an exaggerated consideration, a kind of chivalry which made one uncomfortable. But the reason was not that he was her slave, but that she was his. She adored him: at the heart of their marriage she was completely in his power. It was out of a special gratitude, it was to make a kind of amend, that he was driven to consider her so, in things which mattered less.

To understand his hesitation just then, one needed to have been present that night when Mr March accused her of 'wearing the trousers' – and Charles's smile, unpredictable as forked lightning, lit up the room.

'If you think I ought to,' she said.

'You mustn't decide anything now,' he said, with deliberation, with careful sense. 'But there might be a time when you'll have to, mightn't there?'

Chapter 33

SUMMER NIGHT

AFTER that night I did not hear whether Ann had made her explanations to the *Note*. On my way down to Hasling-field, a fortnight later, I took with me a file of the paper: I wanted to know what legal risks they ran.

It was on a Saturday afternoon that I arrived at Hasling-field. I found Mr March occupied with Katherine's children, telling me that he had had no fresh news from Philip and at the same time rolling a ball along the floor for his grand-son to run after. It was a wet, warm summer day and the windows of the drawing-room stood open. The little boy was aged four, and his fair hair glistened as he scampered after the ball. His sister, aged two, was crawling round Mr March's legs. Mr March rolled the ball again, and told them they were 'making frightful asses of themselves'.

Gazing at them, Mr March said to Katherine and me:

'I must say they look remarkably Anglo-Saxon.'

Each of the children had the March eyes, and it seemed that they would stay fair.

Mr March went on:

'They look remarkably unlike the uglier members of our family. Hannah says that everyone in the family is more presentable when young, but I told her that she must have forgotten Caroline's children in their infancy.'

Katherine chuckled. She and her father were not only be-coming fonder of each other, but the bond of sympathy between them seemed to grow stronger each time I saw them. She was pregnant again, and he had insisted that she came to Haslingfield during July, 'on the firm undertaking', as he wrote to her, 'that you attempt to run the household, though I have never concealed my lack of faith in your abilities in that direction, until a date when your attention is distracted by other developments'.

Actually, she ran the household so that it was more comfortable than I remembered: since her marriage, she had cultivated a talent for comfort. Not even Mr March kept a closer eye on one's physical whims, frailties, likes and dislikes.

That evening, as we waited before dinner for Mr March, I was presented with a Moselle which she had noticed me enjoy on my first visit to Haslingfield, when Charles and Ann were within a few hours of meeting.

Katherine said: 'You remember that night, don't you, Lewis? I was tremendously excited because Francis was coming next day. And you made a remark which might have meant that you guessed I was in love. I lay awake a bit that night wondering whether you really intended it. Francis says that was probably the only sleep he's ever cost me. But I remind him that it was only for an hour.'

She was content. Her third child was due in early August; with Mr-March-like precision, she announced the probable day with a margin of error plus or minus. Also like Mr March, she harried her doctors, wanted to know the reasons for their actions, and would not be put off by bedside patter. Francis had told me some stories about her that were very much in her father's line, full of the same physical curiosity and the same assumption that a doctor is someone whose time you pay for, and whose advice you consider rather as you would an electrician's when he brings a new type of bulb. 'I don't believe you treat doctors in her fashion,' Francis had said, 'unless you have been born scandalously rich.'

Katherine denied it. But as a rule she was content to follow his lead. Just as she had once accepted her brother's opinions, now she accepted her husband's. She had resisted everyone's attempts to educate her: first Charles's, and then Francis's, with some irregular incursions of my own.

Yet I often felt that she had matured faster than any of us.

In a way singularly like her father's after he retired from business, she had become at twenty-seven completely, solidly, and happily herself.

Her anxieties now were all about her chidren. Her self-conscious moments were so mild that she laughed at them. After one of her dinner parties she would keep Francis awake wondering if a remark of hers had been misunderstood, and why a pair of guests left at a quarter past ten; she worked round and round her speculations with the family persistence; the habit remained but the edge had gone.

On this night at Haslingfield, though she kept saying every ten minutes: 'Charles promised to ring up about coming down tomorrow. I'm getting into a state. It will be intolerable if he forgets', it was nothing but the residue of the old habit.

At last the telephone bell rang in the hall, and the butler told her that Mr Charles was asking for her. Having seen her run to the telephone so many times, I found it strange to wait while she walked upright, slow, eight months gone.

Katherine returned and said that Charles was hoping to come down for dinner on the following night, but would have to get back to London to sleep. 'Whether that's because of his practice or Ann I couldn't tell,' she said. 'I should think it's because of Ann, shouldn't you?' Her face became thoughtful and hard. For a moment she looked set, determined, middle-aged. 'That takes me back again to the first time you came here. You realize that I invited Ann specially for you, don't you? I definitely hoped you'd make a match of it. I thought she might be attractive enough to distract you from Sheila. I never thought of her for Charles at all.' She looked at me intently. 'Well, Lewis, my dear, I believe my scheme might have been better for everyone. I know I oughtn't to talk about Sheila, but you must realize that your friends hate to see her eating your life away. And on the other hand, if you had married Ann, you would have kept her in order. She wouldn't have tried to make a different man of you as she's tried with Charles. Yes, it would have been better if my scheme had come off.'

*

The warm, wet wind lashed round the house all Sunday, and I spent the whole day indoors. In the morning I talked for an hour with Mr March alone. He said that Philip was now convinced that the gossip had blown itself out, and accordingly did not consider it worth while to discuss 'ancient history' in the shape of the Howard & Hazlehurst dealings in 1929. Mr March was left apprehensive. I wished I could have told him that Ann and Charles had settled his worries. But I did say that there might be good news for him soon.

After lunch I sat in the library reading the file of the *Note* which I had brought down. The issues ran from the middle of 1935 to the week before; I read with attention, forgetting the beat of rain against the windows and the howl of the wind. I found nothing in the way of a financial accusation, except one tentative hint. But there was a series of facts, bits of personal information, quoted sayings, about people in the circles where Sir Philip moved, the circles of junior ministers, permanent secretaries, chairmen of large firms. Some of the facts I recognized, and I had heard some of the sayings: I knew them to be accurate.

I had tea brought up to the library, and went on reading. In some numbers it was not hard to guess which pieces of information Ann had brought in. Occasionally I thought I could see the hands of other acquaintances. I was making notes, for I thought there was no harm in being prepared when Katherine came in with Charles. 'He's just driven down through the wretched rain,' she said. 'I told him you'd been appallingly unsociable all afternoon.'

Charles came over to my chair and saw what I was reading. 'I didn't know he had such a passion for political information, did you?' he said to Katherine.

He seemed quite untroubled.

'Have you noticed,' he asked me, 'how many of their predictions actually come off?'

'Too many,' I said.

He turned to Katherine. 'Ann does a good deal for it, did you realize that?' He spoke casually, but with affection and pride.

'I take the rag,' said Katherine, 'but I hadn't the slightest idea.'

'I don't suppose you read it,' Charles teased her. 'Do you make Francis read it aloud in bed? Don't you agree that's the only way you ever read anything at all?'

Mr March had come into the room behind them.

'I assume that your lucubrations have been completely disturbed by my family,' he said to me. 'I suggest that it would be considerably less sepulchral in the drawing-room. I don't remember such a July since Hannah came to stay in 1912. She said that she wouldn't have noticed the weather so much in her own house, but that didn't prevent her from outstaying her invitation.'

There were only a few minutes before dinner when I could talk to Charles alone. No, he said, Ann had not yet appealed to Seymour. No, so far as Ann knew, the *Note* had not got any usable facts about Getliffe or anyone else. Yes, she would call the *Note* off for good and all; she was seeing Seymour next week; there was nothing to worry about.

All evening the talk was gay and friendly. Charles showed how glad he was to meet Katherine; he was demonstratively glad, more so than she. His manner to his father was easy, as though they had come together again after all that had happened – come together, not as closely as in the past, but on a new friendly footing where neither of them was making much demand. It was Charles's wish that they should stay like this.

Mr March responded at dinner, more brilliantly even than when I last saw him and Charles together. It was the suspicious and realistic, I thought, who were most easy to reassure. It was the same in love : the extravagantly jealous sometimes needed only a single word to be transported into absolute trust.

Keeping up his liveliness, Mr March told a story of someone called Julian Baring, 'a man I like very much if I am not under the obligation of meeting him'. Then I discovered at last the secret of Mr March's Sunday night attire. The first time I went to Haslingfield, I had noticed with astonishment that on the Sunday night he wore a dinner jacket over his morning trousers and waistcoat. I had stayed there on a good many Sundays since, and I found this to be his invariable custom. Somehow I had never been able to enquire why, but this evening I did, and learned, through Mr March's protestations, shouts, stories, and retorts to his children, that it was his way of lessening the servants' Sunday work. The servants, as I knew, were always Gentiles. Mr March thought it proper that they should go to church on Sunday evening: and he felt that they would get there quicker if they had to put out only his jacket instead of a whole suit.

We went on talking of the March servants. All of them, like Mr March's, were Gentiles. They moved from house to house within the family (for instance, Mr March's butler had started as a footman in Sir Philip's house). They seemed to become more snobbish about the family reputation than the Marches themselves. When Katherine married Francis, some of them protested to her maid – what a comedown it was! To them it was shameful that she had not made a brilliant match. They thought back with regret to the days when the March households had been full of opulent, successful guests. Mr March's servants in particular could not forgive Charles and Katherine for bringing to Bryanston Square and Haslingfield no one but young men like Francis and myself, without connexions, without wardrobes, instead of the titles, the money, the clothes, which brought a thrill into their lives and which they felt in a position to expect.

Most of these accounts came through Katherine's maid. Mr March guffawed as he heard them, but with a nostalgia of his own.

We listened, as we could not help doing that month, to the nine o'clock news. When the items about the Spanish war had finished, Charles switched off the wireless and both he and I were silent. Mr March looked at us, becoming irascible as he saw our concern. He said loudly:

'I say, a plague on both your houses.'

'You don't really say that,' said Charles. 'It wouldn't be quite so dangerous if you did.'

'I repeat,' retorted Mr March, 'it's six of one and half a dozen of the other.'

'It's as clear an issue,' said Charles, 'as we shall have in our time.'

'You're only indulging in this propaganda,' cried Mr March, 'because of the influence of your connexions.'

'No,' I put in. 'I should say exactly the same. I'm afraid I should say more, Mr L. I believe this is only the beginning. The next ten or twenty years aren't going to be pretty.'

'You're all succumbing to a bad attack of nerves,' said Mr March.

Charles said with a grin:

'I don't think so. But remember I've got some reason to be nervous. If it does come to the barricades, Ann will insist, of course, on fighting herself. But she'll also insist on making me fight too.'

Katherine and I laughed, but Mr March merely smiled with his lips. He was preoccupied; his voice, instead of being animated, went flat, as though the mind behind it was being dragged away, dragged from question to question. Charles rose to go. He said goodbye affectionately to his father, and very warmly to Katherine, whom he did not expect to see until her child was born; I went down with him to his car. It was still raining, and a wild night. Charles was in a hurry to get back home by midnight, as he had promised Ann. I mentioned that I wanted to have another word with her, and he said, casually and in entire friendliness, how much she would like that. Then he drove off. I stood for some moments watching the tail-lamp of his car dwindling down the drive.

The next day passed quietly until the late evening. The afternoon was a fine interval among the storms, and I walked in the grounds. When I returned for tea, I found a professional letter had just arrived, which occupied me for a couple of hours. I noticed, without giving it a second thought, that the same post had brought Katherine one or two letters, as well as her daily one from Francis.

After dinner, when we moved into the drawing-room, Katherine rested on a sofa. Mr March was talking to her about her children. Both of them gained satisfaction from providing against unlikely contingencies in the years ahead. The curtains were not drawn yet, the sky was still bright at ten o'clock. It was pleasant to bask there, listening to Mr March, while the short summer night began to fall.

Then Katherine remembered her afternoon mail.

'The only letter I've opened is my husband's,' she said comfortably. 'Being in this state makes me even more lazy than I usually am. Lewis, will you pander to my condition and fetch in the others?'

As I gave them to her, I saw that one was a long foolscap envelope, with her address in green typescript, and I realized that it was her weekly copy of the *Note*.

She read it last. I felt a flicker of uneasiness, nothing more, as she opened the sheets, and went on chatting to Mr March. Suddenly we heard Katherine's voice, loud and harsh.

'I think you ought to listen to this, Mr L.'

She read, angrily and deliberately:

' "*Armaments and Shares*. As foreshadowed in *Note* (Mar. 24 '36) certain personages close to Government appear interested in armaments programme in more ways than one. Hush-hush talk in Century (exclusive City luncheon club, HQ 22 Farringdon St), Jewish candidates quietly blackballed, president George Wyatt, co-director of Sir Horace (Cartel-spokesman) Timberlake – (see *Note*, Nov. 17 '35, Feb. 2 '36, Apr. 15 '36), that heavy killings made through inside knowledge (official) armaments contracts, both '35 (Abyssinian phony scare) and '29. E.g. '29 Herbert Getliffe

KC employed Jan. 2–June 6, advice WO contract Howard & Hazelhurst: £10,000 worth H. & H. bought name of G. L. Paul, May 30, £15,000 worth H. & H. F. E. Paul, June 2, G. L. and F. E. Paul brothers H. Getliffe's wife. Usual lurkman technique (see *Note*, Feb. 9 '36). Have junior ministers, names canvassed in Century, also used lurkmen? Allow for Century's anti-Semitism. But *Note* satisfied background hush-hush scandal. Story, transactions, dates, ministers, later." '

The room was quiet. Then Mr March cried out:

'My son has done this.'

Katherine said: 'It's an outrage. It must be Ann. Don't you agree that it must be Ann? Charles told me that she wrote for them –'

Mr March said: 'He must have known her intentions and he is responsible for it all. He is responsible for it all.'

I broke in:

'I'm sure that is not true. God knows this is bad enough. But I'm sure neither of them knew it was coming. Charles knew nothing last night. Unless he's read this thing today, he still knows nothing now.'

'How can you speak for my son?' Mr March shouted.

I said: 'If he has done this he would have told you. He couldn't have made himself speak to you as he did last night, if he knew this was on the way. It's not in his nature.'

I had spoken with insistence, and Mr March sat silent, huddled in his chair, his chin sunk in his breast.

I had to go on speaking. I tried to explain, without making excuses for Ann, what had happened. I said that she was on the point of going to the *Note* and asking them to keep the story out. After the threat at the end of this piece, it was imperative to say nothing which might make it harder for her.

Mr March gave a sullen nod of acquiescence, but he was looking at me as though I were an enemy, not a friend.

He said: 'I shall judge my son by his actions now. That is all that I can do.'

Katherine said: 'This is her fault. She's not content with crippling Charles. Now she's trying to damage the rest of us. I wish to God she'd never set foot in this house.'

Mr March said quietly:

'I wished that the first moment I saw her. I have never been able to forgive him for marrying her.'

Chapter 34

ANSWER TO AN APPEAL

As soon as I arrived back in London, I telephoned to Ann. She had already seen the issue, she said, and spoken to Seymour. He had guaranteed that nothing more would be published on the story for four weeks: he was himself going to Paris for a fortnight, picking up news, but he would be ready to discuss the problem with her as soon as he returned, and with Charles also if he liked to come along.

'You'll do it,' I said, 'the minute he gets back?'

'Of course.'

'He's not putting you off while he slips something in?'

'He wouldn't do that to me.' Her reply sounded constrained, on the defensive: she did not like my being so suspicious: she could feel that I suspected something else. I thought it more likely than not that Seymour had already got the first piece in without giving her a chance to see it. She resented any such thought: when she gave her trust, as she did to Seymour, she gave it without reserve. Yet she went on to ask me a favour: when she and Charles arranged the meeting with Seymour, would I come too? I was puzzled: what use could I be, I said. She stuck to it. She said, as was true, that I had given Seymour legal advice once or twice; on some things, she went on, he might listen to me.

When Seymour got back, he raised no objection. On the contrary, he rang up on the day they had fixed for the talk, and invited me himself, in his high-spirited, easy, patrician voice. I might even call for him after dinner at the *Note* office, he suggested.

So I duly climbed the five flights of stairs, in the murk and the smell of shavings and mildew. The *Note* office was at the top of a house just off the Charing Cross Road: on the other floors were offices of art photographers, dingy solicitors, something calling itself a trading company: on the fifth landing, in two rooms, was produced – not only edited but set up, duplicated, and distributed – the *Note*. In one of the rooms a light was burning, as Seymour's secretary was still working there, at half past eight. She was working for nothing, as I knew, a prettyish girl with a restless smile. Humphrey (she enjoyed being in the swim, calling him by his Christian name) had been called away, she said, but he was expecting us all at his flat in Dolphin Square.

When at last I got there, he was alone. He was a short, cocky, confident man, nearly bald, although he was no older than Charles; he was singularly ugly, with a mouth so wide that it gave him a touch of the grotesque. His manner was warm and amiable. He put a drink into my hand and led me outside on to the terrace; his flat was high up in the building, and from the terrace one could look down over all western London, the roofs shining into the sunset. But Seymour did not look down: he did not refer to why I was there: he just launched, with a kind of obsessive insistence mixed with his habitual jauntiness, into what he had been hearing in Paris, whom he had seen, what he had been learning about the Spanish war. When I made a remark, he kept up a sighing noise which indicated that he had more to say.

At last I managed to get in my own preoccupation. He was an easy man to be off-hand with, because he was so off-hand and confident himself. I said:

'What about this campaign?'

'What campaign?'

'The one that Ann March and Charles are coming about.'

'Oh that.' He gave a gnome-like grin.

'Why did you start on Philip March at all?'

'Do you think we're really interested in him?' said Seymour with cheerful contempt. 'He's never been more than a city figurehead. No, the chaps we're really interested in are Hawtin and his pals. I think we might be able to put them on the spot, don't you?'

I asked him – what facts had he really got hold of? About

Philip March? About Hawtin? What facts were there, beside those about the Getliffe dealings?

Seymour grinned again, but did not answer. Instead he said:

'Should you say old March cut any ice among that gang?' ('That gang' meant the people who had the real power, the rulers, the establishment: Seymour, like other communists I knew, had a habit of breaking into a curious kind of slang: from him, in his cultivated tone, it sounded odd.)

'That's the sort of thing *you* know,' I said.

'Hawtin's quite a different cup of tea,' said Seymour. 'Now he does cut some ice, and if we get his blood the rest of the gang will feel it, won't they now?'

I asked again, what facts had he got about Hawtin? And when was the next instalment due to appear? To the second question, he gave a straight answer. Not for some weeks. They were not ready yet. If they had to delay for months rather than weeks, he might repeat what he had already printed – 'just to remind some of our friends that we're still thinking about them.'

It was the same answer as he had given to Ann: so there was time, I thought. Meanwhile, as we waited for Ann and Charles, Seymour went on talking, dismissing the 'Hawtin racket', elated and obsessed by 'stories' which, to him, mattered out of comparison more.

Below us, the haze of London was changing from blue to grey as night fell, and through the haze the lights were starting out. From second to second a new light quivered through, now in the Pimlico streets beneath us, now on the skyline. Soon there was a galaxy of lights. It made me think of the press of human lives, their struggles and their peace.

The bell of Seymour's flat rang, and on his way to open the door he switched on his own lights. Outside in the passage were standing Ann and Charles. Seymour grinned up at Charles.

'Late bill,' he said. It was a recognition-symbol, a token of their days at school: I had heard Seymour use it before as a kind of upper-class pass-word.

As we sat down, all of us except Seymour were unrelaxed: but he, just as confidently as he had done with me, started talking: his trip, the 'lowdown' which he had collected, he went on just as with me. It took Ann an effort to say:

'Look, Humphrey, do you mind if we get this over!'

Her voice was tight. I could feel how much she respected him. On his side, he was at once polite and considerate. 'Of course, we'd better if you want to,' he said with a kind, friendly, praising smile.

'I think I've got to bring up this Philip March story,' she said.

'Right,' said Seymour.

Though she looked strained, she began her appeal with extreme lucidity. It was agreed by everyone, wasn't it, she said, that Philip March had had nothing whatever to do with any recent dealings? Seymour nodded his head. Philip March was absolutely in the clear, she said; last year's rumours had nothing to do with him? Seymour nodded. If she herself hadn't brought in the name of Herbert Getliffe, and an almost forgotten piece of gossip, no one would have remotely considered any smear against Philip March?

'Absolutely true,' said Seymour. 'I was just telling Lewis, he never seriously counted, with all due respect to your family, Charles.'

He was sitting back with one leg crossed over the other. For all his cockiness and the tincture of the grotesque, he was a man in whom one could feel authority. It was an authority that did not come just from his commitment, from his position in the party: it was the authority of his nature. Even Charles, leaning forward on the sofa, watching him with hard eyes, paid attention to it. Certainly Ann, more given than Charles to admit authority in others, recognized it. She sat with her backbone straight as a guardsman's by Charles's side, and said 'Well then, I shouldn't ask for anything impossible. I shouldn't ask to call off anything that was important. But it isn't important, is it? I didn't even know that anyone would think it worth while to revive the Getliffe business. I should have thought it was too long ago to count.

I should have thought whatever Philip March did or didn't do at that time, it was too long ago to count. And anyway it's more obscure than the Getliffe business, we couldn't get it cut and dried. I think there would be pretty strong arguments for leaving him alone, in any case. But of course we want him left alone because it's bound to affect my husband's family. It's not often that one can ask for special treatment, is it? I think I can, this time.'

Seymour smiled at her, and said:

'There isn't any such thing as private news, is there?'

She repeated 'I think I can, this time', because his tone was so light that it did not sink in. It took her seconds to realize that he had turned her down flat.

Charles had realized at once. In a harsh and angry voice he said:

'You admit that you've got no foundation at all for any scandal last year – as far as my uncle is concerned. You admit the same about Herbert Getliffe, don't you? Is there any foundation for the scandal at all, even about this man Hawtin? Or are you just wishing that it happened?'

'I don't know,' said Seymour.

'What do you mean, you don't know?'

'Precisely what I say.'

Bitterly Charles went on with his questions. About 1935 there was nothing proved or provable at all: it seemed most likely that there was nothing in the rumour. But, as Seymour said jauntily, the 1929 dealings were on the record – the transactions of Getliffe's brothers-in-law and, as he hoped to demonstrate, those of Philip March.

'You're proposing to use those, in fact,' said Charles, 'to give a bit of credibility to a sheer lie?'

'That's putting it rather more strongly than I should myself. If there was jiggery-pokery some years ago, there's no reason why there shouldn't have been some last year.'

'But you're really pretty certain that there wasn't?'

Seymour shrugged his shoulders.

'I must say,' said Charles, 'it's more dishonest even than I thought.'

'I shan't have time for your moral sensitivity,' said Seymour, his voice suddenly as passionate as Charles's, 'until we've beaten the fascists and got a decent world.'

In the angry silence I put in:

'If you're seriously proposing to print rumours without even a scrap of evidence, the paper isn't going to last very long, is it?'

'Why in God's name not?'

'What's going to stop a crop of libel actions?'

'The trouble with you lawyers,' said Seymour, jaunty once more, 'is that you never know when a fact is a fact, and you never see an inch beyond your noses. I am prepared to bet any of you, or all three if you like, an even hundred pounds that no one, *no one*, brings an action against us over this business. Trust old Father Mouse and bob's your uncle.'

He went on, enjoying himself:

'While I'm about it, I'm prepared to bet you that the paper never runs into a libel action. You trust old Father Mouse. I'm nothing like as wild and woolly as I seem. No, the only thing that could ever finish the paper is that we might come up against the Official Secrets Act. That's the menace, and if we had bad luck that would be the end. I don't suppose I'm telling any of you anything you don't know. Anyway, Ann's seen how we collect some of our stuff and she must have enough documents in her own desk to finish the poor old paper off in a couple of hours.'

It sounded like an indiscretion, like a piece of his cocksureness. Listening, I believed it was the opposite. He had done it deliberately. He was not the man to underestimate just how competent and ruthless other people could be. He took it for granted that Ann and Charles knew that she had it in her power to kill the paper; he took it for granted too, that, after his refusal, having no other conceivable way to protect Charles's family, they would consider it.

He knew her well. It would have been stupid to hide anything, it was good tactics to bring the temptation into the open, brandish it in front of her and defy her with it. He knew, of course, that she was as much committed to the party as he was himself. Outside her marriage, it was her one devotion. It was so much a devotion – only a religious person could know something similar in kind, perhaps – that she had not been shocked when Seymour admitted that he was fabricating a set of scandals. To Charles, it was a moral outrage. To her, so upright in her own dealings, it was not. Any more, oddly enough, than it was to Seymour himself. Both she and Seymour were believers by nature. At times it gave them a purity and innocence that men like Charles never knew: at times it gave Seymour, and perhaps even Ann, a capacity to do things from which Charles, answering to his own conscience, would have been repelled.

As Seymour told Ann that she could ruin the paper next day, I watched her glance at Charles. Their faces were set, but their eyes met with recognition, with understanding.

They left soon after. I stayed behind, so that they could talk alone the minute they got outside.

Seymour did not say another word about them, or the paper. He had the knack of turning off his attention with a click, as though he had pressed a switch. He did not make a comment. Instead, cheerful and unflagging, he insisted on driving me to White's for a night-cap. There, just for once, his cocksureness let him down. A member whom I faintly knew brought in a guest of distinguished appearance. I asked Seymour who he was.

'Oh, that's Lord Kilmainham,' he said, with supreme confidence.

It was not. Enquiring a little later in the lavatory, I found that the guest was an income-tax accountant.

Chapter 35

THE FUTURE OF TWO OLD MEN

SINCE the first instalment in the *Note*, Charles and Mr March had not met nor spoken to each other. Charles had, however, telephoned to Katherine after the visit to Seymour. He had told her, so I gathered, that Ann had done her best to call the paper off. Whether either Katherine or Mr March believed this, I had no means of judging. But they knew I had been present. Within a few days I received a letter from Mr March, telling me that he needed my 'friendly assistance': would I lunch with him at his club, so that we could go together to Sir Philip's office afterwards.

The club servants were surprised to see Mr March there in the month of August, having got used to the clockwork regularity of his life; he had not left Haslingfield during his summer stay for twenty years. Just as, though he went to the club for tea each day he was in London, he had not lunched there since Charles was a child. He did not know where or how to write his order, and had to be helped by the servants. They teased him for it: he, usually so uncondescending, was gruff with them.

He said little at the meal. We had a table to ourselves, but those round us were soon filled. I saw one or two faces I knew, all of civil servants from the departments close by. I felt that Mr March, unable to talk of the bitter anxiety in his mind, was also depressed because he recognized so few. There were only two men he nodded to, and they were very old.

In Pall Mall, on our way to Sir Philip's ministry, he tried to rouse himself from his gloom. We turned into St James's Park towards Whitehall, and Mr March looked over the trees at the dome of the India Office, the roofs and towers, all soft and opal grey in the moist sunlight.

'I must say,' he remarked, 'that it looks comparatively presentable. But I have never been able to understand the fascination which makes my brother Philip and others wish to spend their entire lives in this neighbourhood. I once said as much to Hannah, and she replied that it was sour grapes on my part. No doubt I was envious on account of my failure to cut any kind of figure in the world. Nevertheless, Lewis, if I hadn't been a failure, and had been given my choice of where to have a reasonable success, I should not have chosen this particular neighbourhood.'

His face darkened in a scowl of misery and anger. 'But my brother Philip did. I cannot endure the thought that, because of these happenings, he may find it harder to continue here.'

In the ministry we were led down the corridors to the office of Sir Philip's secretary, who was a youngish man called Williams, smooth-faced, spectacled, dressed for his job in black coat and striped trousers, and full of self-importance in it. 'I will go and find out when the Parliamentary Secretary will be free,' he said, enjoying the chance to bring out his master's appellation. He came back promptly and announced: 'The Parliamentary Secretary will be glad to see you at once.'

We went through the inside door, and Sir Philip came across his room to meet us. He shook hands with Mr March, then said 'How do you do?' to me with his stiff, furrowed smile. As he sat down at his desk by the window which overlooked the park, I saw that his skin had taken on a yellowness, a matt texture, such as one sometimes sees in ageing men. He was seventy-three, only three years older than Mr March, but in the bright summer light the difference looked much greater.

'I expect you're dying of drought as usual at Haslingfield,' Sir Philip began their ritual of brotherly baiting. 'The country is under water everywhere else.'

'I regard the rainfall as having been reasonable for once,' said Mr March. 'And I am pleased to report that I have sufficient water for my requirements.'

These exchanges went on for a few moments. They had made them for so many years, and Sir Philip at least could not let go of them now: Mr March's replies were forced and mechanical. Sir Philip was, as the afternoon began, by far the less perturbed of the two. Soon he said:

'I suppose we must get down to business. I should like to say, Eliot, that I am obliged to you for giving me your time. I should be glad to regard it as a professional service, of course, but my brother informs me that you are certain to prefer it otherwise. I appreciate your feelings and, as I say, I am obliged to you. I think you know some of the facts of this affair. In May there was some gossip about myself and some of my colleagues. We were alleged to have used our official knowledge during the past twelve months to buy holdings in companies where government contracts were soon going to be laid. This gossip also included some names outside the government, one of them being that fellow Getliffe. It has now been published, or at least a first instalment has. I believe you've seen it?'

I nodded.

'I can answer for myself and my colleagues,' Sir Philip went on. 'So far as we are concerned, there's not a word of truth in it. When I came back into the Government last year, I decided to spend the rest of my life being as useful to the country as I could, if they wanted me. It was a sacrifice, but I believe that some of us have got to accept responsibility. These aren't easy years to hold responsibility: I needn't tell you that.'

Even Sir Philip, I was thinking, could not avoid the expressions of convention, talked about 'sacrifice', perhaps used the word to himself – even Sir Philip, who was not a humbug but a hard and realistic man, who loved office and power and knew that he loved it.

'I was prepared to make the sacrifice,' Sir Philip went on. 'I had to resign my directorships when I became a minister, naturally. I also decided to finish with all speculation. I've already told Leonard this.' He glanced at Mr March.

'I acknowledged your assurance,' said Mr March, 'on

hearing it at your bedside during your period of incapacity owing to gout.'

'I finished with it,' said Sir Philip. 'I am not a rich man, of course, but I can get along. I have not taken part in any single transaction since I entered the government last November. I cannot make such a categorical statement for my colleagues whose names have been bandied about, but I'm completely satisfied that they are clear.'

'You mentioned people outside the government,' I broke in. 'I'm also satisfied in the same way about Getliffe.'

'You mean he's bought nothing in the last twelve months?'

'Nothing that could be thought suspicious.'

'What evidence are you going on?'

'Nothing as definite as yours,' I said. 'But I've talked to him on this actual point, and I know him well.'

'I reported Lewis Eliot's observations on this matter,' said Mr March.

Sir Philip's eyes were bright and alert. 'You're convinced about this fellow Getliffe?'

'Quite convinced,' I said.

'I accept that,' said Sir Philip. 'And it makes me certain that the whole campaign is a put-up job and there's no backing to it at all.'

Mr March, who had been listening with painful attention, showed no relief as he heard these words. He looked at his brother, with an expression stupefied, harassed, distressed.

'That being so,' I said, 'your solicitors are telling you to go ahead with a libel action, aren't they?'

'It's not quite so easy,' Sir Philip replied without hesitation, in a tone as authoritative as before. I admired his hard competence. Professionally, I thought, he would have been an ideal client. 'They've tied up this affair with certain other transactions. The other transactions are supposed to have happened when I was in the government in 1929. You will notice that, in the case of Getliffe, they have taken care to tie these two allegations together. It is clever of them. I detest their politics, I've no use for their general attitude, and if I can put them in their place, I shall – but we mustn't imagine that we are dealing with fools.'

'I have never thought so,' said Mr March.

'If they go ahead with these allegations about last year, I should win a libel action, shouldn't I?' Sir Philip asked me.

'Without the slightest doubt,' I said.

'I should also do myself more harm than good,' he went on.

I was thinking how precisely Seymour had calculated the risk.

'There happens to be some substance in what they say about 1929,' said Sir Philip.

We waited for him to go on.

'I may say at once that I've done nothing which men of decent judgement could think improper. But one step I took in good faith which these people may twist against me. I am very much to blame for giving them such a handle. I've always thought it was not only essential to be honest: it was also essential to seem honest. I take all the blame for not seeing further than my nose. That is the only blame I am disposed to take.'

He paused, and gave a sardonic chuckle.

'I should like to distinguish my actions from Getliffe's quite sharply. In 1929 Getliffe made a disgraceful use of information he had acquired professionally. In my judgement, there is no question of it. He knew the government were giving a contract to Howard & Hazlehurst. He used catspaws to buy a fair-sized block of shares. He must have done very well out of it. Howard & Hazlehurst were down to 9s. in 1929: they stand at 36s. today.'

'Thirty-six and sixpence,' said Mr March, as though by sheer habit.

'Getliffe is a twister and I shouldn't have the faintest compunction about going ahead with a libel action if it only meant involving him. If he were disbarred, I should simply consider that he had brought it on himself. He's downright dishonest, and I was sorry that you' – he turned to Mr

March – 'permitted Katherine to marry into the fellow's family. Though I've always liked Francis from the little I've seen of him.'

Mr March burst out, in violent and excessive anger:

'I refuse to accept that criticism at the present juncture. My son-in-law has made an excellent husband for my daughter Katherine in all respects. I refused at the time to penalize them on account of his regrettable connexions, and I still refuse, despite the fact that Herbert Getliffe's name is linked with yours in these deplorable circumstances. I refuse to accept this preposterous criticism. If other marriages in my family had been as sound as my daughter's, we should not be troubled with the discussion on which we are supposed to be engaged.'

Sir Philip seemed to understand his brother's rage.

'Yes, Leonard,' he said, with an awkward, constrained affection. 'But you can appreciate that Getliffe isn't my favourite character just at present, can't you?' His tone became once more efficient, organized, businesslike. 'My own activities were considerably different from that fellow's. I only spent a few months in the government in 1929, you may remember, but of course I knew of the Howard & Hazlehurst contract, and of course I knew of the trend of policy about armaments. Naturally I thought over the implications, which appeared to suggest that, even at the height of disarmament, certain types of weapon would still have to be developed. So certain firms connected with those types of weapon would flourish for the next few years. That wasn't a foolish piece of reasoning, and I felt entitled to act on it. If one struck lucky, one had a good buy. I looked round at various firms. I found one which was in fairly low water, and I backed my guess. The shares were down somewhere that didn't matter, and I put in a fairish sum of money. My guess came off, but I should have preferred it otherwise. For this firm was bought by Howard & Hazlehurst three months after I had put my money in. I had no conceivable foreknowledge of that transaction. I did very well out of it, from the nature of the case. So did one or two of my colleagues, who sometimes follow my guidance in financial matters. It's apparent that an ugly construction would be put on our actions – and these people are putting it. The facts are as I have stated them.'

He looked at Mr March and me in turn.

'I know there are silly persons who, without imputing motives, would still think that what Getliffe and I did were very much the same. I find those silly persons both tiresome and stupid. The point is that Getliffe acted in a way which the rules don't permit, while I kept strictly inside them. That is the only point. There are no absolute principles in these matters. There are simply rules on which all financial dealings depend. If you upset them, you upset the whole structure. If the rules go, then confidence and stability go. That is why I should show no mercy to anyone who breaks them. I should be sorry to see Getliffe escape scotfree.'

He added:

'It would not have occurred to me to break the rules. I blame myself for giving the appearance of having done so. I have had a long life in these matters, and I have never taken part in a transaction of which I am ashamed. The only thing left is to stop this business before it goes further. I want to ask you whether that is in our power.'

His conscience was clear, his self-respect untouched. Mr March had reported, after visiting him when ill, that his brother was 'sick in mind'; but it was not through any inner conflict. He was certain of his integrity. Yet he was desperately taxed. He was an old man, threatened with humiliation. In his hard, simple, strong-willed fashion he had coiled himself up to meet the danger. Throughout the afternoon he had kept his authority. But as he asked 'whether that is in our power' his face was shrunken: he still controlled his tone, but he looked imploring.

I saw that Mr March was stricken by this change. All through the afternoon, he had been torn by a sorrow his brother did not know; but even without that, he would still have flinched from the sight of Philip turning to him for pity and help. It had been painful to him to see the first traces of Philip's anxiety, when he was ill: it was worse now. For Philip had been the hero of his childhood, the brother who did all that he would have liked to do, the brother who had none of his timidities, who was self-sufficient, un-diffident, effective: it was intolerable to see him weak. It filled Mr March with revulsion, even with anger against Philip.

Mr March said in a low voice to his brother:

'As I've already told you, whether it is in our power or not depends on my son's wife.'

'I still don't believe it,' said Sir Philip.

'Will you tell my brother whether she's responsible for this, or not?' said Mr March to me.

'How much do you know about this?' Sir Philip asked me.

'Have you told Sir Philip,' I asked Mr March, 'that she's tried to set it right?'

'I remain to be convinced of that,' said Mr March.

'I assure you.'

'All I can do,' said Mr March, 'is acknowledge your remark.'

'Why are you making it worse than it need be?' I cried. I explained as much as I was free to do of her share in the story, and of how she had made her plea to Seymour and been refused. As I was speaking, Sir Philip's face was lighter, more ready to credit what I said, than his brother's, which was set in an obstinate, incredulous frown. Yet at last Mr March said, as though reluctantly:

'Apparently she has expressed some concern.'

I repeated part of what I had said. All of a sudden he shouted:

'Do you deny that if she wished she could still stop this abomination?'

I hesitated. Yes, she could inform against the *Note*. She could finish it for good. The loyalties that she would have to betray went through my mind, inhibiting my answer. The hesitation made me seem less straightforward than I was really being. Mr March shouted:

'Do you deny it?'

'It's possible, but –'

'Lewis Eliot knows very well,' Mr March said to Sir Philip, 'that it's more than possible.'

'No,' I said. 'It's only possible by a way that no one would like to use. I don't think many people could do it.'

'Can you explain yourself?' said Sir Philip.

I had to shake my head.

'I should be breaking a confidence,' I said.

'At any rate,' said Sir Philip, 'I can take it that this is all part and parcel of her cranky behaviour?'

'In a sense, yes.' I said I could not add to that answer.

Sir Philip became brisk, almost relieved. 'Well,' he said, 'that is the best news I've heard today. Charles must bring her to heel. I've always thought it was scandalous for him to let her indulge in this nonsense. Particularly a young woman as good-looking as she is. He ought to keep her busier himself.' Into the yellowing parchment face there came a smile, appreciative and salacious. It might have been a flicker of himself as a younger man, the Philip who had an eye for the women, the Philip who, so the family gossip said, had kept a string of mistresses.

'I cannot let you delude yourself,' said Mr March.

'What do you mean?'

'You are inclined to think the position is less dangerous because my son's wife is responsible for it.'

The weight of Mr March's words told on Sir Philip.

He replied irritably:

'I don't understand what you're getting at. I've always heard that the young woman is devoted to Charles.'

'I have no reason to believe the contrary.'

'Then she'll do what he tells her, in the end.'

There was a silence, Mr March cried:

'I cannot answer for what my son will tell her.'

'You're not being reasonable.' Sir Philip's tone was harassed and sharp. 'Charles has always had decent feelings for me, hasn't he? You've only got to let him know that this is serious for me. If they go on far enough, they may make it impossible for me to stay in public life. Well then. Be as

considerate as you can, and tell him none of us would interfere with his wife's activities as a general rule, though he
might take it from me that she should have something better
to do with her time. But tell him this is too important for me
and the family for us to be delicate. We must ask him to
assert himself.'

'You don't know how much you're asking,' I broke out.

'If the thing's possible, it's got to be done,' said Sir Philip.

'I will make those representations,' said Mr March. 'But
I cannot answer for the consequences.'

'If you prefer it,' said Sir Philip, 'I am quite prepared to
speak to Charles.'

'No, Philip,' Mr March said. 'I must do it myself.'

Sir Philip stared at him, and then said:

'I'm not willing to leave anything to chance. I expect
Charles to act immediately.'

He looked at his brother for agreement, but Mr March
barely moved his head in acquiescence.

'I shouldn't like to go out under a cloud,' said Sir Philip.
'Of course, we've all got to go some time, but no one likes
being forced out.' Suddenly his tone altered, and he said
quickly:

'Mind you, I'm not ready to admit that my usefulness is
over yet. I've some pieces of work in this department I want
to carry through, and after that –'

Inexplicably his mood had changed, and he began to talk
of his expectations. He hoped to keep his office for six
months, until there was a reshuffle in the government; he
speculated on the reshuffle name by name, knowing this
kind of politics just as he knew the March family. If one
combination came off, he might still get a minor ministry for
himself. For that he was hoping.

It was strange to hear him that afternoon. It was stranger
still to hear Mr March, after a time, join in. Preoccupied,
with occasional silences, he nevertheless joined in, and they
forecast the chances of Sir Philip's acquaintances, among
them Holford's son. Lord Holford – to whose party Charles
had taken me years before – had a son whom he was trying

to manoeuvre into a political success. Both Sir Philip and Mr March were anxious to secure that he did not get so much as a parliamentary private secretaryship.

It was strange to listen to them. No one, it seemed to me, had the power continuously to feel old. There were moments, many of them, when a man as realistic as Mr March was menaced by the grave – as in the club that afternoon, when he saw that his contemporaries were decrepit men. But those moments did not last. There were others, as now, when Sir Philip and Mr March could fear, could hope, just as they would have feared and hoped thirty years before. They were making plans at that moment: Sir Philip at seventy-three was still hoping for a ministry. There was no incongruity to himself: he hoped for it exactly as a young man would. The griefs and hopes of Mr March or Sir Philip might seem to an outsider softened and pathetic, because of the man's age: but to the man himself, age did not matter, they were simply the griefs and hopes of his own timeless self.

Chapter 36

EITHER/OR

AFTER the talk with Sir Philip, Mr March went straight back to Haslingfield. He made no attempt that afternoon to get into touch with Charles; it was several days before he wrote to him. I heard from Katherine that a letter had at last been sent — a noncommittal letter, she gathered, just asking Charles down. We were struck by the procrastination.

Meanwhile, Ann and Charles, in a state when they wished to see no one but each other, did not know what she should do. It was either/or, and whichever she did there was not a tolerable way out.

She did not need to tell Charles what it would be like to betray all she believed in. In fact, I got an impression that they did not talk much about what each feared most, they were too close for that. When I was with them, the discussion was oddly matter-of-fact. If she should decide that the less detestable course was to get the paper stopped, what was the quickest way of doing it? She asked the question without expression. It was not difficult to give practical answers. She possessed, as Seymour had said in his defiant bluff, documents which would do the job: she had only to pass them to someone like Ronald Porson, and an injunction would be out within a few hours.

Charles went down to Haslingfield with nothing settled between them, but resolved to speak intimately and affectionately to his father. None of us knew precisely what was said at that meeting, but it did not go like that. All the news I had came from Katherine, who was, without any qualification at all, on Mr March's side. She felt nothing but hostility to Ann: she had only a residue of sympathy, the faintest residue from the past, for Charles. Yet even she admitted that Mr March had made it more bitter for himself

271

and his son with each word he said. He had never shown less control or less understanding of Charles. He seemed to have exemplified the law of nature according to which, when a human relation has gone profoundly wrong, one is driven to do anything that can make it worse.

Mr March, having delayed for so many days in seeing his son at all, received him with a storm of accusations. He insisted that Charles had deliberately dissimulated, had professed ignorance, had given lying reassurances, whenever Mr March had asked. Charles was outraged. He had gone to see his father with a feeling of guilt: he was in one of those situations where one is half-guilty and half-innocent, or rather guilty at one level and innocent at another. He deserved reproaches, he was forming them against himself — but he was maddened at being accused of behaviour he could never have committed.

Katherine believed that there had been the bitterest words about Ann. It seemed, very strangely, that Mr March had spoken of her as though she were just a slave of Charles's, not an independent human being. What had really been said no one knew but themselves.

They parted in anger, Mr March's wildly possessing him, Charles's hard and strained. But as he went without a good-bye, Charles, still not knowing where to turn in spite of his harsh replies, offered to see Mr March again when he returned to Bryanston Square. It was an attempt to keep a card of re-entry, such as one makes when one is not prepared to face an end. Violently and ungraciously, Mr March accepted it.

*

The second reference in the *Note* was published before the end of August. It went just as Seymour had told me; in itself, it was innocuous. It produced no more facts, hinted at Hawtin as the chief figure in the case, contained nothing which pointed specifically at Sir Philip, and ended by promising to produce the whole story in 'three-four weeks'.

There were no consequences, at any rate none in the open.

I heard some gossip, went to a political dinner party and listened to the hostess moving pieces about the chessboard. Did this mean that Alex Hawtin would soon have a brilliant future behind him? Would there be a reshuffle in the government before long? Would they take the opportunity to put one or two men 'out'? But I was used to that kind of gossip, in which reputations rose and fell in a week : however informed the gossips were, however shrewd, their judgements had a knack of reversing themselves when one was not looking, and next month they would, with equal excitement, malice, and human gusto, be deciding that Alex Hawtin was safely 'in' and that someone else had 'blotted his copybook'.

In the March family, nothing happened for some days : except that Mr March closed Haslingfield and, breaking his seasonal ritual by a fortnight, which had not happened since he took the house forty years before, was back in Bryanston Square by the first week in September. It was known that he had seen the second article, but he said nothing and made no attempt to have another private talk with Charles. In fact, the only action he took as soon as he returned to Bryanston Square was a singular one : he invited Charles and Ann, his niece Margaret March, and several others, including me, to dine with him, on the pretext that he wished to celebrate the birth of Katherine's child.

The child, her second son, had been born a week before Mr March moved back to London. With all his physical exuberance he rejoiced in a birth. He was pleased that Katherine should have called the child after him. But no one believed that this was the true reason for his invitation. Margaret March, who knew most of the facts, thought he was making the opportunity for a scene with Ann : she was nervous at having to be a spectator, although her sympathies were mainly with Mr March.

Others of his relations believed much the same. They knew that a disaster hung over Mr March and Charles, and they felt that Mr March could not endure it any longer. Several of them were apprehensive enough to make excuses not to go. Most of them had learned something of the situation, pitied Mr March, and took his side; this was the case even with the younger generation. They did not begin to understand Charles's position, though he attracted a kind of baffled sympathy from some, simply because he was liked and respected. Ann got no sympathy at all.

Ann herself had no doubt of the reason behind Mr March's invitation. I called at Antrobus Street on my way home one night, just after we had all received the letters asking us to dine; I found Ann alone. For the first time in the years I had known her, her courage would not answer her. She was trying to screw up her will, but she was frightened.

I tried to hearten her. I said that it was possible Mr March had invited us for a much simpler reason. He might want to prove that he had not yet broken with his son. When Charles left Haslingfield, he had shown his card of re-entry and now perhaps Mr March was playing to it.

It did not sound likely. When Charles came in, I saw that she was not only frightened, but torn, just as Charles himself was torn. With her he was tender and protective. It was clear that he had not made her choice for her, and that he was not prepared to.

Nevertheless, that night I believed that, however much he kept from forcing her, however much he respected her choice, she would do as he wanted. I believed it more positively when she mentioned Mr March's invitation, and said that she did not want to go.

'When did it arrive?' said Charles quietly.

'This morning. It's too much of an ordeal, and it couldn't do any good. Even if I did go, it couldn't do any good.' Charles paused and said:

'I'm afraid that I want you to.'

'Why do you?' Her face was open, but hurt and clouded.

'You must see why. He's made an approach, and I can't refuse him. I'm afraid that I want you to go.'

'Must I?' said Ann.

'Yes,' said Charles.

Chapter 37

'WE'RE VERY SIMILAR PEOPLE'

Ann asked me to call for her on the night of Mr March's dinner party. She had been away from home for some nights, and had not seen Charles since she got back; he had an engagement at his old hospital, and would have to go to Bryanston Square direct.

As soon as I caught sight of her I was troubled. She was dressed for the party, as though she had determined to look her best that night. But it was not her dress that took my eye. Her cheeks were flushed; on her forehead there was a frown of strain. At first I took it for granted that these were signs of anxiety because of the evening ahead; then I asked if she were well.

'I've got a cold, I think,' said Ann. 'I felt it coming on a day or two ago. It's nothing much.'

'Any temperature?'

'Perhaps a little,' said Ann.

'Does Charles know?'

'No. I told you, I've not seen him since I went away.'

'Wouldn't it be wiser if you didn't come?'

'Do you think,' Ann said, 'that I could possibly not come now? I've told Mr March that I shall be there, haven't I?'

Suddenly I was reminded of her making herself play on at tennis, her first afternoon at Haslingfield.

'I must make sure that no one takes any notice, though,' she said. 'I'll see if anything can be done about it.' She went upstairs, and was some time away. At last she came into the room, halted in front of me, and said:

'How will that do?'

She had gone over her make-up, hiding the flush on her cheeks, overpainting her lips. One thing alone she could not wipe away, and that was the constricted, strained expression round her eyes.

'You look very pretty,' I said. In our long, comradely acquaintanceship, I had scarcely paid her a compliment before.

She smiled with pleasure. She was vainer than one thought, she distrusted her looks more. She studied herself in the looking-glass over the fireplace. She gave another smile, faint, approving, edged with self-regard.

'I think it will do,' she said.

Again I tried to make her stay at home, but she would not listen.

The September night was fresh, and Ann shivered in the taxi. As we stood on the steps in Bryanston Square just before eight o'clock, the smell of fallen leaves in the garden was blown on the sharp wind. Even for myself, I wished that the evening was over.

In the drawing-room, Margaret March and a cousin whom I scarcely knew were sitting by the fire. Ann began to talk to the cousin, who was a shy, gauche youth of twenty. Margaret said to me quietly: 'I don't think anyone else is coming. And I accepted before I heard what was happening. Otherwise I think I should have got out of it. Perhaps it would have been behaving grossly, but still –'

Then Charles entered, and she became silent. Before any of us had spoken again, Mr March followed his son into the room.

He felt the silence. He looked at Charles, at Ann, and then at the rest of us. At last he shook hands with Ann in a stiff, constrained manner, and said: 'I'm glad to have your company on this occasion. I'm glad that you were not prevented from attending.'

Through dinner, he went on as though trying not to disappoint us. He showed no sign of working up to a scene.

He knew he was expected to show pleasure at the birth, and he tried to act it. He talked of Katherine's children and Katherine herself. He made an attempt, as it were mechanically, to recall the times when 'my daughter had previously made a frightful ass of herself'.

Everyone at the table knew what he was doing. It was no relief to laugh at the jokes. I could not keep from looking at Charles, whose own glance came back time and again to his father. And I could not keep from looking at Ann; once I noticed Charles anxiously watching her. Glancing often from one to the other, I had to maintain more than my share of the conversation, replying to Mr March's mechanical chaff.

Margaret March helped, but the cousin was too shy to speak. In that way we got through dinner, though there was one incident, quite trivial, which chilled us all. Mr March's knife slipped as he was cutting his meat; as he righted himself he knocked his claret glass over. We heard the tinkle, watched the stain seep over the cloth, expecting at any instant that Mr March's usual extravagant stream-of-consciousness grumbling would begin. But he said nothing. He stared at the cloth while the butler dried it up. He did not make a single complaint to save his face.

In the drawing-room, Mr March again attempted to behave as though this were nothing but a celebration. He told Margaret a story at my expense; as he developed it, he became less preoccupied. Then Margaret March made a tactless remark. For she talked about Katherine's children, and said, casually but wistfully:

'If I married, I wonder if I should dare to have a child. I don't suppose I shall have the chance now, worse luck: but I wonder if I should.'

She was getting on into the mid-thirties. I looked at her handsome face, fair and clean-cut.

She added quietly:

'Of course, I know that really I should do the same as Katherine. I should want children, I should start a family. But it would worry me. I'm not sure that it would be wise.'

'Yes,' said Ann, breaking from her silence with feverish intensity. 'Of course you'd have children, of course you would.'

Mr March stared at her. Then he turned away to Margaret March.

'I am not certain that I understand your suggestion,' he said.

She hesitated: 'I mean — when you think of what the world may be.'

Mr March shouted: 'You need not try to respect my feelings. I am not accustomed to having my feelings respected in more important matters. I suppose you mean the world may not be a tolerable place for people of our religion?'

Margaret March nodded.

Mr March cried out:

'I wish the *Jews* would stop being *news*!'

It was a shout of protest: but somehow he said it as a jingle, and as though they were doing it on purpose. Even that night there were lips being compelled not to smile. Mr March could feel the ripple round him. He scowled and went on:

'You need not respect my feelings about such matters. I admit I never expected to see my religion getting this deplorable publicity. I never expected to spend my declining years watching people degraded because they belong to the same religion as myself. But I do not consider that these events should compel any of my relations to cripple their lives. I refuse to credit that they can be affected. And if they should be affected, which I repeat is not possible, they would be better off in the company of their children. If their children turn out to be a consolation, and not a source of grief.'

At that moment, Charles started to talk to his father. That last cry sounded in Charles's ears. The lines of his face became deeper. Across the table he saw the wife whom he adored. He saw her looking strained and ill. With her face before him, he had to speak to his father.

As we listened, nearly everyone there thought there was going to be a reconciliation. It sounded as though he knew which choice must be made. Each word he spoke was affectionate, subtle, concerned. He seemed at first to be talking casually to his father about Haslingfield and Bryanston Square. Yet the words were charged with his feeling for his father, with his family pride, so long concealed, with his longing for privacy and ease with those he loved.

Gradually Charles got Mr March to talk, not in his old vein, but with some show of ease. He soon began to expand on the weather. 'It's been remarkable weather this summer,' said Mr March. 'Only exceeded in wretchedness in my experience by the summer of 1912, which I always blamed for the regrettable misadventure of the third housemaid. It is the first summer since 1929 when there has been no danger of drought at my house in the country. It is the first summer since 1929 that I have not been compelled to make my guests ration the amount of water in their baths.' He turned to me. '1929 was, of course, singularly difficult. I remember that, on your first visit to my house in the country, I was compelled to allow you a maximum of four inches in your bath. The time I issued those instructions to you was immediately followed by the appearance of Ann Simon after luncheon.'

He did not look at Ann.

The name came as a shock. There was a silence.

Charles recovered himself, and said:

'It wasn't a direct consequence, Mr L.'

'No! No! I've always presumed that she was invited through the ordinary channels.'

Mr March was quiet.

'You're not certain that anyone has ever been properly invited to any house of yours, are you?' said Charles.

From his tone, so much more intimate than teasing, I knew that he would not stop trying to persuade Mr March of what he felt.

'You've never been able to trust your children to behave with reasonable decorum, have you?' Charles went on.

'That is so,' said Mr March. 'As I remarked recently, I ought to have been born in a different epoch.'

'I think perhaps I ought to have been too,' said Charles.

'You're better prepared to endure unpleasantnesses than

I am,' said Mr March. 'Whereas I only require to pass my declining years in peace.'

'I'm not as well prepared as you are, Mr L.,' Charles said. 'And I don't like the prospect of the future much more than you do.'

'I never liked the prospect of any unpleasantness,' said Mr March. 'But that's my temperament, I've told you before. I'm a diffident and retiring person.'

'Don't you see that our temperaments are very much alike?' said Charles. His tone suddenly turned urgent and anxious. 'Even though we seem to do different things. I may do things you wouldn't have done, but we're much more alike than most fathers and sons. I wish you'd believe it. At bottom, we're very similar people. Father, don't you know that we are?'

A smile forced itself, as though with difficulty, through to Mr March's face, a smile that became delighted, open, and naïf.

While some of us felt a wave of relief, thought it was all over, felt a sense of relief overwhelming, tired and at the same time sparkling gay, Mr March seemed half-incredulous, half-happy.

He said, in a rapid mutter, that he would like to have a 'consultation' with Charles and Ann 'not later than the end of the present week'.

Charles said yes.

Mr March deliberately changed the conversation, and talked happily to the rest of us, about subjects in which he and we were equally uninterested.

As Charles rose to say goodbye, Ann gave a gasp. As soon as I looked at her, I knew it was a gasp of pain. Charles went to her, asking with extreme anxiety what was the matter.

'I'm not particularly well,' she said.

'You've not been well all night,' he said. He put a hand on her forehead and felt her pulse.

'Why haven't you told me?' he said, in a tone so distressed that it sounded harsh and scolding. He turned to his father.

'I must get her home at once. Lewis, will you ring my partner and tell him that I shall want him to attend to her?'

Mr March stood up and went to him.

'Is she ill?' he said.

'Yes,' said Charles.

'Is it undesirable to move her?'

Charles hesitated, and before he replied Mr March said in a loud voice:

'I insist that she stays in my house. I refuse to accept responsibility if you subject her to unnecessary movement.'

'She would rather be at home,' said Charles.

'I cannot regard her inclinations as decisive. I believe that you would make her stay if it were not for previous circumstances. I cannot accept your recent assurances if you find it necessary to remove her from my house now.'

They looked into each other's eyes. Their faces were transformed from what they had been half an hour before, when Charles made his 'assurances' to his father. They were heavy, frowning, distressed.

'I think I had better stay,' said Ann, who was lying back below them in her chair.

'You're sure?'

'Yes.'

'Will you tell them to be quick? She ought to be in bed at once,' said Charles curtly to his father.

Mr March rang for the butler, and said to Charles:

'If you have no strong objection, I should prefer to send for my practitioner. He is competent as those fellows go, and he can be available without so much delay.'

Before Charles replied, Ann said:

'Yes, let him come.'

The servants worked at speed. Within five minutes Ann and Charles were out of the room; within ten the car of Mr March's doctor drew up outside. The rest of us stayed there. We talked perfunctorily. Once or twice Mr March startled us by speaking with animation: then he relapsed into his thoughts.

It was a long time before Charles came back. His face

was drained of colour, and he spoke straight to his father. His voice was quiet and hard:

'It may be a pneumonia. She's ill.'

A look of recognition passed between them. Mr March did not speak.

Chapter 38

DESIRES BY A BEDSIDE

I CALLED to ask after her on each of the next two after-noons. On the first day I found Mr March alone, distracted and restless, telling me it was beyond doubt pneumonia, in-venting one service after another that he might do for Ann. His car shuttled between Bryanston Square and Pimlico, fetching her belongings; he kept questioning the doctors and nurses; he went out himself to buy her flowers.

On the second afternoon Mr March and Charles both came to see me in the drawing-room. Mr March was still fretting for things that he could do. He behaved as though any action was a relief to his mind: but, when he asked Charles three times in ten minutes what else was needed, he got cold replies. Those replies did not spring simply from suspense. They were cold because of the tension present in the room between them.

In a short time Mr March went out. At once Charles's whole expression changed; his face became at once less hard and more ravaged. He spoke without any pretence.

'It will be days before we know that she's safe. Orange – Mr March's doctor – says that he wouldn't have expected it to take hold of her like this.' He cried out: 'Lewis, I wish I had her courage.'

'I've often wished that,' I said.

'It's the sort of courage I just can't compete with,' Charles said. 'She won't stop thinking about this affair of the *Note*. She told me that it was on that account she must know exactly how ill she is. She wouldn't ask me, but she did ask Orange. She just said that her father and her husband were both doctors, and she wanted to be discussed as though she were a case in front of the class. Mind you,' he said, with an automatic smile, 'intelligent people often ask one to do that.

It doesn't prevent one from lying to them.' He went on: 'But so far as a human being can, she meant it.'

'Did he tell her?'

'He told her that she was dangerously ill.'

He had mentioned 'this affair of the *Note*' almost with indifference. I wondered, didn't he think of connecting it with her illness? She could not have fallen ill at a more critical time; if she had been a stranger, wouldn't he have said that perhaps it was not entirely a coincidence?

Yet he spoke of 'this affair of the *Note*' as though it did not matter: even when he went on to say:

'He told her that she was dangerously ill. When she knew that, she asked to see you before tonight. She wants to tell you something in private – it must be the same business. She wants to see you very much, Lewis. Do you mind going in? Can you spare the time? Are you sure it won't make you late?'

The strain sharpened his courtesy and for an instant he was genuinely worrying about my comfort. On the stairs, going towards Ann's room, he said:

'Do what she asks. Do what she asks – whatever it is.'

As he opened the bedroom door he forced his manner to change.

'Here is Lewis,' he said. 'You mustn't speak for very long. You can let him have his share of the conversation, can't you?'

Mr March's wife had once occupied this bedroom, the largest in the house. The bed itself was wide and high, and was overhung by a canopy; it drew my eyes across the great room, to the figure lying still under the clothes.

She was lying on her right side. Her face was flushed and her eyes bright, and her expression was constricted with strain. She gave a short dry cough, which made her give a painful frown. Her breathing was quick and heavy. There was sweat on her upper lip, and what looked to me like a faint rash.

She muttered a greeting to me, and said to Charles:

'Darling. Will you leave him here a bit?'

'If you want me to,' said Charles, standing by her, looking down at her, unwilling to go.

No one spoke for a moment. There was no noise but the gasp of her breathing. Then she said:

'Please.'

Charles glanced at me, and went out.

When the door closed, she said:

'Lewis, this isn't so good for Charles to go through. He's been here all night. It wasn't a good night for him. We talked about some things. When I was lucid more or less. It's the worst thing – Lewis – feeling that you are soon not going to be lucid.' She had to stop. After a pause she went on:

'They think there's a chance I may die, don't they?'

'I don't know.'

'Be honest.'

'I suppose there's a chance.'

She stared at me.

'Somehow I don't think I shall,' she said.

She broke out:

'But there's one thing I must get settled. I shall feel easier if I get it settled.'

She coughed and paused again.

'There's one thing I haven't talked out with Charles. I can't rely on thinking it out properly now, can I?' she said. 'I mean the showdown over the paper.'

She went on:

'Some people wouldn't be sorry if I were finished with.'

Her voice was faint and husky. Suddenly her will shone out, undefeated.

'I'm not going to back out now,' she whispered. 'If I get over this, then I'll have plenty of time to talk to Charles again. If I don't, will you give him a message? He'll understand that I wasn't ready to back out – the last thing I did –' She was not quite coherent, but I knew that by 'backing out' she meant ruining the *Note*, reneging on the cause. 'But tell him, now he must settle it. He can do whatever he likes. The letters are in my steel filing cabinet under H. He'll find the key in my bag. If Charles decides to stop the paper, he's only got to send them to Ronald or the chap in the Home Office. The letters are mixed up with some others, they'll need a bit of organizing. I couldn't do that now.'

The effort tired her out. She fell asleep, although her body moved without resting. Sometimes she spoke. Once she said, quite clearly, as though continuing the conversation: 'Charles would have to marry again. Someone who wouldn't make trouble. And could give him children, of course.' At other times she called on her father, cried out Charles's name. Most of the time in her sleep she seemed – although when conscious she had spoken so coolly – tormented by anxiety or sheer fear. Her cries sounded as though she were in a nightmare.

Sitting there – through the window the trees of the square shone green and gold in the sunlight – I could imagine what Charles's night by the bedside must have been like. As I watched her, fears seemed to be piling upon her like faces in a nightmare. She woke for a few minutes, lucid and controlled again: she said without fuss that she was afraid of dying. But, when she lost consciousness, quite different fears broke out of her. She cried about the hate that others felt for her. She was terrified of them, terrified that they were persecuting her, terrified that she was at their mercy. She tossed about the bed, calling out names, some of which I had never heard, but among them several times that of Mr March; she called out his name in fright, she was trying to get away from an enemy. Then she seemed to be making a speech.

I went down to the drawing-room, where the afternoon sun was streaming in. Mr March and Charles sat there, but neither spoke.

'How did you leave her, Lewis?' said Mr March at last.

'She was asleep,' I said.

'How did you think she seemed?' he went on.

I did not know how to reply.

'I've not seen enough illness to tell,' I said.

Mr March was fretted with anxiety. His eyes were sombre; he was more restless than Charles.

'I should like to be reassured that everything within human power is being done. I should like to insist that my practitioner is instructed to obtain further advice apart from the fellow he brought in yesterday.'

Charles did not reply to his father. He said to me:

'Did she tell you what she wanted to?'

'Yes,' I said.

'I'm glad of that,' said Charles.

'I shall not be easy,' said Mr March again, 'until I am convinced that everything within human power is being done.'

Charles looked at him and said:

'Leave it to me, that's all I ask of you.'

Part 5

ALONE

Chapter 39

WAITING IN THE DRAWING-ROOM

THROUGH each of those days when no one knew whether Ann would live, the sun shone into the great bedroom at Bryanston Square.

It was a warm and glowing autumn, and she lay in the mellow sunshine, not conscious for many minutes together. But I suspected that, while she was conscious, she had made a request to Charles. All of a sudden he gave orders that no one but the nurses was to visit her room, unless he specially asked them. He told his father so, giving no reason. Mr March knew that it was he himself who had to be kept from her sight.

Charles spent most of each night by her bed. After the fourth night, he rang me up and said she had had a long lucid interval, in which she was worried that she had not made herself clear to me. 'She's worrying about everything that occurs to her. If I can satisfy her about one thing, there's another on her mind before she's stopped thanking me. This *Note* affair is the worst.' As he mentioned it, his voice became harsher. 'I should be grateful if you'd tell her that you understood exactly what she meant.'

When I went into her room that afternoon, however, she scarcely recognized me. Her breathing seemed faster and her skin very hot. The rash on her lip was now full out, and her face was angrily flushed. She coughed and muttered. I waited for some time in the hope she would know me, but, though once she said something, her eyes stared at me unseeing and opaque.

I joined Mr March in the drawing-room, as I had done each day of her illness. He could not bring himself to go to the club; he was deserted, with no one to speak to. He spoke little to me, but we had tea together. He was listening for any movement of the nurses on the stairs so that he could rush outside and ask for the latest news. Occasionally he talked to me, and appeared glad of my presence.

He wanted her to die. He wanted her to die for a practical reason. He believed – he had not discovered the precise situation – that, if she were out of the way, it would not take long to stop the *Note*. He believed, quite correctly, that the means of stopping it would pass to Charles. His family would be left in peace. He took it for granted that there would be a temporary breach with his son. But nothing would come out. In the end they would be reconciled, and he would be left in peace for the rest of his life.

He knew that he wanted it. He was not an introspective man, but he was a completely candid one. Only a man much more dishonest with himself than Mr March could have resisted realizing what his feelings meant. As soon as he knew she was ill, he imagined what the benefit would be if she were dead. He could no more pretend the desire had not risen within him than he could deny a dream from which he had just woken. It was there.

He was too realistic to cover it with self-deceptions. He could not console himself that he was not the first man to watch a sickbed and find his longings uncomfortable to face. He did not think – how many of us have wished, not even for good or tragic reasons, but simply to make our own lives easier, that someone else, someone whom we may be fond of, should just be blotted out? Mr March would not console himself. He wanted Ann to die, whom his son passionately loved, whom he had himself once come near to loving.

It was on this account that he fretted so continuously. He could not suppress his thoughts: but anything he could do to help her he did with as much intensity as if her life had been precious to him. He had, on the second day, made his 'practitioners' bring in the consultant of whom Charles thought most highly; he had sent for the most expensive nurses; he could not have exerted himself more, if this had been Charles ill as a child.

He followed the illness minute by minute. Each time he

could get a word with a nurse, he pressed her for the news. They were all astonished, as were the whole March family, by how violently he felt.

Meanwhile, Mr March thought often about death. He thought of her death and his own. He hated the thought of his death with all his robust, turbulent, healthy vigour.

Realistic as he was, he could not face it starkly in his own heart. On the outside, he could appear stoical, he could refer to the fact, as he did to me several times on those afternoons, that in the nature of things his death must come before long. But, left alone, he did not think of it so.

Death to him meant the silence and the dark. It meant that he, who had been so much alive, would have been annihilated. Other lives would go on, busy, violent and content, ecstatic and anguished, comfortable and full of anxiety, and utterly indifferent to what he had been. Other people would eat in this house, talk in this room, love and get married and have their children, walk through the square, quarrel and come together; and he would be gone from it for ever. Any life, he cried to himself, any life, however stricken with pain, racked by conflict, beaten in all its hopes, is better than the nothingness. It would be better to be a shadow in the darkness, to be able to watch without taking part, than to be struck into that state for which all images are more consoling than the truth – just this world of human beings living out their lives, and oneself not there.

Those thoughts visited him as he waited day by day for news of Ann, never seeing her, forbidden by his son to see her. One afternoon I found him reading the current issue of the *Note*. He read it word by word. 'Pernicious nonsense,' he said. 'But there is naturally nothing further about my brother Philip.'

Reports of Ann's illness went round the March family, and the telephone in Bryanston Square rang many times a day. Sir Philip enquired daily: I wondered whether he too faced his thoughts. There were whispers, rumours, hopes, and alarms. So far as I knew, Katherine put through only one call. But Porson rang me up often, sometimes at Bryanston Square and often at night in my own house. 'How is she?' his voice came, booming, assertive, drunken, distressed. 'I insist that she's always wanted someone to look after her. How is she? You're not keeping anything from me?' Each day he sent flowers, more lavish even than Mr March's. One evening, going home, I thought I saw him watching in the square: but, if it were he, he did not want to be seen, and hurried away out of sight.

Charles paid no attention to any of these incidents. He spoke very little to anyone in the house, and scarcely at all to his father. He was grey with fatigue, so tired that once in the drawing-room he went to sleep in his chair. He was entirely concentrated in Ann. Her sickroom was the only place where he seemed alive.

On the seventh day of her illness, the crisis came. Charles was in the house all that day; his partner had taken charge of his cases for the last forty-eight hours. After tea, Charles came down and said to me, in a hard, uninflected voice:

'She would like to see you again. I must warn you, she is looking much better. You'll probably think the danger has gone. That isn't true.'

Despite his warning, I could not help thinking she was better. She was weak, she could not talk much; but her breathing was quiet now, the fever had gone, and she spoke almost in her ordinary voice.

'You've got it clear, have you? I don't want to force Charles's hand. I've been worrying whether I made that clear. If anything happens to me, he must make a free choice.'

'I've got it clear,' I replied.

'Thank you,' she said. She gave a friendly matter-of-fact smile and said faintly: 'I hope it won't be necessary.'

Charles returned to take me away. He stood by the bedside, looking down at Ann; he made an attempt to smile at her.

With the clumsiness of fatigue, she interleaved her fingers into those of the hand he had rested on her pillow.

'I've been giving Lewis instructions about the *Note*,' she

whispered. 'That isn't finished, you know. Had you for-gotten it?'

'Not quite,' said Charles. 'Not quite.'

For two days after, Charles was ravaged by a suspense and apprehension greater than he had yet known. The consultant had been called in again. They thought she had no resilience left. Mr March's doctor told Charles that no one now could be certain of the end. Then she seemed to be infused by a faint glow of vitality, when they thought it had all gone.

In the afternoon of the ninth day, a warm and cloudless autumn afternoon, we knew that she had been a long time asleep. Mr March and Charles were sitting opposite to each other in the drawing-room, and I was on the sofa. The clock ticked on the mantelpiece, and each quarter of an hour there came its chime, sweet, monotonous, and maddening. It was beyond any one of us to go outside into the sunshine. It would have seemed like tempting fate.

Mr March's face was an old man's that afternoon. The skin beneath his eyes was dark sepia; his head was sunk down, the veins on his temples were blue. Charles was lean-ing forward, his hands locked together; his position did not change for half an hour at a time. Often when he was anxious he smoked in chains: that afternoon he did not smoke. There was no tinge of colour in his face. His eyes shone bright, bloodshot, and intent.

Mr March stared at him and once, with a grinding effort, broke the silence:

'I believe that this sleep may be a good sign. They informed me before luncheon that they had considerably more hope.'

Charles made no sign that he had heard.

At last, it was well after four o'clock, we heard footsteps down the stairs, and a tap on the door. A nurse entered and beckoned Charles. He was out of the room at once. The nurse's manner had not been specially grave, and I felt a touch of relief. Mr March and I exchanged a few words, and then fell silent again. The quarters chimed – half past, a quarter to. Suddenly Mr March sprang up and stopped the clock.

Then there was noise on the stairs, and the sound of a loud, unmuted, orotund voice: 'I think she'll do, March. If we look after her properly, I think she'll do.'

Charles came into the room. He spoke directly to his father for the first time for many hours.

'Did you hear that?' he cried triumphantly. 'Did you hear that?'

Chapter 40

BY HIMSELF

ANN'S convalescence was a slow one, and she could not be moved from Mr March's house. I ceased calling when the danger was past, but heard of her each day from Charles. She had asked Mr March to visit her in her room; it seemed that she had apologized for the inconvenience she had caused him by falling ill; she promised to go as soon as the doctors would let her. From what she told Charles, it had been an interview formal and cool on the surface. After it, Mr March had not spoken to Charles about her.

One afternoon soon after, Charles rang me up.

'You remember when Ann was ill? She gave you a message for me?'

I said yes.

'She said this morning that I could ask you about it. She'd rather you told me than tell me herself.'

I was taken aback, so much so that I did not want to speak over the telephone. I arranged to call at his house. As I walked there along the reach from Chelsea, the river oily in the misty sunshine, the chimneys quivering in the languid Indian summer, I was seized by a sense of strangeness. This new wish of Ann's – for she had, while in danger, said that if she recovered she would tell Charles herself – this wish to have her message given him at secondhand seemed bizarre. But it was not really that wish which struck so strange. It was the comfort of the senses, the warmth of the air and the smell of the autumn trees, assuring one that life might be undisturbed.

Charles was in his surgery. He was not pleased to see me. He did not want to be reminded of what I had come to tell him. He was looking better than when I had last seen him: he had made up sleep, the colour had come back to his face.

But he was not rested. In a tone brittle and harsh, he began:

'I'd better hear what she said. I suppose it's about this wretched paper, isn't it? I'd better hear it.'

I was sure that, since she got better, he had not been able to put the choice out of his mind. I gave him her message, as I should have been obliged to if she had died.

'So she left it to me,' Charles said.

He did not ask for any explanation at all. With a deliberate effort — it was the habit I had got used to when he he was a younger man — he talked of things which prevented me saying any more.

'I've been writing a letter,' he said. 'Would you like to read it? Do you think you would?'

I did not know what to expect. It was, in fact, a letter to the *Lancet*. In August, just before Ann's illness, one of Charles's cases had been a child of three ill with a form of diphtheria, in such a way that the ordinary feeding-tube could not be used. Charles had improvised a kind of two-way tube which had worked well. In the last fortnight, since he knew Ann would recover, he had discovered another case in a hospital, and persuaded them to use the same technique. It had worked again, and now he thought it worth while to publish the method.

'You see, no one has ever been worse with his hands than I am,' said Charles. 'So if I can use this trick, anyone else certainly can. I can't understand why some practical man hasn't thought of it long ago. Still, it's remarkably satisfying. You can believe that, can't you?'

He put the letter on his desk, ready to be typed.

'It's all very odd,' he said. 'When I was very young, I used to think that I might write something. I imagined I might write something on a simply enormous scale. I should have been extremely surprised to be told that my first published work would be a note on a minor device to make life slightly more comfortable for very small children suffering from a rather uncommon disease.'

He was talking to keep me at a distance: but the sarcasm

pleased him. He was genuinely gratified by what he had done. It was good to have aroused a bit of professional envy, to receive a bit of professional praise. It was good to have something definite to one's credit. Concentrated and undiffuse as he was, he had been distracted for a few hours, even at this time, by getting a result.

But I was frightened, because he would not talk about the *Note*. I tried to get him to.

We had been intimate so long: not thinking it out as a technique to soften him, but just because I did not want to leave him quite alone, I confided something about my own marriage – something I had not told him before, nor anyone else. His eyes became sharp with insight, he gave me the support with which he had never failed me. But I did not get any other response.

At last I said:

'Charles, will you let me ask you about something else?'

'What is it?'

'I don't want to add to your trouble. You know that.'

'I know that,' he said.

'Can you tell me what you propose to do? About stopping this paper?'

There was a silence.

'No,' he said. His eyes were steady. He went on:

'I don't know. It's no use talking about it.'

The words were slow, dragged out. Looking at him, I believed he had spoken the precise truth. What his decision would be, he just did not know. But he was by himself, and nothing that anyone said could affect it now.

We went on talking. We even talked politics. I knew by his tone, what I already knew, that whatever he chose, politics would not move him either way.

As I sat with him, I believed that, whatever he chose, he was asking himself – I remembered, with a trace of superstition, the night in Bryanston Square after I had taken Ann to the concert – how much he could bear to dominate another. He had gone through too much in order to be free himself: it was harder for him to choose that she should not be.

Late that night I happened to see him again. I had been dining in Dolphin Square, and was walking home along the Embankment in the moonlight. I saw Charles coming very slowly towards me on the opposite side of the road. His head was bent, he was wearing no overcoat or hat; he might have been out at a case. As he came nearer, he did not look up. Soon I could see his face in the bright moonlight: I did not cross the road, I did not say good-night.

Chapter 41

FAMILY GATHERING

THREE days later, I was surprised to be rung up by Charles. He told me that Katherine, her children, and Francis had arrived the evening before at Bryanston Square. I was surprised again; it was only a month since the baby was born; then I realized from Charles's tone that they had come for a purpose.

They were pressing him to go to Bryanston Square for tea that afternoon: would I pick him up and go with him?

As soon as I saw him, I thought he looked transformed. He was still pale and tired: he was tired but not restless, tired but easy, as though he had just finished playing a game.

At once he asked me, in a relaxed, affectionate voice:

'I'm sorry to be a nuisance, but just tell me again exactly what Ann said to you, will you, Lewis?'

At that moment I knew he had made up his mind.

When I had finished, he was quiet for a few seconds. Then he said, almost as though he were making fun of her:

'I suppose she is much braver than you or me, isn't she? I've always thought she was, haven't you? Yet she didn't want to tell it me herself. She was glad to get out of that.'

He smiled.

'She's been incomparably nearer to me than any other human being ever has, or could be again,' he said. 'She thinks I know her. But I was astonished when she wanted to get out of telling me. Sometimes I think that I don't know her at all.'

On the way to Bryanston Square he asked me if I had ever felt the same, if I had ever felt that someone I knew and loved had for the moment become a stranger – utterly mysterious, utterly unknown. It was like the talks we used to have when we were younger.

Katherine and Francis were waiting in the drawing-room. Charles embraced his sister, held her in his arms, asked about the child. She told him how the delivery had been quick and easy. Charles showed a doctor's interest as he questioned her. She replied with zest; she was physically happier, and more unreticent, than anyone there. She looked blooming with health, radiant as though she had just come from a holiday. The next hour was preying on her mind, she was heavy-hearted, but still she gave out happiness. It set her apart from Charles, or even from her husband, in whom one could see already the signs of strain.

Charles said:

'I must run up and see Ann for five minutes.'

'I suppose,' said Francis, 'that she can't come down for tea?'

'It wouldn't be a good idea,' said Charles. 'Don't you admit that it wouldn't be a good idea?'

There was a sarcastic edge to his tone, and Francis flushed. When Charles had gone, Francis said to me:

'This is intolerable whatever happens.'

He had become more than ever used to getting his own way: but his feelings had stayed delicate. He was still colouring from Charles's snub, and a vein showed in his forehead. He would go through with what he had come to say, just as he went through with any job he set himself. But it cost him an effort which would have deterred a good many of us.

Katherine wanted to begin talking of Charles and Ann. but he stopped her. 'We shall have enough of it soon,' he said. I asked about his work; he was trying a major problem, but had struck a snag. We exchanged some college gossip.

We were beginning tea when Charles came down.

'How is Ann now?' said Francis, with a difficult friendliness.

'She'll be able to leave here next week,' said Charles.

'Good work,' said Francis.

There was a pause. A spoon tinkled in a saucer.

'As a matter of fact,' said Francis, 'it was about her, of course, that we wanted to talk.'

'Yes,' said Charles. His eyes gleamed.

'I think we're bound to ask you,' Francis went on, 'what the present position is about the *Note*. Has Ann stopped that affair?'

Charles answered:

'I shouldn't think so for a minute.'

'What is the position then?' said Katherine.

'I imagine it's exactly the same as when she fell ill,' Charles said.

'You mean, everything's coming down on our heads, that's what you mean, don't you?' she cried.

Francis asked:

'I take it we're right to gather that the only certain way of stopping this business is to get the *Note* suppressed?'

'You're quite right,' said Charles.

'And we're right to gather that it's in Ann's power to do it?'

'You're quite right,' said Charles.

'She would do it if you told her?'

'Certainly.'

'Have you tried?'

For the first time, Charles did not answer immediately. He might have been considering telling them that by now the choice was his. At last he just said:

'No.'

'We must ask you to.' Francis's temper was rising. 'You ought to know that I dislike interfering, but this is too serious to let go by. We must ask you to tell her.'

'I absolutely agree with Francis,' said Katherine loudly. 'It would be gross to interfere between you and Ann, but this is an occasion which we simply can't shut our eyes to, surely you admit that? We must ask you to tell her.'

Charles's voice was quiet, level, self-possessed after theirs.

'I haven't the slightest intention of doing so.'

He looked from one set face to the other. Unexpectedly he smiled.

'I'm sorry,' he said. 'You know how fond I am of both of you. Nothing will affect that, so far as I am concerned, don't you know that? I would do anything for you both.'

'Then for God's sake do this,' cried Katherine.

Charles shook his head. 'I gave you my answer more unpleasantly than I ought to have done. But it's still my answer.'

Francis tried to control himself, to subdue his tone in response to Charles's. 'Look,' he said, 'we can't leave it there. You know, Charles, I feel responsible to some extent. If it hadn't been for my brother Herbert, we might never have got into this mess. He seems to have covered his tracks somehow —'

'You needn't worry about Herbert,' I said.

'Are you sure?' said Francis.

'Quite sure,' I said. 'He's still got a chance of finishing up as a judge.'

'I shouldn't be surprised by anything he did. Not even that,' said Francis. He turned to Charles again. 'Well,' he said, 'you understand that we can't leave it there.'

'I know it's difficult for you. And I'm sorry.'

Francis went on:

'I want to make one point clear. Before I go on. We're not prejudiced by Ann's political motives you know that, but I want to tell you. I think she over-simplifies it all: but if it comes to two sides, we are on the same side as she is. It's the only side one could possibly be on. I'm also prepared to admit that the *Note* has its uses. By and large it's making a contribution. I should just say that it's not such a major contribution — it's not such a major contribution that she's justified in driving on whoever is getting hurt. It is certainly not worth disgracing your family and breaking up Mr L.'

'You must agree with that,' said Katherine. Her voice was angry and menacing: unlike Francis, she was making no attempt to conciliate Charles. 'Anyone in their senses must agree with that.'

'I agree with you politically much more than I do with Ann,' said Charles to Francis. 'In fact, I've always been less committed than you, don't you realize that?'

It was true. Of us in that room, Francis was the furthest to the left. 'I'm much more sceptical than you, I suspect,' said Charles, 'about what Ann and her friends can possibly achieve. You think this paper of theirs has some value. I must say I doubt it. It's different for her. She doesn't doubt it in the slightest. If you're going to lead that kind of life, you must believe from the start that every little action is important –'

Katherine was frowning, but Francis nodded his head.

'For myself,' said Charles, 'I don't think any of that matters.'

'What does matter?' said Katherine.

'Simply that this is something Ann believes in. The suggestion is that I should force her to betray it.'

'You must be mad,' said Katherine. 'You can't give us a better reason than that for getting Uncle Philip into the newspapers?'

'What reason would you like me to give?'

'It's not good enough,' said Francis.

'It won't do her any harm to be forced,' said Katherine. 'If you'd done more of it earlier, this would never have happened. Don't you see that you've been wrong since the day you met her?'

'No,' said Charles. 'I don't see that.'

'We mustn't criticize your marriage,' said Francis.

Katherine interrupted him:

'If your marriage is worth anything at all, this can't make any difference. Don't you see that you can't afford to be too considerate? And we can't afford to let you be. Could anyone in the world think the reason you've given is enough excuse for ruining Mr L.'s peace of mind for the rest of his life?'

Charles said:

'There was a time when you were prepared to take a risk like that.' Katherine looked at him. Her bitter indignation lessened, for he had spoken, for the first time that afternoon, with sadness.

'There was a time,' he repeated, 'when you were prepared to take a risk like that. And that time I was on your side, you know.'

'It was the easy side for you.' Her tone was stern and accusing again.

'I should have taken your side whether it was easy or hard,' said Charles. 'I've always loved you, don't you know that?'

Katherine was near to tears. He had spoken with a warmth and freedom such as she had scarcely heard. She said:

'I can't take your side now. I can't take your side.'

She burst out:

'Don't you see that I can't? Do you think that I don't know you at all? You've never forgiven Mr L. for being in power over you. You've never forgiven him for trying to stop your marriage. And he was absolutely right. Since you married this woman, you've never cared for the rest of us. You've been ready to destroy everything in the family because of her. You're not sorry now, are you? You're not sorry for anything you've done? I believe you're glad.'

Charles had stood up. He leant by the fireplace and spoke with a fierce release of energy:

'I repeat, you were ready to do all these things to marry Francis. I would have done anything on earth to help you. I would still.'

'You won't say this one word which would cost you nothing,' Katherine cried furiously. 'You won't stop your wife finishing off a piece of wickedness she should never have thought of. I know you won't think twice about what this means for Mr L. You've always been capable of being cruel. But is it possible for you to think twice of what it means to us?'

'Yes,' said Francis. 'Can you bring yourself to do that?'

Charles replied:

'You have said some hard things of me. Many of them are true. You have said hard things of Ann. Those you should have kept to yourselves. I won't trouble to tell you how untrue they are. Are you sure that in all this concern of yours you're not thinking of your own convenience? Are you sure that your motives are as pure as you seem to think? It will be a nuisance for you to have a scandal in the family. Aren't you both so comfortable that you'd like to prevent that – whatever else is lost in the process?'

Francis and Katherine sat silent, looking up at him as he stood. Francis, who in much of the quarrel had shown sympathy, was dark with anger, the vein prominent in his forehead. Katherine said, as a last resort:

'You won't trust us. Perhaps you'll trust Lewis. He's got nothing at stake. Lewis, will you tell him what you think?'

They all waited for me.

I said: 'I've already said what I think – to Ann.'

'What did you say?' cried Katherine.

'I said she ought to go to Charles and tell him she wanted to call it off.'

I spoke directly to Charles:

'I should like to ask you something. Will you and Ann talk the whole matter over for the last time?'

He smiled at me and said, without hesitation:

'No, Lewis.' He added, for my benefit alone: 'She did that through you.'

Katherine and Francis exchanged a glance. Francis said:

'There it is. It's no use going on. But we must say this. If Ann doesn't stop this business, we shan't be able to meet her. Obviously, we shan't want to create any embarrassment. If we meet socially, we shall put a decent face on it. But we shall not be able to meet her in private.'

'You know that must include me,' said Charles.

'I was afraid you would take it that way,' said Francis. Charles said:

'There's no other way to take it.'

'No,' said Francis.

'I think you are being just,' Charles said in a level and passionless voice. 'All I can say is this: from you both I hoped for something different from justice. Once, if I had been in your place, I should have done as you are doing. I think perhaps I shouldn't now.'

He added:

'It is hard to lose you. It always will be.'

His energy had ebbed away for a moment.

He sat down. We made some kind of conversation. Ten minutes passed before Mr March came in.

'I should be obliged,' he said, 'if I could have a word with my daughter.'

'I'm afraid that I've given her my answer,' said Charles.

Chapter 42

AN ANSWER

'I assumed that you knew what she was asking me,' said Charles. 'I'm afraid that I've given her my answer.'

He had risen as Mr March came in, and they stood face to face by the window, away from the fireplace and the small tea-table, round which the rest of us were still sitting. They stood face to face, Charles some inches taller than his father, his hair catching the sunlight as it had done years before in the examination hall. Against him his father stood, his head less erect, his whole bearing in some way unprepared.

'I don't want to hear it,' said Mr March.

'You'll hear it from Katherine as soon as I've gone. Don't you admit that you will? Isn't it better for me to tell you myself?'

'I refuse to hear anything further until your wife has completely recovered,' said Mr March. 'I don't regard you as in a fit state to make a decision.'

'I should make the same decision whether she's ill or well,' said Charles. 'I shan't change my mind.'

'What is it?' said Mr March, in despair.

'You don't want me to say much, do you? Katherine has heard it all. All I need say is that, now she's heard it, she and Francis don't wish to meet me again.'

'I knew it,' said Mr March. They looked at each other.

'You can endure being lonely?' Mr March said at last, still in a subdued voice.

'I can endure that kind of loneliness.'

'Then it's useless to ask you to consider mine.'

Charles did not reply at once, and Mr March for the first time raised his voice.

'It's useless to ask you to consider my loneliness. I suppose

I had better be prepared to take the only steps which are open to me.'

'I'm afraid that is for you to decide.'

'You know,' cried Mr March, 'I'm not telling you anything original. You know the position you are placing me in. You're forcing me to deprive myself of my son.'

We each knew that this quarrel was different from those in the past. Always before, Mr March had a power over his son. Now it had gone. Mr March knew: he could not admit it, and his anger rose at random, wildly, without aim.

'You're forcing me,' he shouted, 'to deprive myself of my son. If this outrage happens' – he was clinging to a last vestige of hope – 'if this outrage happens, I shall be compelled to take a step which you will recognize.'

'It won't matter to me, don't you realize that?'

'Nothing that I possess will come to you. You will be compelled to recognize what you've done after my death,' said Mr March.

'I'm sorry, but that doesn't matter.'

Suddenly Katherine cried out:

'Father, why ever didn't you make him independent? When he wanted to marry? I told you at the time it wouldn't be the same between you. Do you remember?'

Mr March turned towards the fireplace, and rounded on her with fury:

'I only consider it necessary to remind you of what my Uncle Justin said to his daughter.' For a second all his anger was diverted to her. 'I reproach myself that I allowed you to make representations between myself and my son.'

'She did her best,' said Charles. 'She tried to bring us together. She tried her best to keep me in your will.'

'Charles!' Katherine cried. He had spoken with indifference: but she cried out as though he had been brutal. Mr March ignored her, and returned to face Charles.

'I should never have spoken of money,' he said, 'if I could have relied on your affection.'

For the first time, as they stood there, Charles's face softened.

'My affection was greater than you were ever ready to admit,' he said. 'Did you hear me speak to you, the night Ann was taken ill? That was true.'

Mr March's voice rang in our ears:

'There's only one thing you can say that I'm prepared to hear.'

Charles had not recovered himself. He said:

'That's impossible for me.'

'Do you consider it more impossible than destroying my family? And showing your utter ingratitude as a son? And condemning yourself to squalor now and after I am dead? And leaving me with nothing to live for in the last years of my life?'

Charles did not answer. Mr March went on: 'Do you consider it is more impossible than what you're bringing about?'

'I'm afraid it is,' said Charles.

The tone of that reply affected Mr March. Since he appealed to Charles's affection, he had reached his son. As though interpreting Charles's reply, which was loaded with remorse, Mr March spoke of Ann.

'If you hadn't married your wife,' Mr March said, 'you would have given a different answer. She is responsible for your unnatural attitude.'

Immediately Charles's manner reverted to that in which he had begun; he became hard again, passionate, almost gay.

'I am responsible for everything I've done,' he said. 'You know that. Don't you know that?'

'I refuse to accept your assurance.'

'You know that it's true,' said Charles.

'If she hadn't begun this outrage, you would never have believed it possible,' Mr March exclaimed. 'If she had desisted, you would have been relieved and –'

'If she had died, you mean. If she had died.' The word crashed out. 'That's what you mean.'

Mr March's head was sunk down.

'You were wrong. You've never been so wrong,' said Charles. 'I tell you this. If she had died, I wouldn't have raised a finger to save you trouble. I should have let it happen.'

The sound died away. The room rested in silence. Charles turned from his father, and glanced indifferently, slackly, across the room, as though he were exhausted by his outburst, as though it had left him without anger or interest.

As Charles turned away, Mr March walked from the window towards us by the fireplace. His face looked suddenly without feeling or expression.

He settled in an armchair; as he did so, his foot touched the tea-table, and I noticed the Tinker-Bell reflections, set dancing on the far wall.

Mr March said, in a low voice:

'Why was it necessary to act as you have done? You seem to have been compelled to break every connexion with the family.'

Charles, still standing by the window, did not move or speak.

'You seem to have been compelled to break off at my expense. It was different with Herbert and my father. But you've had to cut yourself off through me.'

Mr March was speaking as though the pain was too recent to feel; he did not know all that had happened to him, he was light-headed with bereavement and defeat. He spoke like a man baffled, in doubt, still unaware of what he was going to feel, groping and mystified. He forgot Ann, and asked Charles why this conflict must come between them, just because they were themselves. A little time before, he had spoken as though he believed that, without Ann, he and his son would have been at peace. It was inconsistent in terms of logic, but it carried the sense of a father's excessive love, of a love which, in the phrase that the old Japanese used to describe the love of parents for their children, was a darkness of the heart.

'Yes,' said Mr March, 'you found it necessary to act against me. I never expected to have my son needing to act against me. I never contemplated living without my son.'

'Believe what I said to you at that last party,' said Charles quietly. 'I want you to believe that. As well as what I've said today.'

Mr March asked, not angrily, but as though he could not believe what had happened:

'You've counted the cost of this intention of yours? You've asked people what it's like to be penniless?'

'Yes,' said Charles.

'You're ready to put yourself in the shameful position of living on your wife's money?'

Charles had been answering listlessly. He gave a faint smile.

'I may even earn a little myself.'

'Pocket-money. I disregard that,' said Mr March. 'You're prepared to live on your wife?'

'Yes.'

'You're not deterred by my disgrace in seeing you in such a position?'

'No,' said Charles.

'You're not deterred by the disgrace your wife's action will inflict upon my brother and my family?'

'I thought I'd made myself clear,' said Charles with a revival of energy.

'You're not deterred by the misery you're bringing upon me?'

'I don't want to repeat what I've said.'

Without looking at Charles again, Mr March said:

'So, if this calamity happens, you're requiring me to decide on my own actions?'

Even now he was hoping. He could still ask a question about the future.

'Yes,' said Charles.

Charles came into the middle of the room, and said:

'I might as well go now. I told Ann I would see her before I left.'

We heard him run upstairs. Katherine spoke to her father: 'It's no use. I wish I could say something, Mr L., but it's no use. There's nothing to do.' Her mouth was trembling. She added:

'I've never seen him like that before.'

Though she was supporting her father, there was something else in her voice. It dwelt more gently on Charles than any word she had said while he was there. She had made her choice; she could not help but take her father's side. But that remark was brimming with regret, with admiration, with the idolatrous love she bore Charles when she was a girl.

Chapter 43

RED BOX ON THE TABLE

During most of October there was no more news. I saw Francis regularly in Cambridge, but he and Katherine knew no more than I. Charles had already cut himself away from them. We heard a number of rumours – that Sir Philip had seen Charles and threatened a libel action whatever the consequences, that Mr March had visited Ann, convalescing by the sea, that Ronald Porson had visited her, that Charles would not have her back unless she broke with the *Note*.

There were many more rumours, most of them fantasies; but it was true that Sir Philip had seen Charles. Charles mentioned it himself, when I was dining with him on one of my nights in London. He mentioned it with indifference, as though it were a perfectly ordinary occurrence, as though his concerns were as pedestrian as anyone else's. He wanted to regard them as settled; he did not want to see that there was a part of his nature, even yet, after all he had said and done, waiting in trepidation, just as the rest of us were waiting.

The final article in the *Note* was published in the fourth week of October. I did not subscribe to the *Note*, but a colleague of mine used to send it round to me; it was brought to my rooms in college by the messenger, on his last delivery, at ten o'clock on a Friday night. For two Fridays past I had raced my eyes over it, before looking at my letters. On this Friday night I did the same; and, as soon as I had unfolded the sheet, I knew this was it. Though I was prepared, I felt the prick of sweat at my temples.

It was the second item on the first page (the first was a three-line report of a meeting between Edward VIII and the Prime Minister, and it read:

Armament Share Scandal

Note can now give final dope about scandal of Ministers, Ministers' stooges, lurkmen in Whitehall, Inns of Court, official circles, making profits from prior knowledge of armaments programme. Back references (*Note* May 26, August 10, August 24, for background, see also . . .). In '29 Tory Government laid contract of £3,000,000, engine development, with Howard & Hazlehurst (Chairman Sir Horace (Cartelspokesman) Timberlake; on board of Howard & Hazlehurst is Viscount Talland, cousin of Alex Hawtin). Alex (Britain First) Hawtin, Under-Secretary of . . ., rising hope Tory party, groomed for cabinet in immediate future, bought £20,000 – approx. – Enlibar shares. Enlibar subsidiary of Howard & Hazlehurst. Sir Philip March, Parliamentary Secretary, Ministry of . . ., ex-banker, ex-director 17 companies, ex-President Jewish Board of Guardians, bought £15,000 Enlibar shares. Shares in parent firm – quantities not known to nearest pound but over £10,000 – bought by G. L. and F. E. Paul, brothers-in-law of Herbert Getliffe, K.C., legal consultant Hawtin's ministry. Shares also bought by S . . ., H . . . Profits on these transactions (approx.):

Hawtin	£35,000
March	£46,000*
G. L. and	
F. E. Paul	£11,000
S . . .	£5,000
H . . .	£3,000

'35, aircraft programme, same story, contract laid with aircraft firms. . . . Details of investments not to hand, but Hawtin and March repeated gambit. G. L. and F. E. Paul not concerned this round – Getliffe no longer consultant to ministry. S . . ., H . . . took a rake-off, possibly cat's-paws for bigger players, but *Note* not in position to confirm this. Hawtin, March still in Government. Hawtin due for promotion. 'Friend of Franco' speech, Oct. 16, Liverpool; 'Franco is at any rate a Christian' speech, Oct. 23, Birmingham.

* March, old city hand, held on longer.

That was all.

The effects did not come at once. Mr March referred to it in his weekly letter to Katherine, but briefly and without comment. She went to comfort him, but on her return reported that he was composed, strangely passive, almost glad that the words were down on paper; there was nothing to imagine now. He showed no sign at all of taking action. He seemed to have feared that, the instant the words appeared, he would be surrounded by violence and disgrace: but no one except Sir Philip spoke to him about the article for several days. In that time-lag, he had a last hope, strong and comforting, that it would all be forgotten: if he stayed in his house, hid away from gossip, this would pass over, as everything else had done.

We had, in fact, all expected that there would be a blaze of publicity from the beginning. That did not happen; partly because there was another scandal going round the clubs, and people were not to be distracted from Mrs Simpson and the King. The *Note* attack had gone off half-cock. A member of the extreme left asked a question in the House, and demanded a select committee. A few eccentric liberals and malcontents of various kinds (including a conservative anti-semite) occupied a committee room for some hours, but could not agree on a plan of action. There was a leader, so stately and stuffed that it was incomprehensible unless one knew the story, in one of the conservative papers.

Some of the column writers made references. One or two weekly papers, on the extreme right as well as the left, let themselves go. It did not seem to amount to much.

About three weeks after the article came out, however, there were rumours of changes in the government. The political correspondents began tipping their fancies. No one suggested that the changes had anything to do with the *Note*'s article; it was not even explicitly denied. In private the gossips were speculating whether Hawtin would be 'out' or whether he would lose his promotion. He was disliked, he was cold and self-righteous; but to put him out now, after his stand on Spain, would look like a concession to the left. As for Sir Philip, his name was not canvassed much. He had never been a figure in politics; he was old and had no future. The only flicker of interest in him, apart from the scandal, was because he was a Jew.

Meanwhile, Herbert Getliffe was showing the resource and pertinacity that most people missed unless they knew him well. He had a streak of revengefulness, and he was determined that his enemies should pay. He knew that neither Hawtin nor Philip March would bring an action; nor could the Pauls without more damage to himself. So Getliffe concentrated on the minor figures, S ..., H. ... He worked out that there was a good chance of one of them bringing an action which need involve no one else.

He wrote to Sir Philip, suggesting that they should promote an action in H ...'s name. Sir Philip replied curtly that the less said or done, the better. Despite the rebuff, Getliffe approached Mr March, to persuade him to influence his brother; and, leaving nothing to chance, he sent me the outline of the case.

Mr March and Sir Philip each snubbed him again. Getliffe, suggestible as he was when one met him face to face, was utterly impervious when on the make. He wrote to them in detail; he added that I should be familiar with the legal side, if they wanted an opinion; he wrote to me twice, begging me to do my best.

The March brothers were not weak characters, but, like most men, they could be hypnotized by persistence. Ill-temperedly Mr March arranged for me to meet him one morning at Sir Philip's office – 'to discuss the proposals which Getliffe is misguidedly advancing and which are, in my view, profoundly to be regretted at the present juncture'.

That morning when I was due to meet them, a drizzling November day, I opened *The Times* and saw, above a column in the centre page, 'Changes in the Government'. Sir Philip's name was not among them. Hawtin was promoted to full cabinet rank; to make room for him, someone was sent to the Lords. A Parliamentary Secretary and an Under-Secretary were shelved, in favour of two back-benchers. It was difficult to read any meaning into the changes. Hawtin's promotion might be a brushing-off of the scandal, a gesture of confidence, or a move to the right. The other appointments were neutral. At the end of the official statement, there was a comment that more changes would be announced shortly.

I arrived at the room of Sir Philip's secretary a little before my time. He was pretending to work, as I sat looking out at the park. The rain seeped gently down; after the brilliant autumn, the leaves had not yet fallen and shone dazzlingly out of the grey, mournful, misty morning. I heard the rain seep down, and the nervous, restless movements of the young man behind me. He was on edge with nerves: Sir Philip's fate did not matter to him, but he had become infected by the tension. He was expecting a telephone call from Downing Street. Soon he stopped work, and in his formal, throaty, sententious voice (the voice of a man who was going to enjoy every bit of pomp and circumstance in his official life) asked me whether I had studied the government changes, and what significance I gave them. He was earnest, ambitious, self-important: yet each time the telephone rang his face was screwed up with excitement, like that of a boy who is being let into an adult's secret. As each call turned out to be a routine enquiry, his voice went flat with anti-climax. As soon as Mr March came in, Williams showed us into Sir Philip's room. Before we entered, Mr March had time only to shake hands and say that he was obliged to me for coming – but even in that time I could see his face painful with hope, his resignation broken, every hope and desire for happiness evoked again by the news that Hawtin was safe. Sir Philip's first words were, after greeting us both:

'I suppose you saw in the papers that Hawtin's still in? They've given him a leg-up.'

'I was considering what effect it would have on your prospects,' said Mr March.

'It won't be long before I know. This means they're not going to execute us, anyway,' said Sir Philip, with a cackle which did not conceal that he too felt relief, felt active hope. 'As for Alex Hawtin, he's doing better for himself than he deserves. Still, he can't be worse than old ...' Sir Philip broke off, and looked at us across his desk. He had dressed with special care that day, and with a new morning suit was wearing a light-blue, flowing silk tie. It was incongruous, against the aged yellow skin. Yet, even about his face, there was something jaunty still.

'Well,' he said, 'I wanted to consult you about this fellow Getliffe. He's got hold of someone called Huff or Hough – who must be a shady lot himself, judging from the book of words – and they want to bring a libel action if they can get financial support – I needn't go over the ground again. You've seen it for yourselves, I gather.'

'I received another effusion from Herbert Getliffe yesterday,' said Mr March, 'which I regret to say I have omitted to bring. It did not add anything substantial to his previous lucubrations.'

'And you're familiar with it, Eliot?'

'Yes,' I said.

Sir Philip suddenly snapped:

'I don't want to have anything to do with the fellow. No good can come of it. I won't touch anything he's concerned with.'

Anxiety and hope had made his temper less equable.

'I concur in your judgement,' said Mr March. 'The fellow is a pestilential nuisance.'

'I want to stop his damned suggestions,' said Sir Philip. 'Where are they? Why isn't the file here?'

He pushed the button on his desk, and the secretary entered. Sir Philip was just asking for the Getliffe file when in the outer office the telephone rang. 'Will you excuse me while I answer it, sir?' said Williams officiously, once more excited. After he went away, we could hear his voice through the open door. 'Yes, this is Sir Philip March's secretary. ... Yes ... Yes, I will give him that message. ... Yes, he will be ready to receive the letter.'

Williams came in, and said with formality: 'It was a message from the Prime Minister's principal private secretary, sir. It was to say that a letter from the Prime Minister is on its way.'

Sir Philip nodded. 'Do you wish me to stay, sir?' said Williams hopefully.

'No,' said Sir Philip in an absent tone. 'Leave the Getliffe file. I'll ring if I need you.'

As soon as the door was closed, Mr March cried:

'What does it mean? What does it mean?'

'It may mean the sack,' said Sir Philip. 'Or it may mean they're offering me another job.'

At that instant Mr March lost the last particle of hope.

Sir Philip, meeting his brother's despairing gaze, went on stubbornly:

'If he is offering me another job, I shall have to decide whether to turn it down or not. I should like a rest, of course, but after this brouhaha I should probably consider it my duty to accept it. I should want your advice, Leonard, before I let him have his answer.'

Mr March uttered a sound, half-assent, half-groan.

The morning had grown darker, and Sir Philip switched on the reading lamp above his desk. The minutes passed; he looked at the clock and talked in agitation; Mr March was possessed by his thoughts. Sir Philip looked at the clock again, and said irritably:

'Whatever happens to me, I won't have this fellow Getliffe putting a foot in. I won't find a penny for his wretched case and I want to warn him off the business altogether.'

Mr March, as though he had scarcely heard, said yes. Knowing Getliffe better than they did, I said the only method was to prove to him that any conceivable case had a finite risk of involving the Pauls, and in the end himself. I thought that that was so, and that I could convince Getliffe of it. Sir Philip at once gave me the file, and Mr March asked me to go home with him shortly and pick up the last letter. They were tired of trouble. They forgot this last nuisance as soon as the file was in my hand.

The minutes ticked on. Sir Philip complained:

'It can't take a fellow all this time to walk round from Downing Street. These messengers have been slackers ever since I've known them.'

At length we heard a shuffle, a mutter of voices, in the

secretary's room. A tap on the door, and Williams came in, carrying a red oblong despatch box.

'This has just come from the Prime Minister, sir.'

He placed it on the table in front of Sir Philip. The red lid glowed under the lamp.

Sir Philip said sharply:

'Well, well, where is the key?'

'Surely you have it, sir?'

'Never, man, I've never had it. I remember giving it to you the last time a box arrived. After I opened it, I remember giving it to you perfectly well.'

'I'm certain that I remember your keeping the key after you opened that box, sir. I'm almost certain you put it on your key ring –'

'I tell you I've never had the key in my possession for a single moment. You've been in charge of it ever since you've been in that office. I want you to find it now –'

Williams had blushed to his neck and ears. For him that was the intolerable moment of the morning. He went out. Sir Philip and Mr March were left to look at the red box glowing under the light. Sir Philip swore bitterly.

It was some minutes before Williams returned. 'I've borrowed this' – he said, giving a small key to Sir Philip – 'from Sir —' (the Cabinet Minister).

'Very well, very well. Now you'd better go and find mine.'

Williams left before Sir Philip had opened the box and the envelope inside. As soon as he began to read, his expression gave the answer.

'It's the sack, of course,' he said.

He spoke slowly:

'He's pretty civil to me. He says that I shan't mind giving up my job to a younger man.'

He added:

'I didn't bank on going out like this.'

Mr March said:

'Nor did I ever think you would.'

Then Sir Philip spoke as though he were recalling his old, resilient tone. 'Well,' he said, 'I've got a good deal to clear up today. I want to leave things shipshape. You'll look after that fellow Getliffe, Eliot? We don't want any more talk. This will be in the papers tonight. After that they'll forget about me soon enough.'

In the middle of this new active response, he seemed to feel back to his brother's remark. He said to Mr March with brotherly, almost protective kindness:

'Don't take it too much to heart, Leonard. It might be worse.'

'I'm grateful for your consideration,' cried Mr March. 'But it would never have happened but for my connexions.'

'That's as may be,' said Sir Philip. 'That's as may be.'

He spoke again to his brother, stiffly but kindly:

'I know you feel responsible because of Charles's wife. That young woman's dangerous, and we shan't be able to see much of her in the family after this. But I shouldn't like you to do anything about Charles on my account. It can't be any use.'

Mr March said:

'Nothing can be any use now.'

Sir Philip said:

'Well, then. Leave it alone.'

Mr March replied, in a voice firm, resonant, and strong:

'No. I must do what I have to do.'

Chapter 44

COMPENSATION

As soon as we left the office, Mr March reminded me that I was to come home with him to get Getliffe's last letter. He was quick and energetic in his movements; the slowness of despair seemed to have left him; outside in the street, he called for a taxi at the top of his voice, and set off in chase of it like a young man.

We drove down Whitehall. Mr March remarked:

'I presume this is the last occasion when I shall go inside those particular mausoleums. I cannot pretend that will be a hardship for me personally. Though for anyone like my brother Philip, who had ambitions in this direction, it must be an unpleasant wrench to leave.'

I was amazed at his matter-of-fact tone, at the infusion of cheerfulness and heartiness which I had not heard in him for many weeks. He had spoken of his brother with his old mixture of admiration, envy, sense of unworthiness, and detached incredulity, incredulity that a man should choose such a life. He had spoken as he might have done in untroubled days. It was hard to remember his silent anguish an hour before in Sir Philip's room. He said:

'I shall want to speak to my son Charles this morning.'

His tone was still matter-of-fact. He said that he would ring Charles up as soon as he got home. Then he talked of other things, all the way to Bryanston Square. The end had come and he was released. He was flooded by a rush of power. He could go through with it, he knew. He could act as though of his own free will. It set him speaking cheerfully and heartily.

He took me into his study. He gave me Getliffe's letter and said casually: 'I hope you will be able to settle the fellow for us.' Then he asked:

'Are you sufficiently familiar with my son's efforts as a practitioner to know where he is to be found at this time in the morning?' It was ten past twelve.

'He's usually back from his rounds about half past,' I said.

'I will telephone him shortly,' said Mr March. 'I shall require to see him before luncheon.'

He asked me to excuse him, and rang up, not Charles, but the family solicitor. Mr March said that he needed to transact some business in the early afternoon. The solicitor tried to put off the appointment until later in the day, but Mr March insisted that it must be at half past two. 'I shall be having luncheon alone,' he said on the telephone. 'I propose to come directly afterwards to your office. My business may occupy a considerable portion of the afternoon.'

When that was settled, Mr March talked to me for a few minutes. He enquired, with his usual consideration, about my career, but for the most part he wanted to talk of Charles. What would his future be? What society was he intending to move in? Would he make any headway as a practitioner? I told him about the letter to the *Lancet*. Even at that moment, he was full of pride. 'Not that I expect for a minute it is of any value,' he said. 'But nevertheless it shows that he may not be prepared to vegetate.' He sat and considered, on his lips a sad but genuine smile, with no trace of rancour.

'It would be a singular circumstance,' said Mr March, 'if he contributed something after all.'

It was time for him to ring up Charles. When he got an answer, his expression suddenly became fixed. I guessed that he was hearing Ann's voice. 'This is Leonard March,' he said, not greeting her. 'I wish urgently to speak to my son.' There was a pause before he spoke to Charles. 'If it is not inconvenient for you, I should like you to come here without delay.' Mr March did not say any more to Charles. To me he said:

'No doubt it is inconvenient for him, my requiring his presence in this manner.' He paused. 'But I shall make no further demands upon his time.'

Mr March stood up, shook my hand, and said:

'I hope you will forgive me, Lewis, for not inviting you to stay to luncheon. I shall have certain matters to attend to for the remainder of the day.'

He added:

'If you wish to stay in order to see my son, I hope you will not be deterred from doing so. I think you are familiar enough with my house to make yourself at home. I should be sorry if you ceased to be familiar with my house. I shall be obliged if you find it possible to visit me occasionally.'

Chapter 45

'I SUPPOSE I DON'T KNOW YET'

I WENT into the drawing-room, affected by the other times
I had waited there. I sat by the fire, picked up a biography,
and tried to read. The soft rain fell in the square outside.
The light of the wet autumn day was diffuse and gentle, and
the fire burned high in the chimney. I heard Charles's car
drive up, and the sound of the butler's voice greeting him in
the hall.

Again I tried to read. But, within a few minutes, far sooner
than I expected, Charles joined me. He said:

'Mr L. told me that I should find you here.'

He sat down, and looked at me with a tired, composed
smile.

He said.

'He did it with great dignity.'

He said no more of their last meeting.

He began to talk, practically, about his financial condition.
Ann's income would go down now that her father had retired. Charles himself was earning about £900 a year from
his practice. 'It ought to mount up in the next two or three
years,' he said. 'But I shall be lucky if I work it up to £1,500.
Altogether, it will be slightly different from the scale of life
I was brought up to expect.'

He smiled. 'I suppose it doesn't matter much,' he said. 'It
may be a nuisance sometimes not to have a private income –
you used to say what a difference it made, didn't you? I
don't mean for luxuries. I mean there are times when it's
valuable for a doctor to be independent of his job. He can
do things and say things that otherwise he wouldn't dare.
Some of us ought to be able to say things without being
frightened for our livelihood, don't you agree? Well, I shan't
be able to. I don't know how much difference it will make.'

He was showing the kind of realistic worry that I had seen in him so often. It was genuine; for most of his life he had expected that when Mr March died he would become a rich man; he had always lived in comfort, even since his marriage.

He did not restrain his worry. He was not in a hurry to leave his father's house. He spoke about Mr March with a concern so strong and steady that one could not miss it.

'He mustn't be left alone more than anyone can help,' said Charles. 'I've done this, so I can't do anything for him now. But everyone must see that he's got plenty to catch his interest. He finds it hard to be desperately unhappy when there are people round him, you know that, don't you? Even though –' Charles paused. 'Even though he's lost something. He can't be swallowed up by unhappiness while there are people round him. He has to expend himself on them.'

His face was tired, kind. He went on: 'I know it's a different story when he is alone at night.'

He reiterated his concern:

'They mustn't be frightened to intrude on him. When he's unhappy, I mean. It's easy to be too delicate. Sometimes it's right. I assure you it isn't right with Mr L. I think Katherine will know that by instinct. If she doesn't, you must tell her, Lewis. Will you promise to tell her?'

'I'm cut off from them,' he added. 'I can't tell them what to do. But I think I know him better than they do.'

Behind his worry, behind his concern, he was thinking of what he had done.

'I've done this,' he said, repeating the phrase he had used as he gave me messages about his father. 'I've done this. Sometimes I can't believe it. It sounds ridiculous, but I feel I've done nothing.' He gave a smile, completely open, unguarded, and candid. I had never seen his face so brilliant and innocent.

'At other times,' he said, 'I feel remorse.'

The words weighed down. I said:

'I know what you mean. I've told you, once I did something more unforgivable than you've done. I know what you mean.'

Charles said eagerly:

Sometimes it seems the most natural thing in the world to do what one did, isn't that true? Didn't you feel that? And sometimes you felt you wouldn't forget it, you wouldn't be free of the memory, for the rest of your life?'

'I'm not free yet,' I said.

We smiled. There was great intimacy between us.

'Did yours seem like mine? Did it seem you were bound to make a choice? Did it seem you had to hurt one or two people, whatever you did?'

'I hadn't any justification at all,' I said.

'With me,' said Charles, 'it seemed to be wrapped up with everything in my life.'

He waited for some time before he spoke again. His expression was heavy, but not harassed. 'Until it happened, I didn't know what I should have to live with. Live with in myself, I mean: you must have faced that too, haven't you?' He looked at me with simplicity, with a kind of brotherly directness. He said: 'I suppose I don't know yet.'

Did it make nonsense to him of what he had tried to do with his life? More than any of us, I was thinking, he had searched into his own nature, and had distrusted it more. Did this make nonsense of what he had tried to do? To him the answer would sometimes, and perhaps often, be yes.

Sitting with him in the drawing-room, I could not feel it so. Not that I was trying to judge him: all I had was a sense of expectancy, curiously irrelevant, but reassuring as though the heart were beating strongly, about what the future held.

Chapter 46

HIS OWN COMPANY

SOME weeks later I went to dinner at Bryanston Square. As I heard from Katherine, Mr March was inventing excuses to keep his house full; that night he had chosen to celebrate what he regarded as a success of mine. The 'success' was nothing but a formality: I had just been confirmed in my college job and now, if I wanted, could stay there for life. For Mr March it was a pretext for a party; as he greeted me it seemed to be something more.

When the butler showed me into the drawing-room, cosy after the cold night outside, Mr March had already come down, and was standing among Francis and Katherine and a dozen or more of our contemporaries. It was the biggest party I had seen there since his seventieth birthday. He came across to me, swinging his arm, and the instant he shook hands, said without any introduction: 'I always viewed your intention to support yourself by legal practice as misguided.'

It sounded brusque. It sounded unemollient. Taken aback, Katherine said:

'He was doing well in it, after all, Mr L.'

'No! No!' He brushed her aside, and spoke straight to me: 'I didn't regard legal practice as a suitable career for someone with other burdens.'

He spoke with understanding. Although he had not once referred to it, he knew what my marriage meant: this was his way of telling me so. How much time – he broke off shyly – did I intend to devote to my London job? Three days a week, I told him: and I could feel him thinking that that was the amount of time I spent with my wife in the Chelsea house. 'Oh well,' he remarked, 'so long as that brings in sufficient for your requirements.'

As with Francis, so with me, Mr March ignored any earn-

330

ings from academic life. His tone had not altered; apart
from the burst of sympathy, which no one else in the room
recognized, he was talking as he used to do. At dinner he
went on addressing us round the table, just as he had done
on my earliest visits there. The only difference that I should
have noticed, if I had not known what had happened, was a
curious one: the food, which had always been good, was now
luxurious. Mr March, living alone in Bryanston Square, was
doing himself better than ever in the past.

He spread himself on anecdotes: his talent for total recall
was in good working order: there was plenty of laughter. I
looked at Francis. It happened that just at that time there
was a disagreement between us: we had been divided by a
piece of college politics. But still, as our glances met, we had
a fellow-feeling. In that sumptuous dinner party, we should
have been hard put to it to say why we were so uncomfortable, when Mr March himself was not. Perhaps we had
counted on giving him support, which he would not take.

Towards the end of dinner, Mr March drank my health,
and, still holding his glass, got into spate:

'On the occasion of Lewis Eliot first giving me the pleasure
of his company in this house, I observed to my daughter
Katherine that no proper preparations had been taken for
the eventuality that he might prove to be a teetotaller. I
failed to observe to my daughter Katherine on the identical
anniversary that no proper precautions had been taken for
the eventuality that Leonard might not be disposed to
welcome a four-foot-high teddy-bear.'

'Who mightn't like a teddy-bear?' someone cried, apparently nervous in case Mr March was talking of himself.

'My grandson Leonard, of course,' shouted Mr March.
'The anniversary of whose birth, which took place last week,
coincides as to day and month, but not however as to year,
with that of the first visit of Lewis Eliot to my house. Of
course, the opposite mistake used to be made with even more
distressing consequences, though naturally not by my
daughter Katherine.'

'What mistake?'

'Of teetotallers not making adequate provision for non-teetotallers, as opposed to the hypothetical reception of Lewis Eliot, as previously mentioned. On accepting hospitality from my second cousin Archibald Waley I constantly found myself in an intolerable dilemma. Not owing to his extraordinary habit of gnashing his teeth which was owing to a physiological peculiarity and unconnected with any defects of temperament which he nevertheless possessed, and demonstrated by his lamentable behaviour over his expulsion from Alfred Hart's club during a certain disagreement. My intolerable dilemma was of a different nature. I used to present myself at his house – Philip used to say that it was the most inconvenient house in Kensington – and we used to make our entrance into the dining-room in a perfectly orthodox manner that I could see no reason for objecting to. Then however we were confronted as we sat down in our places with a printed card which I have always regarded as the height of bad form, and which did not improve the situation by informing us that we were required to assimilate nine courses. It is perhaps common fairness to point out that at the relevant period it was customary to provide more elaborate refreshments than the fork-suppers we've all taken to fobbing off on our guests.'

'Was this a fork supper, Mr L.?' asked a niece, waving at the plates.

'I don't know what else you'd call it,' said Mr March. 'The over-ostentation of the provender was nevertheless not the main point at issue. One could possibly have contemplated nine courses until one was discouraged by hearing the footman ask "What would you like to drink, sir?" One then enquired for possible alternatives and was given the choice "Orangeade, lemonade, lemon squash, lime juice, ginger beer, ginger ale, barley water. ..." It was always said that when Herbert dined there he put a flask of brandy in his trouser pocket and made an excuse to go to the lavatory at least twice during the proceedings.' Mr March raised his voice above questions, comments, grins:

'The presumed discomfort to Lewis Eliot as a teetotaller

entering this, a non-teetotal house, was in my judgement less than that experienced by myself at Archibald Waley's.' He added:

'In practice, Lewis Eliot turned out not to be a teetotaller at all. As could have been ascertained from the person instrumental in giving me the pleasure of his company. That person being my son Charles.'

No one said anything. Mr March went on:

'At that time there was nothing to prevent me communicating with my son Charles. However, I did not, at least upon the point under discussion.'

He said it with absolute stoicism. It was a stoicism which stopped any of us taking up the reference to Charles, or mentioning him again.

I left early, before any of the others. In the square it was cold enough to take one's breath, and in the wind the stars flashed and quivered above the tossing trees. Trying to find a taxi, I walked along the pavement, across the end of the square, as I had walked with Charles after my first visit to the house, listening to him talk about his father. I was not thinking of them, though: my thoughts had gone to my own house. Just for a random instant, I recalled our housekeeper running down the local doctors, and then admitting, in a querulous, patronizing fashion, that some people in Pimlico spoke of Charles March as a good doctor, and seemed to trust him now. That thought did not last: it drifted into others of our housekeeper, my own home.

Standing at the corner, I stamped my feet, waiting for a taxi. Through the bare trees of the garden, I could see a beam of light, as the door of Mr March's house opened, letting out some more of his guests. Soon the party would be over. He would test the latches and switch off the lights: then he would be left in his own company.

MORE ABOUT PENGUINS
AND PELICANS

Penguinews, which appears every month, contains details of all the new books issued by Penguins as they are published. From time to time it is supplemented by our stocklist, which is our list of almost 5,000 titles.

A specimen copy of *Penguinews* will be sent to you free on request. Please write to Dept EP, Penguin Books Ltd, Harmondsworth, Middlesex, for your copy.

In the U.S.A.: For a complete list of books available from Penguins in the United States write to Dept CS, Penguin Books, 625 Madison Avenue, New York, New York 10022.

In Canada: For a complete list of books available from Penguins in Canada write to Penguin Books Canada Ltd, 2801 John Street, Markham, Ontario L3R 1B4.